Seven Bands of Gold

Book One: First Love

First Love

Seven Bands of Gold Book
Book One: First Love
First Published by Barzipan Publishing 2013
ISBN: 978-0-9573792-4-4
Kindle edition: 978-0-9573792-5-

Second Edition: 2018
ISBN: 13: 978-1723283727

CIP Data: A catalogue record for this book is available from the British Library
Jenny Lees asserts her moral right to be identified as the author of this work.

Quoted extracts:
The Pied Piper of Hamelin, Robert Browning 1842
Treasure Island, Robert Louis Stevenson 1882
Robinson Crusoe, Daniel Defoe 1719

First Love

Seven Bands of Gold

Book One: First Love

Jenny Lees

First Love

For my husband Tony
for being man enough to encourage me in all my ambitious
schemes, for his unstinting support and for his hands-on
research

First Love

Chapter One

From a corner of the smoke-filled room Tom Jones sang *It's Not Unusual*, and Sally smiled inwardly. She was seventeen, it was the swinging sixties and most of her friends had already got through several boyfriends; but here she was, yet again sitting by herself waiting for her father to collect her from a party. The cigarette smoke was beginning to irritate her eyes and she felt desperately in need of some fresh air. Glancing at her watch she realised it would be at least another half hour before her father was parked outside waiting.

Sally had been persuaded by her best friend Caroline to come to the party, with the promise that there would be lots of 'new talent' and that together they would have great fun. Early in the evening Caroline had been seduced away from her side. Sally wasn't sure he was exactly 'talent', although he was 'new', and now all she wanted was to get home. It was late, and she stifled a yawn. There'd be no chance of a lie in the next morning because her mother would have the whole family up early for Mass.

Seeing her girlfriends busily dating one boy after another, like hungry bees flitting from flower to flower, Sally began to wonder if there was something wrong with her. Why couldn't she enjoy the company of the opposite sex the way Caroline did? Perhaps having five brothers was what made Caroline so confident around boys. She knew about boys' stuff like football and cricket, whereas these subjects were a complete enigma to Sally. In stark contrast to Caroline's confidence with the opposite sex, Sally was often tongue-tied as she desperately tried to think of something to say. Then, when she finally plucked up the courage to speak, she would find herself blushing furiously.

As predicted, Caroline had certainly enjoyed herself this evening and no doubt was still enjoying herself with her latest conquest. Apart from the music, which Sally loved, the rest of the evening had consisted of stilted conversations and superficial pleasantries exchanged with uninteresting youths. All the boys could talk about these days was football, as Britain got ready to host the World Cup. It seemed the whole country had gone football crazy. Trying hard to look as though she was having a good time, Sally had refused a cheeky request to step outside for a quick snog and two requests for a date. Thankfully, the music was so loud she could pretend that that she was unable to hear much of the conversation around her.

It was not that Sally was unkind, just that she was totally blind to the fact that during the past few months she had blossomed into quite a beauty. Unfairly, she was getting a reputation for being a bit aloof. Some of the local lads had even laid bets on who would be the first to secure a date with the gorgeous Sally Phillips. The truth was that Sally did not consider herself attractive at all; the nuns at her convent school had knocked any sense of vanity out of her and every other 'young lady' in their charge!

'You'll never get a serious boyfriend, Sal, if you let your dad give you a lift home!' Caroline had teased her, but Sally was much happier when her father offered to pick her up. It was preferable to running the gauntlet of a gang of hormonal youths sparring for who would be the lucky one to walk her home. She could truthfully say she had a lift, and didn't have to say from whom!

The room was emptying now to the strains of *The Sun Ain't Gonna Shine Any More*. Sally wished she'd arranged for her father to pick her up earlier. As couples drifted away, smoke escaped in tendrils through the open door, but it didn't make a lot of difference to the air quality. She checked her watch once more, sighed, then pulled a hankie from her bag to dab at her tormented eyes.

There was a shout of laughter from the doorway and through watering eyes Sally watched, mesmerised, as a handsome young man walked confidently into the room. Tall and slim, he wore blue denim jeans, a pale blue open- necked shirt and a brown leather belt accentuating his trim waist. His dark hair reached his collar and he had a devastating smile that revealed a set of perfect white teeth. The sight of him made her heart flutter – much to her confusion. He was greeted with waves and friendly hellos and was obviously a popular, albeit late, addition to the party. Glancing round the room as he responded to the welcomes with a nod and a smile, his eyes locked with Sally's and he beamed and cheekily winked. Sally felt herself blushing but returned his smile, then quickly looked away.

The newcomer stopped long enough at the improvised bar to fill a pint glass from a small plastic beer barrel set among the bottles, and then walked straight over to where Sally was sitting alone.

'Hello! What have we here? A new blonde on the block! What's your name? Mine's Doug – you don't know me, but I get the feeling you're going to,' he brashly predicted, grinning at her and holding out his hand.

'Er ... it's Sally,' she spluttered shyly, almost forgetting her own name as she drowned in his dazzling smile and cautiously took his outstretched palm. Nonplussed by this direct and self-assured approach, she found herself smiling back up at him. Her experience of her male contemporaries had been restricted to spotty youths with unreliable vocal cords who nervously enquired if she had seen the latest James Bond film. Doug's approach, by comparison, was pure 007. 'May I refill your glass?' he offered, still standing over her. 'What's your preference?' There was a hint of a Scottish burr in his voice that only added to his charm.

Once again, Sally was bowled over and found herself murmuring, 'Just a lemonade, please'. In an overwhelming desire to sound more grown up, she hastily added, 'I've already had too much wine'. The closest that Sally had ever come to drinking alcohol was a Snowball her parents had allowed her to try at Christmas, but for some reason she couldn't fathom, she wanted this handsome stranger to think that she was not only older than her seventeen years but more worldly as well.

Making no comment, Doug picked up her glass and headed back to the bar. Oh God, she thought, I must have sounded so wet! He must think I'm pathetic. Why did I say that? Well, who cares, he probably won't bother coming back anyway.

When she saw him turn and make his way back to her, her stomach did a peculiar somersault. Placing the glass of lemonade on the table, he pointed to the empty seat beside her. 'May I?'

'Yes, of course.' She felt compelled to explain why she was sitting alone on the sofa. 'My friend was sitting there, but she's gone home already. I'm just waiting for my ...' She very nearly said 'father' as she babbled on nervously, but managed to change it to 'lift home' in a further attempt to sound less childish and unsophisticated.

Doug sank down beside her, stretching his long denim-clad legs under the low coffee table in front of them. Nervously, Sally sipped at her drink and, glancing in his direction, blushed when she saw that he was grinning at her. Shyly she smiled back at him. When the next record dropped on the turntable and the Beatles began belting out *I Wanna Hold Your Hand*, the handsome stranger leaned closer.

'Do you know, I'd just love to hold your hand, Sally. Shall we?' He inclined his head towards the few couples who were still shuffling around in the middle of the room, the thick wool pile of the carpet hampering their style.

'Come on, Blondie, don't be shy,' he said, jumping energetically to his feet.

He held out a hand to her and she let him lead her to the centre.

Sally hadn't realised just how tall he was until she shyly placed her hands on his shoulders. He slid his arms expertly around her waist and pulled her close, closer than she had ever physically been to any man other than her father. As they danced, he buried his face in her long blonde hair and nuzzled her neck. Every part of her burned with a feeling she had never experienced; she was excited but scared at the same time. Unsure about what was happening, her mind was desperate to stay in control, but in this stranger's arms her body refused to listen.

'You're as warm and cuddly as a wee kitten,' he whispered, holding her close. The Beatles faded out but Doug continued to hold her tightly to his chest. As the next record dropped on the turntable, Sally decided that it was rather nice being held close and made no attempt to move away.

'In fact, that is what I'm going to call you,' he whispered seductively in her ear.

'I'm five foot eight inches tall and I don't like milk,' she said, laughing up at him. She felt herself follow his lead as they swayed on to the softer tones of Jim Reeves lamenting the call to war of distant drums. Sally wasn't sure whether or not she was relieved when the music ended. Gently, they drew apart and she unwrapped herself from Doug's clutches. There was a moment's hesitation as they stood looking into each other's eyes, then Sally remembered that her father would be waiting for her by now. Glancing at her watch, she saw it was indeed time to say her goodbyes and slip unobtrusively away to where her father would be waiting patiently in his car.

'Thank you for asking me to dance, but I have to go now.'

'Whoa, not so fast, young lady,' Doug said, placing his hands gently on her shoulders. 'How about dinner during the week? I'm not letting you go anywhere until I can be sure I'll be seeing you again.' Sally's heart did a strange little skip as it missed a beat.

'Oh, I don't know. I ... I'm not sure ... You see I ...' she peeped shyly up at him through her eyelashes. She had never been out on a dinner date with anyone before. He was older than the other boys and she was not sure that she should agree. Doug saw the look of doubt in her eyes and grinned at her. 'I only want to feed you, not eat you!' he said, laughing down at her, and again her tummy did a peculiar flip. Yes! She definitely felt she wanted to have dinner with him.

'Well, okay ... er ... yes, that would be nice,' she heard herself saying. 'How about next Wednesday? There's a wee bistro just opened in the town.

Shall we meet there? Seven-thirty? D'you know the one I mean?' 'Yes, yes I know the one.'

'Until then.' Doug winked at her and lifted her hand to his lips. They were warm as he brushed them against her skin and the touch sent a shiver right through her. He watched her leave and then sauntered back to where his friends were congregated, still drinking.

'Cute,' he commented in response to several pairs of raised eyebrows, then reached for a refill of his pint glass.

'Not really your type though, is she?' commented one of the group.

'Well, what would you say is "my type"? It would be useful to know.' Doug lifted his pint to his lips.

'We all know you, Douglas; bright red lipstick, big tits and knickers in her handbag, I would have said.' There was a ripple of laughter.

Doug took the comment with good grace. After all, they weren't wrong; he couldn't understand himself why he had approached the shy young girl, but something had drawn him to her.

That night Sally lay in her bed in the dark, unable to drift off to sleep. There were so many questions that she needed answers to. What were those unfamiliar sensations that had surged right through her whole body? They were nice, though, she smiled to herself in the darkness. Was it love? Am I in love? And why did I get such strange feelings that made me catch my breath when his arms held me? That was nice, she decided. Why did every part of her body come alive when he pulled her in close? God, I'm so confused, she thought. Cloaked in ignorance and rapidly losing courage, she decided it might be better to cancel the dinner date – then realised she had no way of contacting Doug. For a while she contemplated not turning up, feeling perhaps that it was safer that way. Doug had frightened as well as attracted her. Up to that moment, Sally had been incapable of deception and she wondered what had made her tell him that little white lie about the wine?

In the darkness, she shivered – from excitement or fear, she couldn't tell which. Brought up always to be honest with her parents, she decided to mention the date to her mother at the first opportunity. In the past, when she'd felt tempted to make a date with one of the local boys, she'd known her mother would not allow it. If she ran true to form with this date, it would be out of Sally's hands and she would not have to wrestle with her conflicting emotions. With that thought, she fell asleep.

Awakened, as always, by the sounds of her mother preparing breakfast in the kitchen beneath her bedroom, Sally stretched and clambered out of bed. The familiar clatter of cups and saucers and the distinctive crash as the cast iron frying pan hit the gas cooker meant Sally had no need of an alarm clock on a Sunday, or any other day. Her mother insisted the family start every day with a good hot meal, and Sundays before Mass were no exception. By starting early she allowed time for breakfast to be eaten without breaking the rules about fasting time for those taking Communion.

The thoughts that had clouded Sally's mind as she had drifted off to sleep came rushing back. She dressed hastily and ran downstairs, judging she would have her mother to herself for a while before her younger sister Lottie could be prised from her bed.

Rose was just lighting the gas under the frying pan as Sally came into the kitchen. She watched as her mother picked up the slicer and scooped some beef dripping from a bowl and then scraped it against the inside of the big black iron frying pan. It melted immediately and slid into the pan, where it began to sizzle and spit.

'Your father said you weren't outside waiting for him last night, as you usually are. He said he had to wait for you to come out.' Rose smiled across at her daughter. 'Was it a good party? Did you enjoy yourself?' she asked as she adjusted the flame and lowered several rashers of bacon into the frying pan.

Thank you, God, thought Sally as her mother unwittingly gave her the opening she needed.

'Yes, it was quite good. Caroline really enjoyed herself.' Sally stood beside her mother, watching the bacon curling in the heat and feeling that she was beginning to curl up inside herself.

'Huh, she always enjoys herself, that one,' Rose muttered under her breath. From the moment Sally had befriended Caroline, Rose had resented the influence she thought the boyish Caroline MacAvoy had on her daughter. Rose wanted Sally to be a proper little girl and she blamed Caroline in part for turning her into a tomboy. With her curly blonde hair and big blue eyes, Sally was like a doll and Rose desperately wanted her to wear the pretty dresses she lovingly created on her sewing machine. Then along came Caroline, with brothers to emulate, five of them and living far too close! As far as Rose was concerned, Caroline had been allowed to run wild, always in shorts or trousers trying to imitate her brothers – though she could look quite demure in her gymslip and straw boater when she walked to school with Sally.

Caroline had been six years old when she first came to Rose's front door. Ever so politely, she had asked if Sally could come out to play. Rose hadn't recognised her and thought it was a little boy on her doorstep. When it dawned on her who was standing on her front porch, she thought Caroline looked ridiculous with her short, untidy hair. The child had stood there frantically trying to control the dog she'd brought with her. It wasn't on a lead and it had made a lunge to run inside the house! Ugh! Dirty thing! Rose had tried to send the scruffy child packing, but Caroline had defiantly raised that chin of hers and stayed put. Rose's hand had itched to slap the face of the self-assured little brat! But Mrs MacAvoy, her five strapping sons and her social-climbing husband were a force to be reckoned with in this town. Always having the priest round for lunch on a Sunday! Huh! Giving themselves airs and graces, thought Rose. Think they own this town just because Mr MacAvoy's something on the Council. For all her anger and resentment at what she saw as

Caroline's impertinence, Rose had held her peace and called Sally down.

'Mum, is there anything I can do?' Sally offered, breaking in on her mother's thoughts.

'You could put the kettle on.' She smiled at her daughter. Sally turned away to fill the kettle at the sink.

'I enjoyed myself too ...' Sally said, aware of her mother staring at her back as she stood at the sink. 'In fact, I was asked out on a date.' She giggled nervously. There, it was out. She'd said it and she waited for her mother's reaction.

'What sort of date?' Rose asked suspiciously as she flicked the crisp bacon out of the frying pan and into a metal dish which she placed in the oven to keep warm. Sally didn't know what to say and pretended to concentrate on lighting the gas under the kettle.

'What sort of date?' Rose repeated, cracking the first egg into the frying pan.

'Oh ... er ... dinner. A dinner date, he said. At the new bistro in town.' Just as Sally knew she would, her mother immediately took a keen interest. But Sally was no longer sure she wanted her mother to forbid her going. Overnight Sally had decided that, although the closeness of Doug had scared her a little, being held in his arms had been a wonderful and novel experience and she couldn't wait to see him again. Every time she thought of him, her tummy did funny little somersaults.

'Dinner at the bistro?' Rose flicked grease over the eggs. 'Do I know him?'
'No ... I don't think so.'

'Must have a good job if he can afford fancy restaurants! What does he do?'
'I don't know what he does, Mum.'

'Well, what's his name?' The eggs were prised away from the bottom of the pan, placed on another metal plate and popped in the oven, where they would take on the consistency of rubber joke eggs before anyone got to eat them. Her mother had many talents, but cooking a fried breakfast was not one of them.

'Doug, he said his name was Doug.'

'Doug? And where does this Doug come from, if he's not from around here?'

'From his accent, it sounded as if he's from Scotland.'

'Sounds as if he's from Scotland? Didn't you talk to the boy at all?' Rose had turned her attention to slicing bread for the toast.

'A bit ... while we were dancing,' muttered Sally

'A bit. Well, how old is he?'

'I've ... er ... no idea.'

'Not one of the boys from the church youth club then?' 'No, no. He ... er ... was older.'

'Older? How much older?'

'Oh ... not much ... in his twenties, I think.'

'Dancing with a stranger and all you know about him is he's called Doug and he "might be from Scotland". He's a long way from home.' Rose laid the bread out on the grill pan and slid it under the flames to toast. 'Well,' she said with a smile, 'perhaps you could find out a bit more about him on this date.'

What? Sally thought. That was it? Her mother was not forbidding her to go out with Doug? Sally's tummy churned. Oh help! She felt betrayed by her mother's calm acceptance of the fact that she was going out on a date with an older man. But she was simultaneously breathless and excited at the thought of seeing him again. Her world was turning upside down and she mumbled, 'Shall I set the table now?'

'Yes, please, and then you can give Lottie a call.'

Sally risked a peep at her mother and saw with relief that she had turned back to watch the toast.

'So ... you don't mind if I go out with him?' she asked cautiously.

Rose glanced across the kitchen to her daughter placing a chequered cloth on the table. Just recently she had begun to feel that she was losing what little influence and control she felt that she once had over her eldest. Tears pricked the back of her eyes. My little girl's growing up fast, she thought. Now that Sally was working and earning her own money, Rose knew that, despite the late start, it wouldn't be long before she discovered boys. When, she asked herself, had Sally turned into such a beauty? It had happened almost overnight. Sally asked again, 'So you definitely don't mind then, if I go out with him?'

Rose cleared her throat. 'I just hope you remember all I've taught you about taking care of yourself,' she said, blithely forgetting that she'd actually taught her daughter nothing at all about men and sex. That had all been taken care of by the nuns, thank goodness. She was quite sure that she could trust Sally, but she threw her a sharp look. Men, of course, could be very persuasive. 'You will remember, won't you, what I've told you about men?' she said, with a taut smile.

Sally repeated the mantra. 'About them only wanting one thing?' 'Yes. As long as you remember that, you'll be fine.'

'I'll remember, Mum,' Sally said. Suddenly, she didn't know whether to feel relieved that she could go on a date with Doug or worried that her mother was comfortable with it. Either way, it felt as though she had all at once been cut loose from her mother's apron strings. It was thrilling, unnerving and exciting all at the same time.

'Make sure you do! We don't want any mishaps like the O'Learys' girl.'

Sally recalled Bernadette O'Leary from school and the hastily-arranged wedding that had taken place a few months previously. 'Good job Empire line wedding dresses are all the rage at the moment, or she'd never have got anything to fit her by the time they got her up the aisle,' Rose continued uncharitably. 'If Mr O'Leary had owned a shotgun he would have had it at the church with him. The baby was born last week and they had the brass neck to tell the world that it was premature, when we all know it weighed eight pounds at birth. Fills the whole pram, that baby does, he's that big!'

'Mum!' Sally was shocked.

'If you want to see what will happen if you don't remember what I've told you, pop along to number 62 and ask to see the wedding photos. Head and shoulders all of them, except when she's holding a big bouquet over her huge stomach. Her bouquet was that large, I heard that she was staggering under the weight of it when her father marched her down the aisle!'

Sally giggled, but Rose's next words wiped the smile off her face.

'It's no laughing matter, Sally! You wouldn't do that to your father, or us, now would you?'

'No, Mum.' Sally meekly schooled her features. 'I'll call Lottie,' and she hurried away to wake her young sister, skipping up the stairs two at a time in the excitement of knowing she had a date. Her first real date! What surprised Sally most was that not for one moment had she anticipated her mother's reaction! Despite her doubts in the darkness last night, she knew she was looking forward to seeing Doug again.

When Sally left the kitchen, Rose sat down at the table and lit her first cigarette of the day, placed it between her lips, tilted back her head and drew in deeply. Rose had never enjoyed the best of health, her skin was pale and though she was of average height she was very slim. Her hair was always swept back from her face, kept there by a weekly trip to the hairdresser, where she would be closeted away in a cubicle for a couple of hours, eventually emerging with her hair sculpted into place for another week by a 'shampoo and set'. Her dark hair was in stark contrast to her pale skin and she rarely wore make-up apart from bright red lipstick, which invariably managed to stain her teeth; however her fingernails were always perfectly manicured. Rose worked hard to maintain the figure and looks she had in her youth. Tried a little too hard, for it seemed to Sally that her mother had never moved on from the 1950s. With her wasp waist, pencil skirts and seamed stockings, she seemed stuck in a time warp.

Rose got up and stood by the open kitchen door, it was already warm outside and in the garden the birds were greedily tucking in to four slices of incinerated toast that she had thrown out. Distracted by Sally's sudden announcement of a man in her life, she had set fire to the carefully cut slices; she decided she would wait for everyone to appear before chancing another round. She lit another cigarette as she waited for her family to come down to breakfast. She smiled fondly to think that at last her daughter had her first real date, and remembered her own first date with Joe. She recalled how, once they were officially engaged, they had very nearly given way to temptation. But she had held out until they were wed and she was very proud of the fact. Rose had achieved her own ambition to walk righteously up the aisle in virginal white and she hoped that Sally could wait until her wedding night before she succumbed to temptation.

Every night she knelt by her bed, rosary in hand, crossed herself and prayed that a decent young man would come along to marry her elder daughter. In the past few weeks, her prayers had changed to near-frantic pleas that Sally wouldn't get herself pregnant before she was married. It seemed to be happening to so many young girls from all types of backgrounds around the town. Rose's greatest worry now was the shame and humiliation that would be heaped on the family if Sally, too, fell by the wayside. She heard the gossip outside church every Sunday morning. She had joined in with it at times and, with others, had shown her disapproval by shunning the parents of any unfortunate lass who fell pregnant out of wedlock. No longer were friendly greetings called out to the parents who had failed in their duty to keep their daughter on the straight and narrow. Contact with them was cut off, as if distance from the disgrace would prevent it landing at their own front door. Rose had always carefully monitored her elder daughter's movements, forbidding her to socialise with anyone she considered undesirable or a bad influence. Her own strict and constrained

Catholic upbringing had filled her with inhibitions that she was determined to pass on to her own daughter. Fear was her chosen method of keeping Sally on the straight and narrow. Fear of divine retribution, fear of the priest, fear of what the neighbours might think, fear of becoming used goods, and – the greatest fear of all – fear of unwanted pregnancy!

The last few ounces of puppy fat had dropped off Sally in recent months and the tight pigtails that she had worn throughout her childhood had been cut off the day after she left school. Rose had them safe, a keepsake to remind herself of her little girl's long hair. Now Sally's blonde hair hung loose to her shoulders like a silken curtain. Her eyes were as blue as cornflowers on a summer's day and shone captivatingly above the friendly smile that always hovered on her lips.

'You'd better watch that daughter of yours,' the women had warned her, outside church on Sunday mornings.

'You'll be wanting to get her married off as quickly as possible,' they'd told her, 'before a fate worse than death befalls her!'

'With those looks and half the young boys in this town hanging round her, it won't be long before she succumbs ...'

At first Rose could not understand the fuss, then one day she looked at her daughter and felt she was looking at a stranger. As if a blindfold had been removed from her eyes, suddenly Rose could easily see how men would soon be falling at her daughter's feet. The whole package just spelled trouble with a capital 'T', and clearly others had recognised it too.

Rose began to fret. She lay awake at night worrying. How would they ever cope if Sally got herself pregnant? The very thought of being shunned by everyone brought her out in a cold sweat.

Joe had tried to calm her fears. They trusted Sally, didn't they? Sally might be beautiful but she wasn't stupid, was she? Rose agreed with him, but still she worried and lately had begun to grow weary with the constant anxiety about her elder daughter. As the weeks had turned into months and still Sally didn't seem interested in boys, her fears began to ebb.

Now, waiting for her family to come down to breakfast, she tried to justify why she had decided to encourage her daughter to go out with an older man. If he can afford to take her out to fancy restaurants in the middle of the week, he must have a good job, she thought. How could I stop her, anyway? She's not a child. We can't lock her in her bedroom and I don't want her sneaking out. Would she do that? Well, she might ... She had a rebellious streak in her at times, fed no doubt by that Caroline, Rose thought bitterly. And in any case, she could tell that this young man had set off a spark of interest in her daughter. No, Joe's right, we've got to trust her and ... who knows? Silently, she sent up a prayer that maybe her other prayers were about to be answered: that he would be suitable and kind to her daughter. Sally needs a nice young man, she thought, to look after her. Of course, she argued with herself, Sally was very young, but then she had only just turned eighteen when she married Joe, and they'd had a good marriage.

Chapter Two

Sally won the final argument over what she would wear on her first date. The way her mother was behaving, anyone would have thought it was her date, and if Rose had had her way Sally would have had her hair up in a chignon and worn 'something smart in navy with white accessories and a small corsage'. When Sally left home on that Wednesday evening, she was dressed in her favourite black pleated miniskirt, white ribbed polo neck sweater, gold chain belt and white knee-length boots. Her blonde hair, freshly washed and conditioned, hung loose to her shoulders. Wanting to look older, Sally decided to apply more than the usual dab of pink lipstick and made her first attempt at using mascara. It was a disaster, resulting in black smudges and red, smarting eyes. Luckily, she had begun her preparations in plenty of time and by the time she left the house her eyes had stopped stinging and much of the redness had gone. The second attempt had been more successful. Her blonde eyelashes looked thicker and darker, and she felt she had done a reasonably good job.

Peering through the bistro window, Sally saw Doug already seated at a table. Feeling a little self-conscious, she pushed the door and stepped inside.

Several diners stopped to stare at this striking young girl as she made her way to Doug's table and, as she approached, he stood and gave a quiet whistle of approval.

'Hey, you look great,' he whispered as he gave her a quick peck on the cheek. To Sally's embarrassment, she could feel herself blushing to the roots of her hair. Her uncontrollable blushes were the bane of her life; she hated being the centre of attention and at the slightest hint of teasing or a compliment she would colour up. Doug looked very smart in grey flannel trousers and a checked sports jacket; he'd worn a tie, too, and looked older than the young man in denims she had met at the party. He didn't particularly follow fashion but wore what he was comfortable in. Due to his height and physique, whatever he wore looked good and, combined with his smile and gift of the gab, the whole package meant that he was never short of a lady friend.

Doug pulled out a chair, usurping the over-attentive Italian waiter who, not to be outdone, immediately lifted the green napkin from Sally's place setting and swiftly draped it over her lap. Doug appeared irritated by the waiter, who continued to hover over Sally, describing in detail the evening's menu. In an effort to get rid of him, he brusquely ordered two bowls of spaghetti Bolognese and poured Sally a glass of red wine. Chianti was in vogue and the distinctive raffia-covered bottles made attractive candle-holders once the contents had been downed. A guttering red candle added a colourful layer to the landslide of wax already clinging to the side of the bottle in the centre of their table.

Sally was nervous in this unfamiliar situation but, as she sipped gingerly at her wine, she relaxed. At first she sat quietly, allowing Doug to do most of the talking – she had read in a magazine article on dating that men liked women who were good listeners. Guessing that Sally was ill at ease, Doug opened the conversation – he was an old hand in these situations and there wasn't much he didn't know or hadn't learnt about women.

'I suspect you have guessed I am from Scotland,' he began. 'Edinburgh, to be precise'.

Sally nodded and smiled, and continued to sip her wine.

'I did a degree that included engineering and now I have a job working for a large company involved in the oil business. They have offices all over the UK and other parts of the world besides, and it has been my good fortune to be sent down South, and in the process to have met you.'

Sally felt herself colouring up once more and took a large gulp of wine as a diversion.

'My parents' farm is just outside Edinburgh. I go back whenever I can – I love to walk or sometimes ride the hills with my father. I don't think he's forgiven me yet for not taking to farming quite the way he would have liked me to. I am the proverbial black sheep. The whole family are farmers, you see, and have been for generations.'

Sally nodded once more and smiled. She was thrilled to hear that he actually could ride – common ground at last!

'Well, enough about me,' he said. 'Tell me about yourself or I will blather on all night.'

'There's not a lot to tell. I'm a secretary and I work for a firm of solicitors in town.' The waiter returned to the table and placed two steaming bowls of pasta in front of them, interrupting Sally. Glancing down at the spaghetti topped with rich red meaty sauce, she fervently wished that she hadn't chosen to wear a white top. The waiter returned with a giant wooden peppermill wearing a lecherous smile but the innuendo of the phallic object was completely lost on Sally. Before she could continue speaking, he was back again with the parmesan cheese.

'Is that it? May we begin now?' Doug asked in a tone that left the waiter in no doubt that his presence was not appreciated, and he disappeared rapidly through the swing doors leading to the kitchen.

'Now, where were we? You work for a solicitor in town. Now, tell me about all the young men queuing up at your front door,' Doug prompted, genuinely wanting to know more about this young girl who had, all unknowingly and so innocently, swept him completely off his very experienced feet. Most evenings he would be entertaining any one of a string of girlfriends, safe in the knowledge that he'd get his leg over before the night was out: what was he thinking of? His mates had been right; he had a playboy 'love 'em and leave 'em' reputation, and Sally was definitely not what he usually went fishing for!

'There aren't any,' Sally replied honestly.

'I don't believe you – a good-looking lassie like you.' Doug grinned at her as he picked up his fork and began twirling at the pasta.

'Now you're embarrassing me.' The almost-empty glass of red wine in her hand fortified Sally's direct response. 'Honestly, I have to admit it, you're my first date. I've been out to the cinema a few times with a group of friends, but never for dinner, alone with ... with ... ' Losing her courage, Sally's voice trailed off.

'With ...?' he prompted, his hazel eyes twinkling and gazing into hers as he tried to suppress a smile.

'Well, with a man, I suppose is what I want to say.'

Doug laughed and reached across the table to pat her hand. 'Don't worry, you'll be quite safe in my hands,' he whispered. 'Once I can get hold of you,' he added jokingly.

Sally felt as though giant butterflies were having a party in the pit of her stomach. She was suddenly apprehensive. 'Get hold of her?' Whatever did he mean? Instead of asking him, she decided to concentrate on the almost impossible feat of eating the writhing spaghetti without flicking sauce all over her white jumper.

'Do you have any hobbies, Sal?' Doug asked, catching Sally with her mouth full of pasta and causing her to swallow it quickly.

'Well, my main hobby, I suppose, is riding and I have a favourite horse at the local riding stables. I go most weekends to ride and help out with the young children and their ponies. I like any sort of animal, really, but my mother doesn't allow pets in the house – she says they make the house smell. I also like swimming and tennis. My friend has a dog and over the years she's let me share him. We used to take him out for walks together, but sadly he's getting a bit old and arthritic now.' She smiled at Doug. 'Do you have any other hobbies besides walking?'

'My job takes up most of my time and the walking fills in the rest – then of course there's always a pretty girl to take out to dinner.' He smiled across at her. 'I usually go back home to Scotland for my holidays and help my parents on the farm. That way I can combine work with pleasure! Some of the best walks are right on their doorstep.' Seeing that she had finished eating, he asked, 'Would you like some Italian ice cream or a coffee, or both?'

'Just a coffee would be fine. I'm a bit full.' Sally replied. How grown-up! – her mother had never allowed her to drink coffee at home. Doug ordered two coffees and asked for the bill. Sally tried not to grimace as the bitter, strong taste of the espresso coffee lingered on her tongue.

'It's better with a wee bit of sugar.' Doug offered her the bowl of misshapen brown sugar cubes and she gratefully stirred one into the black liquid that remained in her cup. It immediately made the concoction more palatable.

'Okay, the damages are paid – shall we go?' Doug pushed his wallet into his jacket pocket, stood up and walked round to her chair. She got to her feet and gratefully took his outstretched hand. Although the coffee had in some way counterbalanced her wine intake, she felt a little light-headed.

Once outside the bistro, Doug draped his arm protectively around her shoulder as they strolled to the car park at the back of the building.

'I'd better get you home, young lady.'

To Sally's confusion, her reaction to this offer was a combination of relief tinged with disappointment.

'My car is just over there' – he pointed towards a dark green Ford Cortina at the far side of the car park. 'She's nothing too fancy, but having spent my days driving father's tractors and the old Land Rover, it feels almost luxurious.'

'Compared to my father's old Austin it looks very fancy,' Sally giggled. When they reached the car, Doug hesitated. Stepping round in front of her, he put both his hands on her shoulders and held her at her arm's length. He smiled as he studied the now slightly worried expression on the face that looked back up at him. She was so young, so innocent; what I am doing here? he asked himself. He stared into her sparkling blue eyes. For perhaps the first time in his life, he felt out of control in what to him was a very familiar situation. So many times he had taken a young woman out to dinner, so many times he had taken them in his experienced arms afterwards, but this time, for some strange reason, he felt a little apprehensive. This girl excited and scared him at the same time.

Placing a hand under Sally's chin, he gently tilted her face upwards. He slid his other hand round her waist. 'Would you care to come a wee bit closer, Sal?'

He spoke quietly. Slowly, he drew her towards him. There was no resistance as he brushed his lips softly against hers. Then he kissed each cheek before bringing his lips down firmly on to hers. No further encouragement was needed for Sally, as she slipped her arms around his neck. He pulled her in close and felt her relax and her body mirror the contours of his. At last she was in his arms! He had dreamed of this moment all week and it was all he had thought it might be. He was on fire! With one hand he began to caress the back of her neck – then abruptly came to his senses. Suddenly he pushed her away.

'Woweee!' He chuckled hoarsely, making light of the situation. 'You could be dangerous. Get in the car. I'm taking you home.'

That night Sally had even more difficulty falling asleep. It could have been the coffee, but she lay wide awake in the dark, reliving that kiss a dozen times. She had been kissed properly for the first time in her life and it had been so easy, so natural. She remembered with toe-curling embarrassment the experiments outside the church hall at the Catholic Youth Club. Then, it had been so premeditated: self-conscious, awkward clashes of noses and teeth as the inexperienced participants approached each other's lips from the same angle. All that indecision: how long to keep at it and what noise level was required. Afterwards the girls had invariably got together to discuss technique, while the boys had taken votes on the best snogger. But tonight there had been no game plan, no tactics and no assessment. Tonight she had just been swept up into Doug's arms and well and truly kissed. To her alarm and confusion, her instinctive reaction and response had been to hold on to him tightly and kiss him in return. It must be love, she decided. Yes, that's it, I'm in love with Doug...

With her feelings in turmoil and her body in freefall, she lay in the dark and searched her mind for all she knew on the subject of love and sex. She recalled the painfully embarrassing biology lessons at the convent. Those excruciating hours sitting in a class of red-faced teenage girls trying not to giggle as they were given sketchy details of the act necessary for procreation. The breeding habits of rabbits were used to illustrate the lecture and the irony of this choice was lost on the room full of innocent Catholic schoolgirls. Taught by the nuns in a matter-of-fact manner, there had never been any deviation from the biology books. The inference was that, like female rabbits, copulation was something married women had to endure to have babies. Love and emotions were never mentioned and had not seemed in any way connected with the topic. The nuns painted a very unappetising picture of what a woman must submit to within the sanctity of marriage, made more lurid, no doubt, to deter those who might be tempted to taste forbidden fruits before being joined in holy matrimony. As for the male body, Sally could not begin to imagine what it might look like unclothed; an outline drawing of two copulating rabbits was all that had been proffered. The scant wording in the margin gave the additional information that the male rabbit was on top. There was no mention of the Christian preference for the missionary position.

During her early teens, an approach to her mother – which took days of plucking up courage and many false starts – to ask where babies came from had resulted in the unhelpful information, 'It's like a chicken laying an egg'. Her mother had mumbled these words of wisdom with her head bent over the washing-up bowl, studiously scrubbing at the same clean plate, obviously finding the topic deeply embarrassing. Then, as if it might make things clearer, she had generously added, 'It's just the way it is. It's nature.'

Having assimilated this meagre information, Sally realised she knew little about love and sex and that none of it tied in with the explosion of feelings she had experienced when Doug had kissed her. Eventually she drifted off to sleep, deciding that her mother's information, scant and unenlightening as it was, was probably the most accurate: 'It's nature.' In any case, from the way Doug had reacted to that kiss, Sally came to the conclusion that he would probably never ask her out again. He had dropped her off outside her parents' house with a vague promise that he'd 'be in touch', but he hadn't said how or when this would be. He hadn't even asked her for a phone number. Not that she would have been able to give him one, anyway. Her parents were not on the phone and personal calls were not allowed where she worked – but at least it would have shown he was interested in seeing her again. In the dark, Sally quietly shed a few tears at the thought that she wouldn't see him again.

But she was wrong. A few days later Sally was surprised and delighted when the office switchboard put a personal call through to her. 'It's a young man for you. He said he'd make it brief!' Doris, the middle-aged spinster barked down the phone at her. True to his promise, Doug hastily asked, and Sally quickly agreed, to let him pick her up from home that evening.

As soon as she replaced the heavy black receiver on its cradle, Doris appeared at the door of the small office that Sally occupied as a junior secretary. Thinking she was in trouble, Sally began to apologise. 'I am so sorry, Doris. I didn't give him this number. I only told him I worked for solicitors in town and he must have worked it out.'

'I didn't come along to tell you off, lass, just to warn you to watch that one! He'll be your downfall! Too charming by half! Sell fridges to Eskimos, he could,' she predicted with a wagging finger. Doris always wagged a finger to stress the importance of what she was saying. Sally smiled at her and promised to 'watch out'.

Rushing home after work, Sally felt euphoric. He had taken the trouble to find out where she worked and had asked her out again. Excitedly, she rushed indoors and upstairs, followed by her mother. In the privacy of her bedroom, she quickly explained to Rose about the phone call, unable to keep the sparkle from her eyes. As she talked, Rose knew she had been right to trust her daughter. But this 'Doug' was certainly clever if he had found out where Sally worked and, in spite of that old harridan on the switchboard, had actually managed to get put through to Sally! She had only tried once to speak to her daughter at work, when Lottie had fallen over at school and been rushed to hospital. Rose had tried to call her from the phone box outside the hospital, frightened and tearful, and knowing she could not disturb Joe at the bank.

'Well, is her sister dangerously ill?' the switchboard operator had asked. 'Er ... no, not dangerously. They think she's broken her ankle ...' Rose had sobbed down the phone.

'A broken ankle?'

'Or maybe ... they said ... it might just be badly sprained,' Rose had tried to explain between sobs.

'Now it's a sprained ankle, is it?'

'I don't know ... I need Sally ... to help me.' Rose had wailed down the phone.

'What about your husband?'

'He's at the bank, at work.'

'Well, Sally is at work too. I could lose my job and so could she if the boss finds out she's had a personal phone call put through to her "because her little sister has a sprained ankle".'

'Please let me talk to my daughter.'

'Listen, love, I'll tell you what to do. You find out just how badly hurt your little girl is and if she's in any danger, call back and I'll ask if I can put you through. Okay?'

Rose lost her courage as well as the last of her change and tearfully put the phone down. The whole episode had deeply upset her and she'd been unwell for days afterwards, and never again had she dared ring Sally at work.

He must really like her, Rose thought, otherwise why would he bother? Briefly, she wondered what he'd said to get put through. Rose was impressed – he was obviously no fool. She was insistent that Sally had something to eat before she went out, but Sally's tummy was doing cartwheels and, after a few attempts to swallow, she left her tea and ran back upstairs to wash and change. Between choosing an outfit, brushing her hair and applying her make-up, she hurried intermittently back and forth to her parents' bedroom to peek through the net curtains to watch for the arrival of Doug's car. She didn't know why, but she didn't want Doug to meet her mother, not yet. She wanted to skip out of the house before he had a chance to ring the doorbell and bring both her mother and Lottie hurrying to the front door.

But Rose had other plans and was a step ahead of her daughter. As his car pulled up outside the garden gate, Rose opened the front door and, before Sally could get down the stairs, had greeted Doug and invited him in. He stood in the hallway, politely answering Rose's probing questions. He'd be taking Sally ten-pin bowling, if she'd like to do that, he was explaining.

He turned to Sally as she reached the bottom stair. 'Hello, hope I'm not too early for you?'

'No, you're bang on time, I'm ready.' Sally hastily opened the front door and ushered Doug out. She prayed that he had not heard her mother's parting stage whisper, 'What a nice young man, so polite. Good-looking, too.'

The bowling alley was busy and the thunder of the heavy balls crashing down towards the pins made the ground shudder. Doug was wearing grey flannel trousers and a white shirt under a casual tweed jacket. As he removed his jacket and rolled up his shirtsleeves, Sally couldn't help focusing on a few dark hairs peeping out of his open-necked shirt. She was shocked to find it aroused both her curiosity and excitement, but as her emotions seemed like a hand grenade with the pin pulled, she really wasn't sure what she was feeling.

Fascinated, she watched the muscles tighten in his strong arm and his back arch in one graceful movement as he launched the heavy bowling ball with ease. It was completely off centre and ended up in the gully, leaving all the pins safely standing to attention. He turned to Sally, laughing.

'Okay, kitten, your turn ...'

Sally stepped forward and picked up a ball. Momentarily she held it up in front of her and then slowly and deliberately sent it on its way. Oh, no, she thought, as the ball hurtled in a straight line towards the centre pin. It's going to be a strike! Her mother had always told her that a woman should never attempt to win when playing games against a man. It was unladylike to be competitive and was something men didn't like. If a girl wanted to keep a man, she should always let him win. As all ten pins somersaulted out of sight, Sally felt herself blushing and heard Doug laughing behind her. Just for a second, she contemplated apologising for a 'lucky hit'. Just for a second longer, she thought about 'throwing the game', but that rebellious streak took over. During the past few days, she had grown tired of feeling so out of control and at the mercy of the strange emotions being stirred up inside her. *So what if I am good at something?* she thought, and turned to grin back at him, settling for a shrug of her shoulders. Sally began to relax and the game progressed much as it had started.

'Now I know why the boys weren't queuing at your front door – you were down here practising,' he smiled ruefully at her. 'Well, maybe there are some things I can teach you,' he whispered in her ear as they walked hand-in-hand to the coffee lounge to the side of the bowling lanes. Sally sat at an empty table while Doug collected two frothing cappuccinos from the counter.

'I'm busy for the next few days, but how about going to the cinema on Saturday? If I ask you now, I don't have to chat up that awfully suspicious lady on your switchboard,' he said as he placed the cups carefully on the table and sat down opposite her.

'You mean Doris? She's okay, really. It's all very sad. She lost her fiancé in the war and has never looked at another man since. She talks about him quite a bit and she brought his photograph into work one day to show me. He was wearing an RAF uniform and looked so young.'

'There are a lot of those war virgins around. Kept themselves for their man coming home from war and, when he didn't, it became a lifetime's habit they couldn't kick,' Doug said.

Sally blushed to the roots of her hair at the word 'virgin'. She had heard it used regularly in church, but there it seemed somewhat detached from its biological meaning. To hear Doug referring to Doris as a virgin seemed so personal.

Seeing the blush that spread over her face, Doug put his hand over Sally's.

'I'm sorry, that was tactless of me. She's your friend.'

'No, no, it's nothing like that ...' Sally began and then wished she hadn't.

'Oh! Do I detect we're on difficult ground?' Doug leaned forward. 'Is virginity a taboo subject?'

Not knowing where to start, Sally sat in silence; then, in a quiet voice she said, 'It's just that I've never talked about ... well ... those sort of things before. The nuns taught us, they said that ladies didn't discuss women's things with men ...' Before she could say any more, Doug gave a chuckle.

'I'm sorry, Sal, I'm not laughing at you, honestly I'm not, but the thought of yon nuns advising and preparing young ladies for the outside world is laughable.' He leaned forward and lowered his voice further. 'Take their vows, for instance. They're predominantly a list of "Thou shalt nots". Then there's the lifestyle – closeted away from the real world and any sort of temptation. In my experience the fruit of their doctrines is either a totally frigid woman or the complete opposite.' He resisted the temptation to ask in jest which one she might be.

'Come on, let's go back to the car and sit and talk for a wee while. It's getting a little bit too crowded in here.' The café had been steadily filling with thirsty bowlers and the noise of their excited chatter as they held post mortems on their games was beginning to make holding a quiet conversation impossible.

When they reached the car, Doug startled her by opening one of the back doors. Seeing her hesitation, he said, 'It's okay. You're quite safe. I've never taken an unwilling woman in my life and I'm not about to start now.'

The innocent remark surprisingly produced a twinge of jealousy and she found herself wondering who these 'willing women' had been, or if any of them were still around. Was he really busy all week, she wondered, or was he amusing himself with her youth and inexperience and returning to a 'willing woman' between the times he spent with her? Her mother's warnings about the devious ways of men came to the fore ... they only wanted one thing and they 'got what they wanted and left soiled goods'. And 'No decent man wanted you if you were second-hand,' with the emphasis on 'decent'. Sally was sure she shouldn't do it, but she pushed the warnings aside and slid down onto the back seat anyway. She wanted to know about love and sex. All her other friends had been having fun for years, it seemed to her, while she had watched from the side lines. It was her turn now and besides, she thought, I've got to start somewhere.

Doug got in beside her and gently placed his arm around her shoulders, drawing her head down onto his chest. He could well imagine what sort of preparation and advice Sally had received on courtship and men, and braced himself for the ensuing conversation.

He guessed Sally was innocent and inexperienced, but dangerous too. It was fine having a bit of fun with some girls but when he found himself inadvertently caught up with an innocent, he would make good his escape before he could be lured into doing something that most certainly he would later regret. Particularly those with mothers like Sal's. In this sort of situation, he would normally have made some kind of 'let 'em down gently' excuse and left – permanently! But he was drawn to this young girl like no one he'd ever met before. He was infatuated with her. He thought about her constantly. He was amazed at himself

– he could have dated any one of half a dozen young girls and been well and truly laid by this point in the evening. He took a deep breath.

'Now Sal, it's just you and me. I want you to put aside for a minute or two all the things that you've so obviously been taught. You know, all those warnings about the evil ways of men. Men and women can talk together, you know, it's quite a normal and natural thing to do. So if you have any questions, don't be shy. Just ask away and I'll answer them as honestly as I can.' His voice was gentle and encouraging and it gave Sally the confidence to speak up.

After a short silence she said, 'There is something I would like to know ...'

'Go on,' he prompted gently.

'Why did you push me away after kissing me on that first date? Did I do something wrong?'

'Oh, no, no, you did nothing wrong. You were so lovely, you mustn't think you did anything wrong. But I might have, if I had not stopped it right there.'

'Oh! Why was that?'

Doug sighed and silently cursed the Catholic religion for its ignorance and secretiveness. He was genuinely amazed at how little groundwork had been covered at the convent and how completely ill-prepared Sally seemed for adulthood.

'Look, I'm not sure if I'll be very good at this, but I'll try and explain.' Never in his life had he started a love affair with a biology lesson. The girls in Edinburgh needed very little tutoring – in fact, he had learned a lot from them! Doug was usually so confident with women, but this girl was making him feel nervous. 'Well, Sally ... when you kiss a man the way you kissed me, it physically excites him ...' he paused. Oh Hell! How could he explain something like this to her? 'Okay, I see ... and is that a problem? You being excited?' she asked him innocently.

Realising she had completely missed the point, he took a deep breath and ploughed on.

'Well, it can be. Not the kiss. That's not a problem, but things can get out of hand ...' He hesitated, not sure how far to take this, but persevered. 'It's just that certain ... er ... physical changes take place when a man gets excited. He becomes physically aroused. When you pressed your body against mine, the way you did, well ... things happened ...'

'So what happened when we kissed?' She asked.

While Sally was becoming more at ease talking to him, in contrast, Doug was becoming more and more uncomfortable with the way the conversation was going!

'Kitten, do you know anything at all about animal reproduction?'

'Oh yes!' She chirped, relieved she could show Doug that she wasn't completely ignorant of the facts. 'We did that with Sister Frances,' she said, hoping to impress him with her knowledge. 'Sister explained that the male plants a seed and it grows in the female. She told us all about rabbits.'

Doug sighed. Rabbits! Bloody rabbits! Perhaps he should never have started this conversation. Although his parents were farmers, which meant he was probably more familiar with the subject of animal reproduction than many, he was finding the task he had taken on extremely daunting. He wondered just how little Sally did know. He took another deep breath. 'Now for the six million dollar question. Do you know how the seed is planted?'

'Vaguely ...'

'How vaguely?'

Sally went quiet. Once again she felt totally inadequate and in a tearful voice, barely audible, she said, 'Well, there was this drawing of two rabbits ...'

Doug's arms encircled her. 'Whoa! Stop right there! Forget about the bloody rabbits,' he said, giving her a squeeze. 'What we have here is no' a big problem and believe me, sweetheart, there's a cure, so don't get upset about it. Come on. Let's get you home, I don't want to disillusion your mother. I believe she thinks I am a "nice young man" and modesty forbids me to repeat the rest of what I overheard.' He laughed and planted a kiss on her nose. Sally groaned, 'Oh no, I could throttle my mother. I was praying that you hadn't heard all that.'

Chapter Three

The next day at the office Sally was thoroughly miserable; she felt betrayed by the sex education the nuns provided at the convent and felt stupid with all her talk about rabbits that had made Doug laugh at her. She had no context for the strange sensations Doug aroused in her: the feel of his strong arms around her and his kisses! The question played like a loop in her mind – Was it love? Am I in love, whatever love is? How would I know for sure? In vain, she tried to concentrate on her work, but the questions kept thrusting themselves to the front of her mind as she struggled for an answer and, more importantly, a solution.

Her office door opened and Doris stepped in, carrying a cup of tea which she placed on Sally's desk.

'Cheer up! Where's our happy-faced secretary? We've not had a smile from you since you came in. It's not like you. Tell Auntie Doris all about it before Mr Thomson sends down for you to take the morning's dictation.'

Doris wasn't particularly tall but her ample bosom made her seem larger than she was. Stout and looking older than her forty-five years, Doris was a northerner with a heart of gold and it was well known that her bark was worse than her bite.

Despite the tough time she had given Sally's mum on the phone, she had, in fact, let Sally know that her little sister had had a fall. Doris had told her that her mother was upset and that if Sally wanted to get off early, she'd cover for her. Sally had thanked her and reassured her that her mother was always upset where her little sister was concerned, but she had taken Doris up on her offer. When Sally got home, her little sister had been stretched out on the sofa with a sprained ankle that the hospital had strapped up. Her mother was all smiles as she fed Lottie ice cream from a bowl. It was a treat after the accident, her mother said. Sally had been upset! Her mother hadn't even noticed that she had arrived home early, and as for feeding Lottie ice cream! For heaven's sake, her sister was nine years old and her mother still insisted on treating her like a baby! But Sally knew it was pointless to say anything where Lottie was concerned. Lottie, in her mother's eyes, was a 'proper little girl' and Rose doted on her.

Sally looked up at Doris's homely face and quickly looked away again. 'I can't tell you,' she replied in a whisper, blushing. 'It's too ... difficult ...'

Sally suspected Doris was the last person who could help her. But Doris lingered by her desk and lit a cigarette.

'It's that new young man of yours, isn't it? If he makes you unhappy he's not worth having around. Take it from me, a girl like you can take her pick of any man. Now, my Bill ...' Her eyes took on a faraway look and she sighed. 'Treated me like a princess, he did, even though we had our moments. Mind, we always made up after rows and I liked to send him back to the war with a smile on his face, even that last time.' Doris had been watching Sally's face and as Sally's eyes opened wider in surprise, Doris drew on her cigarette and winked at her, blowing the smoke out of the corner of her mouth. 'It was like that in the war. You never knew, you see, so you had to, really. We all did it, if truth were known. They had to have something to take back with them, see, warm memories of home, like. There wasn't much time for weddings and such but he always intended to do right by me when the war was over.' She patted Sally's shoulder lightly and, without another word, hurried back to her switchboard.

Sally stared down at the cup of tea Doris had brought her. Doris! The office virgin! Who would ever have believed it? As the significance of what Doris had just said sank in, Sally picked up the cup and saucer and went through to the switchboard office where Doris sat cheerily answering the phone and re-routing the calls through to the various solicitors' offices. Putting a caller on hold, Doris smiled up at her. Glancing round to make sure that no one else was in earshot, Sally whispered, 'Doris, I need your help. I can't ask my mum again, the nuns didn't tell me very much, and even then it was about rabbits, and ...'

'Oh, I think I can guess what this is all about,' Doris broke into Sally's outpouring of uncertainty. 'I thought something was clouding your mind. Let's not go into it here, lass. Come and have some tea with me this evening and I'll see if I can't find you a book.' She paused as she scribbled down her address, tore the piece of paper from her notebook and handed it to Sally. 'I knew something was worrying you and I thought it had to be something to do with that young man. You're playing out of your league with that one. Mind, I had the same problem meself when I met Bill. Completely ignorant of the facts of life I was, I was that innocent. It all came as quite a shock, I can tell you.' She winked at Sally again and whispered, 'But once you know what's what, there's a lot of pleasure to be had from a good man,' and, with a girlish giggle, she turned back to the busy switchboard.

The rest of the day passed quickly enough and after work Sally popped home briefly to change out of her work clothes and set off to catch the bus across town, calling out to her mother as she left that she would be back in time for supper. Luckily, her mother assumed she was visiting Caroline and neither asked any questions nor made any comments.

Sally glanced at the address and directions Doris had given her and soon found Park View Terrace. Try as she might, she couldn't see a park and wondered fleetingly whose idea it was to call it 'Park View' when there wasn't a patch of green in sight. Walking past several neatly-kept terraced houses, she rang the bell of number 45 and Doris opened the door. There was no hallway and Sally found herself stepping straight into a small, homely sitting room.

'Come on in, lass, and make yourself at home. The kettle's on.'

While Doris was busy in the kitchen, Sally looked round the tiny sitting room, which was neatly furnished with a small two-seater sofa facing the fireplace and an armchair on either side. Seeing an unopened book on the arm of one of the chairs, Sally sat down in the other one. A low coffee table stood between the sofa and the fireplace; on it sat an ashtray, a table lighter and a silver cigarette box, rather like the one that Sally's mother had. On either side of the chimney breast, both alcoves contained glass-fronted cabinets. One displayed an old-fashioned china tea set, complete with teapot, sugar bowl and milk jug, and in the other were numerous sepia photographs of unsmiling adults in old- fashioned frames. In one, a young couple stood rigidly side by side, the woman dressed in an early 1900s-style wedding dress with a halo of orange blossom around her head and the groom wearing an Army uniform. Sally wondered if they were Doris's parents. Several frames held photos of overdressed children, glumly posed on plump cushions. Possibly Doris was among them, but it was hard to tell. She would have liked to look closer at all the photos, but was reluctant to intrude on Doris's privacy. She glanced at the mantelpiece, where a large clock ticked loudly, then turned her head to gaze around at the rest of the room. Against the far wall, behind the sofa, stood a dark oak sideboard on which, in pride of place, was a photo Sally recognised. It was the one Doris had shown her of Bill in his RAF uniform.

'Here we are, then.' Doris returned and placed a tray carefully on the coffee table. 'I don't know,' she tut-tutted as she poured the tea, 'you'd think in this day and age that the lasses would be given more information. Be better prepared, like. I can understand how it happened years since. I never had a word from my own mother nor, no doubt, she from hers, but nowadays I thought everything was supposed to be more easy-going, more out in the open. Like I said, when I met my Bill I hadn't a clue, but I soon learned. He'd been about a bit, and it's not a bad thing to have an experienced man. From the sound of yours, I'd say he's no beginner either. Anyhow, I popped into the library on the way home and got you this book. It's not much, but it's a start.' She picked up the book from the arm of her chair and handed it to Sally. 'Take it home with you and bring it back when you've finished. You've got two weeks on it.'

She paused to open the cigarette box and offer it to Sally. Sally shook her head. Smoking was something that she could not bring herself to do – what was the point of filling your lungs with smoke? Doris took a cigarette and lit it. Taking a deep drag, she blew the smoke up towards the ceiling and settled back in the armchair.

'My best advice to you is to let him teach you. Nobody knows better than a man what pleasures him most – you can only get so much out of a book. But I'll warn you, don't think the first time is going to be all roses and violins. Just bite the bullet and get it over with. Then, if you have a good man, there is a deal of pleasure for both of you. Don't take any notice of these women who reckon it's your duty. Oh, and make sure he uses protection, you don't want any slip-ups.' Doris patted her belly and raised a meaningful eyebrow. Satisfied with one deep drag on her cigarette, she delivered the rest of her advice without taking another. It wasn't an easy subject but, despite her own sense of embarrassment about disclosing her past to this young girl, she wanted to help Sally. She flicked ash into the ashtray, thinking that she wouldn't want to help any of the hoity-toity young madams in the office, always whispering in corners, giggling and poking fun at the old spinster on the switchboard. Oh yes, Doris knew what they thought about her and she also knew that they only spoke nicely to her when they wanted a favour, like asking her to put through a call from one of their boyfriends. Sally was different – well-spoken, polite, always friendly and pleasant. She had no idea why, but to her Sally had an air of vulnerability and she wanted to help her.

'Doris, I'm not planning to jump straight into bed with Doug. I don't think I should unless I'm married ...' Realising how that must have sounded, Sally blushed and hastily added, 'as there isn't a war on, I mean. I think I should wait. I just want to know what to expect if ...'

Thankfully, Doris interrupted her. 'War or no war, let me tell you something else, lass, something that them there nuns wouldn't know anything about. It's all well and good them saying, "not till you're wed," but when a man you feel something for sets his hands on you, every part of you will want him.' Yes, oh yes! Sally thought she knew exactly what Doris was saying. 'It takes a strong will to fight it. Much stronger than I ever had, anyway.' Doris took a sip of tea and a drag on her cigarette. 'When Mother Nature has got your body where she wants it, curved in all the right places and hormones on full steam ahead, no Mother Superior's warning is going to stop you. Unless you're frigid, of course.'

'What does "frigid" mean?' Sally asked, recognising the word from her conversation with Doug.

'Frigid is what some women become. I doubt they are born that way. Frigid, you see, well, frigid women ... how can I explain this ... well, they can't ever abide a man near them. But I shouldn't bother your head about that. You wouldn't be asking me these questions if that was your problem.'

Sally smiled and nodded. She felt a little uncomfortable, wondering if not being frigid meant that she might be at the other end of the scale. If Doris could already tell she wasn't frigid, maybe she was nearer to becoming what her mother called a 'loose woman'. Sally knew only too well what the 'slip-ups' were that Doris had referred to, but there was something else she didn't quite understand.

'Doris, what did you mean by "use protection"? Protection from what?'

'Oh dear, lass, you're not safe to be out on your own,' Doris laughed as she leaned forward to stub out her cigarette. She said in very quiet voice, 'it's something the man puts on himself, down below, so his seeds don't get through to you.'

'Oh!' Sally blushed furiously.

'More tea? I can make another brew.' Doris reached for the teapot.

'No, no thank you, Doris. I have to catch the bus back in time for supper at home. I really appreciate all your help and the advice. Thank you. There is no way I could have talked to my mum about any of this.'

'Me neither, lass, me neither.' Doris smiled and shook her head sadly. 'But I'm always here, lass. These talks are our secret. I swear they think I'm nowt but a dried-up old spinster back at the office. Wouldn't want to shock them all! Don't forget your book.'

As Sally got up to leave, Doris handed her the well-thumbed book from the armchair where Sally had left it. At the door, Doris put her arms around Sally and gave her a motherly peck on the cheek.

Soon after supper Sally started yawning and, using tiredness as an excuse, took herself off to bed for an early night. Once in the privacy of her bedroom, she reached into the bottom of her roomy handbag and pulled out the library book. Flicking through it, she stopped at the page showing an outline drawing of the naked body of a man. Suffused with guilt and a strange private embarrassment, she studied the drawing of the flaccid penis with curiosity. So that's what it looks like! Well, she certainly didn't remember seeing anything like it on the school rabbits. Next she turned to the chapter on 'Making Love' and as she read it, was aware of an intense, inexplicable feeling of excitement growing deep within her. She had an overwhelming desire to reach down and feel those private sensual parts of her body referred to in the book. But that would be wrong – Sally had learnt that when she was four years old. Her mother had caught her with her hand, placed innocently and absent-mindedly, as young children do, down the front of her knickers while reading one of her Ladybird books. She had been slapped soundly and told off. It had left its mark on her, as had her mother's hand. Sally read the library book until her eyes closed and it slipped out of her hand onto the floor.

The following morning she woke with a guilty start. Her bedside light had been switched off, so she knew that her mother must have come in to turn it off for her after she had fallen asleep. Sitting up in bed, she began frantically searching for the book, wondering where it had disappeared to in the night. Fearing that her mother had found it, she was relieved to see it that it had fallen to the floor on the other side of the bed. She quickly retrieved it and hid it high up on the top shelf of her wardrobe under several jumpers.

On Saturday evening Sally dressed early and looked out for Doug's car. This time she managed to get down the front garden path and into the passenger seat before her mother had a chance to drag him into the house for further questioning.

'Are you eager to see the film or are you in a rush to get to me?' he grinned, pecking her on the cheek.

'I was trying to save you the embarrassment of another round of questions and answers with my mother,' Sally replied.

'Och, she means well. I suspect she's never had a big bad man after her daughter before. Maybe she wants to know just how dishonourable my intentions really are.'

Sally pulled a face and gave Doug a fixed grin. She was slowly becoming accustomed to his teasing and no longer felt threatened by it. They were late arriving at the cinema and the lights had dimmed as they edged along to their seats in the centre of the back row.

The film Doug had chosen for them was a new release, a raunchy X-rated comedy for the adult audience. Sally had never been to an X-rated film before and was unsure of what to expect. There were several sex scenes, involving writhing semi-naked bodies and a lot of moaning and groaning, plus occasional shrieking. Sally was glad of the darkness to hide her blushes and embarrassment. When Doug slid his arm along the back of her seat so that her head rested on his shoulder, she willingly leaned against him, enjoying the closeness of his body. After a while, he put one hand under her chin and turning her face towards his, he kissed her, long and slow. His tongue probed Sally's mouth. His breath was sweet and minty and she followed his lead. She held him tight, drawn to his strength and excited by his nearness. In no time at all, it seemed, the film had ended and, as the credits scrolled and the heavy red velvet curtains in front of the screen drew slowly together, there was a stampede of those anxious to leave before the playing of the National Anthem. Sally and Doug, in no mood to rush anywhere, loyally stood until the final bars faded away.

'How about a quick drink in The Crown?' Doug offered as he held out her coat.

Sally giggled. 'Will they serve me?'

'Being a gentleman I can hardly say that you look older than your years, but I think you might just get away with it.' He winked at her cheekily.

Inside the pub, Sally peered through the haze of smoke and looked around the lounge bar. So this is what a pub looks like on the inside, she said to herself. It was the first time she had ever been inside a public house and, at seventeen, was still under the legal age to be drinking. Her father didn't drink much at all, maybe the occasional half-pint of beer at weekends or on holiday and a small whisky for celebrations. On the rare occasions when her parents had gone to a pub, Sally was always made to wait outside in the pub garden with her younger sister, a glass of pop and a packet of crisps.

Doug escorted her to a small table in a quiet corner, then walked over to the bar. A few minutes later he was back with a glass of white wine for her and a whisky for himself. Sitting down opposite her, he took a sip of his drink and leaned across the table to take Sally's hand. He hesitated. There was something he had to say to her, something he needed to get off his chest. He wanted Sally. What he felt for her he had never felt before in his life, but he also wanted to be fair. He had played the field and he knew that she was everything he desired. He also knew that she had no experience of life whatsoever and to lay claim to her at such a young age worried him deeply. Probably, he thought, she would want some time to have fun with boys of her own age. He was seven years older than her. That's not a large age gap, he thought. In years to come the gap would not be so significant but just now, at this time of her life, he must seem like an old man to her. He squeezed her hand gently and attempted to explain his thoughts.

'You're very special to me, Sal, but you're so young. It seems unfair to keep you for myself when you might want to go out and have some fun,' he began.

Sally's stomach lurched. Doug was preparing to cast her aside, using her youth as an excuse. He was doing it very kindly, but she knew where this was leading. Sally felt she was good at summing up situations.

'I'm sorry, I expect I bore you because I'm not experienced, like all the "willing women" you've had in your life,' she mumbled.

Doug realised that she had totally misunderstood his intentions, but he had not missed the hint of jealousy in her voice when she mentioned his 'willing women'.

'Absolutely not, Sal, it's nothing to do with experience, willingness or anything like that. You're only seventeen. I'm nearly twenty-four. Do you really want to hang around with an old man of twenty-four?' Sally looked deep into his eyes as he smiled at her with one quizzical eyebrow raised.

How could she tell him that she thought about him most of the day and night? That she had been so worried after their first date that he might not contact her again? That she found him scary but exciting and how he made her feel so grown up?

'Yes actually, I think I do,' she replied bluntly.

'Well, that's settled, then. Consider yourself stuck with this old man.' He raised his glass and chinked it against hers. 'If you've finished your drink we'd better get going.'

Doug had parked his car in a secluded corner of the car park. He opened the back door of the Cortina and inclined his head towards the back seat. This time she climbed in without hesitation and in one smooth movement Doug was beside her, gathering her into his arms. His kissing had a certain hunger that was new to her and he held her firmly where he wanted her. Feeling that she had no choice but to comply, she placed her arms around his neck and returned his kisses. His mouth left hers and she felt his hot breath as it trailed past her ear, and then the warmth of his lips on her neck. Her breath was coming in short gasps of delight as her body began to tingle with excitement and expectation. Doris had been right. On a scale of one to ten, her resistance had just plummeted to minus one hell of a lot! Doug was now tracing a line of kisses down her neck but as his hand slid expertly inside her blouse, she froze. Suddenly, she felt shy and embarrassed by what she considered were the inadequacies of her body. The thought of Doug discovering these shortcomings brought her sharply back to her senses. Aware of a sudden reticence on her part, Doug removed his hand and drew away.

'Sal, it's okay, I'm sorry,' he murmured huskily. 'I won't if it bothers you ...'

Shivering slightly, Sally whispered back, 'It's just that I've never ... and they're very small and my feet are too big and ...'

'Is that all it's about ... ? Whssssht now, I think you are perfect. I love everything about you, small, big, whatever ... trust me, and it's all perfect, just as it is.'

Doug caught hold of her once more and it wasn't long before she felt herself relax into his arms. As he kissed her, he undid her bra with practised ease. She gasped as his hands again found her small, firm breasts and began gently to stroke and caress her erect nipples. Then, as was his style, he teased her, 'There's a green light on with these two'.

With the waves of ecstasy washing over her there came a willingness to join in. But she was unsure what she was supposed to do, so just edged herself in closer. Sensing her uncertainty, Doug slowly loosened one of her arms from around his neck and, taking hold of her hand, he guided it down to his chest. Sally could feel the hairs through his shirt and caught her breath. It excited her! Feeling brave, she undid several of his shirt buttons and with innocent curiosity her hand began to explore inside. Running her fingers through the coarse curly hair of his chest, her hand brushed against a nipple and she was surprised to find it hard and erect. The warmth of his skin and the musky smell of his aftershave aroused deep within her indescribable feelings and unfamiliar sensations. Doug's kisses became more urgent. Sliding his hand out from inside her blouse, he began to massage her thigh. Sally followed his lead and gently withdrew her hand from his chest: but instead of finding his thigh, her hand accidentally fell straight into his lap. Her breath caught in her throat and her hand froze. She could feel a bulge, a hardness, and suddenly felt frightened and just a little shocked.

Concerned that perhaps he had been rushing things, slowly Doug removed Sally's hand. 'I'd better get you home, young lady, if I'm to be allowed to take you out again.' He sat up slowly and helped Sally into an upright position. As he buttoned up his shirt, Sally sat self-conscious and confused. She was shaking so much that Doug had to help her fasten her bra and he kissed her on the nose as he buttoned up her blouse. She was in a complete dither, her senses were reeling and she felt hot and flustered: she vaguely wondered whether this was the normal reaction to being kissed by a man or was she going down with flu?

'Okay?' Doug asked her gently.

'Fine.' She responded automatically but, in truth, she had no idea how she really felt.

When Doug stopped the car in front of her home, Sally tried not to notice the front bedroom curtains twitching. As she reached for the car door handle, Doug put his hand on her shoulder. She turned towards him, her eyes closed, and he kissed her. The partially-open door had activated the interior light and her mother clearly saw the kiss. Doug caught hold of Sally's hand and kissed her fingertips.

'Would you go out with me again, or have I frightened you away for ever?' he asked, half joking and half concerned.

'Of course I want to go out with you again, old man.' Sally leaned forward and kissed him briefly but boldly on the lips. 'It's okay, I'm not frightened, it's just that I don't know anything and ...'

'I understand, Sal, and I'm sorry – it was stupid of me. I promise to behave myself in future.'

Sally let herself in quietly through the front door, and tiptoed along the narrow hallway and up the stairs. As she reached the top stair she almost fell back down them as she heard her mother's voice, hissing at her in a stage whisper.

'He's a bit forward, isn't he? Expecting a goodnight kiss! It's only your third date.'

Scarlet with guilt, Sally was relieved that she had not put the stairwell lights on, certain that if she had, her mother would have been be able to tell that the evening had involved much more than just a goodnight kiss!

Chapter Four

The summer of 1966 was a glorious one, not only for the England football team but for Sally, too! Doug became her steady boyfriend and they dated regularly throughout the warm summer months. Doug took her to parties, dancing in the discotheque and out for meals. They revisited the bowling alley several times and Sally continued to win every match. To Sally, it seemed that the whole world around her was celebrating and her love and longing for Doug grew each day. England's triumph in the World Cup seemed to be the topic of everyone's conversation but to Sally's relief Doug was not a football enthusiast. During the long summer evenings after work they would often walk in the park and sometimes just sit outside a local pub talking and making each other laugh. Sally didn't care what they talked about – in his company she felt so happy, loved and cared for. Petting became a part of it all, and each time Sally was left wanting more, wanting Doug to go further.

Doug wanted her equally badly, and he surprised himself by his restraint. He knew it would be Sally's first time and he wanted it to be special – not a rushed job on the back seat of his car. The flat that he shared with his work colleague didn't feel right either, not least because they ran the risk of being interrupted at the crucial moment.

No, he would wait, he would find a 'right time'.

From time to time Sally caught up with Caroline but, now she was dating Doug on a regular basis, their relationship had become strained. Sally had introduced them when they ran into Caroline and her latest boyfriend at the bowling alley. Right from the start, Caroline made no secret of the fact that she didn't like Doug. Uncharitably, Sally put this dislike down to jealousy because he had become a rival for Sally's time and affection, which had been Caroline's for many years. Doug was older than the boys Caroline hung around with, and he was better looking than most of them, too. He had a car, unlike many of the local young lads, and he took Sally everywhere in it. Recently, when Caroline called round to ask if Sally wanted to go shopping with her or to the pictures, Sally usually had to decline, having already made arrangements to meet up with Doug. After their first meeting, at the end of a fraught evening at the bowling alley, Doug had picked up the hostile vibes emanating from Caroline. He'd christened her 'Sally's Jack Russell', and admitted to Sally that she terrified him.

'There's not a lot of her, but what there is needs watching!' he had announced to Sally.

'She's my best friend,' Sally had protested. 'We went everywhere together when we were younger and she let me walk her dog because I wasn't allowed to have one. I think our friendship really kicked off when we found that we had a mutual love of Champion the Wonder Horse.' This admission made Doug laugh out loud.

'It's true, and even though I suddenly grew six inches taller than her in the first year of senior school she's always been my bodyguard. Nobody bullied me while Caroline was around. She's so petite but she's always been the stronger willed of the two of us. Probably having all those brothers made it so that she had to be tough to get herself heard,' Sally told him. 'There are five of them, you know, all older than ...'

'Trouble is,' Doug interrupted her, 'you really are a big girl now and you've got me to look after you.'

'Which is exactly why Caroline thinks I need protecting! And she's probably quite right,' Sally responded with a laugh.

Caroline's first impression of Doug had been that he was drop- dead gorgeous but he reminded her too much of her older brother, Christopher, who unashamedly dated several girls at the same time! Chris prided himself on his ability to keep them all blissfully unaware of each other's existence. He would assure each one of them that they alone were the love of his life. Watching these gullible girls coming in and out of her brother's life and hanging on his every word, Caroline had learned to be wary of good-looking smooth talkers and she placed Doug firmly in this category. For her friend's sake, she would be pleasant to Doug and hope that her assessment of him was wrong.

But Sally did feel just a tad guilty every now and again when she and Caroline met at the stables. Caroline never kept a boyfriend for more than a few weeks before she dumped him and, in between boyfriends, she would ask if Sally wanted to go with her to see the latest film. In return, Sally would ask Caroline if she wanted to come out with her and Doug to a party or wherever else they might be planning to go that evening, but Caroline would pull a face.

'Oh yeah! If you think I'm playing gooseberry with you two, you've got another thought coming!' she would mutter.

'I think we're growing up, Caro,' Sally had told her. 'Going our separate ways. You'll find somebody special soon, the man of your dreams. Then we can really make up a foursome.' But Caroline remained sceptical, about both her ability to find the 'man of her dreams' soon and Doug's continued faithfulness to Sally.

Apart from the fact that he was not a Catholic, Rose felt that her daughter could not have picked a more perfect young man to go out with and saw in Doug her future son-in-law. He always collected Sally from the house and brought her home on time. He was punctual and when he called for her, if Sally wasn't quite ready, Rose would always invite him to step inside. Sally would hear them at the foot of the stairs exchanging pleasantries. Doug was courteous and Rose dimpled whenever he paid her a compliment. She smiled on their courtship, giving it her blessing.

As the summer drew to a close, Doug's parents were due to celebrate their silver wedding anniversary. There was to be a big party in September and Doug wanted to take Sally home to Scotland with him to meet his parents. Taking a girl back home was totally out of character, but he wanted them to meet Sally and to gauge their reactions to her. It scared him when he finally admitted to himself that what he would actually be seeking was their approval of her. He had no doubt they would welcome Sally and that she would walk straight into their hearts as surely as she had walked into his own. He began to dream about making the journey to Scotland over a couple of days instead of the one long drive that usually took him the best part of the day and night. The whole scenario was, of course, wishful thinking. Sally's parents would never hand their daughter over to him for safe keeping – who in their right mind would? They'd never allow it, he thought, but he went ahead and invited Sally to the party anyway.

Sally desperately wanted to go with him. He had drawn such vivid pictures of his family and their farm that she couldn't wait to meet them. She shared Doug's doubts that she would be allowed to go, but promised that she would ask her mother anyway. Doug made her feel so special, so grown up and she yearned to get away, at least for a little while, from her mother's clutches and the endless questioning before and after every date.

Sally had known about the trip for a couple of weeks now and each time she saw Doug he asked if she had discussed it with her parents yet. They were meeting again this evening, and this time Sally wanted to give him an answer. She resolved to find the courage to broach the subject with her mother before teatime. The problem was how to handle her highly suspicious mother. Once her mother's permission was secured, she knew that her father would be no problem; his response to any request had always been, 'Ask your mother'.

While she helped Rose peel the potatoes and wash the salad, she casually mentioned that she had been invited by Doug to go to Scotland. Her mother listened in silence as Sally rambled on about never having been to Scotland and how much Doug wanted her to meet his parents and how there was to be a big party to celebrate their silver wedding. Fearful that if she stopped to take a breath her mother would say the words she dreaded hearing, Sally kept on talking, expressing complete surprise at the invitation and enthusing about how wonderful it would be to see Scotland, particularly having heard Doug talk so glowingly about the countryside and his parents' farm. Eventually she finished her well-rehearsed speech and hoped that she had said enough to steer her mother's suspicions away from her true reasons for wanting to go away with Doug: she wanted the opportunity for them to be on their own; she wanted more than the heavy petting in the back of his car, she wanted to go the 'whole way' with Doug, but in a town where she knew practically everyone, it was difficult to get away from their prying eyes. Sally wanted to know what 'it' was like – would it hurt, would she enjoy it, would she feel differently afterwards? There were so many questions, but no one that she trusted who could answer them. Certainly not her mother, and she didn't feel it was right to ask Doris again. She didn't even feel she could discuss it with Caroline.

Knowing her mother's high opinion of Doug, she hoped she had put enough emphasis on the fact that he was such a gentleman that her mother would never even begin to suspect what was going on in either of their minds. Aware of her mother's own inability to talk about sex, she was confident that Rose would not want to open a discussion about it now and, in any case, Sally was ready to defend herself and remind her mother yet again of Doug's gentlemanly behaviour.

Finally she stopped talking and, in the interminable silence that followed, Sally prepared herself for the argument.

But Rose was nobody's fool! Obviously, Sally's young man was taking her daughter up to Scotland for his parents' approval. That was plain to see. Handled carefully, at this rate Sally could be engaged and married within the year to a polite young man with a university degree and a good job – the fact that he was also handsome and charming was a bonus. If only that could happen before Sally succumbed to his charms, all Rose's worries would soon be over. She looked keenly at her daughter. She must be strong-willed, Rose thought, to have held him off until now. She liked Doug and wanted to believe that she could trust him with her daughter. It would be a risk, letting her go off alone with him, but she was confident of her daughter's innocence and Doug's good behaviour.

Rose's biggest worry, however, was what her neighbours would say if they found out she had let Sally go away with her young man. Sally was bound to tell Caroline, and once Mrs MacAvoy knew then the parish priest was sure to hear all about it. Rose put her hand to her head, a sure sign that a headache was coming on, and with a sigh sat down at the kitchen table. Retrieving her cigarettes and lighter from her apron pocket, she lit up. Sally knew the signs: Rose needed to think.

'Shall I lay up the dining table, Mum?' Sally asked. When her mother absent-mindedly nodded, Sally hurried out of the kitchen. Well, at least her mother hadn't said no straight away, and that was a good sign – there was just a chance that she might say yes. Sally had learned over the years that at times like this, when her mother needed to make a decision, it was best to let her be. If she tried to say more at this delicate moment, it might prompt a hasty response – and not necessarily the one she wanted.

Rose drew heavily on her cigarette and tried to think. Why was life so difficult? Doug had been seeing Sally for nearly six months – why didn't he just propose to her?

Her daughter was beautiful – she knew it and everyone else said so, too. Allowing a daughter who was engaged to visit her future in-laws would be quite acceptable. But Doug had made no mention of marrying her daughter. In their little chats in the hallway, Rose had tried to draw him out about his 'future plans' and, while she was always delighted with his polite answers and the cheeky way he had of winking at her, she was none the wiser by the time he left. Rose reasoned that many young girls of Sally's age were going off to university nowadays. How does anyone manage to keep an eye on what they get up to then? she wondered. I think I should write to his parents to thank them for inviting Sally. Then I will extract a promise from Sally that she behaves herself! – although how she would define 'behave', if Sally queried it, she had no idea! The nuns had kindly taken on the awkward task of looking after Sally's sex education and Rose was grateful to be relieved of this embarrassing task. Rose's thoughts turned to the time when she and Joe had got married. In Joe, she had made what her mother had called 'a good catch' and now, twenty years later, she knew her mother had been right. Within a year of their marriage they had been able to put down a deposit on a four-bedroomed semi in the leafy suburbs of Middlesex and this had been their home ever since. Rose loved her home and took pride in keeping it neat and tidy. Joe had made steady progress at the bank and was now Assistant Manager. He'd always been careful with money and made sure his family had never gone short.

Rose frowned. After Sally's birth, two miscarriages had clouded their lives until Charlotte had arrived safe and sound. After eight years as an only child, Sally had a sister, but the two girls were like chalk and cheese, Rose thought. Sally's not like Lottie at all; she's so strong and robust. When Rose had been unwell after her miscarriages, Joe would take Sally out with him on his long walks, so that Rose could lie down and rest for a while. By the time Rose discovered that Joe had been taking Sally along to the local stables for pony rides, it was too late to stop Sally's infatuation with animals in general and horses in particular. He turned my little girl into a tomboy, she thought bitterly. Then Sally had met that dreadful Caroline and the transformation had been complete.

When Rose had recovered her health, she had tried to reclaim her little girl, making pretty dresses for her and tying her hair in pale blue ribbons which matched her eyes. Sally hated them and would run crying to her father, who would tell her she needn't wear a ribbon in her hair if she didn't want to. Sally is his child, Rose thought bitterly, but Charlotte is mine.

Charlotte was everything that Sally was not, and Rose thought her everything a little girl should be. Lottie loved pretty dresses and playing with dolls and was as fastidious as her mother about cleanliness. Rose had been charmed when Lottie came running to her one day, exclaiming that she had collected 'fairies' in a jam jar! Inside the jar were fluffy parachute seeds from dandelions, which had turned to down. They'd sat on a blanket on the lawn and Rose had watched as the little girl had shaken her 'fairies' out of the jar and waved as they were gently carried skywards on a summer breeze.

Sally had collected caterpillars in her jam jar and given them names! Urgh! Feeding them until each one turned into a chrysalis, the sight of which made Rose recoil in horror! It had been Joe who had allowed Sally to join the Brownies and Girl Guides and Rose blamed these organisations for encouraging her daughter's interest in such ugly, dirty things! Well, she had put her foot down about that sort of thing where Lottie was concerned. Lottie had joined the Guild of St Agnes and, for special saints' feast days, Rose loved nothing better than making Lottie a new white dress to wear under the red satin cloak of the Guild. Rose was proud of Lottie when she walked in procession round the church with the other young girls, carrying the banner of St Agnes before them. When she grew older, Rose would encourage her to join the Children of Mary. The older girls didn't have to wear white, but Rose was looking forward to making Lottie something special to wear beneath the blue satin cloak that all the Children of Mary wore. It was such a pleasure making clothes for Lottie, who loved dressing as a little girl should, and playing nicely with her dolls and having her friends round for a tea party. Sally, Rose thought, was only ever happy when she was wearing trousers or those awful jeans! She would go off to play at Caroline's house, often coming home oblivious to the leaves in her hair from climbing trees and the hairs on her clothes from playing with the dogs. Rose shuddered with disgust. Dogs! Dirty, smelly things. She smugly consoled herself with the thought that the MacAvoy household probably reeked of animals. Then it was horses, and Sally came home from the stables these days covered in filth and smelling of the stables!

Rose wondered what she had done wrong to deserve a daughter like Sally and over the years had convinced herself that it was all Joe's fault. He had spoilt the child, encouraging her to run wild with that friend of hers! If only she was more feminine, Rose thought, perhaps Doug would have proposed to her by now. Rose had been confident that, having raised her daughter in the bosom of the Catholic Church, everything else would fall into place. Mass on Sunday mornings, Sunday School in the afternoons and a convent education. The nuns had told her that they did their best to turn each young girl into a young lady by the time they left school. She was not so sure they had succeeded in Sally's case!

It could have been worse, I suppose, thought Rose. At least she's shown no inclination to become a 'mod' or a 'rocker'! Under the watchful eye of the parish priest and several responsible adults at the local Youth Club, such tendencies were frowned upon and very few of the teenagers who attended showed any more than a passing interest in such extremes. Now that Sally was earning her own money, Rose knew that it would become increasingly difficult to prevent her daughter from spreading her wings further.

Rose sighed. It felt as if she had spent half her adult life worrying about Sally and she was growing tired of it. She had done all she could to keep her on the straight and narrow. I'm sure I can trust her, she thought. Haven't I always waited up for her; made sure that I asked questions when she came in about where she had been and what she had been up to? Sally blushed furiously when she lied, but Rose had so far never caught her out. She even secretly checked that Sally's periods arrived on time every month. Sighing even more deeply, Rose reflected that Lottie was so much easier and now she wanted to devote more time to her younger daughter.

Maybe it's time to let go, she thought. It seemed a sensible plan in view of Sally's own transition from caterpillar to butterfly.

Cautiously, Sally returned to the kitchen.

'I've laid the table, Mum,' she said quietly so as not to exacerbate the headache she knew was threatening to descend on her mother.

Rose suddenly made up her mind. 'I'll talk to your father about you going up to Scotland, but if we do let you go, you've got to promise one thing.'

'Er ... yes, of course, what is it?' Sally coloured up, suspecting what was coming.

'You don't tell a soul. Especially that Caroline, d'you hear?'

'Oh, yes, Mum.' Sally sighed with relief. 'I mean no, of course not. Er... why?'

'Because if you do, that MacAvoy woman is bound to tell the priest and then he'll be round here. Then the neighbours will be wondering what he's doing coming here. I mean it, Sally! If the priest turns up on the doorstep, you won't be going anywhere.'

Sally hid her relief. 'I promise, Mum. I won't tell a soul.' For a minute there she thought her mother's worry was more personal. She should have guessed the priest would be involved.

'And, before we do anything else, we'll need his parents' address in Scotland.'

'Yes, Mum.' Well, at least she hadn't said no! And it sounded as if she was saying yes. Sally was amazed.

'And maybe it's time he came here for a meal, so that we can all meet him. Properly!'

'Yes, Mum,' Sally said meekly.

That evening she told Doug what her mother had said. 'Oh aye!' he laughed, 'they're checking up on me.'

'You don't mind?'

'Of course I don't, lassie. They want to know where it is I'll be taking you. Any parent would want to know that.'

Rose wrote a friendly informal letter to Doug's mother, congratulating them on their forthcoming anniversary and thanking her for the kind invitation to her daughter to attend their party. Almost by return of post, Rose received a pleasant reply from Doug's mother, saying how much they were all looking forward to meeting Dougie's girl and how they needn't worry. Sally would be well looked after and they would be delighted to welcome her. Armed with this response, Rose spoke to Joe. He wasn't keen for Sally to be travelling up to Scotland with her young man, but he also felt the weight of Rose's blame for him turning their elder daughter into a tomboy. Fear was the tool she used to control Sally and guilt was the tool she used to get her own way with her husband.

Sally's initial joy at being allowed to travel north with Doug was somewhat overshadowed by Rose's offer to make her daughter a 'nice frock' to wear to the party. In fairness, her mother was an excellent seamstress, but her fashion sense was firmly embedded in the styles found in 1950s romantic movies. Knowing her mother's interpretation of a 'nice frock', Sally immediately envisaged a dated creation of soft pink tulle over several net petticoats. It would naturally have a ballerina-length skirt, a short-sleeved black velvet bodice, and matching accessories such as black elbow-length gloves and a black satin clutch handbag.

Her fears were not entirely unfounded. Sally arrived home from work a few days later to find that her mother had been shopping for dress material. It wasn't to be pink tulle, it was worse! Folded neatly on the sideboard were several yards of pale yellow dimpled nylon. Balanced on top was a brown paper bag which, when she peeped inside, Sally found to her horror contained a large flower motif made entirely of black sequins. Realising that Sally was home, her mother dashed into the room and reached excitedly for the folded material. Draping the yellow nylon up against Sally, she felt inside the bag for the shiny black sequin flower arrangement and proudly held it against Sally's left shoulder.

'There! Isn't that lovely?' she asked, not meeting Sally's eyes. 'Yellow really suits you. I think it should have a modest scooped neck, a bit of a dropped waist, small puff sleeves and a really full gathered skirt.' All Sally could do was to smile weakly, cringing inside at the spectacle that she knew she would make wearing such a monstrosity in public.

'Ballerina length always looks nice, very flattering. Of course you'll need some elegant black elbow-length gloves, just to set it off.' Sally pulled a face and, mistaking the reason for it, her mother added generously, 'That's okay, you can borrow a pair of mine'.

Sally cleared her throat and managed a weak, 'Thanks, Mum,' as she tried to erase from her mind the image her mother had just painted of the finished garment. She did not have the heart to dampen her mother's enthusiasm. Moreover, she felt it would be unwise to upset her and, in the process, jeopardise her trip to Scotland, so she went along with all the measuring and subsequent fittings. As the dress took shape, Sally could see that the price of her freedom was pretty high.

A few days later, walking home from work through the park's rose garden with Doug, Sally told him that he was invited to tea on Sunday. 'Sorry about that, but somehow I think you're on the menu.' She wrinkled her nose and smiled at him. 'Expect to be grilled.'

Doug loved that habit of hers and smiled back at her, imitating her wrinkled nose.

'Well, they surely cannae have any more questions to ask than my parents have asked about you. Ever since I told them I was bringing you, my mother hasn't been off the phone. I have a confession to make – you see, you are the first girl I've actually taken home. My mom is beside herself with curiosity. She wants to know what's different this time.'

'What have you told her?'

'Just that you are a right bobby-dazzler.'

'A what?'

'"Bobby-dazzler". It's what we call real stunners in Scotland.'

'Doug! You didn't really say that!' As Sally playfully poked him in the ribs, he caught her wrist and, pulling her to him, kissed her briskly on the lips. It made her giggle. Doug was fun, she thought, a born teaser.

He was also a romantic. Since their first date, billets doux and cards had been arriving at the office addressed to her personally with just one line written on them: 'How about "it"?' or '"It's" not so bad!' Sally would blush and hurriedly hide them away in her handbag. He had been thoroughly amused at Sally's revelation that the nun who attempted to teach them the facts of life had been unable to bring herself to use the words 'sexual intercourse'. Instead, the nun had constantly used the word 'it' to explain the act necessary for procreation, and Doug loved to tease Sally by referring to 'it' in his love notes to her. Handing her an envelope on one occasion, Doris had given her a knowing smile before adding, 'Something he wouldn't want your mother to see, eh? Enjoy yourself, lass, but take care; remember what I told you about protecting yourself. A child is a burden, especially without a father. Mind, I sometimes wish I'd been less careful. I would've had something real to remember my Bill by, something of him. Not just memories and a pile of fading old photographs. But it wasn't meant to be.'

Despite Sally insisting to Doris that Doug had not put any pressure on her to sleep with him, Doris had interrupted her protestations with a 'Huh- humph!', a shake of her head and a playful wag of her finger.

'You're going off alone with him, aren't you? He might well not put any pressure on you to sleep with him but, mark my words, if he does, then the temptation to do so will be very strong.' Despite Sally's promise to her mother not to tell a soul, the day after her parents agreed to let her go away with Doug she hadn't been able to resist confiding in Doris, knowing her secret would be safe with her.

Doug's voice cut through her thoughts and brought her back to the present.

'Penny for them?'

'Sorry, I was miles away, just thinking of what needs to be done before I leave for Scotland,' she replied, blushing slightly.

'I could see you were miles away. Anyway, when do I get grilled, kitten, and how much do I have to admit to?'

Sally had been staring straight ahead as they had walked along, lost in her thoughts. Now she turned and stared at him, her mouth wide open.

'What?' she exclaimed. 'You don't have to admit to anything. Please don't tease me, I'll be on pins as it is.'

Doug squeezed her hand, laughing at the look of horror on her face.

Despite her pleas, he continued to tease her.

'Don't worry, I'll tell them that your honour is quite safe with me, but as a canny Scotsman I may have to economise en route to Scotland! So it's two to a room!'

'Doug, you cannot possibly say that! They'll change their minds and definitely won't let me go away with you,' groaned Sally.

'How about, "You dinnae have to worry, Mrs Phillips, because she won't let me do "it"?'

'Doug!' squeaked Sally. 'Please stop it!'

'Ah! Those oh-so-familiar words yet again – "Doug, please stop it",' he mimicked, laughing at her. 'Okay, Sunday tea it is, and I promise I'll be on my best behaviour, honest. Should I bring a Bible and say I've been to the kirk on the way?'

'Absolutely not! Stay well off the subject of religion!'

Doug walked Sally the rest of the way home. At the gate he nodded furtively towards the house, turned up the collar of his jacket and asked, 'Do you want a quick peck on the cheek or the works?'

Sally's response was to put her arms around his neck and press her lips to his. He held her close and returned her kiss, then, drawing apart from her, he started back down the street. After a few paces, he turned to wave. Sally waved back, blowing him a kiss and, with a lightness of foot that only those in love know, she walked into the house.

Lottie had moved from her lookout behind the sitting room curtain and was waiting for Sally when she came in through the front door. Now an irritating ten-year-old, she had been watching out for her sister to come home from work. She hadn't expected to see Doug with Sally, but viewed them with great interest as they had kissed. She was ready to indulge in her favourite pastime – goading her sister. If there was any fallout, she could always rely on her mother to take her side.

'Yuk, I don't want boys to kiss me like that. What does spit taste like? Yuk.' Lottie pulled a face and, bending forward, pretended to vomit by thrusting her tongue out as far as it would go. Sally, fed up with the performance and cross at being spied on, retaliated, 'I shouldn't lose any sleep over it! Nobody's going to want to kiss a horrible little girl like you!' At which point Lottie burst into tears and went off to 'tell mummy'. Sally sighed and resigned herself to the lecture she was sure to get from her mother about being mean to her dear little sister.

Chapter Five

The following day, Doug phoned Sally at the office.

'It's Romeo,' announced Doris, chuckling as she connected the call – obviously Doug had been laying on the charm.

'Hello, kitten, just a quickie. Would you like to come over to my place for supper this evening?' Sally had been there before, but only briefly, and she wasn't sure what her mother would say if she knew she was going to Doug's bachelor pad for a meal. But she heard herself saying, 'Yep, okay'.

'Mind, I can only cook about three dishes, so you can try the first of them this evening. If you survive maybe you'll come back for another at a later date.'

'Sounds lovely. What time?'

'How about seven o'clock?'

'Okay, see you then.' Sally kept the call brief.

Sally didn't tell her mother that she was having a meal at Doug's place, merely that she was going to eat out. By this time, her mother had ceased to be quite so inquisitive about Sally's movements, and with luck she wouldn't ask too many questions when Sally got home that night, either.

In a large converted Victorian house on the outskirts of town, Doug shared a bachelor flat with Pete. Sally read the nameplates of the building's occupants and spotted one casually labelled 'Doug and Pete'. She didn't have to wait long before she heard the clatter of feet on the stairs. The door opened and Doug swept her into his arms.

'Come along, Pete's still here, but once he's been fed we'll have some peace and quiet as he's away to his evening classes.' Sally followed him up the broad staircase to the first floor and through the door marked Flat 1A. As Doug ushered Sally into the large and comfortably-furnished sitting room, his flatmate hauled himself to his feet from the depths of the sagging settee and Doug swiftly introduced them.

'Pete, Sally, Sally, Pete. Now I have to rescue the dinner.' In two strides he'd left them and was through the door to a small adjoining kitchen. Sally smiled at the tall, slim, mousy-haired young man who was staring at her. So this is his flatmate, she thought, and all her old shyness came back to her as she stood desperately trying to think of something to say. She tried to remember what Doug had told her about him.

'Talk among yourselves for a wee while,' Doug called out from the kitchen, and Pete finally smiled at Sally. He indicated for her to sit on the settee and sat himself down at the opposite end of it. The clatter of pots and pans continued from the kitchen.

'Smells good,' Sally said lamely, in an attempt to break the embarrassing silence that had settled between her and Pete.

'Yeah, Doug's multi-talented. Have you known him long?'

'Er ... a few months or so. I haven't really stopped to think how long we've been going out.' The conversation was stilted and Sally was grateful when Doug reappeared to announce that supper was ready. He placed a large bowl of chips in the middle of the small table set with three place settings, a mustard pot, a bottle of red wine and three glasses. Sally and Pete stood up as Doug disappeared briefly back into the kitchen. He returned with a frying pan and served up three medium rare steaks cooked to perfection.

'Come along, sit yourselves down.' He drew back one of the dining chairs for Sally to sit.

Doug's speciality of the day was washed down with the ubiquitous bottle of Chianti. Supper over, and fortified by the wine, the two men continued a discussion begun earlier, about the existence of God. Doug leaned towards atheism while Pete declared his belief in a God, although he was not sure in what shape or form. Sally sat in silence, not daring to express an opinion for fear of divine retribution. Her Roman Catholic beliefs, instilled in her from a very young age, consisted of guilt, fear and superstitions held in place by threats of varying degrees of punishment. It seemed that if you could manage to live the life of a complete saint here on earth, there was a remote chance of your soul being allowed into heaven! Sally was convinced that the stringent qualifications required even to stand outside the Pearly Gates were beyond any mortal. Short of offering to be burned at the stake for her religion, she couldn't see herself getting in through the gates of heaven. Besides, when she had been told that animals have no souls and that there was no place for them in heaven, she wasn't so sure she wanted to go there anyway. To Sally, an environment full of righteous people and no animals wouldn't be heaven at all, it would be hell. Her eyes filled slightly as she remembered the gist of a short verse that she had read. It went something like, 'What sort of place must heaven be if my dog isn't waiting there to welcome me?' In addition to her already repetitive list of regularly confessed sins there was now Doug, and all the temptations she found in his arms. She couldn't imagine confessing these new sins to Father O'Daly and expecting absolution!

While Doug and Pete continued to exchange their views on religion Sally, lost in thought, recited to herself the Ten Commandments, drilled into her at school. As she had not actually broken any of them yet, she came to the conclusion that maybe heaven with all its angels was not totally out of the question. But before trying to work her way into heaven she would have to double-check on the animal situation.

'Sal?' Doug touched her arm.

'Oh! Yes, sorry, I was miles away, thinking about heaven. It must be all this talk about religion and the wine. Did you know Jesus's first miracle was to change water into wine?'

'Is that so? Well, maybe he's not such a bad chap after all,' Doug said. 'Now, if you've had enough to eat, Pete wants to get off to his evening class and is anxious to help get the dishes cleared away.'

'There's no need to be late for classes, Pete – I can do the dishes. It's the least I can do after such a nice meal. The chef can put his feet up,' she said as she rose and began collecting up the dirty plates.

'Thanks, much appreciated,' Pete called after her as she walked to the kitchen. He pulled on his jacket and headed for the door. 'Lovely supper, Doug. Be good. I'll be back about ten, but I promise I'll make a lot of noise opening the door.'

Pete had often arrived home unnoticed by Doug and his latest conquest copulating on the settee. He had heard all about Sally and he could see now why Doug was so taken with her. The last thing he wanted was to stumble in on them thrashing around in the sitting room in the throes of love-making and embarrass them all. It seemed to Pete that Doug had a passion so uncontrollable that, once ignited, it rendered him incapable of dragging his bird the last few yards to the privacy of his bedroom.

In the kitchen, Sally was blushing at his implication and in her embarrassment found she had squeezed far too much washing-up liquid into the plastic bowl. Doug carried the remaining dirty dishes into the small kitchen and placed them on the draining board. He stood behind Sally and slipped his arms around her waist, gently easing her away from the sink.

She held out her bubble-covered hands as he turned her round to face him. 'Hey, this heaven you were so deep in thought about just now – it can be a place on Earth, you know.' He gently kissed her cheek and, half turning, reached for the kitchen towel, holding it out for her to dry her hands.

'Come along, I don't want you to spend time washing dishes. It's the first opportunity I've had to get you completely to myself.'

Taking Sally's hand, he led her across the room to the shabby settee and pulled her down beside him. Sally curled up close and laid her head against his shoulder while he talked about his plans for showing her his home town of Edinburgh. He ran his fingers idly through Sally's silky blonde hair as he spoke. He omitted to say he wanted Sally to himself for a few days on the way up north because, once they got to his parents' house, his mother would be behind his every move. He had no doubt bedrooms would be prepared at different ends of the big old farmhouse, with his mother and several yards of squeaky floorboards in between. Not that he had any plans to seduce Sally under his mother's roof. He knew that Sally found it difficult to lie: in any case, her blushes gave her away, so the less she knew about the travel arrangements the better. That way, she needn't worry about having to lie to her parents. Cradling her in his arms, he asked, 'How does that sound?'

Sally thought the whole trip to Scotland sounded exciting, but quite honestly she didn't care where she was as long as she was with Doug. Tentatively, she pressed her lips to his. It always stirred Doug deeply when she kissed him voluntarily and he clutched her hungrily to him. Their kisses became long and probing, searching each other's mouths. Sally ran her tongue over his perfect white teeth.

Doug broke away and said, 'I don't know how long I can resist you if you do that. I want all of you in every way, but I don't want to frighten you.' His voice was husky with passion as he gently pushed her away. He wanted Sally to understand a few things. He wanted to tell her so she understood, to warn her.

'Sally?'

'Mmm?' Still leaning against him, she stretched herself out on the settee to make herself more comfortable.

'Sally, do you know what the biggest turn on is for a man, the thing that excites him most?'

'No. I have no idea.' She kissed his neck and Doug sighed.

'Well, I'll tell ye. It's knowing he is wanted by the woman in his arms. It's when she shows him by some little sign that she is not just tolerating his advances because she thinks it's what she ought to do. When you put your lips on mine just now, that was tantamount to an invitation and you had better know, my sweet lassie, that I find it nigh impossible to refuse such invitations.'

Sally giggled. 'That does seem to put the ball squarely in my court. I'm not sure where to invite you and what games to play.'

'When two people are in love, they can play anything they like, anywhere they want, all day and ... ' he added softly, 'all night.'

Sally sat up and looked into Doug's eyes, 'Did you say "in love"?'

'Unless there is someone else in the room with us, I suppose I must've done.' Doug chuckled and pulled her in close, his lips silencing any further questions.

Held tightly in his arms, she moaned softly when at last his hands moved to her breasts. Following his lead, she slid her hand inside his open shirt and moved it slowly over his chest, feeling the curls of black hair that had fuelled her curiosity when she had first glimpsed them. It grew in a thick line down the centre of his chest and tracing the line of hair downwards with her fingers always made Sally want to explore further. She removed her hand and placed it boldly on Doug's lap. Driven on by some inner demon, Sally moved her fingers around Doug's 'hardness' feeling the outline of what lay beneath his jeans. She heard the familiar catch of his breath, but her hand pursued its roaming. In her ignorance, Sally had tried to imagine what a real man's penis might actually be like, and now she began to realise! It seemed to her that she had grossly underestimated the dimensions! It scared her a little, but thrilled her too.

Slowly she unzipped his trousers and slipped her hand inside. Doug placed one hand at the top of her leg and gently rubbed her thigh, then expertly inched his hand up under her skirt and on to the flat of her stomach. Sally shivered with excitement, aware of the warmth of his hand as it slid under the elastic of her knickers and his fingers touched and stroked those places that made her yearn for him to continue. The sensations were electrifying, overpowering even. Suddenly, unexpectedly, she began to tremble, so much that her teeth chattered against each other. Doug sat her up and held her close. 'What's wrong? Are you all right? Why are you shaking?'

'I don't know,' replied Sally. 'It's silly, but I just can't stop.' He held her until the shaking subsided. 'I feel so stupid.'

'Mind, I've never had that effect on a woman before,' Doug teased her gently. 'I'm quite flattered.'

'Please don't talk about your other women, especially the willing ones. It makes me feel inadequate,' Sally stuttered.

'Dash, and there I was hoping it would make you feel jealous. Anyhow, it felt to me like I had a very willing woman in my arms tonight.' But Doug was resolute. He couldn't let Sally's first time be here, with the risk that Pete would come back in. He wanted something a bit special for her. Gently, he pushed her away and stood up. 'Would you like a cup of tea – because any minute now Pete's going to come crashing through that door, and those deliciously pink cheeks and shiny eyes of yours are a dead giveaway of what you've been up to.'

He strode towards the kitchen and Sally followed him. 'Which way is your bathroom?'

Using one hand to turn on the tap and the other to hold the kettle while it filled with water, Doug inclined his head towards a door on the far side of the sitting room. 'Second door from the right of the front door.' The bright bathroom was neat and tidy and as Sally peered into the bathroom mirror she realised Doug for once hadn't been teasing her. She had rosy pink cheeks and her eyes shone as never before. As she was splashing her cheeks with cold water she heard the front door open and Pete's voice call out.

'Okay, make yourselves decent, I'm back.'

The cool water did little to reduce the heightened colour in her cheeks and, as she returned to the sitting room, Pete's knowing smile suffused her face anew. Doug's mischievous grin and seductive wink behind Pete's back added to her guilt-laced discomfort.

'Tea, anyone?' offered Doug. 'Then I'd better drive you home, or you might be grounded next week. I've also got to survive the tea party on Sunday and I want a clear conscience when I sit down with your parents.'

Pete hooted with exaggerated laughter, a pint or two at the local on the way home having eroded his shyness and loosened his inhibitions. 'Bugger off, Doug. You haven't got a conscience, never mind a clear one,' he muttered

Surprised by his language and the comment, Sally looked sharply at Pete and turned to Doug with one eyebrow raised in a question.

'Och, take no notice of our Pete, he cannae hold his booze and likes to crack a joke – usually at somebody else's expense,' Doug said, brushing the comment aside and stepping closer to Sally.

Doug had never worked with a clean slate before and, if he was honest with himself, the thought made him extremely nervous. His friends had bragged about having virgins, but Sally would be Doug's first. He surely wanted her, but not as a trophy, not to share stories with his mates. He did not know why he wanted her so much, nor why he was holding himself in check. Tonight, he had mentioned love – it had somehow just slipped out. Love was a word he had studiously avoided mentioning to any of his previous girlfriends. But when he was with Sally, he felt protective, excited, frustrated, content, so many emotions rolled into one; perhaps he really was in love with her? Maybe, he thought, there is such a thing as love at first sight, after all.

'Come along, Sal, it's time I got you home, before our Pete here forgets any more of his manners in front of a lady.'

Doug stopped the car in front of her house. 'Here we are, safe and sound.

Now let me see, you're going to ask the Jack Russell to go shopping with you on Saturday and I'm working 'til late, so I need a really big kiss to last me until four o'clock on Sunday. Then it's best suit, best smile and best behaviour and not a word to your parents about what a racy piece their daughter is turning out to be.'

'Racy! Doug, stop it, you're embarrassing me.' She playfully smacked his knee.

'Hey, a little higher and I'll have to accept your invitation to meet the "beastie".'

Sally giggled. 'Now you're being immodest and I think there's some exaggeration. Don't forget I know you a little better than I did.'

'Ha! But you've only known the "beastie" when he's confined. Unleashed, he's formidable!' Doug enjoyed flirting with her in this way and was delighted that Sally now felt confident to give back as good as she got. She might not know much, and she had been painfully shy to begin with, but she was proving to be a quick learner and fun to teach.

Sally's response was immediate. They kissed and, as they drew apart, Doug leaned forward and rubbed noses Eskimo style.

'No, I don't think that's quite enough to last until Sunday,' and he covered her mouth with his own. 'Now off you go! Enjoy your shopping with yon Jack Russell and I'll see you on Sunday.'

First Love

Chapter Six

Sally walked over to Caroline's the following evening and, as she was not yet home from work, left a message asking if she wanted to go shopping on Saturday. Caroline had a high-profile secretarial job in central London, which often kept her late in the office.

Caroline was thrilled when she got the message and they met as arranged, at two o'clock in their favourite coffee shop just off the High Street. Over a frothy cappuccino, Caroline demanded a full update on Sally's love life.

'Okay, how is macho man? Do tell. Where is he this afternoon and why your sudden interest in shopping?'

Remembering her promise to her mother, Sally shrugged her shoulders. 'Oh, I just wanted some new clothes for the autumn,' she said, trying to control the blush that she knew was spreading over her cheeks.

'And you didn't want to drag lover boy along?' Caroline asked scornfully. 'Is he cooling down a bit, or have you had enough of him?' Caroline was plainly fishing now.

'No ... no, he's working and I thought it would be a good chance for us to do some catching up,' Sally replied, sipping her coffee and avoiding eye contact.

'And ...?'

'And what?' She looked directly at Caro, her eyes alight with the excitement that shone whenever she thought about the forthcoming trip with Doug. So far, Doris was the only other person that she had told but somehow it didn't seem right to trust Doris and not her best friend.

'Uh-huh! I thought so! You're up to something.' Caroline paused. 'He's proposed! That's it, isn't it?' Caroline said, and began to laugh.

Sally giggled. 'No he hasn't, and stop fishing. Really, there's nothing to tell...'

'Oh God! It's not ...? You're not ...?' Caroline said, suddenly all serious.

'Caroline! You're worse than my mother and no, I am not!'

'So what's going on then? You know you want to tell me. He hasn't proposed but he's going to? Is that it?'

'No,' Sally said, but she had difficulty keeping a grin off her face. 'What then?'

'Caroline ...' Sally leaned across the table to whisper. 'If I tell you, you've got to swear on the Bible that you won't breathe a word to a soul.'

'Yes, yes, I swear. What's happening?' Caroline leaned eagerly in towards Sally.

'I mean it, Caroline! Particularly as far as your mother is concerned! You won't tell her, will you?'

Caroline's eyes danced with amusement. 'Do you know, my mum misses not seeing you around the place? Keeps asking where you are these days, as if she didn't know!'

'Probing for information, more like.'

'Well, yes, of course, but then she follows it up with why can't I find a nice young man? Your boy certainly seems to be a hit with everyone, except all the local boys, who are green with envy, including a couple of my brothers. Keep asking me if you're still dating him!'

Sally started laughing, but Caroline persisted.

'So come on then, tell me what's happened or I shall go home and tell mother that you're up to something and won't say what it is!'

'No! You wouldn't do that!' Sally recoiled with horror and it was Caroline's turn to laugh. They both knew the consequences of a remark like that to Mrs Mac! Caroline's mother would make it her mission to uncover the truth and was just as likely to make a direct approach to Sally's mum and ask her outright what was going on. And if she made a show of it outside church on a Sunday morning, rumours would spread like wildfire.

'Caroline!' Sally said fiercely, 'that's blackmail!'

'Yep! Serves you right for trying to keep a secret from me.'

'You're about as good as I am at lying to my mother and if I tell you and then you tell your mother ... Oh God!' Sally shuddered.

'Well ... I'll just sigh and say what I always say, "I don't know, out with lover boy again", I guess. I've missed you too, Sal. So come on, tell me what's happening.'

Sally eyed her friend warily.

'If you betray me, Caro, I'll never speak to you again.'

'I won't. Promise and I swear I won't breathe a word, to anyone.'

Sally told her about the trip to Scotland, relieved at last to be able to tell someone else her exciting news.

'Do you know, I just can't believe your mum and dad are letting you go off with him!' Caroline said when Sally had finished telling her. 'I'm really shocked.' 'You can't be any more shocked than I am. Mum has been going on and on about "trusting me" all week and they've asked Doug to tea tomorrow. God, I hope they don't start asking him awkward questions. I'll curl up and die of embarrassment.'

'What if he makes a really serious pass at you when he has you to himself? What are you going to do? I bet he's had more women than we've had breakfasts between us. How are you going to handle him with the bog standard and basic bedroom knowledge that we were pushed out into the big bad world with?'

Caroline slurped at her coffee.

'I know what you mean. I can't see anything that Sister Immaculata or Sister Frances told us about copulating rabbits being of any use. But don't worry, I've been doing some homework and Doris has been a gem. D'you know, I can really talk to her? She reckons we should all enjoy ourselves, but just be careful not to get pregnant.' Sally lowered her voice as she leaned forwards, 'Doris says that sex can be fun for the woman as well as the man.'

'Doris!' shrieked Caroline, clamping her hand across her mouth. 'Sorry, I didn't mean to be so loud,' she whispered. 'Doris! Doris? I just can't believe that she's been advising you on s-e-x.' Caroline spelt the word in hushed tones, taking a quick glance to see if the middle-aged couple at the next table had registered her outburst.

Too late, Sally realised she had betrayed Doris. She hadn't meant to, it had just slipped out. God, she thought, why am I so useless at keeping secrets?

'Yes, Doris - and please, please, Caroline, don't tell anyone, she would be so embarrassed,' pleaded Sally. She knew that she could trust Caroline to keep quiet but she still felt guilty about revealing Doris's involvement in furthering her sex education.

Sally made as it to leave. 'Come on, let's get some shopping done.'

'Not until you tell me which number you're up to?' Caroline grinned up at her.

'What d'you mean, "number" – what number?' Sally was momentarily puzzled by the question.

'Oh come on, don't play the innocent ... you must remember! Have you got to Number Ten yet?'

Sally sat down again, grinning back at her friend. She'd almost forgotten! During their third year at school, based on the sketchy outline of the act of reproduction that the nuns had given them, Caroline and Sally had irreverently rewritten the Ten Commandments. Closeted away in Caroline's bedroom they had laughed hysterically and whispered for hours as they had made their shameful list. Cheekily entitling their work: 'How to Make a Rabbit', it began: Number One: 'Meeting the man of your dreams'; Number Two: 'Holding hands', and so on. Together they had created a sequence of events leading to the ultimate outcome, the act of conception – Number Ten on the list. Even with a term's worth of sex education to digest, they still had precious few facts to work with. However, with the fertile imaginations of 14-year-olds, what details they lacked were easily made up.

'Of course we haven't got to ten!' she snorted. 'Honestly, Caroline! What do you take me for?'

'Come on!' Caroline said in disbelief. 'You must have got to number five, at least! He doesn't look the sort that would hang around.' Sally did a quick calculation to work out what number five referred to. For the first time in their lifelong friendship, Sally felt that she didn't wanted to share her secrets with Caroline. She was torn between the two; she felt it would be disloyal to Doug to tell anyone about their time together, but she also knew Caroline's questions were based on a 'need to know'. It was a girlie thing, sharing the mysteries of growing up. When Caroline had started her periods before Sally, she had shared every detail and had made it less disturbing for Sally when she had started hers. Sally suspected that Caroline was still as ignorant as she herself had been when she first met Doug. Thankfully Doris had come to her rescue with the library book and her personal advice. Sally ran through the sequence in her head once more and was going to honestly declare a number six, but she bottled out and hissed, 'Five, now let's get going.'

'Five? Five! You let him see your breasts! Wow! Mind you, I'm surprised he could find them!'

'Ssssh! Keep your voice down. Now let's go, I kept my part of the deal.' And Sally headed for the café door to hide the tell-tale blush creeping up her neck and face as a result of that little white lie.

Three hours later, festooned with carrier bags, they staggered back into the café for another coffee.

'Which bits of shopping are you going to show your mother when she asks? Because if I were you, I wouldn't flash that new underwear under her nose, or you'll be going nowhere! Black lacy bra and knickers! It's a bit of a contrast to the white cotton Aertex you bought in the sales last time we hit town. If Doug claps his eyes on you in that outfit, you'll be up to number ten before you know it!' Caroline sipped her coffee and grinned at Sally's obvious discomfort.

'Caroline, will you stop winding me up? I just thought it would be nice to have something a bit glamorous. Anyhow, I don't intend going to number ten, so you can stop that sort of talk.'

'Yep, I can stop. The question is, can you?'

'Give us a break, Caroline; I have Sunday tea to get through tomorrow.'

To Sally, Caroline was ever the sensible one who never allowed herself to get into awkward situations, whereas she herself stumbled innocently into them all the time – and once she was there, Caroline delighted in turning up the heat.

From the brief encounter Caroline had had with Doug, she thought she knew exactly what he had in mind, and Sally's purchase of the black underwear had worryingly confirmed to her that she was a willing participant. Caroline couldn't work out if Sally was just being incredibly naïve or was really up for it. She also sensed that Sally had moved ahead of her in the growing-up stakes and she was envious that Sally's parents seemed to be encouraging her. Not that any boy had asked Caroline to go away with him, but she knew that if one had, hell would freeze over before her parents and protective brothers would allow it.

Although Caroline envied Sally's new-found freedom, she was genuinely alarmed that her friend might be getting in too deep too quickly. Nonchalantly heaping sugar into her second cup of coffee and watching it sink slowly through the layer of frothy milk, Caroline continued teasing Sally.

'Tomorrow should be fun with your mum, dad and lover boy. Is your awful sister going to be there, sniggering away, as well? I bet your dad will act all suspicious and I can just see your mother – my money is on her going all giggly. I bet she's reliving her own courtship through yours. Shall I come along and put in my two pennies' worth and give you some moral support?' Caroline joked.

'No thanks! I can do without you and your big wooden spoon stirring things up.'

Caroline could see her friend was getting more than a little stressed with the situation. She softened her tone.

'Look, Sal, I can see you're pretty well besotted with Doug, and who can blame you? But be careful. He might well turn out to be the one for you. I just feel he's too good to be true. Don't get hurt, that's all. Now, I promise to say no more on that subject and I'm going to stop winding you up. Go to Scotland, have a great time and when you get back I want to hear all about it – and I mean all!' Caroline smiled. 'I have to admit he is quite sexy. Does he have a brother?'

'He has quite a nice flatmate called Pete. He might suit you. He's a bit intense and likes to tease. Remind you of anyone you know?' she asked, grinning at her friend with raised eyebrows. Caroline grinned back. 'When we get back, I'll suggest a foursome.' Sally glanced at her watch. 'Come on, let's move. I need to get home and hide some of my shopping before my mum sees it.'

As they waited for the bus to take them home, Caroline studied her friend's profile. Who would have thought that Sally would have been the first to attract a serious boyfriend? When they were growing up, Sally had been rather plain and ungainly and her waist-length, tightly-plaited pigtails hanging behind each ear did nothing to improve her image.

Until Doug had come along, it had always seemed to Caroline that Sally was totally oblivious to the opposite sex, her passion being firmly fixed on horses and rescuing stray animals. Perhaps that was it, Caroline thought; maybe Doug needs taking care of, and Sally has fallen for his puppy dog act? But then she considered Doug's character – she could see through him, even if Sally couldn't. No, he was far too confident to need the likes of Sally. He was the archetypal tall, dark, handsome guy liberally laced with charm. A man like that could have any woman he wanted and probably did! Caroline was well aware that her friend had turned into a stunner and it didn't take much imagination to see what any man would want with her!

By three o'clock on Sunday, Sally was nervous to the point where she began to shake. It was to be a light tea of cold meats, salad and cakes and she helped her mother set the table. Her mother's cooking had never been very imaginative and the menus, unchanged throughout Sally's childhood, were set forever in a seven-day cycle. You could tell which day of the week it was by what was served up on the table. Sunday lunch was always roast beef, popped into the oven just before they went off to Mass, and Sunday tea was invariably cold meats and salad served at five o'clock.

Once the dining table was set to her satisfaction and most of the food prepared, her mother disappeared upstairs to change into a smart dress. In sharp contrast, her father had made very little effort. His sole concession to making an occasion of it was to wear his favourite tie, and awaiting Doug's arrival he had tucked himself away in the front room with the Sunday newspapers and the television. Joe had invested in a television set to watch the World Cup matches and although he enjoyed watching TV he was too nervous to concentrate on it this particular afternoon and the set remained switched off. He had managed to get his pipe alight and was puffing away as he tried to concentrate on reading. His fondness for his pipe was a family joke, as it seemed to everyone that he spent more time cleaning and filling it than actually smoking it. He would never admit it, but he was bothered by the imminent arrival of his daughter's first boyfriend. Lottie had been closeted away in her bedroom since she had finished lunch and Sally dreaded her reappearance. Lottie had no inhibitions and her direct questions were often a source of embarrassment to all, especially Sally. It seemed that her mother encouraged her precocious younger sister in this by allowing her to think of herself as cute and amusing.

Promptly at four o'clock, the doorbell rang. 'I'll go!' yelled Lottie as she came crashing out of her bedroom door, leaping down the stairs two at a time. To Sally's amazement, Lottie was wearing her best party frock, a chocolate box creation designed and made by mother, of course. It consisted of a full skirt of gathered, pale blue taffeta with strategically-placed dark blue velvet bows. Sally had opted for black trousers with a black-and-white striped shirt and had tied her blonde hair back in a ponytail with a multicoloured chiffon scarf. By virtually falling down the last two stairs, Lottie managed to get to the front door just ahead of Sally.

From outside, Doug could hear the banging and crashing caused by Lottie's anxiety to be first to the door and when it opened he stood there smiling and holding out a bunch of flowers.

'Well, what a reception.' He handed her the flowers. 'You must be Lottie. I'm pleased to meet you. Would you take these to your mummy, please? I think they need some water.'

Instantly smitten, and delighted at being singled out for such an important task, Lottie turned and gave Sally a self-satisfied smirk, before sauntering back along the hall towards the kitchen, clutching the flowers and sniffing them loudly as she went.

'How does the land lie, kitten, is it safe to come in?' Doug whispered.

'Well, mother is all dolled up and still in the kitchen, father is reading the Sunday papers in a cloud of pipe smoke and, as you've already seen Lottie, thankfully I don't have to attempt to describe the effect that your visit is having on her.' She grinned at him. Doug ruefully grinned back, aware that it must be obvious to her that he too had made a big effort. Sally had taken in the dark blue suit, pale shirt and Slim Jim open-weave blue tie, and thought that he looked devastatingly handsome. He was about to plant a quick kiss on her lips when a noise at the end of the hallway made them jump apart.

'How are you, Doug?' enquired Rose. 'Come along in. At last we have time for a proper chat. You're usually whisked away by Sally before we even get a chance to say hello.'

Throwing her daughter a meaningful glance, she took Doug's arm and led him into the sitting room, where her husband was waiting.

His pipe had gone out and Sally, following behind them, was pleased to see that the room had virtually cleared of smoke. Seemingly unaware of its demise, her father still clenched the pipe between his teeth; it didn't occur to Sally that this was a measure of his anxiety at meeting Doug. He removed his pipe and cleared his throat as he stood up to be introduced.

'Joe, this is Doug.'

'How do you do?' both men chorused as they shook hands.

'Sit down, Doug, and make yourself at home.' Joe pointed to the chair opposite him.

'Come along, Sally, I need a hand in the kitchen, please.' It was more of an order than a request.

As she was marched towards the kitchen by her mother, Sally's stomach turned a somersault. It was obvious that the whole thing had been stage-managed and there was a reason why Doug was being left alone with her father. Surely, she thought, he wasn't going to do the protective father bit, asking Doug about his intentions!

In due course, when Sally put her head round the sitting room door to announce that tea was ready, Doug was listening politely to one of her father's tales. Her dad was a good storyteller and even though she had heard most of his stories many times she still loved to listen to him. 'He's not telling you how he had to walk two miles to school in the morning and then had half an hour to run home for his lunch and get back to school for the afternoon classes, is he?'

'No, not at all,' Doug said with a smile.

'No,' her father chimed in, 'nothing to do with that, it was men's talk.' Sally was taken aback when suddenly and uncharacteristically her father winked at her. 'Come along. If your mother's got the tea on the table we'd better not keep her waiting.'

Once they had all congregated in the dining room, Sally's mother directed Doug towards the chair on her right. Without being asked, Lottie, in a sea of rustling taffeta, brushed past Sally and sat next to him. Sally was furious with her, but dared not show it – Lottie's tongue could be dangerous if provoked. She bestowed on Sally another smug smile. Sally moved round to the far side of the table and, when everyone was seated, the arrival of the food created a welcome diversion to their individual tensions. Recognising sibling rivalry, Doug attempted to defuse the situation by focusing on Lottie. He began chatting to her.

'Do you go horse riding?' he asked while buttering his bread.

'No, but Sally does,' Lottie replied, pouting.

After a pause and a few more mouthfuls, Doug tried again. 'Do you swim?'

'No, but Sally can,' Lottie replied in a slightly exasperated voice.

Sally, knowing the advantage of keeping her sister's temper sweet, decided to help Doug out.

'Lottie's a very good dancer, aren't you, Lot?'

'Oh, really? What sort of dancing do you do?' Doug asked, and Lottie's face lit up.

'Ballet and tap and we're practising for a Christmas concert. Would you like to come and watch me?'

'I would love to!' Lottie gave Sally a look of triumph. The little minx is flirting with him, thought Sally, but knew she dare say nothing. She was the epitome of sugar and spice, but Sally knew her sister could become slugs and snails in an instant. And when Lottie was upset, her not-so-innocent tongue could be unleashed and things could become very embarrassing. She realised that she would just have to play along with this little charade until the meal was over.

When everyone had finished eating, Rose began to draw out Doug about the proposed trip to Scotland.

'So tell us, Doug, what are your plans for next weekend, for getting up to Scotland? Are you going by train?'

Sally had been expecting this. She had so far evaded her mother's questions by saying that she had left all the planning to Doug. It was hardly surprising, therefore, that her mother should now be quizzing him. Sally was impressed by his unflustered response.

'With your permission, Mrs Phillips, Sir,' he began, glancing towards Joe, 'I'd like to pick Sally up after work on Friday evening. As you know, it's a long drive to Edinburgh. I usually leave about five in the morning, and it can take all of ten hours or more, depending on the traffic. I would nae want to put Sally through such an arduous journey. So with your permission, I thought we could make a start early Friday evening. Sal, perhaps you could get away from work a wee bit earlier?' Sally nodded. This was the first she had heard of his plans. 'There is a very respectable little bed and breakfast place I've occasionally used, just outside Nottingham. Then, if we make another early start on the Saturday morning, we could be in the Lake District by lunchtime. As Sally's never been to the North, I thought she might like to see some of the Lake District and Border country on the way up to Edinburgh. It's very beautiful. Of course, if you would prefer, we could go by train, but that would mean travelling into London early on Saturday morning. There again, we could catch the overnight sleeper on Friday or Saturday night. But if we did that, Sally would see very little of the countryside until she woke up at Waverley Station in Edinburgh. To be honest, I'd rather have my own car at the farm. That way, I can take Sally out to show her some of the local beauty spots.' He finished the carefully-rehearsed explanation with a casual shrug of his shoulders and gave Rose his most charming smile.

'What's an overnight sleeper?' Lottie interrupted.

'It's a special train with beds on it,' Doug explained to her. 'You get on in London in the evening and while you're sleeping it carries you all the way up to Scotland.'

Lottie looked at Sally, back at Doug and asked, 'Will you be in a bed with Sally, kissing her goodnight, like you do when you bring her home?'

Doug, glancing from the innocent expression on Lottie's face to the bright red blush on Sally's cheeks was, for once, momentarily lost for words. Rose and Joe exchanged glances and the ensuing silence round the table was deafening until Joe spoke up.

'Lottie! That's enough of your silly questions. You will leave the table and go to your room, right now!'

Lottie always obeyed her father without argument and, with a sly grin, she bolted out of the room and up to her bedroom. She was astute enough to realise that not only had she scored a hit over her sister but that her banishment to her room was an excellent excuse not to help with the washing up!

'Doug, would you like some more tea?' Her mother offered.

'No thank you, Mrs Phillips, I'm completely full.'

'Please, do call me Rose.' Sally, still scarlet with embarrassment, rose to her feet and gathered up the teacups, quickly making her way to the kitchen. As her mother began to clear the table, Sally's father also stood up.

'Come on, Doug, let's leave these women to their devices. If it's not too early for you, I have a very nice whisky in the cupboard in the sitting room.'

Sally heard her father and called out to Doug as they made their way back down the hall,

'Dad's famous for using a thimble to measure it out, so ask for a double'.

'Thimble!' Joe paused in the hall and turned with laughter in his voice. 'What do you mean, I measure it out in a thimble? That's enough of your cheek, young lady. No doubt you have your reasons, Doug, but I can't think why anyone would want to take that cheeky minx anywhere.'

There had always been a lot of teasing, laughter and leg pulling in their relationship. There was no doubt that Sally was 'daddy's girl', and she got along with him more easily than she ever did with her mother. Sally was close to her father and enjoyed being able to tease him. There was no such lightness in her relationship with her mother. Rose made no attempt to disguise her disapproval and disappointment in Sally, with her constant, unfavourable comparisons between Sally's tomboy ways and Lottie's petite femininity. Lottie was pretty enough to look cute in a fluffy net tutu and light-footed enough to be good at ballet. Sally felt that in Lottie her mother had the daughter she had always wanted; a dainty little girl who played with dolls and loved to be dressed in party frocks.

In the sitting room, Joe filled two glasses with generous measures of whisky and handed one to Doug. From the first introduction, Doug had immediately felt at ease with Sally's father and the two men sat opposite each other in not-uncomfortable silence, each staring into the amber liquid that half-filled the lead crystal glasses. Joe was not sure what he was expected to say to this pleasant, polite young man that Rose had obviously earmarked for Sally. But Sally was so very young and she had seen nothing of life yet. Then again, as Rose had reminded him, neither had he and Rose when they had got together. They had grown up three streets apart and their teenage friendship had somehow turned into an engagement and then marriage. Joe had hardly noticed it happening – one minute he was taking Rose to the cinema and the next he was at the altar! He looked across at Doug and cleared his throat.

'Now, about this trip to Scotland.'

Doug sat up anxiously and braced himself for the grilling that Sally had warned him about.

'What would be the arrangements at this "very respectable bed and breakfast" place you mentioned?' Joe asked.

Doug reached into his jacket pocket. 'I've already taken the liberty, Sir,   of booking two single rooms. I have the receipt here.' He held it out to Joe. 'I know it's a lot to ask, but I would never do anything to hurt Sally and I'd not do anything to cause you to mistrust me.'

Joe took the piece of paper held out to him but didn't read it. 'And this trip to Scotland is to ... to what?'

'I want my parents to meet her, Sir. Sally is the first girl I've ever taken home, and she's very special to me, you see ...'

'You'll behave yourselves?' Joe muttered uncomfortably as he tried to find the right words.

'I hope you can trust me, Sir.'

Joe handed back the unread receipt. He wasn't sure that he did trust Doug, but neither was he sure that he could stop Sally from going anyway, and damn the consequences. He didn't want that. He loved his elder daughter and, after all, Rose had reminded him that he was the one who had said Sally was not stupid and that they had to trust her. Very well then, he would put his trust in Sally, even if Doug was an unknown quantity. He cleared his throat and reached for his pipe. After tapping it on the hearth, he refilled it, lit a match and put the flame to the tobacco. Once his pipe was well and truly alight he sat back in his chair and eyed Doug. Doug leaned back and tried to look unconcerned but, as the seconds ticked away, it became more and more difficult. Eventually, Joe removed the pipe from his mouth and cleared his throat.

'Will you be doing much walking? Sally likes to walk in the countryside, you know. We've walked a fair few miles together over the years.'

Doug sat up in relief. 'I'm hoping that we'll have time to do some walking.' He took a fortifying sip of his whisky as he waited for the next question.

'You see, it's like this, Doug. From our walks Sally knows quite a lot about nature, wild flowers, trees, insects and so on ...' Joe leaned forward. 'But man to man, I'm not so sure she knows much about the birds and the bees ... so I trust you'll be sensible. Now, let's have another drink.'

Doug shifted uncomfortably in his chair, unsure if the 'grilling' was over, then quickly downed the dregs in his glass.

'Thanks, don't mind if I do,' he replied.

Chapter Seven

Although the days were becoming shorter, the warmth and sunshine of high summer spilled over into September and Sally took advantage of bright sunny mornings to walk to work in an attempt to get fitter. Doug had talked in some detail of the many walks he wanted to share with her and she had built up a romantic image of striding over the hillsides hand-in-hand with him. She didn't want this idyll shattered by the more probable scenario in which she would be following in Doug's wake, gasping for breath and begging him to wait until she caught up with him.

Sally's last few evenings prior to their departure were spent in her bedroom in a frenzy of packing and unpacking the smart brown suitcase Doris had lent her. Her parents had never travelled and the need for a suitcase had never arisen before. Her father had teasingly offered her his old khaki kitbag from his days as a conscript in the Army. Sally's bedroom began to resemble the local church hall during a Girl Guides jumble sale. Clothes were piled high on chairs and strewn across the floor, evidence of her nervous energy and complete indecision. Although she had bought several new items on her shopping trip, she would need to take with her more than just her recent purchases. Old favourites were tried on and carefully folded into the case, only to be lifted out the next day and replaced with something completely different.

Her battered and beloved one-eyed teddy bear, who usually sat squinting out across the bedroom from his place of honour on the chest of drawers, was now sitting with his face to the wall. Sally had turned him round as a reminder to pack the risqué new underwear hidden away out of sight under the paper lining of her knickers drawer. Convinced that her mother would thoroughly inspect the contents of her suitcase while she was at work, Sally decided she would slide the new undies into her case at the very last minute. With her faithful Ted's help, she would remember to pack them.

Thursday evening was set aside for personal grooming as advised in a ladies' magazine article which she'd read and cut out, entitled 'Pamper Your Body'. She'd spent her whole lunch hour shopping at the beauty counter in the local chemist for items on the list. That evening, closeting herself away in her bedroom with the bag of 'essentials', she decided to start by applying a sachet of 'home facial' cream before getting to work on her nails. The instructions warned that the contents of the sachet should be left on her face to dry for a minimum of ten minutes. For maximum effect, she decided to leave it on for twenty. It was Sally's first attempt at looking after her young skin and she felt very grown-up as she sat in front of her dressing table mirror and spread the cream 'infused with cucumber' all over her face and neck, leaving only her blue eyes peering out from a pale green mask. Satisfied that she had followed the instructions to the letter, she turned her attention to her ragged cuticles. Head down, she concentrated intently on her nails and only looked up when her bedroom door flew open and Lottie burst in. As the instructions had quite definitely stated 'Do not smile or speak', Sally felt unable either to yell at her sister to get out or to risk a smile of reassurance, for fear of cracking her facemask. Lottie, unnerved firstly by the silence and then by her sister's green face and staring eyes, fled the room screaming for her mother. Sally fought the desire to burst out laughing and crack the mask. When the first coat of nail polish was dry, she made her way along the landing to the bathroom, armed with a tube of depilatory cream for the next step in her beauty regime. She locked the bathroom door against further intrusions, then jumped as she caught a glance of herself in her father's shaving mirror; it revealed the reason for Lottie's hasty departure. By now the cream on her face felt worryingly tight and had dried fluorescent white, giving her a ghostly pallor. She hurriedly began to rinse her face, but it took several basins of tepid water before every last bit of the caked-on mask was removed.

Turning her attention to the depilatory cream, she opened the box. A wooden spatula dropped to the floor as she searched for the instruction leaflet. 'Squeeze enough cream on to spatula to smooth over unwanted hair and wait ten minutes, then scrape off cream with spatula.' Well, that seemed simple enough. She held up an arm in front of the mirror. Her blonde hair was barely visible to the naked eye but, on closer examination, there in her armpit lurked half a dozen straggly hairs and they had to go. A quick glance under the other armpit revealed similar stragglers. Retrieving the spatula from the floor, she squeezed some paste on to it and applied it to the hairs under each arm. When she checked her legs, thankfully there didn't seem to be any unwelcome growth there. The dreadful smell of the cream permeated the bathroom. Surely, she thought, her mother would smell it, too, and know what she was up to!

Wishing the required ten minutes would hurry by, Sally went on to the next phase of the 'Pamper Your Body' beauty regime. She had never bothered with her eyebrows before, but at lunchtime she had purchased some eyebrow tweezers and with some trepidation she now peered closely in the mirror.

Cautiously, she took hold of a stray hair that she could see sprouting from the bridge of her nose. Bracing herself, she tugged firmly at the offending growth, and immediately dropped the tweezers with a clatter as the stinging pain made her eyes water! For several minutes   it was impossible for Sally to see the remaining twenty-odd hairs that, according to the facial diagram in the magazine article, still needed removing.

When she had finally finished plucking her eyebrows, an angry red patch of bare skin throbbed between them. Sally dabbed the area with cold water and hoped it would soon be gone. She didn't recall having unwanted hair before reading the magazine, and now she was covered in the stuff. Turning her attention back to her armpits, she was astonished to find that the cream had magically dissolved the hair. With the wooden spatula, she scraped away at the glutinous mush of hair and smelly cream. Urgh! It was a messy business and the bathroom stank. She realised with horror that the smell lingered under her arms as well! She vigorously rubbed a highly fragrant soap bar into her armpits, but the overpowering odour remained.

Sally ran a bath and poured some of her mother's bath salts into the swirling water. She soaked herself until well after her ration of hot water from the immersion heater had finished – but the smell still filled her nostrils! Returning to her bedroom, with the stench of the depilatory cream still all- pervasive, Sally liberally sprayed deodorant under one arm and immediately felt an excruciatingly painful stinging sensation in her armpit. Rushing back into the bathroom and bending low over the basin, she splashed cold water up into her armpit in an attempt to cool the burning sensation. Holding her arm up to the mirror, she groaned; an angry, disfiguring red rash had formed. Sally sat on the edge of the bath and, when she had finished gently patting herself dry, glanced through the instructions for use of the cream. Well, she thought, that'll teach me to read the full instructions in future.

That night she attempted to sleep with both arms behind her head to allow air to circulate around her armpits. In the morning she was relieved to see that the redness between her eyebrows had vanished and the rash in her armpit was less angry. The smell had mellowed somewhat, too; either that or she had got used to it. Her evening of 'Pampering Your Body' had been torture, but twelve unwanted armpit hairs had been dissolved and twenty stray eyebrow hairs, eventually and very painfully, had been tweezed out. Her fingernails looked neat and she fancied that the home facial had improved her skin tone as well as traumatising her sister – one and sixpence well spent!

Sally had requested, and been granted, permission to leave work early on

Friday, but it was Rose who hovered nervously by the front door. Now that the time had arrived for Sally to leave, she needed to get her away without the neighbours seeing the suitcase! The question was how to get the suitcase into Doug's car quickly and quietly without it being seen? The fewer people around to witness Sally leaving the better, even Lottie had been encouraged to go home with a friend after school and was not expected back until nearly bedtime.

Knowing that Doug was always punctual, and pink with excitement, Sally was ready to leave just before six o'clock. Ted Bear now sat in his usual position with his back to the wall looking out across the bedroom at her. Sally felt sure that his one good eye had looked accusingly at her when she had lifted out the black lacy underwear and hastily slipped it into her suitcase. She wore the less risqué pale blue bra and pants set, allowing for the fact that, should her mother decide to poke around in the suitcase, she would only see the pale lemon set that Sally had recently bought; the black lacy set remained a secret. The suitcase was now packed with new outfits as well as some old favourites and the illicit undies! It also contained the yellow, dimpled nylon dress that Rose had carefully folded between layers of tissue and the compulsory pair of black gloves and sateen clutch bag.

For the journey, Sally had pinned her hair up into a neat French pleat and wore a smart blue lambswool dress with a cowl neck. Over this she pulled on a dove-grey tweed jacket, which matched her gloves, handbag and shoes. Looking in the mirror, Sally thought she looked quite grown-up – almost ladylike!

As she left the suitcase in readiness in the hallway, she collided with her mother, who had suddenly appeared from the sitting room muttering to herself, 'God-given opportunity not to be missed ...' Sally watched in amazement as her mother scooped up the suitcase and rushed down the front garden path with it. Bewildered, Sally watched as Rose placed the case underneath the thick privet hedge to the right of the front gate, out of sight of the road, before hurrying back inside and quickly closing the front door. The vigilant Rose had seen Mrs Clancy, an old and revered gossip who lived opposite them at number 12, heading off towards the top end of the avenue. When her mother returned, Sally looked at her enquiringly but just then Doug's car could be heard pulling up in front of their house, and once more Rose disappeared hastily out through the door. When Doug opened the garden gate he was surprised to see Rose hurtling down the front garden path towards him.

'Good afternoon, Rose. Is Sally ready?'

'Open the boot of your car,' Rose hissed at him. 'Her suitcase is right there,' she pointed towards the hedge. 'Be quick!'

A bemused Doug caught hold of the case and within seconds he had opened the boot, placed the case inside and slammed it shut, suppressing a smile. Luckily, he had put his own luggage on the back seat, otherwise the exercise would not have been quite so slick.

'Yes, she's ready. I just wanted to help her with the suitcase. Sally!' she called out. Where was the stupid girl? She'd been right next to her in the hallway. Sally, totally unaware of the little pantomime that had just taken place, was having a final look in the hall mirror and a last-minute rummage through her handbag to make sure that she had picked up everything she needed. As she hurried down the garden path to where her mother and Doug were waiting, her tummy somersaulted. She had looked forward to this for so long but, now that the actual time was here for her to leave, she suddenly felt nervous. But there was Doug, holding the gate open as he smiled warmly at her.

'Bye, Mum ...' she said hesitantly, wondering if her mother would use this opportunity to impart any final words of advice to her. But Rose was eager for them to leave, in case the remaining neighbours were watching and would jump to all the right conclusions – that she was allowing her daughter to go off with a packed suitcase, in a car, with a man she wasn't married to!

Joe was not back from work, and Sally was relieved yet sad that he was not there to wave farewell to her. As she paused by the front gate, her mother leaned forward for a token kiss on the cheek and without a word hurried back up the path. Doug opened the passenger door and stood patiently while Sally waved to her mother, who now stood at the front door. Rose wished that they would get a move on and leave before old Mrs Clancy waddled back into view.

Rose had already reminded her daughter many times during the past few days to use her good manners while she was away. In years gone by, such instructions meant not leaving the table without permission and remembering to say 'thank you for having me' after a friend's birthday party. While she had given the subject of sex a wide berth, she had also frequently added that Sally should 'behave herself', leaving Sally to assume, from the embarrassing silences and gaps in the conversation, that her mother was not referring to table manners.

'Cheerio, Rose. Don't worry, I'll take good care of her,' Doug called out. Blowing her a kiss, he slid down into the driver's seat. Rose's eyes darted left and right, praying no one had heard him before she stepped back inside and shut the door. At least no net curtains twitched, nor could she see anyone within earshot of Doug's parting promise.

Had she done the right thing? she wondered, as the door clicked to behind her. Well, too late now – they were on their way. Besides, she reasoned, Doug was definitely a good catch for Sally, and what else was there for her but to be a good wife and mother? What more could any girl wish for? In Doug, Rose felt that Sally had done pretty well for herself. As she continued in this train of thought, Rose persuaded herself that she had indeed done the right thing and, with resignation that there was nothing to be gained by worrying about it now, she set about preparing tea for Joe.

'Okay, away we go.' Doug turned the key in the ignition and the car roared into life. By the time they had reached the first bend in the road he had burst into song.

'Ye'll tak the high road And I'll tak the low road

And I'll be in Scotland afore ye!'

Sally, who had never felt so liberated in all her life, joined in. 'But me and my true love

Will never meet again

On the bonny bonny banks Of Loch Lomond!'

And they both burst out laughing as he turned the corner and they were really on their way!

'Did you get any last-minute warnings and instructions from your mum, back there on the doorstep?'

'No, that chat came a few days ago. Usual stuff, remember my table manners and say, "thank you for having me".'

'Is that all? Thank God for that. I thought she might be giving you a few last-minute hints on fornicating rabbits. Mind, that bit about "thank you for having me" might come in handy this week ... with a bit of luck.' Doug was smiling but kept his eyes on the road ahead as he teased her.

'Have you run out of words to your song already?' Sally asked, refusing to be led where Doug was trying to take the conversation. Doug grinned and took the hint.

'There's a map on the floor in front of you, if you'd like to see where we're going. I've a pretty good idea of the route, so don't worry too much about navigating for the time being, but I might need some help when we get up into Grasmere tomorrow. Just now we'll head north on this road.' He put his hand briefly on Sally's knee and gave it an affectionate squeeze. 'There's a present for you on the back seat. You should be able to reach it.'

Surprised, Sally turned and picked up a beautifully-wrapped gift box covered in silver paper held in place by a pink silk ribbon tied in a large bow. The packaging looked expensive and she stared at it in amazement.

'Go ahead, open it,' Doug encouraged her.

Sally tugged at the ribbon and stripped off the paper to reveal a silver box. She took off the lid and from among the soft white tissue paper lifted up a pale blue silk top. A row of lace daisies across the front continued up over the shoulder to form the straps. Looking into the box, beneath more tissue, she found matching panties to the baby-doll pyjamas.

'Doug! It's lovely. I've never had anything like this before ...' she gasped with surprise. Sally was enchanted and held the top up against her.

'Maybe you've not, but I'm going to spoil you this week, starting right now. I'm glad you like it. Mind, I might well expect to see it on you later – and will you not hold it up quite so high! The chap driving towards us nearly went off the road.' Sally laughed and carefully folded the pretty pyjama top back in the box.

For the next couple of hours, they chatted and laughed as the car sped northwards.

'We're making good time despite the traffic and should be getting onto the A6 shortly. We'll get a few miles further and start looking out for a place to stay for the night.'

'What about this respectable B&B you told my parents about?'

'Oh aye, that place. Well, it's a way further on but I'm beginning to feel a bit weary now. If I can get my head down we can get an early start tomorrow and be up into the Lake District by the afternoon. D'you know, it's been a horrendously busy week and I've really been looking forward to this break.'

Shortly afterwards, Doug indicated, slowed the car and turned into the car park of a large roadside pub advertising good food and accommodation.

'This might do. Wait here, Sal, while I go in and check availability,' he said, getting out of the car. A few minutes later, he strolled back across the car park and, opening the door, smiled down at her. 'We're in luck, but sadly they only have one room – it was a case of take it or leave it. We'll have to share, but I'm quite happy to drive on if that doesn't suit you, kitten?'

'If you're tired, it'd be dangerous and silly to keep driving. I'll take my chances!' Sally replied, grinning up at him. She had longed for this moment – to spend a whole night in Doug's arms!

'Good lass!' Doug hesitated before adding, 'And, um, by the way ... when you sign the register, it'll be as Mrs MacDonald and perhaps you'd better put your gloves on, at least on your left hand. The nosy besom behind the desk has eyes like a vulture.'

Sally's tummy flipped, but this time it wasn't with excitement; she had not considered that such deception would be involved.

'Oh ... No! Wait ... Doug ... Look, I don't know if I can go through with this. She will know! I'm bound to give the game away!' she stammered as panic began to overwhelm her.

'Of course you can, kitten,' he whispered reassuringly. 'Just smile and sign.' Leaning into the car, he kissed her on the cheek. 'By the way, it's MacDonald, with an "a". Better get it right,' he grinned as he held out his hand to help her out of the car.

It was typical of Sally's attitude to life that she had not really thought out the practicalities of spending days and, more importantly, nights alone with Doug. Her mother called it 'living in a dream world' and it had got Sally into all sorts of awkward situations in the past. Setting off to see Scotland and being alone with Doug had seemed a very exciting thing to do, but this was no daydream! This was here and now!

The scenarios of her daydreams had not stretched to posing as his wife, nor even being alone in a hotel room with him. Reality was waiting for her in reception, and after that? She didn't even want to think about that. The excitement that she had felt earlier was draining away, together with her confidence; suddenly Sally felt tired and she shivered. Taking a deep breath, she pulled on her jacket and gloves and picked up her handbag. She reached over for the parcel on the back seat while Doug lifted her case from the boot. He retrieved his own from the back seat and, having locked the car, led the way to a side door.

Waiting for them in the reception area was Mrs Richardson, the landlady. For thirty-five years she had run the Dog and Pheasant, through good times and bad. During the war, she had been proud of the fact that she had managed to keep the place going, not only without any staff but also, at times, without any beer, either. The war over and her husband dead, the brewery queried the appropriateness of a woman running the establishment on her own. They hadn't had a problem with it during the war, she protested, to which the suave brewery representative had condescendingly replied, 'Desperate times needed desperate measures, Mrs Richardson, and the war's over now!' However the brewery had seen sense and relented.

Bitterness and frustration with the hand life had dealt her had left its mark. Her mane of auburn hair, once her shining glory, was now grey and pulled tightly back into a bun at the nape of her neck. Her neat figure had expanded so much that now the only reliable means of support for her incredibly large bosom was the broad waistband of her apron. The reception desk was just the right height for her to rest them on, so that it too could play a supporting role in defying gravity. From behind the weight of these magnificent specimens, she watched the young couple with small, beady eyes as they made their way to her front desk.

Sally stood at Doug's side, smiling sweetly and saying nothing, having taken his instructions literally. Doug signed the book and then handed her the pen. The landlady stared at the silver box with the pink ribbon around that Sally had placed on the counter while she signed the register. Sally could feel the woman's eyes watching her every move as she laboriously signed an unpractised 'Sally MacDonald' beneath Doug's confident scrawl and started when Mrs Richardson suddenly spoke.

'Holiday or honeymoon, dear?'

Doug smiled at the harridan. 'We're on our way up to Scotland to visit my parents, so we're just passing through. Now if I could have the room keys and some directions, we won't keep you standing around any longer, so late at night. It's gone nine o'clock.' Doug's smile and concerned response had the desired effect.

'Of course, Mr MacDonald. D'you need a hand with your suitcases? I can't get up them rickety old stairs on my pins,' she nodded towards the staircase at the far side of the reception area, 'but I could ring for someone to come through if you'd like some help?'

'I wouldn't dream of it – we'll manage, thanks.' Doug smiled at her again and she mellowed under his charm.

'Would you like some supper?' she asked.

'That would be very welcome, if it's not too much trouble. Just give us ten minutes and we'll be back down. A pint of your best beer and a snack would be much appreciated.' He flashed another smile in the direction of his latest conquest as he moved towards the narrow, uneven stairs to the first floor. Sally followed behind, relieved to be away from the scrutiny of the suspicious woman.

'It's a nice room,' Doug remarked, as they made their way along the narrow hallway at the top of the stairs. 'It's got the rare luxury of having its own bathroom. That's why I chose it.'

'Chose it? I thought there was only one vacancy? A case of "take it or leave it," you said.'

'Oops! My mother's quite right, a liar needs a good memory,' Doug chuckled over his shoulder. Sally wasn't sure what to make of his calm admission that he had just been caught out, but his laugh was infectious and she found herself grinning at his cheek.

Outside Room 19, Doug put the suitcases down as he fumbled with a large old-fashioned key to unlock the door. When it finally turned, he lifted the suitcases and Sally moved forward to help by pushing open the heavy door. As they stepped into the room, she gasped with delight. It was a lovely large room with dark oak beams, which stood out in contrast against the cream walls and ceiling. The floorboards were a lighter oak and polished to a warm honey colour, and against the centre of one wall was a large brass bed covered with a patchwork bedspread. Faded green velvet curtains had been drawn across the windows and Sally felt that, although large, the room had a warm, cosy feeling about it. Doug dropped the suitcases to the floor and strode over to the bed. Sitting on the edge, he bounced up and down and the bed began to squeak its loud objections.

'Come over here, Mrs, let's see if this is to your liking. It feels as though it could be a wee bit on the fast side for me,' he joked.

Sally walked over to Doug and as he patted the bed sat down shyly beside him. Immediately, his arms went round her and as they fell backwards on to the bed his lips sought hers. She had not seen Doug for nearly a week before their trip and was hungry for his kisses; as a result, her uncertainty about the situation disappeared as quickly as it had arisen. Sally had missed the physical contact, too, especially the feel of his arms around her. Kisses and cuddles had been rare in her childhood; it was not in her mother's nature to show such affection and, while Sally had spent many hours walking and talking with her father, he was not the kind of man who felt the need to hold his little girl's hand. Doug's kisses became more demanding but after a few minutes he sat up, pulling Sally back up with him as he did so.

'Let's not get too carried away or the landlady will be hammering on the door with our supper. There's something else, kitten,' he said, reaching into his pocket. 'I think it might be a good idea to slip this on for the next day or two.'

'But it looks like a wedding ring ...' she said, gazing naïvely down at the plain gold band he dropped into her hand.

'Exactly!' Doug winked at her and got up. 'I'll just freshen up, then the bathroom's all yours,' he said, walking across the room.

Sally stayed where she was, staring down at the ring in the palm of her hand, not sure what to make of this latest development. Slowly, she closed her fingers over it, rose and walked aimlessly over to the mirror. Gazing at the reflection that stared back at her, she asked it, 'What are you doing?' She stood for a few moments reliving the deception at the front desk – and now a ring, to be worn as a wedding ring, another deception. Her mind was in a whirl as she stood critically eyeing the reflection of the stranger who stared back at her. At that moment Doug emerged from the bathroom and, as Sally turned to him, he saw the worried look and realised that the smile had gone from her eyes. Sensing that it might be wise to leave her alone for a while, Doug tossed the room key on to the bed as he made for the door.

'Bathroom's free. Lock up when you come down, kitten. I'll wait for you in the bar.' And he was gone.

'Thanks, I won't be long,' she replied, almost in a whisper, as she stared down at her white knuckles where her fingers clenched around the ring. Reality had wakened her from the idyllic daydream that had been fuelled by her desire to be with Doug; fear and panic now clutched at her heart. What am I doing here? she asked herself. Oh Lord! One moment she had appeared to herself mature and in control of the situation and now she felt totally out of control and very, very vulnerable. Slowly, she turned away from the mirror and went into the bathroom. She washed and dried her hands and, with trepidation and an indescribable sense of guilt, she slowly slid the gold band onto the third finger of her left hand. As she tentatively held her hand out in front of her, tears welled in her eyes. All she could see was deceit and subterfuge where she'd naïvely imagined there would be romance and happiness. She fully expected a bolt from the blue to strike her down for such a sinful masquerade. The lack of immediate divine retribution didn't make her feel any better. She just assumed that God would catch up with her at a later date.

First Love

Chapter Eight

When Sally finally found her way through the maze of stairs and corridors into the lounge bar, she saw Doug perched on a stool, halfway through his pint of beer, chatting to the landlady.

'What would you like to drink, Sal? Your usual?' he asked. Sally had no idea what her 'usual' might be! She had never been allowed anywhere near alcohol at home and it was only recently that she had begun to enjoy an occasional, illicit glass of wine. Hoisting herself onto the stool beside him, she took his lead.

'Yes please, darling, I'll have my usual.'

'Gin and tonic please – make it a double, and whatever you would like for yourself.' As the old woman turned to make her way further down the bar, Sally raised her eyebrows at Doug and mouthed, 'Double gin and tonic?'

Doug just grinned at her, shrugging his shoulders, and leant forward to whisper, 'You'll like it. Don't worry; it's a very refreshing drink'.

'But I'll be flat on my back if I drink that much!' she whispered back at him.

Doug's grin widened. 'That's the general idea!'

'Douglas MacDonald with an "a", I thought you were a gentleman!' Sally whispered back to him in mock protest, but she was unable to resist his irrepressible grin and she found herself willingly grinning back at him.

'Oh, I am! You'll see,' he smiled confidently at her as he raised his glass.

With their heads bowed together, they were both still laughing when the landlady returned.

'Well, if you're not on honeymoon, I'd say you haven't been married long,' she said, looking at Sally. 'And from the look of you,' she turned to Doug, 'Well – in my day, young man, you would've been called a cradle snatcher!' She very much doubted that they were married; the girl barely looked old enough to be sitting in her bar, let alone married, but you just couldn't tell these days. If the young man had not been so persuasive, she would have been inclined to turn them away. At least the girl had the decency to be wearing a ring, but she really didn't approve of all the shenanigans that the youngsters got up to these days. What was the world coming to? As she continued with her musings, suspicion evident from her stance, Doug looked across at Sally, who was now blushing, more from guilt than the compliment.

'Well, look at her – she's beautiful! Can you blame me? If I hadn't snatched her quick, somebody else would have,' he said, trying to draw the old woman's attention away from Sally with his questioning.

'Huh-hurmh!' the woman muttered as she placed Sally's drink on the bar without taking her eyes off her. Without being asked, she topped up Doug's pint glass.

Well, she thought, maybe I won't turn you out, but you'll know that I'm not that easily fooled! At least the girl's got the decency to blush, but this laddie's a sharp one all right. He needs watching! Placing his replenished glass on the counter, she turned abruptly and headed off towards the kitchen.

At Doug's suggestion, they collected their drinks up from the bar and moved to a corner table. Just as they sat down, two large plates of chicken and chips were placed before them.

'Well! Isn't that a feast?' Doug complimented the old woman. 'I'm more than ready for this. Thank you very much.' But this time he failed to raise a reciprocal smile from her and she returned to the bar without further comment. Never having had gin before, Sally tentatively sipped at her drink. The taste was quite pleasant and she was thirsty, so she quickly downed most of it. On an empty stomach it was quick to take effect, and she began to feel light-headed. She wasn't particularly hungry, but in a belated attempt to soak up some of the alcohol coursing through her system, she began to pick at the chicken. Doug tucked in to his supper, swiftly clearing his plate and emptying his beer glass.

The landlady had continued to watch them from behind the bar, and she called over to him, 'Would you like another beer?'

'No, thank you, that's very kind but I think we'll be turning in now. It's an early start in the morning for us. But you've been very hospitable, thank you.'

He knew her type and he could tell that she was suspicious. While he was confident of his own ability to fend off searching questions, he wasn't sure that Sally could cope with any more this evening. He thought he had blown it when he told her that she would have to sign in as his wife and had noticed how easily she had blushed just now at the bar. Doug stood up and Sally somewhat unsteadily followed his lead. He held her hand as they left the bar and led her upstairs. Sally began to giggle as she felt herself swaying slightly and by the time they had reached the bedroom door they were both giggling.

'Usual drink, Mrs Mac? Hey, do you know you play the part of Mrs Mac very well?' Doug teased her as he wrapped his arm around her waist to steady her.

'Well, I was actually wondering just how many "Gin and Tonic Drinking

Mrs Macs" there've been?' Sally hiccupped. 'Ooo, pardon me.'

'Aye, well I admit, there've been a few, but let me say, if there was an Oscar for playing the part, it would undoubtedly have to go to you.' He kissed her nose, pushed the bedroom door open and stood aside to usher her in. 'It remains to be seen what other talents you might have. I know ladies take hours in the bathroom, so give me a few minutes and then it's all yours.' Gathering up his dressing gown, he disappeared into the bathroom.

Sally sat down in the armchair clutching her dressing gown, toilet bag and the silver box containing the saucy baby-doll pyjamas. Briefly, a window of doubt opened in her mind and her Dutch courage threatened to evaporate through it. Resolutely she slammed the window shut. She couldn't back out now, not having come this far. We love each other, she thought, and that's all that matters. She could hear water splashing and Doug humming happily in the bathroom and it made her smile.

Eventually Doug opened the bathroom door to reveal himself in a blue silk paisley dressing gown, smelling of cologne and toothpaste. 'All yours,' he said, and bent over to plant a kiss on her forehead.

Hesitantly, Sally stood up and managed a smile, though her heart was hammering against her ribs; whether this was due to excitement or fear she had no way of telling.

In the privacy of the bathroom, Sally placed everything on the stool next to the bath, which was big, deep and made of cast iron. Perched on four ornate feet, it looked inviting and she would have liked to fill it to the top and sink into it, but the archaic hot water system of the old inn would obviously not be up to it. She managed a fairly thorough wash in the few inches of tepid water that worked its way noisily through the ancient pipes and taps and eventually spluttered into the bath.

Still feeling somewhat light-headed, Sally clambered carefully out of the bath, wrapped herself in a towel, cleaned her teeth and brushed her hair. She then reached for the bottle of perfume that had cost her almost a week's wages and put a few drops behind each ear and on her wrists. Sally wasn't sure why she had to put it in those two places but momentarily she could see her mother opening the dark blue bottle labelled 'Evening in Paris' and, tipping a few drops onto her fingertips, showing Sally where to dab the scent. As quickly as the vision of her mother had arisen in her mind, she cast it aside. Her confidence soared, and letting the bath towel drop to the floor she placed perfume in a couple of other places that her mother most certainly had not shown her! Reaching for the silver gift box, she lifted out the silk baby-doll pyjamas and slipped the top over her head. For the first time in her life, she felt the sensation of silk against her skin, and it was one that she would never forget! It was so sensual and, as the material touched her skin, it felt as soft as the flutter of a butterfly's wings. Stepping hastily into the silk panties, she reached for her less sensual, but highly practical, cotton dressing gown and wrapped herself in it. Then, with more confidence than she was now feeling, she opened the bathroom door, and walked back into the bedroom.

Doug was already in bed and from the soft glow of the bedside lamp Sally could see he was naked to his waist. Her heart missed a beat as she wondered if he was also naked from the waist down. By way of a saucy invitation he partially lifted up the bedclothes.

'Okay, now let's see those baby-doll pyjamas modelled. May I suggest you just take a deep breath and go for it?' He chuckled. Sally took off her dressing gown and threw it in the general direction of a chair. The after-effects of the gin kicked in once again and suddenly she had a desire to throw caution to the wind. Adopting an exaggerated model's pose, she attempted a slinky catwalk stroll over to the bed, giving a couple of twirls on the way.

'Bravo!' Doug encouraged. As she reached the bed, he lifted the bedclothes back further and invitingly patted the vacant space in the bed next to him. It was at this point that her courage almost failed her as, catching sight of his naked thigh, she knew without a shadow of a doubt that under the bedclothes he was completely naked. Seeing her hesitation Doug reached out and caught hold of her wrist, playfully hauling her on to the bed. 'Hey, relax ... no pressure, we only go as far as you want to,' he said, pulling her closer. He could feel her heart beating so wildly that for a few moments he just held her quietly in his arms. Gradually she began to relax but he waited a while longer, running his fingers through her hair before speaking softly.

'God, you're so lovely and I want to make love to you so much that it frightens me. I haven't been able to sleep all week thinking about this moment, dreaming of being alone with you in my arms, and now that we are here, together, I have to admit to being more than a little apprehensive.'

'That makes two of us, although my sleepless nights were probably over slightly different fears to yours,' Sally replied, and she started to tremble. 'Oh no! Not again!' she said through chattering teeth. Doug drew her close.

'Hey, come on, now,' he whispered tenderly, pushing the hair back from her face as he spoke.

'I feel so stupid. I don't know why I'm shaking. It just happens and it's beyond my control.'

Trying to lighten the situation, Doug teased her. 'D'ye know what I think? I think it's pure lust! You're shaking in anticipation at the very thought of a night spent in my arms ...' he chuckled.

Sally looked into his eyes and smiled weakly. 'Oh, you think so, do you? I can't help feeling that guilt and fear of the unknown are probably closer to the truth.'

Disarmed by her honesty and acutely conscious of her innocence, for the first time in many years, Doug was at a loss to know what to say or do next. Should he just hold her close or should he push his conscience aside and follow the intense urge pulsating through his body to seduce her?

'Sal, you know I want to make love to you ... but I've to admit to a certain nervousness about this whole situation ...' He kissed the top of her head where it lay against his naked chest.

'It's all right. I want you to. But I'm worried ... I just don't think I'll be much good at this sort of thing ...'

'Whoa, whoa – stop right there! Sal, my sweetheart "being good"? That's not what it's about.' His lips gently brushed hers as he whispered, 'It's not about that at all'. At the feel of his lips on hers, she was on fire and went beyond the shivering as she responded to his kisses.

Finally he broke away and held her gaze with his own. Nobody could ever know how much he wanted this girl. He was head over heels in love with her and he wanted her more than anything he had ever wanted in his life. If only it was tomorrow morning; if only this one night was over; how would he ever control himself? The last thing he wanted was to frighten her or hurt her.

'Sal, if at any point you want me to stop, say so, and you have my solemn promise that I will. Okay?'

'Okay.'

'Might I add, you have the advantage over me at the moment. I feel somewhat naked and vulnerable as you do seem to have an awful lot of clothes on. Don't be shy, let me help you ...'

'I don't believe that you're the one feeling vulnerable,' Sally sighed. 'Well, lassie, you had better believe it, because it's true.'

Confident that there were no unsightly or unwanted hairs lurking in her armpits and that she had got rid of the lingering smell of the depilatory cream, Sally slowly sat up and held her arms aloft. Unaware of her precise thoughts at that moment, Doug lifted the silk pyjama top over her head and, with his thoughts and eyes fixed firmly on the sight of Sally's nakedness, he tossed it to the floor. Slowly he moved his hands along the length of her outstretched arms and onto her breasts. His hands lingered there as he gently kissed and caressed each one before continuing downwards to the silk panties.

'Somehow I thought that this part of the outfit might not be such a good idea,' Doug chuckled as he began to struggle with their removal, 'but they looked so sexy.'

Under his direction Sally raised herself up off the bed, making it easier for him to slide them down over her buttocks and legs. The panties then joined the pyjama top on the floor. Doug pulled her slowly down into his arms and as she sank completely naked onto his chest, she discovered yet another new, even more pleasing sensation than silk on skin; that of skin against skin! She pressed up close to the warmth of his naked body, thankful that her uncontrollable nervous shaking had all but disappeared. Doug kissed and nuzzled her ears, then her cheeks, then her lips. As his tongue probed her mouth, every part of her began trembling again, only this time it was in eager response to his kisses and the caresses of his hand running lightly and sensually over her body. When he reached down between her legs, Sally audibly caught her breath; once again his touch was electrifying.

'Okay so far? How are we doing?' He murmured.

'Mmmm ...' was all she could manage. Then she drew in a sharp breath and kissed him.

As they lay there together, Doug's experienced hands played her body as expertly as an experienced musician would play a musical instrument. To her bewilderment, his fingers caused waves of exquisite sensations that induced her back to arch and muscles that up until now she was unaware she owned to tighten involuntarily. Then, taking her inexperienced hand, he guided it down towards to his penis, holding it there until Sally shyly wrapped her fingers very gently around his firm erection.

'Still okay?' He whispered, nuzzling gently at her neck and ear. Preoccupied with the new and pleasant sensations exploding within her as well as coping with a range of conflicting emotions that were racing through her mind, Sally didn't answer. Despite Doris's good advice, she was still finding it difficult to put aside what she had been taught and continued to be dubious that she would find the entire process as pleasurable as it was, so far, turning out to be. Sex was all about babies and any pleasure from the act of procreation would be the man's. Where was all the pain and discomfort that she had been told about? Why was her body reacting in this way? At what point, she wondered, should she bring up the subject of 'protection'? On and on ran the thoughts jumbling around in her head, while her body continued to undulate and 'dance' to the exquisite tune that Doug's expert hands played upon it. He continued to kiss her passionately and, as he caressed her, he slowly encouraged her legs to open further and further apart. All her anxieties were beginning to sink beneath the torrent of painfully exquisite feelings that she was drowning in. Supporting himself on his elbows, Doug moved to lie between her legs, placing kisses on her forehead and nose.

He smiled down at her. 'I don't see a red light as yet.'

'No red light. Perhaps an orange one, though,' she giggled nervously.

'I take it that's a "proceed with caution", then? Do you know, I can't ever remember seeing a chapter on "Love Making" in the Highway Code.'

They both laughed and while she was laughing Doug's mouth covered hers and once more his tongue probed her mouth as his hand reached down to fondle and tease. Yet again her back arched under his caresses as he probed with his fingers. Then Sally called out as she gave an involuntary sharp intake of breath; there was pressure and a confusion of pain mixed with more, hitherto unknown, sensations of extreme pleasure and sensitivity; it felt as if she was on fire.

Doug became very still, undecided as to his next move.

'Do you want me to stop?' As if from far off, Sally heard the concern in his voice.

Recalling Doris's advice, Sally gasped, 'No, don't stop! Whatever I say, don't stop!'

Once more he brought his lips gently to hers and the warm sensual feelings that this gave her encouraged Sally to respond; spontaneously she pushed her hips up from the bed to meet him as another final sharp pain brought her back to reality and she groaned. Again Doug hesitated; this was totally new ground to him.

'Are you sure you're okay, kitten?'

'I'm fine. What happens next? Show me,' she whispered.

'Don't you think I've shown you enough for one day?' Smiling down at her, he looked into her blue eyes and kissed her nose, relieved that the deed had been done. Sally grinned mischievously and wriggled her hips under him.

'Sal, don't do that, please.'

'I want to, it feels quite nice,' Sally giggled, brazenly pushing herself against him.

'Oh, you little devil, you're on such dangerous ground now!' Doug gently thrust forward each time she pushed against him until suddenly he groaned and rolled off her, onto his back.

'What happened? Did I do something wrong?' Sally asked, suddenly feeling bewildered by his actions.

'No, no, lassie, you did everything right. So right ... I nearly got it wrong,' he said, reaching over to the bedside table for some tissues.

Wrapped cosily in each other's arms, they talked on for a while about their love for each other until eventually Sally unfurled and stretched; in a post-coital state of mind, she felt blissfully happy. The 'guilt trip' would kick in later, but for the moment, she belonged to Doug. Smiling dreamily up at him, she wondered about her new experiences.

'Do you know, Doris was quite right? Mother Nature is very cunning.'
'Doris! Not Doris from your office? In heaven's name, what could she teach you?'

'You might be surprised to know that I took her advice about tonight.'
'Surprised is something of an understatement – and exactly what advice would it have been that Doris imparted?'

'Well, apart from warning me that I wouldn't be able to resist you – which was quite right, I couldn't – Doris said "don't waste time; bite the bullet the first time and get it over with". She said you'd probably be as worried about it as I was. When you admitted you were frightened too, I knew she'd given me good advice, so I "bit the bullet" and "went for it", as Doris put it.'

Doug lay silent for a while and then she heard his familiar chuckle.

'Did she teach you yon bit about wiggling your backside around? Or did you make that up yourself?'

'Oh no, she just said find a good man and let him show you how to please him.'

'Well thanks be to Doris, and as for you, young lady, you certainly are very pleasing to me. Come here.' Doug pulled her in closer to him. 'Do you snore?'
'Why?'

'Because I'm about to,' and gently he kissed her lips.

Sally tried to sleep but just the smallest doubts began to cloud her mind, and the doubts were all delivered in her mother's stage whisper.

'Had what he's wanted now!' 'Second-hand goods.'

'No one wants used goods!'

What would happen, she wondered, if she became pregnant? He hadn't used what Doris had referred to as 'protection'. Well, if he had, Sally hadn't seen anything, but anyway, she thought, I wouldn't have known what to look for even if he had. But as she listened to Doug's slow, easy breathing and he held her safely in his arms, her thoughts quietened and, with her head against his chest, she finally fell asleep.

When she woke the next morning, she could hear sounds of splashing coming from the bathroom. It seemed that the water heater had gathered some speed overnight and Doug was filling the big bath. Just then, he put his head round the bathroom door.

'You're awake! Good. Come and look at this very inviting bath I'm filling.' In the morning light Sally suddenly felt very naked and shy; sitting up in bed, she modestly held the sheets up to her shoulders to cover herself. Doug guessed her feelings and walked further into the bedroom wearing just a towel round his waist. He picked up her dressing gown, smiling down at her as she took it from him.

'Err, bye the bye I've seen it all and it's lovely. Now, come on through and be spoiled. I'm going to scrub your back.'

Wrapping herself in the dressing gown, she slid out from under the covers and joined him in the bathroom. Suddenly she was faced with the predicament of needing to use the toilet but nothing would have induced her to sit herself on the loo in his presence. Sensing her needs, Doug wandered back into the bedroom and left her alone.

'Are you in that bath yet? Don't let it get cold,' he called out as he walked back into the bathroom. Sally, no longer feeling as uninhibited as she had been the previous evening, had opted to give her teeth an extra vigorous brush instead. She quickly averted her eyes when he casually dropped his towel on to the floor before climbing into the huge bath. As she wiped her mouth and Doug invitingly held out his hand to her, she realised how silly this all seemed, after all that they had shared last night.

'Come on in,' he invited, 'there's plenty of room for two.'

Still avoiding his eyes, Sally took a deep breath, removed her dressing gown and, taking his outstretched hand, boldly stepped naked into the bath.

'This bath is designed for two. Look, the taps and plug are set in the middle so there's no argument about who sits at the uncomfortable end.' Self-consciously Sally lowered herself down into the bath to sit facing him, her knees bent up under her chin. In the cold light of day, Sally just could not believe that she was sitting naked in a bathtub with a naked man at the other end of it. Without the Dutch courage of last night's gin and tonic she felt shy and vulnerable.

Suddenly, Doug reached under the soapy bath water and, catching hold of her legs behind the knees, he pulled her easily towards him. Her embarrassment dispersed as he slipped his legs under her bottom, so that she ended up straddling him. With her legs wrapped comfortably around his waist, she began to giggle as they sat face to face in the middle of the bathtub.

'That's better.' Doug kissed her on the nose and handed her a bath sponge. 'Now, if you care to put your arms round me you can do my back and while you're doing that I can put my arms round you and do yours. Oh! And by the way, take no notice of my cheeky friend down there, or else we'll never get down to breakfast!'

Sally laughed out loud. Doug had the magic to transform her shyness into boldness and the last remnants of her inhibitions slipped away as he teased and played with her, until Sally decided that it was time for her to join in.

'Your friend's getting very difficult to ignore. I think he's got some sort of homing device,' she said with a saucy grin on her face. She felt positively wicked, enjoying the feeling of Doug getting harder and rubbing against her stomach. Deliberately pressing herself up against him, she reached round to the centre of his back with the sponge. Then, leaning back slightly, she rubbed soap on to Doug's chest, squeezing the sponge and watching as the rivulets of water trickled through the forest of dark hair on his chest. She became so engrossed with studying his body that she was unaware that he was watching her and smiling.

'Do you like the welcome mat?' he asked, looking down at his hairy chest. 'I love it, I could play on it all day.' She ran her fingers up through his tight dark curls.

'I would willingly let you, but we have to get back on the road. So could you desist and let me get up?'

'But what about this?' Sally reached under the water and ran her soapy hands up and down his erect penis, as he had shown her the night before.

'Well, I was going to use the ploy that, if I ignored it, maybe it would go away. But if you keep doing that, there will be no chance.'

Sally looked Doug straight in the eye and with a smile continued to slide her hands up and down his manhood.

'Really, you should stop, if not he's likely to disgrace himself.' Doug was becoming breathless but Sally, taking no heed of his warnings, continued to stroke and caress, until Doug moaned with ecstasy and climaxed.

Sally leaned forward and whispered seductively, 'I've heard them described as tadpoles; can they swim in bath water?'

'Mind you don't end up with a hutch full of rabbits.' Doug sighed as he lay back, spent, against the end of the bath. Sally playfully splashed water over his face and then quickly stood up. 'I thought you wanted breakfast,' she said as she clambered out of the bath, now totally at ease with her naked body.

'I'll be with you in a minute. I'm not sure I can stand up yet,' he laughed. He scooped up the bath sponge and threw it across the bathroom to where Sally stood wrapped in a bath towel. She caught it and tossed it back at him.

Alone in the bedroom, Sally was smiling to herself as she pulled the new black lace underwear out of her suitcase. Having slipped into the lace panties and then the bra, she pulled on a blue shirt just as Doug, making a pretence of staggering, collapsed on to the bed. Catching sight of her black lacy underwear through the gap in the unbuttoned shirt, he threw his hands up in mock surrender.

'Oh! Christ no! Just cover yourself up, woman! I can't take any more! Black lace! Here I was, expecting fleecy blue knickers from a convent school girl!'

'Fleecy blue knickers? You wanted me to wear fleecy blue knickers?' She laughed. 'Have I wasted my hard-earned cash?' She launched herself towards the bed and sat astride him and again he held up his hands in mock surrender. 'Okay, okay! I give in! Send for the nuns. How do I get the genie back into the bottle?'

'I don't think she ever wants to go back into the bottle,' Sally pouted. 'Does she have to?'

'Absolutely not, but we do have to get down those stairs to breakfast.' He sat up and rolled her off on to the bed.

In no time at all he had put on a clean shirt and casual trousers and slipped on his sports jacket. 'Typical woman!' he tutted. 'Never ready on time. Come along, hurry up, I'm starving.'

Sally had packed away her dress and chosen to wear her favourite needle cord trousers, and was bending over, tying up the laces of the 'sensible' walking shoes that Doug had advised her to bring with her.

'My, that's a smashing bum you have. Your back view's nearly as good as the front. I must remember that.'

Picking up the cushion from a nearby chair, Sally threw it at him. 'I'm ready now.'

Once more, they threaded their way through the maze of narrow corridors and found their way down to a small dining room, where several breakfast tables had been laid. They sat at a table laid for two and eventually a waitress, who looked about Sally's age, appeared at their side to take their order. Mrs Richardson, who carried out the functions of landlady, receptionist, cook and barmaid, drew the line at waiting on tables. Sally smiled up at the young girl, feeling a wave of sympathy for her. Her uniform swamped her and Sally guessed that there was a small, neat figure underneath the shapeless black dress that was pulled in at the waist by the ties of a not-so-white apron. The constant turnover in staff made it practical for Mrs Richardson to buy uniforms in the largest size – a 'one size fits all' system. Thick black stockings rested in wrinkles at the girl's ankles and her long fair hair was tied back in a ponytail with an elastic band; three large hairgrips held the frilly white maid's cap precariously in place on the back of her head.

'Full English breakfast or what?' she mumbled in their direction. 'And do yer want tea or coffee?'

Doug's smile was wasted on her as she stood yawning, with pencil poised to take his order.

'We'll have the full English breakfast please, but could we have some coffee while we're waiting?' The girl licked the end of the pencil, scribbled on her pad and, without another word, slouched off back towards the kitchens.

Piqued at her attitude and lack of response to the smile that he had laid on for her benefit, he leaned towards Sally and in a loud whisper said, 'Dear me! I wonder which school of etiquette and charm she's a graduate of? That expression's enough to sour the milk at this time of the morning! If I hadn't woken up with such an appetite after last night, I'd be tempted to be away from here!'

'Ssssh, Doug ... she might hear you and be upset.'

'How could you tell if the likes of yon lassie was upset or no?'

Without knowing why, Sally felt sorry for the slovenly waitress and wondered if it was because she herself had never felt happier than she did that morning. She felt suddenly grown-up and liberated from her claustrophobic childhood. She didn't want to be ungrateful; her parents were good people and she loved them, but she had always felt so restricted. So many things she mustn't do, so many demands to 'conform to the norm', but now, after last night, she felt that she was free from it all.

Chapter Nine

The country roads on the scenic route to the Lake District were deserted, except for a few locals going about their daily work. They followed a farmer in his rusty old tractor for a several miles, then an open-backed Land Rover with three black-and-white sheepdogs in the back. With their silky black ears flapping in the slipstream, they were obviously enjoying their open-air ride. Two of them sat obediently with their backs to the driver's cab staring at the vehicles following theirs. The third dog was standing up with its front paws on the side of the Land Rover, peering round the side of the driver's cab, facing the oncoming traffic. When Doug pulled out to overtake, this dog barked hysterically at them and rushed back and forth. It all looked very dangerous to Sally and she was worried for the safety of all three dogs. 'Won't they fall out?' she asked Doug.

'I expect they have on several occasions, and then found their way home afterwards,' he chuckled. 'Ha! Sheepdogs, they're extremely intelligent in many ways and totally stupid in others. We have two at the farm. Ours are forever jumping out of the tractor bucket to chase rabbits and then when you get home they're sitting waiting on the doorstep. They have boundless energy.'

In spite of the hold-ups by the slower-moving farm vehicles they had encountered they made good time, and around midday stopped for a light lunch in a pretty country pub. They sat close together at a table in the pub gardens enjoying the warmth of the late summer sun.

'We don't have to worry about finding a place to stay tonight, I've got that sorted,' said Doug and then, leaning closer, he whispered in her ear, 'I've booked something really special. I promised you that I was going to spoil you and I intend to keep my promise.'

'Oh dear, now what?' Sally exclaimed, 'and you don't have to whisper – we're the only ones here,' she continued, sipping at her iced lemonade.

Doug chuckled. 'It's all organised, you'll just have to wait and see. We're getting into the really pretty part of the drive; from here on up, it's rolling hills, green valleys and breath-taking views. If you're ready, we can get on our way again.' Doug's enthusiasm for the countryside they were driving through was more than justified; the views were spectacular. Being born and raised on a tree-lined avenue in suburbia, Sally had never seen so much sky and open space before. Endless swathes of green and purple countryside rolling past the car window were a completely new experience to her. The sky that edged the purple horizon was a vast canvas of deep blue daubed with exploding pillows of brilliant white clouds billowing up into the heavens. Sheep lay in patches of shade at the foot of drystone walls, and overhead birds of prey spread their wings and languidly rode the thermals created by warm air rising from the valley below. This was a world that Sally had only seen in books and its vastness made her feel very small and insignificant. They drove along in silence for a while, Doug enjoying the freedom of being away from the claustrophobia of towns and Sally becoming totally absorbed with a landscape that stretched for miles in every direction.

After a while Sally's mind began to wander, contemplating what sort of reception she might get from Doug's parents. Eventually she broke the companionable silence between them.

'Doug, what are your parents like?'

'Well now, my dad is a tall chap, with red cheeks from being out in all weathers, and my mother is shorter and bakes cakes,' Doug responded in his inimitable fashion.

'Please stop teasing for one minute. What I mean is, will they approve of you bringing someone home? Are they religious? What will they think of us travelling up together like this? Won't they disapprove?'

'That's an awful lot of approval you're looking for,' he joked.

'I'm a bit nervous about meeting them, Doug ...' she replied in an attempt to get him to take her seriously.

'Don't be! I can assure you, my mother will be delighted and will most definitely approve of my choice. My father will be putty in your hands; despite being a regular face at the kirk on a Sunday he can't resist a "bobby-dazzler". As for our travel arrangements, that, my darling, is confidential information. I fully expect some suspicious glances and clever questioning from my mother, but she won't be getting anything out of me!' He patted Sally's knee. 'Do I detect an attack of conscience after last night's antics? Don't worry; she won't know what you've been up to just by looking at your face.'

'Thank goodness for that, because my mother always can!' Sally sighed as Doug laughed.

'I doubt that she can! It'll just be your conscience. I bet you were the sort that pleaded guilty before you were even found out.'

'Yes, that's me, but in fairness I was utterly brainwashed. It seemed everything I did once I was up on my feet and walking was some kind of sin. I was frequently in trouble and I was always being dragged along to church on a weekly basis to confess all, even when I didn't think I had been too bad!'

Sally cast her mind back to those early years. How could a child, so young and innocent, possibly have sinned so much against the God who had supposedly made her in His own image? She remembered sitting on the hard wooden church pews with Caroline, holding conversations in hushed tones.

They would discuss what they'd done during the week and agree what should be confessed to the man in black, waiting for them inside the dark confines of the confessional box. They would try to remember what they had told him on the previous occasion, because repeating a sin was surely, they had reasoned in their innocence, a double sin! They thought that if he remembered their previous confession, and noted that they had committed the same sins again, then their penance might easily be increased from the usual five Hail Marys to ten! On a summer's evening, when they wanted to be outside playing, reciting ten Hail Marys would seem to take for ever! And if he also threw in a couple of Our Fathers, well then it would be an eternity before they could escape! One thing was sure, if Sally had been remotely sinful, then Caroline would have been her accomplice, so a weekly 'pre-confessional comparing of notes' was essential, to ensure that their sins were divided equally. Their aim was to come out of the confessional box with the same penance. Smiling at the memories of it all, she turned to Doug.

'Do you know, Doug, sometimes I would've been really good all week, so I'd sit in that dark, scary confessional box, wracking my brains, trying to think of a sin I could own up to, just to keep the priest happy. I wasn't very imaginative, so eventually it did become a bit repetitive. My father always cracked the same joke; he would say "You could be in there some time, so take some sandwiches and take some for the priest. You might get off with a lesser sentence."'

Sally began to laugh and Doug, laughing with her, asked, 'What kind of sentence do you think you would get if you confessed about last night?'

'Oh, that's easy– probably ordered to return within the week to confess the next instalment!' Sally roared with laughter at her own joke, then felt slightly shocked at her sudden irreverent attitude and hoped that yet again she would not incur the wrath of God.

'The next instalment? My, my! Now that sounds promising ... you're priceless!' Doug laughed as he drove along.

'Tell me more about your brother and sister,' Sally prompted, moving the topic swiftly on from the confessional and away from the night to come. 'Well, Iain's twenty and works on the farm helping my father, and Fiona's eighteen and away at college, though she'll be back at the farm for the party. No doubt you'll meet the rest of the clan, uncles and aunts at the celebrations. The only other person that haunts the place is Moira.'

'Moira? Is she a ghost?'

Doug gave a little laugh, 'Nay, lassie. Moira is Fiona's friend; she's been hanging around the farm with her for donkey's years.' As he spoke, he indicated to leave the main road and, changing down a gear, began to drive slowly along a narrow country lane with hedges so high that in places they made a canopy of green above their heads. 'I think this is the right way,' he said, leaning forward to peer through the windscreen. 'We should pick up signs for the Manor House Hotel shortly.'

'There's a sign,' Sally pointed out to him, 'half-hidden in the bushes. It says to turn left.' Sally directed Doug and as the lane became even narrower it barely seemed wide enough to take one car. A hundred yards further down the lane he drew up in front of an open pair of wrought-iron gates. To the right of the gates, on the grass verge and virtually hidden by tall spikes of bright pink willow herb, which in turn were being choked by rampant bindweed, they could see an old wooden board. Through all the foliage, they could just make out the words 'Manor House Hotel'.

'This is it.' Doug turned up a long tree-lined drive, at the end of which stood a large, imposing house. Doug stopped the car by the colonnaded front door.

'I'll just leave the car here for the moment while we check in and drop the suitcases off. I'll pop out later to put it in the car park.'

The grand entrance hall with its high ceiling and flag-stoned floors made Sally feel nervous and uncomfortable about the deceit that was again being conveyed by the band of gold on her left hand. As she walked into the reception area, she felt self-conscious and intimidated by her surroundings. Doug had explained to her that hotels had been known to turn away unmarried couples trying to book into a double room. He had convinced her that wearing a ring and posing as his wife was a necessary ploy so that they could be together. Sally felt that she had had no choice but to go along with the deception, but it filled her with shame. She followed Doug as he made his way towards an impressive dark oak counter, where a prominently placed brass sign informed all visitors that this was the RECEPTION DESK. A warm glow from a log fire hissing and crackling in a large hearth made the spacious hall feel more homely and, seeing it, Sally felt slightly less intimidated.

This time, behind the reception desk a smartly-dressed elderly man was waiting patiently for them. He greeted them as they approached and Doug introduced himself.

'Oh, yes, good evening, Mr MacDonald, of course, you booked the Victorian suite. Everything is ready for you, Sir. If you wouldn't mind just signing the guest book, please ...' he said, proffering a pen for Doug to use. 'May I ask which newspaper Sir would like in the morning, and would you and Madam prefer tea or coffee with your breakfast?'

'I'll have the Telegraph, please and coffee, but as I'm not familiar with what madam drinks first thing in the morning, I'll have to ask her.'

Sally attempted to stop her mouth dropping open as she stood rooted to the spot, blushing furiously. Frantically she tried to make sense of what Doug had just said, but her confidence was shaken to the core! The man behind the desk immediately straightened up, raising his eyebrows in a haughty manner. His sharp intake of breath was audible and, just as he was about to query the meaning of such a disgraceful remark, Doug held up his hand, a wicked grin spreading across his face.

'I'm only joking, she drinks coffee. Come along, Mrs MacDonald, you need to sign the book.' Sally, her head still whirling from Doug's little joke, shakily stepped forward and signed in.

Reassured, the man behind the reception desk turned away to reach up to a row of gleaming brass hooks on which keys were hanging. He was shaking his head, appalled at some of the things that young people came out with these days! Since the war, he had noticed a sharp decline in the behaviour of many of the younger generation. Shame, he thought; he had seemed to be quite a pleasant refined young gentleman when he had telephoned to make the reservation. To say such a thing in front of his young wife! Well, well ... how embarrassing for her, so young, too. It won't do to encourage that sort of behaviour here at the Manor House! Without looking at Doug, he handed him a large dark metal key with a polished brass tag attached that said 'Manor House Hotel' on one side and 'Victorian Suite' on the other.

'Here is the key to the Victorian suite, Sir. You are on the first floor, overlooking the lake. If you go up the main stairs and turn left, you will find the door to your suite directly in front of you. I will send your suitcases up presently. Enjoy your stay, Mr and Mrs MacDonald.' As he handed Doug the key, he abruptly turned away, tilting his eyes and nose upwards, and Sally thought she heard him sniff with disapproval. It made Sally feel as if they were being dismissed like naughty children.

'Thank you very much. I'm sure we will,' Doug replied, oblivious to the snub.

Together they climbed the wide wooden staircase, which creaked loudly under their tread. The red carpet, faded and threadbare, snaked up the centre of the stairs and was held in place with highly-polished brass stair rods. Turning left as directed, they came to a large wooden door on which 'Victorian Suite' was painted in gold.

'That was easy enough – here we are.' Doug unlocked the door and stood aside for Sally to enter the room; she stood and stared with amazement at the large four-poster bed that dominated it. Her eyes were drawn to the detailed wooden carvings on each of the four posts supporting the canopy high above the bed. The sides were hung with brocade drapes that had once been maroon but had faded to varying shades of pink and brown. Brass handles adorned an enormous wardrobe and the drawers of a dressing table, both of which were made from a highly-polished dark wood. Two old-fashioned winged armchairs, in faded tapestry which had once depicted hunting scenes, flanked a large stone fireplace with a polished brass fender surrounding an empty hearth. In one corner of the room, there was a tall wooden stand which supported an enormous leafy green plant in a large green china pot. Floor-to- ceiling windows on the far side of the room looked out over the lake and, either side of them, faded red velvet curtains hung forlornly in soft folds. In front of the window there was a small oak dining table and two chairs, the seats of which were covered in frayed and faded maroon velvet. It seemed to Sally that the whole place was a combination of polished dark wood, highly-polished brass and shabby soft furnishings. Although now faded, she thought it must have all looked very luxurious and expensive in its heyday. As she stood in the middle of the room, looking round at the sombre dark wood furniture, she couldn't help thinking that it all felt a bit too funereal for her taste.

'Hey!' Doug had walked over to the door that led into the bathroom and he chuckled gleefully as he stepped inside, 'Come and take a look at this bath! It's even bigger than the one we had at the last place.'

Sally wasn't sure that she wanted to spend the night in what looked like a funeral parlour, but she obediently followed Doug into the vast bathroom. Literally taking 'centre stage', in the middle of the room, was the most enormous bath Sally had ever seen. It was roll-topped and free-standing, and rested on six claw-shaped feet on a raised wooden platform. The lavatory was also on a raised wooden dais with a large square-shaped polished mahogany seat. Hanging over it, high up near the ceiling, was a decorative metal cistern, attached to which was a shining gold-coloured chain with a china pull. No wonder it's called the Victorian Suite, thought Sally as she gazed round the bathroom, which was bigger than her bedroom at home. It all looked so majestic, a bathroom fit for a queen.

Hearing a discreet knock at the door, Doug left her in the bathroom and, striding across the bedroom, opened the door to another grey-haired elderly man. Unlike the upright, arrogant man on reception, the porter was stooped and looked well past his retirement age. He tottered smiling into the middle of the room, pushing a trolley bearing their two suitcases. Swiftly Doug stepped forward and lifted both cases off the trolley.

'That's all right, Sir. I was about to do that for you,' the old porter protested.

'No problem. My pleasure,' Doug said, grinning at him. 'But there's something you might well be able to do for me.' Taking his elbow, Doug walked the porter back to the door, pressing some money into his hand as he leaned down to whisper in his ear.

Closing the door behind the old gent, Doug sighed with a sense of well- being. He kicked off his shoes, removed his jacket and stretched out on the bed, weary from all the driving. They were booked in for two nights, giving him a break from continually being on the road as well as a chance for them both to do some sightseeing. Lying on the bed with his hands behind his head, he closed his eyes. He was relieved that the tension and worry of his first night with Sally was behind him. Now he thought they could both relax and enjoy each other's company; a grin began to spread slowly across his face as he anticipated their second night together.

Standing in the middle of the vast bedroom, Sally's eyes lovingly rested on Doug's prone figure stretched across the bed, but her practical side kicked in and she wandered over to her suitcase and flicked open the catches. This was a chance, she thought, for her clothes to lose some of their creases, having been shut away in a suitcase for the last couple of days. She began removing some of them from the case to hang up in the large wardrobe and was pleased to see that they looked reasonably uncrushed. She was glad now that she had taken the trouble to pack them all very carefully.

'Doug, would you like me to hang up some of your shirts?' she offered. 'It's a huge wardrobe with plenty of space.'

'Sure, kitten, that would be fine, just open my suitcase and help yourself,' Doug responded without opening his eyes. 'Give me ten minutes' shut-eye and I'll be as right as rain.'

Sally reached into Doug's suitcase, lifting out two shirts and slipping them on to individual hangers. She then lifted out a pair of corduroy trousers, and as she did so an envelope dropped from the pocket and fell back into the suitcase, spilling out a photograph. Picking it up, Sally saw that it was of an attractive young woman with dark hair. The girl was laughing, displaying a set of even white teeth. It was none of her business, she told herself; there was probably a perfectly reasonable explanation; it might even be his sister, she thought, feeling guilty as if she had been deliberately prying. But as Sally hastily stuffed the photo back inside the envelope, she could see the word 'love' and several kisses written on the back, and felt a pang of jealousy. As she continued to hang up the clothes, she began to ask herself why Doug would carry such a photo around with him. Eventually she decided to dismiss the jealous thoughts in her mind; it was probably nothing to worry about and therefore not worth mentioning. Closing the wardrobe doors, she walked over to the bed. Doug immediately opened his eyes.

'Have you finished your household chores?' he joked.

'Everything that needs to be hanging is in the wardrobe, though I expect we'll smell of mothballs for the rest of the week.'

As she leaned over him, he reached up and pulled her down on the bed and kissed her. 'What would you like to do? We have some daylight left if you'd like to drive somewhere to see some of the local sights.'

'No, you've done enough driving. Let's go for a walk in the gardens and get some exercise,' she suggested.

'Aye, well, if it's exercise you want, I've plenty of that in mind for later!' Doug chuckled as he swung his legs off the bed and slipped his shoes back on. 'Come along, then. Once round the block, but bring a jacket – it can get cold very quickly this far north.'

The gardens around the hotel were clothed in the last colours of summer and the first of autumn. Beds of bronze and maroon chrysanthemums stole the eye away from the soft pink of the last of the summer roses. It was late afternoon and the sun cast long shadows across the lawn, which was as green and smooth as a billiard table. The lawns swept down to a large lake, where mallards and moorhens were busy seeking their final meal of the day. Some sifted and searched in the tall reeds at the edge of the lake, while others partially submerged themselves in the deeper water. It was all very tranquil as Sally and Doug stood quietly for a while, watching with amusement the antics of the ducks on the lake. Two upended ducks, having caught separate ends of the same tasty morsel underwater, had surfaced and immediately began a tug of war. Attracted by the noise, several mallards scurried across the lake to join in and a free-for-all ensued. Their wings beating on the water and their loud quacks broke the peace and quiet of the evening. The last rays of the setting sun on the water disappeared and the lake and surrounding gardens were left in complete shade. Without the sunlight twinkling on the lake, it suddenly felt cooler so, having been entertained by the brawling ducks, they continued their walk hand-in-hand around the lake and back up into the formal gardens. Seeing a red squirrel running along a nearby oak tree branch, Sally was delighted when it ran down the trunk and along the ground right in front of them. Suddenly it noticed Sally and Doug close by and retreated back up the tree at speed. The evening was becoming ever cooler, making Sally thankful that she had her jacket and Doug, noticing the chill in the air, put his arm around her shoulder and pulled her in close.

'They say the further north you go it gets two or three overcoats colder than down in the south, but it's well worth it. Come on, let's head back. By the time we tidy ourselves up and get changed it'll be supper time.'

When they returned to their suite, it was immediately obvious that during their absence someone had been into the room. Flames from a recently-lit log fire danced and crackled in the hearth and reflected off the polished brass fender. Although the hotel had central heating of a sort, it had retained all the original fireplaces in recognition of the fact that the archaic heating system on its own was not sufficient to adequately heat the large rooms with their high ceilings. The fire was a welcome sight.

'Oh, isn't that just perfect? Now I just need a big sheepskin rug in front of that and you on it, preferably naked. Shall I see if reception have one?'

'Doug MacDonald, don't you dare,' Sally said as she made her way over to one of the winged armchairs and, kicking off her shoes, sat down and began toasting her toes. Doug followed and, standing in front of her, held out his hands, hauled her sharply to her feet and sat in the chair before quickly pulling her back down on to his lap. Instinctively she rested her head against his shoulder.

'Is something bothering you, Sal?' he asked, hugging her close.

'What makes you think that?'

'Just a feeling I get. You've been awfully quiet.'

Somehow, she couldn't tell him about the photo that had fallen out of his trouser pocket. Even though he had told her to open his suitcase, she still felt inexplicably guilty and didn't want him to think she'd been prying.

'Nothing serious is bothering me. It was just that thing you mentioned about Moira – is she your girlfriend?'

'How can she be my girlfriend? I thought you were?' Doug responded with humour and another gentle hug.

'Yes, I know, but what I meant to ask is, was she your girlfriend?'

'Let me explain. Moira has been around for years. I did feel under a bit of pressure to date her when she was back from college last summer and staying at the farm with Fiona. I was there, visiting my parents for a few weeks. Moira's parents have known mine for years and I suppose they were all, in some ways, encouraging us. She's not a bad lass but it was starting to feel like too much was being taken for granted, almost as if I was sliding into an arranged marriage. Although Moira was very willing to go along with the idea, I was not. So please don't worry your head about her.'

Sally did worry, though. Was Moira the girl in the photo? Before she had time to say more Doug stood up, tipping her playfully off his lap and back onto the chair.

'Quick wash and tidy up, then we must dress and go down for dinner. Me first, then I'll make myself scarce so you can have the run of the place.' He disappeared into the bathroom and she could hear him singing out of tune as he washed. When Doug reappeared he was still wearing his trousers but was stripped to the waist and the sight of his naked chest sent a thrill through Sally. A towel was casually draped over one shoulder and he used one end of it to continue to wipe his now clean-shaven face and neck.

'Okay, your turn. You've got ten minutes.'

'But I'm sure you took much longer than that,' Sally objected.

'It takes me longer to make myself beautiful, whereas you, my darling, don't need to work so hard at it,' he joked, tossing the towel on to a chair. Then he almost disappeared from sight as he reached into the cavernous wardrobe for a clean shirt.

'I'll be with you when I'm ready and not a minute before,' she called out to him, getting up from the chair.

'Rebellious streak, eh? I'll make a note of that,' Doug called back, as Sally headed towards the bathroom. Once there, she stripped down to her undies, had a quick wash and dabbed on some perfume before making her way back into the bedroom.

Walking across the room she was aware that Doug was watching her and, despite their recent intimacy, his eyes on her partially-naked body made her feel self-conscious. Reaching the wardrobe, she quickly lifted out the plain blue dress that she had bought on the shopping trip with Caroline and dropped it over her head. Feeling more comfortable, Sally moved back to the dressing table and brushed out her shining blonde hair from its ponytail. Peering critically into the mirror, she aimed some pale pink lipstick at her lips.

'You look lovely – you'll do, let's go.' Doug unfolded himself from the fireside chair where he had been sitting, silently observing her.

Chapter Ten

There were diners already seated when they entered the dining room and some of them looked up and smiled as Sally and Doug were shown to their table by the window. Sally automatically returned their smiles. The waiter stood behind her chair, and she bent her knees to sit down as he skilfully slid the chair into place. As Doug seated himself, the waiter handed them heavy leather-bound menus and, having recommended the chef's speciality, left them to browse through the selection of other dishes on offer.

'That was very neatly done – have you been practising?' Doug asked, nodding towards her chair.

'That was one of the few fun subjects taught at the convent. They may have shoved us through the bedroom door without a map and compass, but everything else was very well rehearsed. Sister Mary used to teach us what she called "etiquette" twice a week; she was a lovely person. Her ambition was to turn us all into "ladies", and she taught us when to stand up and how to sit down, as well as how to blow our noses discreetly in public, and how to address various ranks and dignitaries. We even had to practise curtsies. Her lessons were always great fun because she didn't mind us laughing. She always maintained that what she taught us might seem ridiculous in the classroom but that it might come in very useful one day.'

The waiter had returned while she had been talking and stood waiting politely for Sally to stop so that he could take their order. They both decided on steak and Doug ordered a bottle of red wine from the abundant wine list. Once the waiter had moved out of earshot, Doug leaned forward to whisper, 'Well, I'd be delighted to take over from where your happy nun left off and complete your education. You seem to learn extremely quickly,' he said, winking at her, making Sally blush.

'And what would you teach me? How to torture people? You're a terrible tease – that poor man at reception was speechless when you told him that you didn't know whether I drank tea or coffee with my breakfast.'

'Yes! His face was a sight to behold,' Doug laughed. 'But let me tell you, yours was even better!'

Sally aimed a playful kick at his ankle under the table but she was rather too successful in her aim. Doug was still rubbing his shin when the waiter returned to their table clutching a wine bottle with a pristine white napkin wrapped around its neck. The waiter opened the bottle and poured a little of the ruby liquid into a glass for the ritual tasting and Doug lifted the wine glass to his nose and sniffed appreciatively before taking a sip.

'That's fine, thank you very much.'

The waiter filled Sally's wine glass, topped up Doug's and placed the wine bottle on a nearby sideboard.

'Here's to us and a good trip,' Doug said, raising his glass to Sally's.

The steaks arrived on large oval plates and they eagerly tucked into the generous portions, suddenly realising how hungry they were. Eventually they were faced with the sweet trolley and when they were finished Doug asked, 'Would you like coffee, Sal?'

'Yes, please.'

When the waiter returned to their table Doug ordered coffee for two.

'Would you care to withdraw to the sitting room, Sir? It's just through that door; make yourselves comfortable and I will bring your coffee through to you presently,' he offered.

Sally had never been in such a spacious sitting room; large Chesterfield sofas and leather armchairs, arranged in little clusters around low coffee tables, made it comfortable and inviting, and many of the other diners had already made their way in there. She lowered herself onto one of the large sofas while Doug wandered round the room looking in the glass-fronted display cases containing dead fish invisibly suspended against painted backdrops of pond life. Glancing around, Sally was dismayed to see the heads of several deer, glass-eyed and expressionless, their antlers festooned with cobwebs. On another wall, long-dead and doubtless long-forgotten gentry stared eerily from the canvasses of large oil paintings in gilt frames. There was a display of dusty old hunting trophies including foxes' heads and tails nailed to wooden boards, which impressed Sally even less. Faded floral brocade curtains were partially drawn across tall windows and doors that opened out on to a garden terrace.

'Some of those catches are quite impressive; the weights and measurements are on a little plaque on each of the cases,' Doug said, sitting down beside Sally.

'I think shooting deer and sticking their heads on the wall is a dreadful thing to do,' she said quietly.

'Do I gather you are not so impressed?' Doug smiled sympathetically. He had momentarily forgotten that Sally was not a country girl, and to an animal-loving townie the pursuits of country folk would seem barbaric. He tried explaining to her that the deer had to be culled for their own good before each winter, otherwise the old and the infirm would slowly die from starvation.

'How can you shoot something for its own good?' Sally bristled.

Doug smiled. 'I can see this is a debate I'm not going to win.' Conveniently for him, the waiter chose that moment to appear with the coffee tray and petits fours and, unlike the poor fish, it let Doug off the hook and he swiftly changed the subject.

'I think we should have a drive around the area tomorrow and you must remember to put on those sensible shoes of yours. Apart from the fact that we might find some nice walks, I'd love to see you bend over to tie the laces again.'

'Doug MacDonald!' She found herself using her mother's stage whisper, 'You have a one-track mind.'

'I know. Does that bother you overmuch?'

'What do you think?'

He leaned towards her, his forehead almost against hers as he said quietly, 'I think the nuns did a good job keeping the lid on you as long as they did, and I think I want you back up those stairs.'

Coffee finished, Sally and Doug walked hand-in-hand back across the sitting room, oblivious to the knowing smiles that the older couples exchanged between them. As they reached the stairs, Doug skipped ahead of her, taking them two at a time, and Sally laughed out loud when he turned at the top and waited for her with his arms outstretched. He gathered her into them, steering her towards the door of their suite and when he opened it he was pleased to see that, once again, the old man's memory had not let him down and his request had been fulfilled. The curtains had been drawn across the windows, shutting out the blackness of the night, the fire had been built up and the bedside lamps had been lit. The soft lights and the fire had transformed the room and Sally felt more comfortable about spending the night in it.

Set in a corner of the room, on a stand specially designed for the purpose, was a silver ice bucket with the neck of a champagne bottle peeping over the top. Two tall champagne flutes stood on a silver tray placed on another small table next to the ice bucket.

'What's that?' Sally pointed to the ice bucket. 'That is the best champagne in the house.' 'I've never tasted champagne.'

'Well, I did promise to spoil you. So sit over by the fire while I open the bottle, and prepare to be thoroughly spoilt!'

Pulling some cushions on to the floor, Sally dropped down onto them and leaned back against the large fireside chair as Doug popped the cork and expertly filled the two champagne flutes.

'One glass of giggle water coming up ...' he said, chuckling as he handed Sally a glass. He lowered himself down to the floor and stretched out beside her, raising his glass to hers in a toast.

'Here's to love!'

'To love!' Sally lifted her glass.

'To our love!' Doug held his glass aloft again, but this time Sally did not join him.

'Isn't it a bit sudden?' she asked, looking at him over the rim of her glass. She sipped the champagne; the bubbles played on her tongue, taking her by surprise and making her cough a little.

'That's usually my line,' he said ruefully, grinning. 'But somehow, Sal, you've managed to turn the tables on me. I've only known you a few months but already I can't imagine my life without you. It might sound a bit corny but I can't even remember what my life was like before I met you.'

Sally chose her next words with care, but she wanted to be truthful. Doug seemed so sincere and, if he was in earnest, she did not want to hurt his feelings intentionally. She knew that Doug thought she was very naïve about many things but she didn't want him to be under any illusions that she was being naïve about their current situation! Sally had been fourteen when, unlike many of the other girls at the Youth Club, her mother would still not let a young boy walk her home alone, warning her that they only wanted 'one thing'. When Sally had innocently asked her mother what that 'one thing' was, her mother could only imply what it might be with dark looks and a red face that meant absolutely nothing to Sally at the time. Eventually she had worked it out; she knew what that 'one thing' was; it was about a boy telling a young girl that he loved her purely to seduce her.

'Doug, you don't have to say all those nice things, you know. I'm here because I want to be here, with you, now, not for whatever might happen in the future.'

He pressed his forehead against hers.

'Oh, Sal, you don't realise what I'm saying to you, do you, kitten? Perhaps I should put it plainer. I think I'm in love with you. No. That's wrong. I don't think I am. I know I am! You are everything I've ever wanted: a beautiful playmate; a friend; someone who makes me laugh, and I'm crazy about you!'

Taking Sally's glass out of her hand, he placed it on the hearth as he tipped her head back to look deeply into her eyes before leaning forward to brush his lips tenderly against hers. Softly she returned his kisses, not knowing quite what to say after his outburst. His arms enfolded her and he held her tightly as slowly they stretched out in silence on the floor in front of the warm glow of the fire, her head against his chest. For a while they both watched the flames dancing off the logs, neither wishing to be the one to end this tender moment, until eventually Sally plucked up the courage to speak.

'Doug ...'

'Hmm ...?'

'Doug ...' she hesitated, choosing her words carefully, not wanting to say the wrong thing and spoil the mood, but driven on by a need to try to explain her true feelings. 'Doug, I don't think I know what love is. Not the sort of love I think you're talking about. But what I do know is that I want to be with you all the time and when I see you my heart goes bump and my tummy knots up. Is that love, do you think?'

Touched by her innocence and chastened by her honesty, he was filled with emotion at her admission and he gave her a loving hug, holding her even closer. When he felt his emotions were under control again he gently whispered, 'Well, even if it isn't, I'll settle for your heart going bump. It's plenty to be going on with for now.'

He doubted whether this girl would ever know how to be anything else other than truthful and honest. Granted, she was very young and he knew instinctively that she had not yet been subjected to situations in life that might make her cynical and harden her attitude. As he thought about it he prayed that, whatever life threw at her, she would never become embittered. He just could not imagine her ever becoming devious or dishonest; it just didn't seem to be in her make-up. Suddenly he sat up.

'Now, how about a real treat? How about I fill that big bathtub up to the top with bubbles? Then while you soak away the cares of the day, I'll refresh you with champagne!'

'Champagne! In the bath! I'll feel like a film star!'

'Your wish is my command,' he joked, 'and which one would you like?'

'Which what?'

'Film star! You said you feel like a film star, let's act out your fantasy. Which one would you like?'

Sally laughed out loud. 'Don't be silly, I didn't mean that.'

'I know exactly what you meant. I was just teasing. But let me try and guess who your favourite film star would be? It would probably have to be someone on a horse. I know – a cowboy! How about Roy Rogers on Trigger, or possibly the Lone Ranger on Silver, galloping up to rescue you from some bad guy like me?' His grin was infectious, but Sally put her head on one side and thought for a minute. After a short pause she grinned back at him.

'Not necessarily a cowboy; what about a handsome sheikh in the desert? He could gallop up on a pure white stallion to rescue me from your clutches.'

'Ah! Of course, the Rudolph Valentino fantasy! I could never understand why women found him such a turn-on. Perhaps it wasn't the guy himself? It's more likely the romance of Arabia and a sheikh in the desert. Take my advice, stick with the cowboys or you may well be very disappointed. I worked in the Middle East for a wee while and in my experience it's just hot, sticky and full of smelly camels. Not a sheikh in sight ... or a galloping horse, for that matter.'

Sally laughed. 'I'm sure all of it will remain a fantasy. America and Arabia are a long way from here and in completely opposite directions.'

Doug kissed her on the nose and stood up. 'Now I'm away to fill that swimming pool they call a bathtub.'

After wine at dinner and now the champagne, Sally felt a little light-headed, so she stayed put for a few minutes before getting up slowly from the fireside. Staggering a few steps, she stopped and concentrated on putting one foot in front of the other until she reached the bathroom door. Peering in, she saw Doug on his knees pouring out a purple liquid from a tall glass jar and stirring it into the foaming water. She came up behind him and, reaching into the bath for a handful of the bubbles, playfully blew them in his direction, making him laugh.

'Okay, that's ready.' He stood up and, stepping towards Sally, he removed the champagne flute from her hand and carefully placed it beside the bath. Taking her in his arms he held her close and kissed her, deftly unzipping the back of her dress at the same time. It slipped smartly off her shoulders and slid to the floor, swiftly followed by her bra and then her lace panties. He ran his hands hungrily over her naked body before helping her climb into the bath and as she sank beneath a froth of bubbles he handed her back the champagne glass. Sally cautiously leaned back, enjoying feeling the bubbles gently engulf her. Doug made his way back into the bedroom only to reappear a few minutes later, naked but holding the champagne bottle strategically placed in front of him.

Sally giggled from the depths of the warm, soapy suds.

'Ah, now you're being modest, that's not like you. Might I remind you that I've seen it all before,' she said, mimicking his Scottish accent. Recognising his own words to her that morning, he laughed out loud. At the sight of his handsome laughing face, Sally's tummy flipped over.

Topping up both their glasses, he put the bottle down by the side of the bath and, clambering in, sat down opposite Sally with his glass held aloft.

'What have I done to deserve such luxury? Cold champagne, a warm bath and a hot woman! I'm so afraid I will wake up and find it's all a beautiful dream.'

Sally brushed her glass against his and then sipped at her champagne.

'I seem to have completely lost track of time. It seems ages since I left home and yet it was only yesterday. But we have done so much that the time is flying by. Does that make sense?' Through her alcoholic haze of well-being, Sally felt she wasn't quite explaining herself and wondered if what she said was actually what she meant.

'Sweetheart ...' Doug began, 'after two glasses of wine and two of champagne, I don't really expect you to make much sense. But I think I know what you're trying to say.'

They lingered in the bath for a while longer and then Doug stepped out and grabbed a towel, wrapping it around himself before holding out another for Sally. They were the biggest, fluffiest, towels Sally had ever seen, snow white and very soft. As she stood up, Doug placed the towel around her shoulders and, taking her hand, steadied her as she clambered out of the bath. He then gave her a quick hug.

'Come along, we'll sit by the fire a while and dry off.'

At some point while Sally had been in the bathroom, Doug had removed the eiderdown bedspread and all the pillows from the four-poster bed and laid them out in front of the fireplace.

Sally raised her eyebrows at him and he smiled coyly, shrugging his shoulders.

'Well, I couldn't find fur rugs, so I improvised,' he offered by way of explanation.

Wrapped only in their bath towels, they sank on to the eiderdown in front of the fire and as Sally leaned back against Doug her long blonde hair tickled his naked chest and he began to run his fingers through it. The soft firelight and warmth of the log fire, combined with the effects of the champagne and Doug's nearness, swept over her in a wave of complete and utter happiness.

'Penny for them?' Doug asked.

'Oh, I was just remembering what you said, about finding heaven on earth. The way I am feeling just now must be pretty close to it.'

'I think you can get even closer,' he whispered seductively in her ear. Taking her in his arms, he kissed her gently and as her bath towel dropped away from her shoulders she could feel his bare skin against hers. Hot with desire, she wanted to throw open her legs and feel him inside her, but Doug was in no hurry and chuckled as she wriggled invitingly underneath him. Rolling away from her, he reached for his glass and, pushing Sally down on to the pillows, he knelt between her outstretched legs and poured champagne slowly over her breasts so that it trickled down to her navel and on to her flat stomach. Then, leaning forward, he kissed her breasts, licking the champagne from around her nipples. Sally could hardly breathe, as with his tongue he followed the rivulet of champagne, tasting and kissing, tracing the flow of it, as it made its way down to her stomach. Sally lay breathless and helpless as Doug made his way back up her body, planting small kisses en route, until his lips reached hers, and this time his kiss was not so gentle. The weight of his body came down on her and as Sally felt him slip easily into her, she wanted to scream and cry out. The build-up to this moment had been so intense and she responded to Doug's gentle thrusting by clinging to him, with her arms around his neck and automatically lifting her legs to clasp them around his waist. Urged on by such exquisite feelings, she pressed into him and as his movements became more urgent he whispered, 'God, Sally, I love you so much.'

'I love you too, Doug,' she responded and clung to him tighter than ever.

It was exactly what he wanted to hear and, throwing all caution to the wind, he sighed and, shuddering, he came inside her. She was his, so what did it matter? They lay wrapped in each other's arms; Doug blissfully happy, while Sally inexplicably felt tears stinging the corners of her eyes.

'Hey, what's all this?'

'I don't know, I suppose I always cry when I'm happy,' she whispered, kissing him gently on the lips. They settled down to lie entwined. After a while, one of the logs collapsed into the fire with a shower of sparks and the remaining logs settled further down into the grate and Doug whispered, 'Come along, the fire is dying down, and that big old bed looks awfully comfortable and inviting.'

He got to his feet and smiled down at her, then held out his hand. After helping Sally to her feet he gathered up the pillows and bedspread with one arm, using the other to place around her waist as they made their way to the four-poster bed. Falling into each other's arms once more, it wasn't long before they were sound asleep.

Chapter Eleven

Early the next morning a persistent knocking at the door awakened them.

Doug jumped out of the bed and, reaching for his dressing gown, pulled it round himself, tying up the cord as he went across the room to open the door. Peering from beneath the sheets through half-open eyes, Sally caught a glimpse of the old porter from the previous night; he was standing in the doorway behind a large wooden trolley. Embarrassed by her nakedness, she huddled well under the bedclothes out of sight. Hearing cutlery being moved and the clatter of plates, she chanced a furtive peep and she could see that the elderly porter was setting breakfast on the table by the window overlooking the lake. She'd snuggled back down into the bed feigning sleep when suddenly the bedclothes were whipped completely away from her naked body. Sally shrieked.

'Okay! Out you come! He knows what you've been doing, so there's no point in hiding under there,' Doug said in a loud voice.

'Ssssh! Doug, stop it!' Sally hissed at him as she made a grab for the bedclothes.

'It's okay! He's long gone!' Doug said, laughing at the startled expression on her face, and Sally grabbed a pillow, playfully hitting him with it as he collapsed laughing onto the bed beside her.

'I wish I'd had a camera to take a picture of your face when I pulled yon covers off you. I told you I was going to spoil you, so I ordered room service. Mind, I didn't think nine o'clock would come round this quickly,' Doug chuckled. 'Remind me, is it coffee or tea you have in the mornings?'

'What I don't have much of is a sense of humour first thing in the morning, so watch it, Haggis!'

'Well now, I'm quite sure I could put a smile on your face, but in the meantime the breakfast would get cold,' he said. Getting up from the bed, he handed Sally her dressing gown. 'Come along! Breakfast is served.'

'Shall I be mother?' Sally volunteered as she made her way over to the table and started to pour the coffee, breathing in the delicious aroma of the brew escaping from the percolator.

'After last night, I hope that's not a prophecy,' said Doug, sitting down at the table and holding out a cup for her to fill. Having poured coffee into one cup,

Sally paused in the act of filling Doug's. Slowly she sat down, searching his face for some explanation of his comment.

'Hey! Don't look so worried. You're mine and I'm never letting you go. So there's no problem, whatever happens. Do you understand?'

'Yes, but even so, what you're suggesting is not the best way to start a life together, and it's not what I want,' Sally said bluntly. As she continued to fill his cup, she saw the expression of surprise and hurt on his face and felt compelled to explain herself. 'Doug, it's not that I don't want to be with you, I do; but I don't want to go from one prison to another. I've only just escaped from the confines of school and my overzealous parents. I've seen what happens when babies arrive. I would like children, eventually, but I want to have a life first.'

Sally had vivid memories of the arrival of her sister. The whole household had suffered sleepless nights for months. Her mother, continuously short-tempered through lack of sleep, was very impatient with everyone. While her father tried to reassure her that things would get better once the baby 'settled', it was twelve long months before the household got any beneficial sleep and back to any semblance of normality. By that time Charlotte was walking, bringing yet another set of problems to beset them all. 'Watch the baby', she was always being told, but it seemed to Sally that the baby had some kind of death wish! Charlotte climbed stairs at an alarming speed and had an insatiable curiosity for electrical sockets; everything that was not fixed securely in its place ended up in her mouth. No, Sally was in no hurry to embrace motherhood.

Unaware that her first-hand experience with babies had been such a deterrent, Doug thought Sally's argument sounded very mature and was genuinely surprised. His experience so far with young women was that they all seemed determined to get him up the aisle as quickly as possible! More than once he'd had to do some nifty footwork to avoid getting himself trapped into proposing marriage. He had not, until now, been able to settle down, recognising in himself that he was not ready for the responsibility of a wife and children to take care of, but with Sally he welcomed the thought and had been confident that Sally would too. Now his confidence was jarred and it was a new experience for him. Not since his teens had he had any difficulty in attracting the opposite sex and now he could not quite believe what he was hearing, but he had one last card up his sleeve.

'Well, selfishly I might have seriously jeopardised your plans last night.' But again he was surprised when, instead of looking alarmed as he had expected, Sally just smiled at him from the other side of the table.

'Probably not. Although they were very vague with the detail of exactly what it was we had to abstain from, the nuns did teach us about the fertility cycle and the rhythm method of birth control. I think we'll be all right,' she said in a matter-of-fact tone as she helped herself to some toast.

'You mean ... you had it all worked out?' Doug was incredulous.

'Well, I'm pretty sure that it's safe this week.'

He was stunned – she had been one jump of ahead of him all the while! He'd reasoned with himself that he wanted Sally, and if anything went wrong he was prepared to marry her. Last night he was careless, something he had never been before and, although he had brought contraceptives with him, in the throes of passion all his good intentions had gone out of the window. Several girls he had known would have jumped at the chance to trap him into marriage. For the first time in his life he felt something different stirring, and slowly it began to dawn on him what it was. Respect. Her inexperience and naivety had made him feel protective towards her, but it was becoming apparent to him that, if it came to it, she could probably take care of herself and he loved her even more for it.

'You might only be a teenager, but you're going on twenty-seven up here,' he tapped his head. Over the rim of his cup he studied her face as he continued to sip his coffee and Sally smiled at him again.

'Anyway, what did you mean, just now, about not letting me go?' Sally asked.

'I think you know what I meant,' he said, grinning at her. 'Well, it sounded as if you were proposing marriage?'

'Would you accept if I did?' Doug's hand covered hers where she'd placed it on the table.

'Mmmm ... I might do. Try it sometime ...' Over the toast and coffee, they shared a long and loving kiss.

'Have you had enough? Shall we get dressed and go and enjoy the day?'

As they got ready Sally lay on the bed and wriggled into her tight blue jeans.

Doug shook his head. 'Aye, well, that's the movement that was my downfall last night. No red-blooded man could withstand that! Now if you're going to bend over to put those shoes on, I'm away to the bathroom to clean my teeth, or we'll never be out of the bedroom before it's dark.'

Grinning broadly, Sally stood up and hugged him.

By ten o'clock they were in the car and heading towards the village of Grasmere.

'It's the wrong time of year to see any of those famous daffodils. Mind, yon daffodil piece is not my favourite poem – being made to learn it word-perfect at school has left me scarred for life. We had a ferocious teacher, so even though

I learnt it fairly well, when I stood up to say the words my mind went blank. It didn't help my memory any when the old dragon shouted, 'Pull yourself together, Douglas MacDonald'. It was always at that point that my knees would threaten to give way and I would be seriously in danger of wetting myself. My bladder was only controlled by the shame I felt when I was five years old and got sent home in the school's spare pair of pants, clutching a bag with my wet ones in it. Somehow I didn't think I'd have got my mother's sympathy if I'd done that again at thirteen!'

Laughing out loud at Doug's school memories, Sally joined in.

'I had to learn the whole of The Pied Piper of Hamelin. I can still remember it now; it's dinned into my brain for ever.' And she began to recite:

'Hamelin town's in Brunswick By famous Hanover City, The River Weser deep and wide Washes its banks on the southern side A pleasanter spot you never spied.' She started to laugh. 'Yuk! It was all about rats – at least yours was about pretty flowers.'

As they drove on through the valley the impressive scenery put a stop to further conversation. The wooded slopes cradling the famous village were dressed in early autumn colours of red and yellow. The morning air was crystal clear so that in the distance they could see majestic hills rising up to meet a deep blue sky.

'Grasmere is not a big lake,' Doug explained. 'It's about a mile long and half a mile wide but it's so very pretty and with the history attached to this place I thought you'd enjoy looking round the village. Then maybe we can find a nice lakeside walk.'

The tourist season was virtually over but being a Sunday there were quite a few visitors wandering about the village, which had retained its old picturesque appearance despite being a popular tourist spot. They walked hand-in-hand to the small churchyard, where Doug showed her Wordsworth's tomb, and then strolled back along the road to the Wordsworth Museum. Before going inside, they paused to read a plaque stating that the building, known as Dove Cottage, had been the home of William and Dorothy Wordsworth from 1799 to 1808. They had the museum to themselves until suddenly the peaceful ambience inside the cottage was disturbed. A party of American tourists began to file in and from their noisy chatter it was obvious that they could not conceal their delight at being surrounded by so much history. Sally and Doug hurried out into the September sunshine.

'Did you see the chap in the bright yellow crimplene suit?' Doug asked her, rolling his eyes.

'How could I have missed him? He was so loud and huge. D'you know, I think if he'd fainted on the hillside, the locals would think it was spring? There was enough yellow crimplene in that suit to represent more than a host of daffodils.'

Doug roared with laughter. 'Come on! Let's look for some lunch and then we'll take a longer walk. I'm starving.' He added suggestively, 'Somehow being with you gives me an appetite'.

They found a small café which listed 'home cooking' on a hand-written sign in the window.

'This looks promising.' Doug pushed open the door and a hidden bell jingled to announce their arrival. As they made their way into the café, a middle-aged woman with a welcoming face beamed at them from an open doorway at the far end of the room.

'Be with you in a minute, make yourselves at home ...' she called out.

Choosing a table set for two by the window, they sat down. After a few moments, Sally leaned towards Doug and whispered, 'Darling, I'm having a wonderful time, thank you'.

'Darling? I've never been called that before. It sounds very nice.'

'You don't really expect me to believe that, do you?'

'What?'

'That nobody has ever called you "darling".'

'Well, they haven't. I've been called a few other things, some of them complimentary and others not so, but I'm pretty sure I've never been called darling. I quite like it.'

Just then the owner of the friendly face made her way over to their table.

'Now, what can I tempt you with?' she asked, still beaming at them. 'It's all local produce and home-cooked. I've a piece of beef roasting, or if you want something lighter I can make you a salad with home-boiled ham and fresh bread I baked this morning.'

'The salad sounds appetising and about right,' Sally said.

'Fine, that'll be two salads then, please and a pot of tea,' Doug ordered.

'I'll be straight back. You timed it just right. I've twelve Americans coming in shortly. They booked a week ago, insisted they wanted a traditional roast beef lunch, English style, that's why I could offer you the beef.'

'Ah, yes, I think we met them in the museum, so they're not far away,' Doug informed her.

They were halfway through their lunch when the American party duly arrived, led in by the man wearing the daffodil-yellow suit. The owner of the café had placed several tables together to seat them in one large group and now they filled the small dining room. The man in the suit organised and reorganised the party until finally he had got everyone seated to his satisfaction before turning his attention to the English-looking couple sitting in the window. Along with his fellow Americans, he just loved an English accent, so he set about engaging them in polite conversation.

'Howdy,' the head above the yellow suit nodded towards Sally and Doug.

They smiled back at him, not wishing to seem unfriendly, and Doug raised his hand in a half-hearted 'Howdy to you too' wave.

'Are you folks from around here?' the large yellow-clad American called over to them.

'No, I'm from Scotland, and Sally here is from the south of England.'

'My name's Bob and I'm from Beaumont, Texas, and this is my wife, Geraldine. I have Scottish ancestors,' he grinned at Doug, 'but then most of us like to lay claim to having roots somewhere back here in the old country. But truly, my grandmother was a McDonald.'

Doug laughed. 'Welcome to the clan. My name is Douglas MacDonald.'

With a loud whoop and a show of great excitement, the American jumped to his feet as fast as his bulky body would allow and hurried over to their table, where he pumped Doug's outstretched hand.

'Honey! Honey! Will you listen to this? This young chap's a McDonald!' 'That's nice, hun.' His wife, who was busy applying even more red lipstick to her already very bright red lips, turned her head briefly from the compact mirror to smile over towards them, before turning back to peer at herself critically in the mirror again. Smiling up at the huge American as he loomed over their table, Sally decided that it was time to turn the tables on Doug.

'Is that MacDonald with or without an "a"?'

'Och! It doesn't really matter how you spell it,' Doug said, as he saw the bemused expression on the American's face.

'Oh really? But what if you were booking into a hotel as husband and wife? It would need to be the same then, wouldn't it?' Sally smiled sweetly at them.

'Beg pardon, ma'am?' The American looked from one to the other of them, momentarily confused and lost for words. These Brits sometimes talked in riddles.

'Take no notice,' Doug smiled up at him. 'It's a little private joke,' he said, knocking Sally's foot under the table.

'Oh ... okay, buddy ... I understand you don't care to share the joke if it's private, that's okay,' the American smiled.

'Where are you headed from here?' Doug said quickly, to change the subject. No, he certainly did not want to share the joke!

'Well, we've been in England a week. We've done London and the Lake District and for the next three days we're doing Scotland. Then we've got two weeks to do Europe and then it's back to the US of A.'

'That's a hectic schedule and a lot of history and geography to cover in a relatively short space of time.' It was Doug's turn to be intrigued now, wanting to know just how, exactly, the Americans were going to 'do' Scotland in three days when there were still places he hadn't seen after 23 years of living there!

'Yep! I expect three days is pushing it a bit, but we have to get back home to the States to plan our next trip,' he explained. 'You see, we thought we would take a couple of weeks and do Africa.' The American spoke with such conviction that Doug began to wonder if he himself had been a little slow in 'doing' his homeland!

Just then, the traditional English roast beef was served up to the Americans and Sally and Doug used this as an excuse to say their goodbyes and hurriedly left the little café for their planned walk.

Later that afternoon Sally leaned back in the seat of the car.

'Wow! My feet are squeaking! I don't think I've ever walked so far. It was very pretty; I've never seen so much countryside close up.' Sally was enthralled with it all.

'Wait until you see Scotland! Some parts are just as pretty as this, while others are rugged and will completely take your breath away!'

'I've no doubt they'll take my breath away if you're going to march me along at the speed we clocked today!' she laughingly shot straight back at him.

'You'll get fit pretty quickly,' he said, patting her knee and then gently squeezing her thigh. 'I do believe I can feel you muscling up already,' and they both laughed.

Arriving back at the hotel Doug told her, 'We'll have to have an early start in the morning; it's still a goodly run on the final leg up to Edinburgh tomorrow.'

'Sounds like an early night then ...' Sally said, chuckling quietly.

'You shameless hussy! Are you after my body again?' Doug laughed and reached over to tap her bottom as she got out of the car in front of the hotel, then drove to the parking area.

Sally collected the key from reception, where the same man that had booked them in the previous day was on duty at the desk again. When Sally smiled at him, he politely volunteered the information that, while it was too late to have afternoon tea in the sitting room, he could arrange for her, if she wished, to have a tray of tea delivered to their suite. Sally thanked him and as she made her way up the creaky stairs, she was relieved that they hadn't arrived back at the hotel in time to have their tea in the sitting room. She hadn't really enjoyed being in there the previous evening, overlooked by so many deceased people and moth-eaten glassy-eyed stuffed animals.

While they had been out, the fire in the bedroom had been lit and, leaving the bedroom door ajar for Doug, Sally seated herself on the floor in front of the fire with arms clasped around her knees, a childhood habit she had not outgrown. Doug and the elderly porter who'd brought their breakfast that morning arrived at the same time. The cups and saucers rattled as the old man made his way shakily across the room and placed the tea tray on the table by the window. Doug poured out two cups of tea and brought them over to where Sally was sitting in front of the fire, and handed one to her. He sank down gratefully onto the high-winged fireside chair and Sally rested her head against his knee.

'Doug, I'm so happy, it's been a wonderful day,' she said, staring dreamily into the flames.

Reaching out, he ruffled her hair. 'This is just the start, kitten. There's going to be a lifetime of fun for the two of us.'

As she turned to look up into his eyes, he leaned forward to kiss her and then, taking her hand, helped her to her feet, kissing her again. Slowly he guided her towards the four-poster bed, kissing her every step of the way until they fell on to it laughing.

'What are the chances of me being able to peel off those jeans?'

'Plenty, if I help you,' she giggled, already thrilling to the idea of what she knew was coming.

'You're a brazen woman, Sally Phillips, and I love you for it. Come here.'

He dragged her playfully to the centre of the bed and sat astride her as he unzipped her jeans. She retaliated by opening his belt and unzipping his trousers. Kneeling back on the bed, he tugged at her jeans and as he did so his own trousers fell from his hips.

'Hey, you're cheating,' Sally giggled, as her jeans and pants came off in one swift tug. Sitting up, she launched herself at Doug, reversing their positions. Sitting astride him, she pushed him down onto the bed and a struggle ensued to remove his trousers.

Doug was surprised and delighted. 'Wow! I've never been stripped by a woman in my life!'

Sally stopped what she was doing and her eyebrows came together in a frown as she looked down at him.

'I don't believe you. You said you've had loads of willing women,' she said, putting an emphasis on the word 'willing'.

'Well, loads was a bit of an exaggeration, and when I say willing, they willingly submitted, more than willingly participated.'

'Have I got this all wrong, then? Should I be doing this?' she asked, puzzled by his explanation.

His arms went round her, 'Oh, no, no, no, no, absolutely not! You've got it all right and believe me you can do this ... anytime you please.'

She leaned forward until their lips met and as they kissed, he held her close with one arm, while with his free hand he sought and found the tell-tale warmth between her legs. Sally gasped at his touch. Still sitting astride him, she managed to divest him of his jumper and shirt and then ran her hands over and over his chest, occasionally leaning forward to kiss him. Quickly he undid her blouse and bra, tossing them away to join the rest of their discarded clothing. The anticipation of pleasure was curling her toes as he pulled her forwards towards his erect penis. Running his hands over her firm nipples he traced a line down from her breasts to her waist and then, holding her gently, he encouraged her up on to her knees and willingly she lowered herself onto his full erection. She was hot and wet with anticipation and the feeling as he entered her was exquisite, and she gasped in ecstasy.

'Take care,' he warned, 'you're in total control of this situation.'

Leaning forward, she began to gently rotate her hips, 'You mean if I do this, you can't stop me?'

Doug moaned with pleasure. 'No. I mean, if you do that, I can't stop me!'

Chapter Twelve

By mid-afternoon the following day they had reached the outskirts of Edinburgh and for most of the journey Sally had sat silently beside Doug, gazing out of the window. As they had driven away from the hotel earlier that morning, it was with a sense of relief that she had taken off the ring and handed it back to him. But the relief did not last long. It had quickly been replaced by renewed apprehension at the forthcoming meeting with his parents. Sensing that her thoughts were elsewhere, Doug was content to concentrate on the driving, revelling in his own sense of well-being that always increased as he neared his childhood home.

Gradually, the view from the car window began to change dramatically. No longer were there acres of open fields or moorland spread out on either side of the road and framed by the purple-clad hills beyond. As they drove into Edinburgh, tall gloomy buildings began to surround them. Their black-stained walls blocked out even the smallest sliver of sunlight. Doug exploited his first-hand knowledge of the back streets to snake his way across the city. The old cobbled stone roads he chose shook the car until Sally's teeth began to rattle in her head: either that, she thought, or my nerves are getting the better of me!

As Doug drove along, oblivious to her mounting anxiety, he pointed out familiar landmarks to her, overjoyed to be back in his hometown.

'We've to drive into the centre of Edinburgh and out the other side. It's very attractive in parts and an interesting city, full of history. We can explore on foot one day and I'll tell you all about it,' he said, glancing over at her profile. He was rewarded with one of her lovely smiles. 'No doubt you will have heard the tale of Greyfriars Bobby? The wee dog that slept on his master's grave?'

'No, I haven't, and just from that brief description I'm not sure I want to know. It's going to make me cry, isn't it?' To add to the gloom of this grey-looking city, she noticed that it had begun to drizzle and the last thing she wanted to hear now was a sad tale about a faithful dog.

'Not much doubt about that, so I'll leave Bobby's story for another day. There's a hill over there on your left which they call Arthur's Seat. It's said that if maidens go up there and wash their faces in the first dew of summer they stay young for ever. I suspect some quick-thinking lads centuries ago thought that one up, to get the girls up the hill and away from their mothers. It's quite a climb. We'll drive along Princes Street. It'll take us a bit longer but it's a very famous part of the old city and you should see it. There are shops down one side and beautiful gardens on the other. You'll be able to see Edinburgh Castle sitting up on its granite throne. I'll try to fit in a visit to the castle while we're here.' Doug changed gear and turned right into the road leading to Princes Street.

The mention of the castle stirred childhood memories in Sally. 'I had a jigsaw puzzle of Edinburgh Castle, with a lovely pink sunset sky behind it ... or that might have been the Windsor Castle one and the Edinburgh one had the blue sky,' she mused out loud.

'I would nae have thought you had the patience to sit and do a jigsaw puzzle!'

'I don't! I only did them when I was under house arrest.'

'House arrest?'

'Can't think of any other way to describe it, really. If I had a cold or if it was raining my mother would incarcerate me with my sister, jigsaw puzzles, crayons and colouring books! It was awful! When I was eventually allowed to go out, I would have to wear so many layers of clothing I could hardly move!'

Doug hooted with laughter. 'Life was a bit hardier on the farm. My mother believed fresh air cured all, so we were wrapped up and booted out the door.'

'I wish I'd been brought up in the countryside,' Sally said wistfully. 'I'm really looking forward to seeing the farm and all the animals, but I'm still nervous at the thought of meeting your mum and dad.'

'Don't worry, they'll be fine. There we are, up to your left on the skyline, there's the castle and this is the famous Princes Street.'

Sally looked up to where the dark, forbidding castle stood high on a mound of grass and rock and noticed that, like the rest of the buildings in the city, its walls were also blackened, as though they had been deliberately smeared with grime.

'Why is everything so black and ... sooty-looking?' Sally asked. She had very nearly said 'grimy' but didn't want to upset Doug by insulting his home city. Doug guessed she was being tactful and smiled. He had heard it called much worse.

'It's due to the coal and wood fires that were burnt for warmth in the city's homes over the centuries; it's affectionately known as Auld Reekie, because of the smell given off by those fires.'

Having driven through the heart of the city and out into the suburbs the other side, it was not long before they were in open countryside again. Although it was no longer raining, dark clouds still hung low in the sky threatening more rain, and to Sally it seemed that the weather reflected her feelings. Would they like her? Would she like them? What if they asked her about the travel arrangements? What would she say to them?

Doug's voice broke into her thoughts. 'Look, now you can see the Pentland Hills in front of you.' Sally peered ahead through the windscreen; even on a wet day it all looked very beautiful. They drove on, along high-banked leafy lanes that became so narrow that they had to use designated passing places when they met another vehicle coming towards them. Eventually Doug turned off the lane onto a private road and, as they rounded a bend, Sally could see a large grey stone farmhouse surrounded by barns nestled in the hillside. Cows and sheep grazed in fields either side of a long winding track which disappeared behind the farmhouse. Some lifted their heads and watched inquisitively as the car climbed slowly up the steep, rutted roadway. When Doug drew up in the cobbled yard, the farmhouse door opened and his mother, eager to see her son and meet his girlfriend, hurried down the path to the garden gate. She had greying hair, a kindly face and a welcoming smile, just as Doug had described her. Doug leapt out of the car and walked towards his mother. They exchanged an affectionate hug, Doug towering above his mother as he bent forward and planted a kiss on her forehead. Sally stood by the car tactfully waiting until the reunion was over.

'Mum, this is Sally,' he said, leaving his mother's embrace as he held out a hand to Sally, slipping an encouraging arm around her waist to draw her nearer to his side.

Sally held out her hand. 'How do you do, Mrs MacDonald.'

To Sally's surprise, Doug's mother ignored her outstretched hand and, before Sally realised what was happening, she had been swiftly gathered into Mrs MacDonald's arms and kissed on the cheek. Sally was momentarily embarrassed; she was not used to such displays of affection and she wasn't quite sure how to react.

'I do very well and please call me Liza – everyone else does. Now, leave that strapping lad of mine to get the cases and you come along in – it's getting a wee bit chilly.'

Tucking her arm through Sally's, she swept her up the path and into the farmhouse. All Sally's apprehension vanished in that instant; overwhelmed by the warmth of such a welcome, she forgot all about being nervous as Liza led her into the large farmhouse kitchen. The most delicious smells of home-cooked bread and meaty casserole assailed her senses and Sally, who had not eaten very much since the previous night, suddenly felt very hungry. Liza waved her towards the large wooden kitchen table, talking all the while about the unpredictable nature of the weather as she turned her attention to the kettle that stood ready on the range. Sally nodded and smiled, immediately   at ease with Liza in the homely kitchen. As she went to sit at the table, she saw a tabby cat and a very old dog lying side by side, fast asleep on a rug in front of the range. Sally went over to them and knelt down to gently stroke the dog. The sheepdog, partially deaf through old age, lifted his head in surprise as he felt strange hands on his fur and through eyes veiled by cataracts he squinted up at Sally. His muzzle was grey and Sally realised that he must be very old; she thought it was a shame that age had not only dulled his eyes but also taken its toll on his fur, which looked moth-eaten.

Liza held her breath as she watched, relieved not to hear a warning growl from Cloud, whose reaction to strangers even in his younger days had always been unpredictable, to say the least. Now he spent most of his time asleep in front of the range but, even though he couldn't see or hear too well, he let it be known that he did not take kindly to strangers. Although he no longer had the teeth to back up the threat, his growls could still sound menacing.

'That's Cloud. He's pensioned off,' explained Liza, 'but he was a good dog in his day. His grandson's now doing all the sheep and cattle work. He'll be along presently with Hamish. Cloud is quite deaf but he's a cunning old dog and could be pretty hard of hearing in his younger days too, if he chose to be!'

Liza felt that she was babbling, but she had been determined to welcome the girl her eldest son was bringing home to meet them. She could see why Doug was smitten; she was a beauty! The fact that Cloud had succumbed so quickly to her was also significant in the eyes of Liza. For a moment, she stood by the range smiling at the memories; where had all the years gone? she wondered. It seemed only yesterday that Hamish would cuss the young Cloud for his wilful ways. Shaking her head, she filled the teapot and glanced kindly at Sally as she continued to stroke the old dog, who lay inert, flat on his back, ecstatic at the attention he was receiving. Riddled with arthritis, he had made the effort to roll over in order to take full advantage of this unexpected but very welcome massage.

'I see you are fond of animals.'

'Oh yes, I love animals, but I've never been allowed to have any. My mother says they make a house smell ... oh ...'

It was an innocent remark based on years of indoctrination and the words were out of her mouth a split second before she realised, with horror, how impolite it sounded. If she could have caught the words in mid-air and stuffed them back into her mouth she would have done so. She coloured with embarrassment and hastily added, 'It's because we live in a town, I suppose

... but I spend all my weekends at the riding stables. They have dogs ... and cats there, as well as all the horses ...' Sally's nervousness caused a torrent of reminiscences to pour forth. 'I've had pets, of a sort ... rescued them ... like wild birds that were sick or injured; hedgehogs, too, only I wasn't allowed to keep them in the house. They had to stay in the garden shed, but sometimes I'd sneak them into my bedroom when my mum wasn't looking ... to keep them warm. My mother would have murdered me if she'd found out, especially as the hedgehogs always had loads of fleas ...'

As Sally blundered on, Liza continued to make the tea but now she turned to smile down at this lovely young girl that her son had brought home. She had taken an instinctive liking to Sally; knowing that the girl had not intended any criticism, she was moved by her obvious discomfort and attempts to make amends. When Sally ran out of conversation, there was a short silence while Liza tried to think of some way to reassure her.

'I can remember a time when Cloud found a wee hedgehog in the yard and rolled it along very gingerly with his paw and his nose. When he looked up his face was a mass of fleas and by the evening his scratching and snuffling had driven us all to distraction.' She chuckled at the memory of it. 'So he had to suffer the indignity of a bath in the sheep dip so we'd all get a night's sleep.' As she spoke, she placed several china mugs on the kitchen table and just then Doug came into the kitchen.

'I've left the suitcases in the hall – I wasn't sure which bedrooms to take them up to.'

'Ye ken fine where your bedroom is! It hasn't moved these twenty-three years and Sally is in the one next door to mine and your father's ...' his mother replied without looking up. 'Sit down and have some tea and a chat, and you can bother about the suitcases later.'

Doug winked at Sally behind his mother's back and she smiled back at him, relieved that the first hurdle had been overcome. Doug's mother was a sweet, gentle woman and had made her feel very welcome. Cloud had struggled up on to his legs to follow Sally as she made her way over to the table and had   sat himself on the floor beside her chair, his head pressed against her knee. Sally, unaware of the honour he was showing her by condescending to move from the warm comfort of his rug, idly continued to rub his ears. The old dog shuffled his front feet and pressed even closer to Sally. His once-brown eyes, now milky with age, were partially closed as he enjoyed the gentle massage.

'Cloud will take any amount of that,' Doug said. 'Where's my welcome then, Cloud? Given it away to someone else, have you?' The dog thumped his tail at the sound of his name but didn't move; unless there was a very good reason, he moved about as little as possible these days. 'I see – enough said.'

Just then, the back door opened and Cloud hauled himself up on his old shaky legs, his tail wagging slowly to welcome home his master who strolled into the kitchen with Cloud's young grandson at his heels. Doug's father was a tall, well-built man with a mop of unruly hair and a weather-beaten complexion. Grey, bushy eyebrows could not hide the twinkle in his eyes and a big friendly smile spread across his face when he saw Sally. He made his way across the kitchen and father and son shook hands, then clasped each other's shoulders, obviously delighted to be in each other's company again.

'Hello there. You must be Sally,' he said. 'Ye are quite right, son, she's a fair bobby-dazzler!' They both laughed as he stepped round the table to greet Sally, who had turned pink with embarrassment. Once more she was swept up into a welcoming hug and pecked swiftly on the cheek.

'Welcome to Home Farm, lass. I see ye've got the first mug of tea. There'll be an endless supply of those in this kitchen. The whole world gets put to rights over Liza's teapot,' he said, sitting down and taking the steaming mug that Liza passed to him. Sally could only smile her response, as once again she was overwhelmed by such a genuine display of affection. Feeling a wet nose nudge her fingers, she looked down. Cloud's grandson was vying with his grandfather for her attention. The difference between the two dogs was striking. Skip was slim and sleek; his coat had a healthy sheen and his eyes and ears were alert and tuned in to everything going on around him. Cloud gave him a nudge with his head and the young sheepdog immediately dropped until his tummy was touching the floor, wriggling in total submission to his elderly grandfather. Sally chuckled at Skip's behaviour. She couldn't remember a time when she had ever felt so at home and content as she did at that moment.

'Well, children, drink up your tea and you can go and sort rooms and suitcases out,' Liza said, sitting herself down at the table. 'Dinner is in the oven and will be ready in about an hour. Iain should be back by then. I thought we'd have a family supper in the kitchen tonight; it's cosier than that big old dining room. Fiona gets home tomorrow, then the whole family will all be back together. There's something very comforting about having all my bairns together again under the same roof. I'm fair looking forward to that.' With a sigh of content, she beamed at the three of them. With Doug away from home so often with his work and Fiona away at college, she missed the family gatherings round the kitchen table.

'If you've finished, Sal, I'll show you to your room.'

Sally nodded and as Doug stood up she smiled shyly at Liza. Remembering her mother's instructions about manners, she thanked her for the tea and followed Doug into the hallway. He picked up both their suitcases and led the way up a wide staircase which opened out on to a large, square landing. Doug stopped at the first door to put his suitcase down.

'Just as I predicted! Opposite ends of the house with mother and yards of squeaky floorboards in between us!' he whispered, grinning ruefully.

'She obviously knows you well,' Sally teased.

'Less of your cheek, little lady. Leave the door open and I'll be along in the night. Now let me see, where were those two squeaky boards?' Doug walked up and down the hall, testing the polished oak floorboards.

'Doug, you can't do that!' Sally hissed in a fierce whisper. The very thought of him attempting to creep past his parents' room to hers in the night made her panic.

'Can I not?' He winked at her, his eyes sparkling mischievously. 'Follow me.' He led the way across the hall to the end bedroom and, once inside, placed her suitcase on a large wooden chest under the window. He went back to the door and gently pushed it shut.

'Come here, you little beauty.' He kissed her passionately. The ordeal of meeting his parents over, Sally sank thankfully into Doug's arms and returned his kisses.

'Have I ever told you that I love you?' he whispered to her.

'I think you might have mentioned something along those lines.'

'Well I do. I love you, Sally Phillips, I love you a lot,' and he kissed her again. Sally held him tight, her arms around his neck as he continued to hug and kiss her, until they were suddenly interrupted by a shout from downstairs.

'Doug!'

'That's Iain,' he whispered. 'I'd best go and say hello. There's a bathroom at the end of the hallway on the left, if you want to freshen up. Come down when you're ready and I'll introduce you to my baby brother.'

Her bedroom was warm and welcoming; with a feeling of relief, Sally sat down on the bed. She had been dreading meeting Doug's parents but it hadn't been such a bad day after all. They seemed kind, and now he'd told her once again that he loved her. She was breathless with happiness.

Wandering over to the suitcase, she began to unpack her clothes and felt a bit guilty as she left the yellow, dimpled nylon dress lying in the bottom of the suitcase. She hadn't yet made up her mind what she was going to wear for the party, but nothing would induce her to wear that dress! Having hung up the rest of her clothes neatly in the tiny wardrobe in the corner of the room, she sat on the bed again – it felt so much softer than the one she had at home. It was such a pretty room, with flower print curtains framing a window that looked out over the back of the farmyard onto rolling fields and nearby hills. Not another house in sight, thought Sally – so unlike the view from her bedroom at home, where she looked out onto her father's neat lawn and shrubs which ended abruptly at their boundary fence. And beyond the boundary fence, other neat little gardens and, as far as the eye could see, row upon row of red-brick houses. Smiling to herself, she ran her hands lightly over the pretty patchwork quilt that covered the bed. Not only did she love Doug, she decided, but she loved his parents, his home, this room and she even loved the black iron bedstead with its brass knobs on each corner.

After a quick rinse of her face and hands, she brushed her hair and made her way back downstairs. At the kitchen door she hesitated, listening to the sound of laughter from within. Suddenly she felt shy but, plucking up courage, she grasped the door handle firmly as she recalled the advice given by the nuns at the convent.

'Don't creep into a room, child! Never sidle round a door as if you are ashamed to be seen entering a room! Shoulders down, head up, smile and walk in!'

Sally took a deep breath and opened the door. The two brothers sat side by side at the old oak table, engrossed in conversation. As she appeared in the doorway, Doug immediately rose, took her by the arm and escorted her into the room.

'Sally, this is Iain, my baby brother.' Iain stood up and held out his hand. He was slightly taller than Doug, fairer in complexion, and through the heavy cotton of his shirt Sally couldn't help but notice the outline of the muscles on his torso and upper arms, testimony to the strenuous manual work on the farm. His face mirrored the disarming smile of his elder brother.

'Hello, Sally.' Her outstretched hand disappeared in Iain's large callused grasp, as he took her hand in his and placed his other hand over the top of hers. 'Now, tell me, what's a pretty girl like yerself see in the likes of him?' He jerked his head towards Doug.

'Take no notice, Sally! He always wants to steal my best toys.'

There was more laughter and, despite her deep blushes at Iain's compliment, Sally couldn't help joining in. Iain released her hand and they all sat down at the table.

'Doug tells me that ye're a good rider. The back of a horse is the best way to see the countryside round here. If the weather stays kind, you can take the ponies out onto the hills.'

'Ponies! Do you have ponies here?' Sally's face lit up as she looked at each of them in turn.

'Highland ponies, aye – we keep a couple for shepherding. We use them for bringing the sheep in off the hill for lambing or shearing. They're very sure-footed and clever. If ye ever get lost in bad weather they even know their way home ...'

'Eih, ye're right enough there, son, they even ken their way home from the pub in the dark with nae help from their riders!' their mother added, without turning from her preparations at the range as a united roar of laughter erupted from the brothers.

'Mother will never forgive us for that one!' Doug shook his head, his eyes brimming with mischief, but it was Iain who answered the quizzical expression on Sally's face.

'It was a hot summer's day and we'd taken sheep up to the far hill. On the way home we were really thirsty so we stopped for a swift half at the pub. One half followed another. Eventually, when we fell out of the pub it was dark – but luckily the ponies were where we'd left them, tied to a gate. We just about managed to clamber up on to their backs but the pair of us were asleep on their necks by the time they brought us back into the farmyard.'

'Aye! And neither one of ye old enough to have a legal drink!' Liza exclaimed. 'If the local bobby had seen you, there would have been trouble.'

'Did ye not know that he was there with us? His bike was in the woodshed at the back of the pub, hidden out of sight of his missus, and he bought us the first round to buy our silence,' chuckled Doug.

While they were all still laughing, the door opened and Hamish joined them at the kitchen table. Liza began to lay out the cutlery for dinner, working round the men. Sally stood up, offering to help.

'Thank you, dear. You just sit yourself there for now, but I'll be glad of some help after, to tidy away.'

Reaching into the oven, Liza brought out a large earthenware casserole dish and placed it on the table, quickly followed by another two dishes containing a selection of vegetables and potatoes. A freshly-baked loaf of bread was placed on the breadboard. Once Liza was seated, she lifted the lid off the casserole to release a mouth-watering aroma. She ladled the rich brown stew onto the plates and passed them round.

'Help yourself to the vegetables,' she said to Sally, passing her a large serving spoon.

Momentarily, the conversation subsided as everyone began eating.

Hamish was the first to break the silence. 'Did you have an easy drive up?'

Sally's tummy flipped over and she nervously glanced up from her plate.

'I see ye've changed the car – they must be overpaying you,' Hamish continued, mopping his gravy with a crust of bread as he glanced at his elder son.

'It was an easy enough trip, father, and I had to change the car – the other wasn't worth repairing.' Doug kept his reply simple as he helped himself to more stew.

'Ye should've got the old one back up here for your Uncle Bob to fix. Ye know he can keep any machine on this earth going and in working order.'

'Oh aye,' replied Iain, 'but somehow I don't think our Dougie wanted a car held together with a bit of Uncle Bob's rough welding and a roll of baling twine!'

'Aye, true enough,' admitted Hamish, as they all laughed. 'His repairs are no' exactly stylish, but some of his tractors that are still working are the original ones. Aye, and we used horses afore that!'

As the light-hearted banter between the men continued, Sally was suddenly overcome with tiredness. The long car journey combined with the food and the warmth in the kitchen was making her feel very drowsy. Seeing her trying to stifle a yawn, Liza leaned towards her with a concerned look on her face.

'I expect ye're very tired after the journey up.' Liza smiled at her. 'It's quite a way, is it not? Dougie says he has to start at five in the morning to get here the same day, so you must be in need of an early night.'

Sally's tummy took a nosedive again.

'Mother, have you made one of your special apple pies?' Doug quickly chipped in. He knew how to flatter his mother and his request was enough to distract her from further questions about their journey.

'Aye, I have that, son. Eat up and I'll get some custard on the go.' She bustled over to the range. Doug gave Sally a quick wink and she smiled her thanks to him across the table. For a moment there, she had felt like a rabbit in the headlights and was relieved at Doug's skilful diversion.

Once the meal was over, Sally helped Liza clear away the dishes. To her surprise, as Liza washed and Sally dried, Doug and his brother also helped, putting away the clean crockery and kitchen pots where they belonged. At home, the kitchen was very much her mother's domain – 'women's work', her father would say – and as a result he rarely set foot in it, let alone helped to wash up. When the dishes were done, Sally was ushered through into the sitting room where a log fire burned brightly in the large open hearth. Cloud and Skip had already claimed prime positions and were stretched out side by side on the fireside mat in front of the warming flames. Doug wandered over to where his father was busy pouring generous tots of amber liquid into small tumblers, and Sally made herself comfortable on the floor, leaning back against one of the armchairs with her legs stretched out beside the two dogs. Absent-mindedly, she began stroking Cloud again and he let out a sigh of contentment.

'If you smell burning fur, it usually means Cloud's on fire,' Doug said. 'So you'll need to wake him up. He sleeps so soundly and he's so deaf these days, he doesn't hear the logs spitting. Sometimes a spark will land in his coat and still he doesn't wake up! In years gone by, at the sound of the fire sparking, he would've leapt to his feet, like young Skip still does.'

'Oh, poor Cloud ...' Sally felt sorry for the old dog, understanding now the moth-eaten look of his coat. It had obviously been regularly singed.

'Well now ...' Hamish said as he handed Doug two small tumblers, 'I think we should partake of a wee dram to welcome Sally into our home.'

'I'm not sure Sally has a taste for the whisky,' Doug said gently, not wishing to dampen his father's welcoming gesture.

'Och ... if that's the case, then we'll start Sally off with a wee drop of liqueur whisky. I'm sure she'll soon get a taste for that,' he said, turning to a bottle of Drambuie and pouring a generous amount into another tumbler. As Liza entered the sitting room at that moment, with a wicked grin on his face he added, 'It didnae tak your mother long to get a taste for it! Now, look, I have to mark the bottle before I leave the house!' Everyone roared with laughter and Sally began to relish the affectionate good nature of this family.

'Hamish!' Liza mockingly reprimanded her husband, struggling to prevent her own face from splitting into an ear-to-ear smile. Unabashed, he waited while everyone settled down on the comfortable settee and easy chairs arranged in a semicircle around the welcoming fire. Doug claimed the armchair by Sally and the drinks were passed round. When the laughter had died down, Hamish held up his glass.

'To Sally - welcome to Scotland, lass, and if ye're not put off after this visit, we'll be pleased to see you here among us anytime.' They all raised their glasses. Sally, overwhelmed by their welcome, felt tears of happiness prick her eyes and she glanced shyly up at Doug. He leaned forward, brushing her forehead with his lips and neither of them saw the knowing smiles that passed between Hamish, Liza and Iain.

The light-hearted chatter and leg-pulling continued for a while before conversation turned to the state of farming in general, the effect of the recent weather on the summer's harvest and the market prices of livestock. Suddenly, the large wooden clock high on the mantelpiece interrupted their conversation by chiming its tuneless way laboriously to ten o'clock.

'Well, that's my bedtime song,' said Hamish. 'We rise early on the farm, Sally.' Obeying the clock's monotonous demand, he stood and took a large key from behind its case. Opening up the glass that protected the clock face, he slotted the key into a hole and gave it five quick turns.

'This old clock has seen many generations of MacDonalds get themselves to bed early enough to rise fresh of a morn. Now, Sally, if you want to look round the farm and see the animals, ye're very welcome to come with me, so I suggest you heed the old clock too.' Nodding to where his sons were topping up their whisky tumblers, he added, 'I doubt I'll be seeing either of these two before noon tomorrow. Sleep well, Sally. Goodnight, boys!'

'Goodnight,' all three responded as Liza stood up to follow her husband. 'Goodnight, Sally. If ye're tired, don't wait up for these two. They'll be blathering half the night. I daresay they've a lot to catch up on.' Sally smiled up at her from her position on fireside rug between Cloud and Skip.

'Not too late now, boys,' Liza called out, and she too was gone.

For a while Sally listened to the brothers conversing, as she gently stroked Skip. On one side of her the old dog lay snoring, while Skip had positioned himself close enough to Sally so that he could roll over and have his tummy scratched. Soon the external warmth from the fire and the internal warmth of the Drambuie began to take effect. Her eyelids were heavy and the temptation to let her head droop forward was becoming too much to ignore.

'Shall I show you up to your bed now?' Doug asked, noticing that she could hardly keep her eyes open.

'It's okay, I can find my way. You stay and talk to Iain,' she said as she began to get up from the floor.

'Not at all, the least I can do is walk you to the door,' Doug said, getting up and helping Sally to her feet.

'That's not "the least" you can do, that's "the most" you can do, with mother's ears tuned in to your every footstep,' chuckled Iain.

'Very funny! I'll be right back.'

'Too right, you will be!' grinned Iain, continuing to goad his older brother.
'Goodnight, Iain.'

'Goodnight, Sal.' Sally smiled at him, thinking how similar the two brothers were and how much she liked their easy-going natures.

Doug followed Sally into her bedroom. Closing the door behind him, he took her into his arms and kissed her.

'See, I knew they would like you. Have you got over the nerves now?'

'After the first glass of Drambuie I really felt fine,' Sally giggled, nestling into his arms. 'Everyone is so kind.' Reaching up, she held his face between her hands. 'And there's something else ...'

'What's that?'

She kissed him. 'I love you, Doug,' she whispered.

'Oh, Sally,' he looked deep into her eyes. 'Sally ... Sally ... Sally ...' he murmured, pulling her to him and hugging her close. 'Oh Sally, I want to stay here with you, all night.'

'You can't do that, Doug. You had better go – Iain will be waiting. Go on ...' and she playfully shooed him out of the room.

Sitting on her bed, glowing from the warmth of his kisses, she imagined that she could still feel the strength of his arms around her; Sally had never felt so happy.

Loving and being loved in return, she decided, was the most wonderful thing she had ever experienced! Sighing to herself, she undressed and put on a sensible nightdress, not wanting to be seen in the seductive baby-doll pyjamas that Doug had bought her. What, she shuddered to think, would Liza make of her, if she saw her in those? As soon as she climbed into the big brass bed she sank into the feather mattress and, resting her head on the pillows, fell fast asleep.

'Doug?' Sally whispered. Gradually aroused from her sleep, and aware that she was not alone in the bed, fearfully she sat up. There was no reply. Cautiously she reached out into the darkness. She almost screamed as something cold and wet nuzzled her hand but then the gentle thump of a tail soon identified her bed mate.

'Oh! Cloud! It's you!' Relieved that Doug had not risked creeping into her room as he had jokingly threatened to do, Sally lay back against the soft white pillows and once more drifted into a deep sleep.

Chapter Thirteen

When Liza took Sally a cup of tea the following morning she found Cloud stretched out on the bed alongside her, the pair of them sound asleep.

'Well there's a picture, you old devil ...' she whispered. 'I'd never have thought those old legs would carry you this far, let alone launch you up onto the bed.' At the distant sound of her voice, Cloud wagged his tail without opening his eyes, but Sally opened hers.

'I'm sorry, Liza, he came up in the night. Is he allowed on the bed?' she said as she yawned and stretched her arms out above the sheets.

'Officially, no, but he kens well enough which is my blind eye. Come on, old fella, out and do your business – ye can see the lass later.' She ushered the stiff old sheepdog off the bed and out of the bedroom, and Sally could hear his long old claws tapping on the wooden floor as he slowly made his way across the hall and down the stairs.

Sally washed, then dressed in jeans, shirt and a warm jumper and went down to the kitchen where the moreish smell of fried bacon greeted her nostrils as she walked in. The clock on the wall showed it was eight-thirty.

'Good morning, Liza, am I very late getting up? Is everyone up and out already?' she asked, looking round the empty kitchen. She was mindful that most farmers worked from dawn until dusk and sometimes beyond.

'No, no, only Hamish and Skip. It'll be a while before those two boys of mine appear! They had a good enough catching-up session into the wee small hours of this morning. It was one of them that left the kitchen door open and Cloud made good use of that to escape and find a warm cosy place to sleep.'

Sally laughed. 'I hope you didn't mind. I think he's lovely to sleep with. He didn't move all night – it was like having a huge, furry hot water bottle.'

'And I hope you didnae mind me waking you up with an early-morning cuppa? Only, Hamish is going to take a pony up onto the hill to bring down a few stray ewes. It's a beautiful morning and I thought you might like to take the other pony and go with him?'

'Oh, thank you! No, I don't mind at all being woken up to go riding. That would be heavenly. I'd love it!'

'Aye, well, sit yourself down and I'll get you some breakfast. Ye'll need something inside you afore ye go. Hamish will be along presently and he'll be ready for his breakfast too – he's been in and out feeding the stock since six.'

Just then Sally heard the back door open and the scuffling sounds of someone removing their boots in the back porch. Hamish walked into the kitchen wearing a smile, cord trousers, a jumper and colourful woolly socks that looked home-knitted. He sat down at the table opposite Sally.

'Good morning. Did ye sleep well, lass? I hear there was a stranger in your bed, isn't that right, Cloud?' The old dog didn't move from where he now lay, next to Hamish's multicoloured feet, but at the mention of his name his tail thumped appreciatively. Hamish leaned down and patted his head.

'Oh aye, ye've got good taste, old lad.'

'I slept really well, thank you,' Sally answered shyly, blushing at Hamish's reference to 'a stranger in her bed'. They were not to know that, when she had awakened during the night, she had been half hoping, half fearful that it had been their son who had crept on to her bed.

'Has Liza told ye yet about giving me a hand this morn?' When Sally nodded, he continued, 'Okay, lass, let's get some of Liza's breakfast into ye and we can get saddled up. We've to go up the valley a way – some of our ewes have strayed during the night and I want them back closer to our own ram.' Then he lowered his voice as he leaned over the table towards Sally. 'If I don't keep an eye on these old girls,' he said playfully, glancing over to where Liza was busy at the range, 'they tend to wander off and find themselves a younger ram to entertain them. Then in the spring we won't know who has fathered what ... bit like our village.'

'Hamish, shush now!' Liza was smiling as she came back to the table with plates of egg, bacon, sausages and tomatoes and, mistaking the reason for the blush on Sally's cheeks, threw him a warning look.

'Liza, this is a farm, it's going on all the time! The lass will have to get used to such talk,' he said, tucking into his breakfast.

'Aye, I know, but Hamish ...'

'Dinnae "but Hamish" me, woman,' he said between mouthfuls. 'Before the lass gets halfway across the farmyard she's liable to trip over that cockerel of yours, treading his hens. I dinnae ken what you feed him – the beggar never stops for breath!'

Liza brought her own plate to the table and sat down to join them, relieved that, despite her blushes, Sally was laughing.

'Aye, that new Rhode Island cockerel is a bit too keen on his job, it can be embarrassing. When the Minister delivered the kirk magazine last week, I was trying to hold a conversation with him in the front yard and Rhodey trod four!

Right in front of us! There were hens crouching down squawking and feathers flying everywhere! I didnae know where to look for decency!' As she spoke, Liza sliced thick chunks of bread, passing it round and rolling her eyes up to the ceiling, making Sally laugh even more.

'You cannae blame the cockerel! He's only being a good Christian. Going forth and multiplying and filling the earth,' chuckled Hamish as he used the bread to mop up the remains of the egg yolk on his plate.

'Eih, but the Minister! He's an old bachelor and none so broad-minded ...'

'Rubbish!' hooted Hamish. 'Away with you, woman! He may be an old bachelor, but that hasnae stopped him getting his cocoa from the postmistress for nigh on forty years! Oh aye! A spinster she may be, but she'll no have

"Returned Unopened" on her tombstone!'

Liza was chuckling so much that she only had the breath to fondly chastise her husband yet again with the words, 'Hamish ... please!' before casting her eyes up to heaven and shaking her head in exasperation.

Sally, who was having difficulty controlling her own giggles, loved it all. This was so very different from breakfasts at home, where such light-hearted banter first thing in the morning was unheard of!

Breakfast over, Sally followed Hamish out to the porch.

'Ye might have to use a pair of these old boots. It can be boggy in parts if we have to get off the ponies at all.' After trying on several pairs of well-used boots, they finally found a pair that fitted Sally and Hamish handed her a waterproof coat off the row of hooks.

'Tak' that with ye, tie it to the back of the saddle. Ye never know when the weather will change up in the hills. It's no very pretty but it'll keep you dry.'

Sally took the dark green waxed coat and followed Hamish out to the big stone barn. The interior of the barn was sectioned off into pens and, standing together in one of the larger pens, knee-deep in straw, were two sturdy, broad-backed ponies with long manes and forelocks that came down over their eyes. One was pure white and the other a creamy dun with a black mane and tail and a black dorsal line. Sally reckoned that they were just over fourteen hands high.

'Oh, they're gorgeous!' she exclaimed as she followed Hamish into the pen. 'I've seen pictures of Highland ponies but I've never seen a real one. They're bigger than I imagined.'

'Eih, well they're strong beasts and can easily carry a man or the dead weight of a full-grown stag up and down a mountainside. The white one is Heather, the other is Molly. You can tak' ye choice; they're both honest and kind.'

Sally decided on Molly. Hamish was impressed as he watched her skilfully tack up the dun-coloured mare with the saddle and bridle he'd lifted from the saddle rack and rested against a near-by haybale. All the while they were tacking up the ponies, Skip waited, flattening himself to the ground. His head never moved from resting on his front paws, but his hazel eyes followed their every move. Hamish led Heather out into the hazy, early morning sunshine and Sally followed with Molly. The ponies' hooves clattered on the cobbles as they rode out of the yard, then across a front field and on to the lower slopes of the hillside. Skip ran along in front of them, his nose to the ground. Occasionally he would take off at speed, only to stop a short distance away, where he would frantically go round in circles for a few moments before dashing back to them, then take off again a few moments later.

'Rabbits,' Hamish said to explain Skip's erratic behaviour. 'He's reading the early morning news, following the scents of rabbits, foxes and anything else that moved in the night.'

Sally watched in amazement as suddenly the young dog gave a yelp and set off at great speed. This time, Hamish whistled him back before he had gone too far.

'If the blighter gets too well onto a rabbit, he'll be away out of sight and gone for the day,' he explained. 'Then we'll have to do the young beggar's job of rounding up the sheep ourselves,' laughed Hamish.' I dinnae ken about yeself, but I cannae run that fast.'

'Me neither,' Sally laughed. 'I was always last in the races on school sports day, so you'd better keep Skip close by.'

Having only ever ridden along narrow bridle paths in the woods adjoining her local riding stables, Sally was unaccustomed to the vast openness of the countryside. Momentarily, she felt dizzy and overwhelmed by the space around her. As she looked skywards to the hills, shyly she mentioned to Hamish how she felt.

'Aye, I can understand what ye're saying, lass, even though I've never been confined myself. I have to say I feel very sorry for those that have never had the chance to feel this freedom and to see God's handiwork at close quarters. No doubt there's some folk who would never leave the towns and cities. Each to their own, but this is the only place on earth I can survive. Even our Dougie has to come home regularly to recharge his batteries.' As the sure-footed ponies continued to pick their way along the narrow track, Hamish went quiet as he contemplated how his eldest son could ever have left his homeland in the first place. 'He's very different to Iain, is Dougie, needed to spread his wings and fly a little. Clever at school, too, with passing all those exams and going off to university for his engineering degree.' They continued climbing steadily, the track so narrow in places that Sally had to drop back into single file, making further conversation difficult. She could see a cluster of buildings on a distant hillside and when the track widened out again Hamish slowed so that Sally could come back alongside him.

'That's my brother's farm over the way, on the far side of the valley, and it will all come to Dougie one day. It's a big place, with a lot of good low land as well as grazing on the hill.'

He wanted this lass to know how things might turn out in the long run. From the short time he had spent in Sally's company he could see she had the makings of a good farmer's wife. He liked her, and anything he could do to encourage the union with his son would not be a bad move, in his estimation.

'Who knows, perhaps by the time he inherits, he will be done with his roaming the world and be ready to return to us and settle down. There'll be nae pressure; everyone has their own life to lead. I would never tie him down or make him feel beholden.'

Hamish was a man happy with his lot and had put no pressure on Doug to follow him into farming. Even though he was unable to comprehend why his son was not content to stay at home, he was wise enough to give Doug the time to find out exactly what he wanted from life. He smiled at Sally, sitting completely at ease on Molly's broad back, the reins loose in her hands. They rode on in amiable silence, Sally loving the serene beauty of the surrounding hillsides. It was all so quiet and peaceful here; the only sound was the breeze whistling and rustling through the nearby trees, accompanied by the occasional creak of the leather saddle she was sitting on. Clouds scurried across the sky and Sally watched fascinated as their shadows raced over the landscape all around her. The dizzy, overwhelming sensation of a few moments before had passed.

Hamish sent up a silent prayer that Doug would not do anything to upset this union. Although she was a townie, she obviously enjoyed being in the countryside and sat a horse well, too. The dogs loved her, and that was always a good sign in his eyes – and anyone with eyes in their head could see that his son was totally besotted with this young lass. He looked at her wind-reddened cheeks and sparkling blue eyes and thought how young she was. But despite her youth, he decided she would suit his eldest son very well. He knew Doug had been a rake; many of the girls in the village had fallen for his charms and Hamish had no doubt that he had sown more than his fair share of wild oats. Thankfully, to date it seemed they had all been sown on barren soil! Just then,

Sally turned her head; she realised Hamish had been studying her profile but she had been so deeply engrossed in enjoying her surroundings that for   a moment she wondered if he had spoken to her and she had not heard him.

'I really didn't know there could be so much space and sky,' Sally said apologetically, breathing in deeply to cover her embarrassment.

'Enjoy God's handiwork, lassie, and the air. 'Tis like wine on a clear day like today. D'ye know that generations of the same family of sheep have grazed these hills? Aye, for centuries the same families have mapped out these hills with sheep paths for the shortest routes to the best shelter belts and most reliable water supplies. We cannae just go and buy strange sheep and put them on the hill. We always have to keep a few sheep of our own breeding because only they know how to survive on this particular patch.'

'That's fascinating,' Sally said, 'and it makes sense when you think about it, because each generation teaches the next.'

They continued their steady ascent in single file, the native ponies never faltering as they picked their way along the narrow paths. At various places along the way, streams of crystal-clear water trickled out of the undergrowth and cut shallow gullies across their path, before cascading over the edge to continue the journey down the hillside to refresh the lake below. As they reached the summit, the path levelled and widened out and Hamish reined Heather in as Sally brought Molly alongside.

'Aye, here we are now. I thought this is where we might find them.' Hamish pointed down to a small, wooded valley that spread out below them and Sally could see a dozen or so sheep grazing there. They started downhill and when they finally reached the valley floor Hamish whistled Skip. The collie had been enjoying a drink from a stream nearby but responded immediately to his master's whistle. He flattened himself to the ground and crept along silently on his belly until he was on the far side of the unsuspecting sheep. Then, following Hamish's instructions, the dog darted left and right, bunching up the sheep as he drove them slowly forward.

'That'll do, Skip! Aye, hold to them there! Good lad!' The dog lay down in the lush grass that covered the valley floor and the sheep relaxed, lowering their heads to resume grazing once more.

'Now, if I ride up the front and lead the way, will you bring up the rear with Skip? Don't worry, they should all follow and Skip will round up any stragglers. There's a lot of truth to the saying "following like sheep",' chuckled Hamish.

Sally was enthralled at the sight of the sheepdog working, for it seemed to her that Skip could control the flock by eye contact alone. He lay flat, perfectly still but staring straight ahead, his gaze never wandering from the sheep in his charge. Occasionally, one of the ewes would walk towards him and stare as if trying to read his thoughts, but the dog never moved a whisker and the ewe would soon put its head down and continue grazing.

'Okay, Hamish, leave the rear end to me. If I get it wrong, I'm sure Skip will put things right,' Sally offered, sounding more confident than she felt.

They set off for home with Hamish on Heather leading the way and the sheep in a crocodile line following behind. Sally was entertained by the loud bleats from the disgruntled sheep protesting at their interrupted grazing. Skip spent the time running back and forth along the line, making sure that no sheep broke ranks as they slowly made their way home. The sun was high in the sky when they eventually reached the bottom fields below the farmhouse, for they had taken a different and longer route back. Sally envied Hamish; it must be wonderful to live in the countryside and be so familiar with the landscape that the trees, hills and unmade paths became natural signposts. Reaching a heavy wooden gate, Hamish leaned from his pony and pushed it open, whistling to Skip to send the sheep on through as he did so. When the last ewe ran passed him, he slammed the gate shut.

'That's a job well done, lassie!' he said as he smiled across at Sally. 'Now let's get back and see if those lazy sons of mine have come up for air from their beds.'

She followed Hamish on to a narrow lane and they trotted side by side until they reached the entrance to the field that edged the roadway up to the farm. It was a long field with springy green turf that swept upwards to the boundary of the farmyard. Turning into it, suddenly Hamish called out, 'Right, Sally! Molly and Heather have a bit of a ritual here. Hold tight! Last one home makes the tea!'

To Sally's astonishment, Hamish dropped the reins on Heather. The sure-footed Highland mare shot forward up the hillside homewards. Knowing the game and not waiting to be asked, in one leap Molly was up alongside Heather, nearly toppling Sally backwards out of the saddle in the process. Sally shrieked with laughter as she regained her seat and the two mares raced neck-and-neck up the field towards the farmhouse. The wind swept Sally's hair back from her face and stung her eyes until she could feel wet tears on her cheeks. Exhilarated by the chase, she dug her heels into Molly's side, urging the mare on, leaning forward and yelling excitedly in her pony's ears. Molly, carrying considerably less weight than her companion, found the extra speed and they reached the top of the field well ahead of Hamish on Heather. Throughout it all, Skip, caught up in the excitement of the race, ran alongside, barking hysterically at the ponies' heels. Finally, Sally eased Molly to a standstill at the edge of the field and turned, out of breath and laughing, to watch Heather and Hamish canter their final couple of strides to her side.

Doug had watched the scene from the farmyard, waiting for their return, and he heard his father call out congratulations to Sally as they came to a halt.

'Well done! And well ridden!'

Doug could hear the laughter in his father's voice and thought that it had been a long time since he had heard him enjoy himself so much.

'It certainly looks as if I'll be making the tea, lassie. Although, to be fair, I think Molly had a definite weight advantage over poor Heather here,' he said, patting his mare's sleek neck as Doug strolled towards them.

'Well, father,' he said with mock disapproval, 'not only do you steal my girl, but you disgrace the family honour by letting her beat you home.' He held Molly's bridle as Sally dismounted. She reached up and kissed Doug on the cheek, grinning and glowing with the exhilaration of the race.

'Aye, and yon lass has been of more use to me today than either of you two lardy puddings!' his father replied as he dismounted. 'And by the bye, I didnae allow her to win, she had me well beat.'

'Could that be because you're a bit of a lardy pudding yourself, father?' Doug winked at Sally.

Looking out from under his bushy eyebrows with a merry twinkle in his eyes, Hamish wagged a finger at his elder son. 'Aye, that's as maybe nowadays, but we'll have less of your cheek, young man.'

They were all laughing as Doug took Heather's reins from his father and led the pony back across the yard. 'We'll get both the ponies fed, Dad. I expect you need a cuppa after all that excitement,' he said.

Hamish was about to protest but stopped himself in time, guessing that his son wanted to be alone with Sally. He couldn't blame him. She was a bonny lass.

'Thank you, son. I'll go in and sit myself down for a spell.' Sally and Doug continued to make their way over to the barn as Hamish walked away to the kitchen porch, where he removed his boots before going in.

'Did you find all the missing ewes?' Liza asked from where she stood at the kitchen sink, scrubbing mud from the home-grown potatoes.

'Aye, they're back safe now, down in the lower Bank Fields. I closed the gates on them for a while so they don't stray right back up there. Grass will always be greener...'

'... and how did the lass enjoy herself?'

'She liked it fine, sits a horse well, too. Loved the countryside! A nice lass altogether. I hope that boy of ours treats her right; she's way younger than his usual pieces but I've nae doubt she would suit him very well.' Hamish voiced out loud the thoughts and fears that had occupied his mind during their ride. Liza recognised that they exactly echoed her own hopes and concerns.

'Well, maybe this time our boy has found someone who will clip his wings and steady his roving eye. She's the first one he's brought home to stay over. I've to agree with you, Hamish, she's very young, but then that might not be such a bad thing. He seems fair taken with her, been stood in that yard for half an hour since, waiting on you both getting back.'

'Aye, that's why I left them alone to feed and bed down the ponies.' Then, still with a twinkle in his eye, he added, 'Daresay he'll need to get some more hay down from the old hayloft ...' As he spoke, he moved behind Liza and put his arms around her waist; she half-turned to glance up at her husband with a shine in her own eyes that matched his. Guessing what his son might have had in mind, he whispered, 'It's been a while since I rolled you in the hay, Liza, my dear.'

'Away with you, Hamish MacDonald! Ye're making me blush!' and she turned back to her potatoes. 'And don't you go getting silly ideas – it'd take me most of my time these days to get up that ladder into the hayloft.'

'Ye never used to think it was silly. And if I remember rightly, it was you that led me astray.' Hamish kissed the top of her head.

'Don't you let my old mother hear you say that, or I'd still be in trouble, even at my age!' Liza giggled like a schoolgirl and turned completely to look up at her husband. The light of love still shone brightly in her eyes for this gentle giant of a man. 'Besides,' she lowered her voice, 'if I hadnae made the first move, ye'd never have left your mother's apron strings.'

Suddenly, Liza's feet left the floor as Hamish caught hold of her, lifted her up in his arms and kissed her soundly on the lips. It was true he had been painfully shy and, although he had worshipped Liza from afar, he knew he would never have had the courage to make the first move. Liza had waited and waited, until one day she had walked straight up to him and kissed him on the lips, bold as brass! He was confident that he would have got around to proposing to her eventually but Liza had run out of patience and had finally proposed to him. Now, 25 years later, he had two strapping sons and a pretty little daughter. He often wondered where Doug got his seductive talents from, certain in the knowledge that it wasn't from him. Iain too, seemed pretty clued up with women. He had come to the conclusion that his sons took after their mother, while his sweet daughter Fiona was like him, very shy.

'My, my, having a couple of lovebirds in the house seems to have given you ideas,' chuckled Liza.

'Aye, them and possibly that new cockerel of yours,' murmured Hamish, still holding her tightly.

'Away with you now! Let me get the kettle on before someone comes in on us,' and, still laughing, Liza wriggled out of his grasp.

Back in the barn, Sally put a feed of oats and chaff into the manger for Molly and Heather while Doug lifted the heavy saddles up on to the racks at the end of the barn and hung each bridle up beside them. When he came back, he leaned over the stable door, watching Sally stroke Molly's ears while the contented pony buried its muzzle in the feed and crunched on the oats.

'The wind and fresh air has dared put roses in your cheeks, and that's my job. Come over here.'

Sally did as she was bid and, walking out of the stall, took hold of Doug's outstretched hand. He pointed towards a wooden ladder that led upwards to a square hole in the roof. Looking up, Sally could see a hayloft.

'Up you go.' Doug raised his eyes towards the opening. Obediently Sally let go of his hand and climbed carefully up the ladder and through into the loft where the sweet smell of the hay reminded her of newly-mown grass on a warm summer's day. Doug had been to the barn earlier and, in anticipation of this moment, had spread out a blue tartan blanket on the soft mound of loose hay among the bales. Sally laughed as Doug followed her and gently pushed her over onto the makeshift bed before dropping down beside her. Lying on her back among the hay bales, Sally stared up at the centuries-old oak beams which supported the barn roof. Luckily she wasn't scared of spiders, for between the beams these permanent occupants of the hayloft had been busy spinning webs. Many of the webs held gossamer-wrapped bundles of mummified insects, evidence of a larder filled by the spider's kiss of death.

Sally sighed. 'Doug, I'm having such a wonderful day.'

'Aye, and it's not over yet.' Doug leaned forward to kiss her and, slipping his hands under her jumper, he began to trace the shape of her breasts through her shirt.

'Doug, you can't! Not here! What if someone comes?'

'Nobody will come. Iain's already away to town.' Ignorant of the antics going on in the kitchen, he added, 'And father will be well asleep in front of the kitchen stove by now'.

His mouth covered hers and she eagerly returned his kisses. Doug held her close in a warm embrace. 'Sal, I was so lonely without you in my bed last night.'

'But we've only spent three nights together,' she gently chided him.

'I know, but I like it that way. You in my bed. I'll need to do something about that, so that it's a permanent arrangement.' He tugged at her jeans and expertly removed them; he began to run his hands over her body and she trembled involuntarily under his touch. Her hands travelled down over his flat stomach and searched playfully inside his already unzipped trousers. Slowly, Sally began to fondle Doug and he gave an appreciative murmur as she gently sought out and caressed his most sensitive parts in the way that he had shown her. She was not shy to use what she had learned. He slid down beside her and, supporting himself on his elbows, moved to lie between her legs, his hazel eyes looking deeply into her blue ones all the while as he slowly pressed himself into her and she raised her hips to meet him.

'Ah! Ha! You're an eager one, and no mistake,' he murmured as he kissed her nose and lay still. 'Not so fast, young lady,' he said, withdrawing himself fractionally from within her.

'Stop teasing,' she whispered, biting at his ear. She thrust her hips against him, urging him back inside her again.

'Oh, no ... I can't resist that!' Doug gasped, teasing at an end. Completely inside her, he began rocking gently. He continued to smile down into her sparkling blue eyes.

'I really love you, Sal.' His mouth slowly covered hers once more and Sally kissed him back, probing his mouth with her tongue. She was completely on fire now and brought herself up to meet him, following and matching his slow rhythm. His kissing and thrusting suddenly became more urgent and he groaned and whispered her name.

Rolling onto his back, Doug held Sally close in his arms.

Sally snuggled up close to him, waiting for the fire within her to settle down. She enjoyed Doug's love-making, the feeling of joining with him in such an exciting and intimate way. Oh yes, she had learned a lot from Doug – how wrong those nuns were to lead people to believe that it would be something that women had to 'endure'. Giving herself to Doug had been a pleasure, not a chore, and it left her feeling naughty, a little guilty even, but always wanting more.

'Mustn't let you get cold, and I think we should put in an appearance for the mid-morning cup of tea.'

'What! Right now? Doug, I don't think I can face your mother. Not just yet.'

'Of course you can. The fresh wind off the hill and galloping Molly put those roses into your cheeks; I just added the finishing touches.' He brushed the hair back from her face and removed a few tell-tale strands of hay from it. 'Come on, trust me, you look just fine.'

They climbed down the ladder, holding hands as they walked across the farmyard. Unaware that they were being watched, they stopped every few paces to share just one more kiss before they reached the house. Removing their boots in the back porch, they opened the kitchen door and were greeted with delight and laughter by Hamish and Liza who were standing at the kitchen table. With a joyful cry, Doug stepped forward.

'Fiona!' Doug hugged his sister and proudly introduced her to Sally. 'Fiona, this is Sally.' Fiona was slim, pretty, diminutive against her brothers and more like her mother in looks; her pale complexion and green eyes were fringed by naturally long dark lashes and her striking dark auburn hair had a strong natural curl which refused to be tamed by the black velvet ribbon attempting to contain it. Sally noticed that Fiona had the same open, easy smile as her brothers. Fiona stepped forward; this time Sally was ready and without restraint the two girls hugged.

'I hear father has been working you already,' Fiona said shyly as the two girls separated.

'It wasn't really work, riding a lovely Highland pony in beautiful countryside.' Before Sally had finished speaking the kitchen door burst open and Sally's tummy lurched as she recognised the girl who stood in the doorway. There was no mistaking that beautiful face; it was the same one that she had seen in the photograph which had fallen out of Doug's pocket.

The jovial atmosphere in the kitchen seemed to change in an instant. Ignoring everyone else in the kitchen, Moira stood in the doorway and looked across at Doug, who was standing at Fiona's side. Without a word, she turned her head to stare at Sally. She had been hoping that the gossip about Doug's new girlfriend had been unfounded but, glancing out of Fiona's bedroom window a few moments before, she had seen them walking across the yard, hand in hand. They were coming from the direction of the hay barn and from their behaviour Moira had a pretty good idea of what had been going on. All the way across the yard, she had seen that Doug couldn't keep either his hands or his lips off her. Now, here she stood, her cheeks flushed, her blue eyes sparkling, and as blonde as Moira was dark. Damn it, even Moira had to admit the girl was a beauty! Her stare took in the long, untamed blonde hair that fell loosely onto Sally's shoulders and immediately she felt that her own raven-black, bobbed style was too severe, despite being the height of fashion. How dare this blonde piece trespass on what was rightfully hers?

It was an awkward moment. They all stood there looking at Moira as she stared coldly at Sally. Doug stepped forward, his arms open to greet her as a friend and ready to give her a brotherly peck on the cheek.

'Moira ...'

Moira quickly closed the space between them and, smiling up at Doug, she threw both her arms around his neck, reaching to kiss him full and hard on the lips. Cursing himself for not realising her intention, Doug quickly removed her arms from around his neck and held her wrists firmly in order to prevent a repeat performance as he took a step backwards.

'Moira ... this is Sally,' he said as he let go of her wrists. Expecting her to turn away to greet Sally, he realised that she had caught hold of his hands; tossing an indifferent 'Hello' in Sally's direction, she held onto him, laughing up at him, as she continued to gaze adoringly into his eyes. Doug felt trapped and foolish as he stood there, embarrassed by Moira's behaviour and unsure what to do or say.

Liza shook her head in disbelief as she stared across at Moira and noticed that while Moira had been upstairs, she had unbuttoned her blouse to expose more cleavage than any decent girl should dare to show. The fashionable broad belt at her waist had been tightly pulled in, accentuating both her tiny waist and the curve of her hips and she had re-applied enough bright red lipstick to look as though she'd been in a road accident. When she had kissed Doug, she had transferred most of it on to his face so that he resembled a pantomime dame! If the situation hadn't been so fraught and embarrassing, it would have been funny. Moira's behaviour angered Liza; it had embarrassed them all, but in particular her eldest.

Sally, meanwhile, had remained rooted to the spot, not knowing quite how to handle the scene that had been acted out in front of her, but well aware that it had been played out for her benefit.

'Hello, Moira,' she'd mumbled, uncertainly.

Hamish was seething at the bad manners displayed by Moira towards a guest in his home; prompted by a look from Liza, he cleared his throat.

'Sally, it's time Cloud and Skip had their lunch. Would you like to help me feed them?' He had never particularly liked Moira; she was far too sure of herself for his liking. There had been a while back there last summer, when it seemed as if she was getting her hooks into Doug. He had been relieved when he realised that his son had not fallen under her spell. He would leave it to Liza

145

to handle the situation. The look she had given him as he left the kitchen left Hamish in no doubt that she would have words to say to Moira once he had removed Sally from the scene.

Sally gratefully followed Hamish through to the utility room, where he handed her two earthenware dog bowls with meat and biscuits already in them.

'Here we are, it's all prepared,' he said, handing her one of the bowls. 'We just have to add a wee bit of warm water to Cloud's biscuits to soften them up. Sadly, the few teeth he has left are not much good to him now,' he said, pouring warm water from the kettle that he had picked up from the range as he left the kitchen. Sally lowered her head, embarrassed by the tears welling in her eyes.

'Now, don't let that silly besom in there bother ye. She set her sights on our Dougie a while ago but he's more sense than to take that one on.' Sally raised her eyes, blinking away the tears and Hamish winked at her, smiling knowingly.

'Besides, I somehow get the idea that boy of mine has made his mind up and I cannae say I blame him. I guarantee old Cloud here will approve his choice, too,' he said. He turned to look behind him, where both dogs were patiently waiting for their feed. Cloud was a pretty good judge of character, he thought, and obviously the dog adored her. Grateful for his words, Sally took Cloud's bowl from Hamish and placed it on the floor.

They stood and watched as the dogs ate, Hamish explaining that this was to make sure that Skip, who could bolt his food down far quicker than his grandfather, did not then attempt to elbow the old-timer out of the way. If there was no human pack leader there to ensure that Skip could be banished as soon as he had finished, he might just find the courage to rob his grandfather of his lunch.

Gradually, Sally regained control of her emotions and couldn't help laughing at the tales Hamish was telling her about the dogs. She knew that this giant of a man was trying to help her and, sensing an ally, gratefully smiled her thanks at him.

When Hamish and Sally had left the kitchen, Liza took charge.

'Moira! I'll no have that sort of behaviour in my home, for whatever reason! D'ye understand that? Ye've been coming here since you were a wee bairn and we've taken you into our family. Ye've been most welcome but that doesnae mean I'll tolerate such rudeness from you, any more than I would the other three. D'ye understand me now?'

Over the years, Moira had grown to love and respect Liza, who was so different from her own mother, and it hurt and embarrassed her to be admonished thus, particularly in front of Doug and Fiona.

Deflated but still defiant, she tearfully looked first at Liza, then at Fiona and Doug as they stood in silent embarrassment, watching her.

Choking back the tears, she blurted out, 'But why did he bring her here? She doesn't belong here, does she?' Seeking reassurance from them and not getting it, she turned and ran out of the kitchen.

'Fiona, go with Moira, please,' Liza commanded her daughter and Fiona too fled from the scene, confused and hurt by her friend's behaviour.

'Mum ...'

'Aye, I know what ye're going to say, son, but there must have been something said or done last summer for her to think you were hers.'

'Mum, I swear ...'

'I dare say ye do, but it needs sorting before someone gets hurt. Get that mess off your face.' And she turned away from him.

Chapter Fourteen

Upstairs in the large bedroom that had become a second home to Moira, Fiona sat on one of the beds and prepared for the tirade she knew would come after Moira's meeting with Doug's new girlfriend.

Fiona loved Moira and was grateful for her friendship, recognising that her life would have been very lonely growing up on the farm without a surrogate sister. When she was small her brothers, out of sight of their mother, had teased and tormented her. They had inherited a sense of humour and fun from both their parents and never meant any harm, but sometimes their pranks would leave Fiona bewildered and tearful. When she had first brought Moira home for tea, the focus of their attention was redirected and the boys quickly realised that, in Moira, they had met their match. Fiona admired Moira's quick-witted retorts and the way in which she had competed with them, and wished she could have been more like her friend. Her easy-going nature had made it possible for Moira to take the lead in all their escapades; as a result, Moira was encouraged to behave as if she was Fiona's older sister.

By contrast, Moira was an only child, born long after her parents had given up hope of having children. From birth, her parents were delighted with their beautiful little girl and had cherished and cosseted her as a precious gift. Until she went to school, Moira had been the centre of adult attention, her every whim indulged. Arriving at school, finding she was just one of many other children competing for the teacher's attention came as a bit of shock to her. It wasn't long before she was teased about being the teacher's pet and a spoiled brat. It was Fiona, finding her sobbing in the corner of the playground one day, who had befriended her and soon Liza invited her to stay at the farm. The two girls would pretend to be sisters and, together with Doug and Iain, the four of them would play together throughout the school holidays; Moira could pretend that Doug and Iain were her brothers too. This happy state of affairs had continued until Moira reached puberty and had earmarked Doug for her very own.

Now she just could not accept that he would choose another instead of her, and had confidently arrived at the conclusion that this clever, calculating blonde had somehow tricked him. Surely, she thought, he would come to his senses now that he was home among his own kind.

Fiona sat nervously on the edge of her old bed while Moira stalked the floor, intermittently swearing, finding fault with Sally and uninhibitedly giving vent to her feelings. As she listened to Moira pouring her heart out, Fiona didn't know whether to feel sorry for her friend or her brother.

'What does he see in her? Just tell me that? What does he see in her?' Moira desperately wanted a cigarette but, mindful of the uproar it had caused some years previously when they had been caught experimenting with their first cigarettes, she dared not light up in the house again, however strong the urge.

'Well ...' Fiona thought she could see exactly what her brother saw in Sally and suspected that Moira could, too. 'We don't really know her yet ... I think we should give her a chance,' Fiona ventured, to answer her friend's questions.

'What?' Moira hissed. 'Give her a chance? A chance to do what? Ensnare him completely? That brother of yours is obviously besotted with her. I bet you he's just fucked her in the hay barn.'

'Oh please don't ...' said Fiona flinching at the language.

'Don't what?'

'Use that word, it's horrible.' Fiona stared at her feet in embarrassment.

'Well, it's the right word to use and if it upsets you then that's just too bad! It's what they've been doing, whichever way you want to put it. What would you call it?'

'Well ... I think I'd prefer to call it "making love".'

'"Making love"?' spat Moira. '"Making love" ...! Which planet are you from? God, Fiona you're so bloody naïve! Your brother has never "made love", as you so sweetly put it, in his life! He's an animal! He uses women! Well ... he has fucked me once too often!'

'Well then ...'

'Well then what?'

Fiona hesitated, not wanting to bring Moira's tirade down on her own head. 'Well ... if he is like you say he is, why are you making such a fuss?' Fiona blanched as Moira turned to stare at her. 'I mean, let her have him,' Fiona said weakly, and fell silent.

Moira stared at her friend for a moment longer, strode over to her own bed and threw herself down on it. Quite suddenly she burst into tears.

'She can't have him! She can't!'

'But Moira ... you just said ...'

'I love him!' Moira whispered through her sobs and tears. 'I love him. He's mine – he's got to be mine ...'

Doug could do no wrong in Fiona's eyes, but then she felt the same way about both of her brothers. If only Moira would forget the stupid idea of marrying Doug, so that they could be real sisters. It was a plan that Fiona had been enthusiastic about herself when they were seven years old but somewhere over the years she had grown out of the idea, while Moira never had.

Getting up from the bed, Fiona fetched some tissues and went to sit beside her friend, putting an arm around her shoulders as Moira sobbed uncontrollably. Handing her the tissues, Fiona doubted if Moira really did love her brother. She suspected it might be the old story of Moira not wanting anyone else to play with the toys she considered her own. She sighed; there was nothing she could do to help either of them. If Doug really had chosen another, she was hopeful that, once Moira realised it, she would probably declare that she hadn't really wanted him after all!

While Moira lay across the bed, sobbing and drumming her fists into the pillows, Fiona's thoughts turned to the girl she had just met downstairs. From the few minutes she had spent with Sally, she thought she seemed very nice. She had a lovely smile, and it was the first time that Doug had ever brought a girl home to meet them all – a significant fact. It must be serious and, from Moira's reaction, clearly she thought so, too.

Fiona glanced down at her friend. She knew that Moira was capable of anything when she didn't get her own way. Fiona guessed that they were all in for a rough time during the next few days but hoped that Moira would not do anything to spoil her parents' party.

After feeding the dogs, Hamish went out into the yard and Sally cautiously returned to the kitchen. As she peered round the kitchen door, Sally received a reassuring smile from Liza and was relieved to note that Moira had disappeared. Seeing Doug sitting at the kitchen table, Sally made her way over to him. He'd removed the lipstick from his face, and now sat dejected and alone at the table, peeling a mountain of potatoes. Liza continued to bustle about the kitchen, occasionally disappearing into the dining room to make it ready for the evening meal.

'I can help, if you like?' Sally volunteered as she sat down next to him.

'Okay, Sal, you can do the carrots,' Doug said with a sigh, and handed her a small peeling knife as he pushed the bowl of carrots towards her.

'Sorry about Moira- she was a bit rude. She'll come round,' he said, glancing anxiously at her.

'I doubt it,' Sally replied, smiling at him. 'I'd better sit with my back to the wall for the next few days.'

Doug laughed, relieved that Sally had taken it so well and that she did not seem too upset by Moira's behaviour.

'I think you're getting the idea. You can see my problem though – she's very determined.'

Sally leaned forward and planted a kiss on Doug's cheek.

'Can't say I blame her.' She held up one of the carrots from the bowl.

'Hey, this one reminds me of you,' she whispered, with a mischievous grin on her face. 'Oh, that small, eh! Cheek! You don't realise how lucky you are, miss,' and they leant towards each other, giggling like naughty children.

They were still laughing, heads together over the peelings, when Fiona and Moira came back into the kitchen. With Moira right behind her, Fiona was only too aware of the impact that such a scene of togetherness would have on her friend.

'What's this? Share the joke,' Fiona said, smiling at the pair of them as she made her way towards the table.

'Private joke, honestly. Nothing very interesting at all. Come on, sit down and tell me about college and if your typing speeds are improving? I don't know why you're bothering to learn shorthand – I can't see any difference between that and the squiggles you call handwriting.'

As Fiona sat down she automatically reached for a peeling knife, happy to help with the preparations for supper.

'Don't start picking on me, big brother,' she said, laughing.

Moira, disdainfully ignoring the mountain of vegetables, sat down opposite Doug and Sally.

'How long are you home for?' Moira suddenly asked Doug, rudely cutting across the cosy conversation between the siblings.

'Sally and I have to leave on Saturday. We're both back at work next week so we'll have Friday to get over the party and we'll have to be off back down south,' he replied, unaware that references to Sally and her inclusion in his travel arrangements were reigniting Moira's already intense jealousy.

Moira pointedly continued to ignore Sally, steadfastly avoiding any eye contact with her rival, but her icy behaviour afforded Sally the opportunity to study her without being accused of staring. Sally's overall impression was of someone worldly, sophisticated and well groomed; petite – but the word 'voluptuous' came to her mind as Moira had left her blouse arranged to show maximum cleavage. Sally could clearly see that she had something that Sally had not: an ample bosom! A striking girl, thought Sally, with her jet black hair cut in a bob and a fashionably long fringe partially covering her eyes, which Sally could just make out were golden, with little specks of green in them.

Dainty long, pale fingers were tipped with beautifully-manicured nails, painted deep red. Sally looked at her own hands; there was no sign now of the manicure that she had carefully applied last Thursday night. This study of her rival had the effect of making Sally feel awkward and clumsy and she wished she had taken the time to go up to her room, brush out her windswept hair and apply a little lipstick; but it was too late now.

Moira, keeping a wary eye on Liza, waited until she had once again hurried out of the kitchen.

'Well, I suppose we should be grateful you could spare the time to come home to see us at all!' she hissed, with barely-concealed sarcasm.

Doug squirmed with discomfort and was grateful when his mother reappeared. He knew his mother's presence would curb the worst of Moira's behaviour and that she wouldn't want another reprimand, quite so soon, from Liza.

'As well as coming home for the party, I thought I might just as well make it a week's holiday and take a few extra days' leave to show Sally around; she hasn't been to Scotland before, so we might go over to Pitlochry tomorrow,' he said, smiling at Sally. 'That's if father doesn't kidnap her again to go shepherding with him before I get up.' He was hoping that Moira would get the message that any spare time he had this week would be spent with Sally.

Moira got the message, loud and clear!

'Oh, but I love Pitlochry! Fiona and I can come along – we need to blow away some of the cobwebs from that stuffy college, don't we, Fi?' she said, looking to Fiona for confirmation and support of her plans.

Fiona paused in the act of slicing a potato in half and stared open-mouthed at her friend. Trapped between a rock and a hard place, and aware that both Doug and Moira were staring at her, waiting to see which she would chose, she felt herself blushing.

'Of course we can all go together – that would be fun,' Sally innocently responded, thinking she was coming to Fiona's rescue. Naïvely, she thought the best thing she could do was try to make friends with Moira.

Doug, who had been willing his sister to deflect Moira's intention to accompany him and Sally on this trip, swivelled his head round to stare at Sally. He had desperately been hoping that his sister would, for once, refuse to go along with one of her friend's ideas. There were things he hadn't told Sally about his relationship with Moira and he was sure that, in her present mood, Moira would relish a chance to exploit Sally's ignorance about them.

Moira could not believe her luck. Sally's response only served to confirm her suspicions that she was a very dumb blonde indeed! Already Moira was picturing the outing as providing her with ample opportunities to outsmart her rival. Ignoring Sally's generous response, Moira continued to address her remarks to Doug.

'What d'you say, Doug? Will that be okay?'

It was Doug's turn to feel well and truly trapped into playing Moira's games. He felt he had no choice but to agree with Sally, even though it meant pandering to Moira's suggestion.

'You heard fine what Sally said, and if it's okay with her then it's okay by me,' he said rather lamely. He knew without looking at her that Moira had a triumphant grin on her face.

How could he have been so stupid? He had always resisted Moira's blatant advances but briefly last summer, in between girlfriends, he'd come home to visit his parents. Moira had been back from college and hanging around the farm most days with Fiona. One warm summer's evening he had been unsaddling the ponies in the barn after helping his father on the hill, when Moira had suddenly appeared and, uncharacteristically, offered to help. With her tanned legs exposed in a pair of shorts and a low-cut sleeveless top, her ensemble left very little to the imagination. They had chit-chatted for a while and, without warning, as he turned from reaching up to put Molly's saddle on the rack, she had wrapped her arms around his neck, stretching up on tiptoe, and had offered him her lips, pressing herself against him. Automatically, his hands had encircled her tiny waist as his lips came down to meet hers. It had been a while and Doug, with his healthy sexual appetite, was hungry. Before he could stop himself they were in the hayloft and he was making love to her. Oh yes, it was good! A little too good for Doug, who wasn't so sure that he liked his women to be quite so experienced. He remembered thinking to himself that the comprehensive list of skills Moira's secretarial college taught wasn't just confined to shorthand and typing!

That summer, Moira was there, willing and available. But in Doug's mind, the whole thing was just another affair and after the holidays he had returned to his job in the south. Putting Moira out of his mind, Doug engaged in several simultaneous new love affairs, as was his style. Too late, he realised how wrong he had been, as it became clear that, as far as Moira was concerned, their brief affair marked the beginning of their life together, just as she had always planned it. She had returned to college believing Doug was finally hers and began sending him love letters. That year, he had refused to go home for Hogmanay, using 'a heavy work schedule' as his excuse. He hoped that his absence from the festive season would give Moira a cooling-off period and fervently prayed she would meet someone else in the meantime. It was not that he did not like Moira; he thought she was both attractive and intelligent, if a little too controlling sometimes, but that was all part of the fun and the challenge. He reasoned with himself that it was probably just that he was not ready for commitment. Then he had met Sally and for the first time in his life knew what it felt like to fall in love.

After a somewhat fraught dinner, Sally slept surprisingly well and woke early to the sounds of the cockerel. Wrapping her dressing gown around her shoulders, she wandered over to the bedroom window. In the field below she could see Rhodey's shiny red and emerald-green feathers as the cockerel perched precariously atop some rusty old farm machinery. Having finished his crowing, he was preening himself for action while eyeing the unsuspecting hens searching for slugs in the long grass. With their heads down and their bottoms up they were easy targets for his 'affection'. As Sally watched, Rhodey leapt from his perch straight on to the back of one of his wives. Moments later he dismounted, only to set off again in hot pursuit of another. Sally giggled as she saw hysterical hens fleeing back to the relative safety of the hen house with the amorous cockerel in hot pursuit.

Yellow climbing roses clung to the wall of the old farmhouse and had grown so high that they framed her window, and some peeped into her bedroom. The sun was not yet warm enough to evaporate the rainbow droplets of dew that each rose wore and they glistened like small diamonds. But down in the valley a thin white mist cloaked the ground and there the early morning sun had enough warmth to lift it off and, little by little, tiny wisps trailed upwards before vanishing. Sally felt relaxed and happy; then she remembered the events of the previous day and braced herself, knowing that an ordeal lay ahead of her. Hearing a quiet tap at the bedroom door, Sally hastily clambered back into bed and pulled the covers over herself.

'Come in.'

Two steaming mugs of tea appeared round the edge of the door, followed by Doug, who smiled briefly but looked serious.

'Good morning! I'm glad you're awake, kitten – we didn't have much opportunity to talk last night.' He placed the mugs carefully on the bedside table and sat down on the edge of her bed.

'It was a bit awkward.' Sally was still at a loss to understand why Moira had been quite so venomous and didn't know what else to say.

'Aye, well, Sal, there's something you should know, before you get told, because I've no doubt you will be!' Doug hesitated. 'It's about Moira and me. You see, I did something very stupid last summer. I wasn't exactly fair to her and I did myself no favours by it either.' Briefly he outlined the events of the previous summer, while Sally sat quietly listening to him with a sinking feeling in her tummy. When he finished, she continued to sit there, staring down at her hands, not knowing what to say. Her silence frightened Doug. 'Sal, I'm being honest with you. It's over, but she won't have it that way. Maybe now she will accept it when she sees how it is with me and you.'

'Did you tell her you loved her?' For the inexperienced Sally this seemed to be some kind of benchmark. Had she been fooled? she wondered; taken in by his declarations of love?; did he mean it, or was this something he said to every female that he made love to? Was she really more to him than any of the other girls that he had known before her?

'No, I didn't,' he explained gently. 'It wasn't like that with her. She was there and she was more than willing.' Her heart sank - so Moira was one of his willing women? She continued to sit in silence, staring down at her hands. Never a good conversationalist in the early morning, she was having difficulty absorbing it all, and struggled to organise her thoughts.

Doug was trying to gauge her reaction to his confession; her silence was unnerving him. 'Come on, Sal, look at me,' he said, taking hold of both her hands. 'I really do love you. You're different. I want you to be mine forever.'

She smiled at the look of concern that showed on his face. 'Forever is a long time,' she said quietly.

'It won't ever be long enough for me, I promise you.' He took her into his arms and tears of relief ran down her face as he kissed her. But when she looked up into his eyes, to her astonishment she saw that his eyes were misty too. Surely men don't cry, she thought, especially not men like Doug?

Having eaten an early breakfast, Hamish was already out by the time Sally arrived in the kitchen. He'd had enough of Moira the previous evening and couldn't be sure of holding his tongue if she started her ceaseless campaign over breakfast. When the last knife and fork clattered to rest on the breakfast plates, Liza, thankful that the meal had passed in virtual silence, ordered, 'Leave the dishes! Off you go and have a lovely day!'

'Well, Doug, you'll be the envy of Pitlochry with these three beautiful lasses in tow. I'm off to the top meadows. See you all this evening.' Iain left the table, chuckling at his brother's truly unenviable situation. Well, it serves him right for playing so close to home, he thought. Everyone knows the golden rule about not crapping on your own doorstep. The trouble with Dougie, he decided, was that the ladies found him irresistible and he couldn't keep his pants buttoned up!

As they walked across the cobbled yard to the car, Doug called out light-heartedly, 'Okay, all aboard'.

'I'll have to sit in the front! I don't travel well in the back – I might throw up!' Moira announced, sweeping past Sally, and before Doug or anyone else could object, she had climbed into the front passenger seat. Without a murmur, Sally opened the back door and sat next to Fiona. Sally and Fiona flinched as Doug slammed the driver's door shut with unnecessary force.

'Sally?' Doug caught her eye in the rear-view mirror. 'We'll be going on the new suspension bridge over the Forth and you'll also be able to see the infamous Forth Railway Bridge,' he said over his shoulder as he drove down the bumpy farm track to the road. 'It's said that they never stop painting it, because by the time they get to one end it's time to start painting it again at the other.' Sally could only smile her response.

As they drove along, Doug tried to break the ice with little bits of local history and information, all the time thinking that this was not what he had envisaged at all! He had wanted Sally all to himself and had been looking forward to showing her his beloved Scotland.

Fiona sat silently during most of the trip, not wanting to say anything that might upset Moira and set her off on another tirade intended to upset Sally. Fiona was quite worn out by her friend's attitude. She had listened and tried to be sympathetic towards her plight all the previous afternoon and half the night as well and, not for the first time, wondered if Moira was just using their friendship to stay close to Doug. At first, she decided she didn't really mind if that was the only reason Moira remained friends with her, but during the last 24 hours she had been embarrassed by her friend's behaviour in front of her parents. So, having smiled and shrugged her shoulders apologetically at Sally when she had got into the car, Fiona had remained silent, keeping her face turned away from Sally and firmly towards the window. She would have liked to chat to Dougie's girlfriend but feared that any sign of friendliness would further inflame the situation. Worse still, she herself might be the target of one of Moira's scathing attacks! Fiona sighed and continued to stare out of the window.

Moira began rummaging around in her handbag and eventually brought out a packet of cigarettes and lighter.

'Don't even think about it,' Doug growled at her.

'Never bothered you before ...'

'Well it does now!'

157

'If it bothers you that much, I'll open the window. Sally, would you like one?' Moira asked sweetly.

'Sally doesn't smoke – and neither do you in my car!'

'Oh, really? She doesn't smoke? Why am I not surprised?' Her sarcasm was undisguised.

'I'm warning you, Moira, that's enough!'

Replacing the cigarette, she tossed the packet and lighter back into her bag and reached across to pat him on the thigh.

'My, my! Aren't we tetchy?'

Doug grabbed her hand. 'Moira, if you carry on like this I'm driving to the nearest railway station where you can wait on the next train back into Edinburgh!'

Trying to close her ears to the bickering from the front of the car, Sally turned to gaze out of the window. The views on the drive up to Pitlochry were truly spectacular and Sally decided to concentrate her attention on appreciating the beauty of her surroundings. Eventually, Doug pulled into a small car park in a wooded clearing. As soon as they were all out of the car, Doug caught hold of Sally's hand, allowing his sister and Moira to walk ahead. Moira had already marched off ahead of all of them, crossing over a small footbridge and lighting a cigarette as she went. Fiona was left to make her way across the bridge on her own and as she reached the other side she turned round and called back to her brother and Sally.

'Come on, you two, don't get lost!' though what she really wanted to say was, 'Please don't leave me alone to deal with Moira while she is in this mood!'

Doug squeezed Sally's hand. 'I'm sorry, this is turning out to be such a rotten day for you. I must really be naïve! I just didn't think Moira would behave quite so badly,' he said dejectedly.

'It's okay, don't worry.' She gave his hand a squeeze back and smiled up at him.

Doug leaned into her and kissed her ear. 'I love you,' he whispered.

'I love you too,' Sally responded shyly.

As they reached the spot where Fiona and Moira were standing waiting for them, they came to a halt and there was an awkward silence. Moira leaned against a tree, drawing agitatedly on her cigarette, blowing smoke into the air above her head.

'Let's see if the wee teahouse is open,' Doug suggested. 'Then after, we can go for a walk around the top road. There's a circular walk that will take us out into the countryside and back around to the village.'

'Walk! How far?' Moira protested.

'Far enough to put some fresh air into your lungs, which they could well do with after all that smoke.

'Huh!' was Moira's response. 'Well, I'm not walking bloody miles!'

'Pleased to hear it! Perhaps you would care to wait until we return. I think I, for one, have had enough of your company just now!'

'Oh really! Well, how times have changed! You couldn't get enough of my bloody company last summer, especially on your blue blanket in the hayloft.' She stubbed her cigarette out with her heel and turned to Sally. 'Has he taken you up there yet?' she sneered.

Sally blushed. It was not the reaction Moira wanted. She hadn't wanted to believe it when she had seen the pair of them sauntering across the yard from the barn yesterday, but now she knew for sure. 'Oh! I see! I guessed as much when I saw the pair of yous coming back across the yard! You couldn't keep your bloody hands off each other!' Moira lit another cigarette and sucked on it greedily, several times in quick succession.

Doug realised that he would be allowing Moira to lead him further into the mire if he jumped to Sally's defence.

'Come along, Sal.' Doug caught her hand and turned to Fiona. 'Sally and I are walking – you two are free to do what you like. Plenty of places round here for an early lunch, so we'll meet you back at the tea rooms by four-thirty. Have a nice day.'

Fiona would have preferred to be a hundred miles away right now, but a glance at her childhood friend showed her that she was needed. Not waiting for a reaction and still holding Sally's hand, Doug walked briskly up the road towards a sign indicating a recommended walking route.

Silently, Fiona reached into her handbag and drew out a bunch of tissues and handed them to her friend.

'I told you this was a bad idea. It would have been much better if we had stayed at home,' she said gently to her distraught friend. 'I really think you should just forget Doug in that way – just be friends, like it was before.'

'Oh, shut up!' Moira hissed. 'What would you know about being in love? Answer me that. What would you know?'

She's right, thought Fiona, what would I know? Although any number of boys had tried to get to know her, shyness had always prevented her from accepting an invitation for a date. So far, she had never been sufficiently attracted to any of them to make her want to spend a whole evening alone in their company. At least, not in quite the same way as her friend always wanted to be alone with the boys that she had met.

As the distance between them and the two girls grew, Doug threw an arm around Sally's shoulder and gave her a hug. 'I'm truly sorry about that. I knew she might be difficult, but even she stepped over the bounds of decency back there.'

Shocked by what she had just heard, Sally remained very quiet, not quite able to get the mental image of Doug and Moira rolling together in the hayloft out of her mind. Not getting a response, Doug took hold of her hand again and they continued along their way in thoughtful silence.

'Sal, are you okay?'

'I'm just a bit overwhelmed. I'll be all right in a while.'

'Come and sit here for a spell – it's peaceful and the view will help. It's a favourite spot of mine,' he said, guiding her towards a fallen tree.

'Oh? And what about Moira? Is it her favourite spot as well?' It sounded petty and Sally wished she hadn't said it.

'Let's have no more mention of her name. I told you in all honesty what happened. That episode in my life is history. I was stupid and it was a mistake, and the sooner she realises that the better.' He took Sally in his arms and kissed her. 'Now, are we going to let her spoil our day? Come on, Sal, I've been so looking forward to spending this time with you.'

Sally looked up at Doug's concerned face, and fervently hoped he was right. Moira was history and he was hers now. She smiled at him.

Chapter Fifteen

Early the next morning Sally sat alone in her bedroom, out of reach of Moira's talons, waiting for the knock at the door that would let her know that Doug was ready to leave. The week had gone by so quickly and already it was the day of Liza and Hamish's wedding anniversary party, which was taking place at a local hotel. Doug had suggested to Sally that they could drive into Edinburgh early in the morning and he would show her a little bit of the old city. He was careful to keep his plans quiet from Fiona and Moira, and warned Sally to do the same. The last thing he wanted was a repetition of their nightmare trip to Pitlochry.

As Sally sat on her bed, she thought about the imminent gathering of Doug's relations and friends, and was still undecided about what to wear to the party. Seeing the end result of her mother's creative talents hanging on her wardrobe door when she had arrived back from work one afternoon, she had quickly packed another couple of dresses. If the party had been a ballroom dancing competition, most definitely her mother's creation would have been the envy of them all!

Undaunted by Sally's less than enthusiastic response to her latest creation and confident that once she saw herself in it Sally would be as enthralled with it as she herself was, Rose had slipped the dress over Sally's head. Zipping it up, she'd tweaked the shoulders so that the black sequin motif sat at the correct angle. Then she'd taken a step back to admire her daughter and her handiwork before dashing off to fetch the long, black velvet gloves and evening bag. In her mother's absence, Sally had cautiously opened the wardrobe door and dared to look at herself in the full-length mirror on the inside. Just as she thought, the pale lemon colour of the dress against her complexion and blonde hair had made her look insipid and, worse still, the excess material from the dropped waist was gathered at the exact point where it would accentuate her hips; it made her look and feel enormous. Rose had smiled proudly as she'd added the 'finishing touch' of black gloves and clutch sateen handbag. Sally felt that she only needed a beribboned yellow straw bonnet and she could have auditioned as an extra for Gone with the Wind!

The dress remained folded in tissue at the bottom of her suitcase, alongside her mother's elbow-length gloves. Sally felt a pang of guilt, knowing that her mother had put a lot of effort into making it for her. Now, having met Moira, she was glad that she had packed a couple of extra dresses and any lingering doubts and guilty thoughts about not wearing her mother's creation vanished. A quiet tapping at her bedroom door interrupted her thoughts.

'Sal,' Doug whispered. 'Are you ready?'

'Just coming,' she whispered back and, picking her wool jacket up off the bed, she made her way quickly to the door.

'Come on – let's get going before those two get up. We can have something to eat in Edinburgh,' he whispered. They crept quietly down the stairs, past the kitchen where they could hear Liza preparing breakfast and out through the front door.

They breakfasted in a little café and walked hand-in-hand through Princes Street Gardens, passed the Scott Monument. Ahead of them, Sally could see the famous outline of Edinburgh Castle dominating the skyline.

'This is lovely!' Sally said with a sigh as she gazed around, enchanted by her surroundings. 'Gardens, castles, shops, cobbled streets and historical monuments. If I had to live in a big city, I wouldn't mind living in Edinburgh. There's so much here and it's all so close by.'

'Well, I have to say I'm relieved to hear that, because I'm being moved back up north to take charge of the Edinburgh-based branch of the company. You see, just before we met, I'd applied for a position up here and I've just had news of the promotion and that my transfer has been approved. I start my new post here in Edinburgh at the end of November.'

Sally was unsure how to react. Her first thoughts were that such a move would mean that Doug would be far away from her, quickly followed by the corollary that it would place him within easy reach of Moira.

'Oh! That's nice for you. You'll be near your parents. And you obviously love being in Scotland ...' She tried to make it sound as if she was really pleased for him, but it came out as a subdued whisper.

Doug stopped walking and, turning to face Sally, he saw the dismay on her face. He realised that she was struggling with her emotions and hurriedly went on to explain.

'I was going to ask if you'd be willing to move up here to Edinburgh with me, Sal.'

Looking into his eyes, she said truthfully, 'I would love to live in Edinburgh with you, but I can't see my parents agreeing to it'.

'Sal! My sweetheart! I am not asking you to live with me in sin! I am asking you to marry me and come up here as my wife! I told you the other morning in the hotel that I am never letting you go.' Before she could respond, Doug pulled her to him and kissed her. As they drew apart he whispered, 'I wasn't planning to blurt it out quite like this. I thought I would select a romantic time and place and propose properly, but when you mentioned that you'd like to live in Edinburgh, I rather overtook myself. Before you answer, I think you should know that I couldn't come up here without you, whatever you say.' Once more he swept her up into his arms, oblivious to the elderly couple who squeezed past them, tut-tutting their annoyance as they tried to avoid stepping off the narrow path and onto the flowerbeds. Unable to stand the suspense, Doug whispered, 'I love you so much, Sal, please, please say yes – say you will marry me.'

She looked up into eyes that sparkled with love and anticipation. His face mirrored his love and her heart filled with joy. Everything he'd said to her she now believed; he'd meant it! He really wanted her. He really wanted to marry her. She'd been right to cast aside her mother's suspicions and warnings.

'What about my parents? I would need their consent, wouldn't I?'

'For goodness sake! Sal, is that a yes?' He was holding her at arm's length and searching her face for a more positive response.

Realising how off-hand her reply had been, Sally smiled. 'Yes, Doug! It's a yes!'

He swept her into a bear hug once more and as their lips met, he fervently hoped that if the park keeper came along he would forgive such behaviour under the circumstances. He had found out on many an occasion in his teens that amorous displays were frowned upon in Princes Street Gardens.

'We'll worry about your parents next week. I'll do things properly and ask your father as soon as we get back down south. Come on, let's have a celebratory cup of tea in Mackie's, then I'm taking you to the famous Edinburgh Tartan Shop. I want to buy you something special. Now! Today! To celebrate! As well as an engagement ring, but we'll get that sorted once I've spoken to your dad. Now that you're almost a MacDonald I fancy you should own a skirt in the family tartan. You could wear it to the party. I think that would be in keeping. What do you say?'

Relieved to think that she might have something special to wear that night and happy in the knowledge that it would be something that Doug had chosen for her, Sally nodded in complete agreement. She was more than happy for Doug to select what she should wear to his parents' party – after all, he was the one that she should be anxious to please from now on, not her mother.

Doug squeezed her hand affectionately and led her out of the gardens up a flight of steps, onto Princes Street and across the road into Mackie's. After enjoying light fragrant tea from elegant china cups and saucers and downing several helpings of the establishment's famous shortbread, they headed along Princes Street to the Edinburgh Tartan Shop.

A bell tinkled as they stepped inside and Sally saw that it was exactly what the sign said it was: a shop full of tartan! Tartan kilts and skirts and bolts of chequered materials lined the walls; stacked ceiling-high, they represented every clan in Scotland and many others besides. 'Ready to wear' kilts hung on rails at one end, while in the centre of the shop tall glass display cabinets held a large selection of traditional highland dress accessories. As they wandered towards the cabinets, Doug pointed to the huge ornate till standing proudly on the counter. On the back of the till was a grubby yellowing notice informing customers that, should they care to give their name to the shop assistant, their ancestry would be traced and matched to a tartan.

Doug whispered to her that nobody went away empty-handed; a tartan would always be found to please visiting great-grandsons or -daughters of long-ago emigrants. He had explained to her over tea in Mackie's that people travelled from all over the world to seek their roots in Scotland and now he proudly pointed out the notice to her as proof of this.

Sally was not too enamoured with the display of authentic birds' claws, set with gemstones and mounted on large pins. It didn't help when Doug told her that they were kilt pins and highly popular. She was revolted at the very idea of incorporating parts of dead animals to wear as a decoration and, pulling a face, she turned away. Spying a beautiful display of silver Celtic crosses and swords similarly inset with gemstones in another cabinet, she walked over to take a closer look. A small sign in the cabinet informed her that these were also kilt pins and she decided that these were preferable to the others.

'Good morning,' Doug greeted the stern-looking shop assistant, using his most disarming smile. The woman gave no sign that she had heard him as she continued to stand tall and straight, staring out across the floor space with her hands lightly resting on the counter. The slim, middle-aged woman had been watching the couple, wondering if these were more browsing tourists or potential customers. Slightly unnerved by her unsmiling stance, Doug decided to try again. He knew that it would do no good to show the assistant he was irritated by her lack of response. He was on home territory now and these stern Scottish women with their fierce looks had even fiercer tongues when provoked. Favouring her with one of his cheekiest grins, he continued, 'I'd like to buy a family tartan, please.'

'Aye? Well, no doubt if you do, you've come to the right place. I expect I

can help you. It's all depending on the name, mind, as to whether or no we have something in stock or whether we have to send away for it. We pride ourselves on having every known tartan but we do occasionally have some smart Alecs coming in here ...,' she paused, looking Doug up and down, 'trying to catch us out.' She had spoken slowly and with no hint of emotion appearing on her thin, angular face. If ever she had seen a smart Alec, here was one standing at the counter now and it didn't pay to be too friendly. Over the years she had become immune to such boyish charms, having been on the receiving end of some elaborate jokes. She still blushed when she recalled the name that had been presented to her by a very charming young man. 'MacHine,' he had told her. Although it was not a name that she was familiar with, she had treated him with courtesy and respect and had spent some time trying to trace the line of ancestry, until eventually, thinking it was a huge joke, he had informed her that the word was pronounced 'machine'! He and his young friends had staggered
. out of the shop shaking with laughter at how easily she had been taken in.

'I think my request is probably an easy enough one for you. It's MacDonald.' Doug watched the woman's face, waiting for her reaction to such a familiar Scottish name, and maybe a hint of a smile, but it never came.

'You're quite right there, Sir. I'll have no problem finding a MacDonald cloth.' She walked briskly and silently out from behind the counter and Sally thought she looked every inch like a schoolteacher. Her hair was iron grey and cut in a mannish style. Her blouse was made of fine white linen, long-sleeved and buttoned up tightly to the throat, where a small brooch was neatly pinned. The blouse was tucked into a smart, calf-length tartan skirt, below which there was just a glimpse of shapeless calves in dark nylons disappearing into thick-soled, lace-up black brogues.

Placing a small wooden stool in front of the wall of tartans, she stepped up and tugged out a roll of material that was predominantly dark green, crossed with narrow lines of blue, black and red. Bringing it to them, she expertly flipped the bolt of cloth, unravelling it across the counter, and invited them to see and feel the quality of the material.

'Aye, that's the one right enough but ...' Doug hesitated. 'I've just had a wee thought. Before I order anything to be made up, would you have a long evening skirt already made that might fit this young lady?'

Her expert eye darted to Sally's waist and without a word she disappeared behind some curtains to the left of the counter. In less than a minute she was back, carrying, almost reverently across her arms, a full-length skirt in the MacDonald tartan.

'Here we are, Madam. Lucky for you the MacDonalds were a prolific clan. Naturally enough, as it's a popular tartan, we carry quite a large stock.'

Briefly, she held the skirt against Sally and as their eyes met, Sally was relieved to see a glimmer of warmth in her eyes. At the prospect of a buying customer, her reserve was quickly thawing. When Sally held the skirt up against herself, trying to gauge the length and fit, the shop assistant suggested that she pop into the changing room at the back of the shop to try it on. Sally smiled her thanks and was rewarded with a surprisingly warm smile in return. Once in the changing rooms, Sally realised with relief that the skirt fitted as though it had been made for her and the weight of the material meant it hung well over her hips. She loved it and couldn't wait to wear it.

While he waited for Sally, Doug had selected a Celtic-style pendant with a deep purple stone in the centre as an extra little gift for her and, in the process, rose even further in the shop assistant's esteem. And so it was that when Sally shyly stepped out of the fitting room, they were both smiling and chatting away like old friends. Sally was thrilled with the skirt and delighted to have something more suitable to wear that evening and, when Doug showed her the pendant, she thought that she had never seen anything more lovely and said so.

With the purchases wrapped and paid for, the happy couple walked out of the shop and along Princes Street. They were engrossed in conversation when suddenly a deep resonating boom made Sally jump. Several pigeons perched on a nearby monument soared into the air, engulfing them in a flurry of beating wings and feathers as they did so.

'What was that?' Sally gasped, looking round wildly. For all the world it had sounded like an explosion, but Doug only grinned. Catching hold of her hand again, he carried on walking.

'You'll have to get used to that if you're going to live in Edinburgh. That'll be the firing of the one O'clock Gun. It's fired every day from the castle battlements at precisely – would you believe – one o'clock.'

'What on earth for?'

'It was originally done so that the captains of ships berthed in the Forth could set their chronometers to the correct time at least once a day while they were in the harbour.'

'What's a chronometer? Is it some sort of clock or a watch?'

'Ah, I can enlighten you, having learnt all about it at school. The chronometer is a navigational instrument invented by a Yorkshireman during the 18th century and used by Captain Cook when he sailed off to explore the Pacific.'

Sally was intrigued by the history of Edinburgh and she was eager to move here and learn more about the whole city. Doug continued to share the facts drummed into him by his zealous schoolmistress, and Sally enjoyed a brief history lesson.

'Originally, they used a ball on a mast on a tall building that dropped down at precisely one o'clock, but occasionally Auld Reekie lived up to its name and produced so much smoke that some days folk couldn't see if the ball had dropped or not. So they decided to use a back-up system and put the gun in. After much banging and firing in different parts of the city, they decided that the battery at the castle was the best place to get maximum coverage. So there it remains to this day. It not only reminds everyone what the time is but frightens the life out of unsuspecting visitors,' he chuckled. 'Let's walk back up through the gardens and have some lunch, then I think we need to head back to the farm. If we boys give father a helping hand feeding the stock this afternoon, Iain and I can get him finished early and scrubbed up in plenty of time for tonight.'

When they arrived back at the farm, the place seemed deserted; Liza had treated herself to a rare trip to the hairdresser and had not yet returned and, thankfully, Fiona and Moira were nowhere to be seen. Giving her a swift peck on the cheek and encouraging Sally to make herself a cup of tea, Doug hurried outside again to search for his father. Having no idea where Moira might have gone or when she would be back, Sally decided not to linger in the kitchen. She took the parcel up to her bedroom and mercifully reached it unnoticed. Carefully unwrapping her packages, she laid the ankle-length skirt out on the bed. She reached into the wardrobe and lifted out a new long-sleeved white blouse trimmed with lace at the neck and cuffs. She had fallen in love with the blouse as soon as she had seen it, and had bought it with a vague notion that she would wear it with one of the skirts that she had packed. Now, placing it against the skirt on the bed, she could see that they would be perfect together. Then she gently arranged the pendant Doug had given her around the neck of the blouse. Standing back from the bed to get a better view of the ensemble, she was overjoyed. It was perfect; her outfit for the celebration tonight was now complete and, with happiness in her heart, she made her way along to the bathroom. After a quick bath and with her hair washed and wrapped in a towel, she returned to her bedroom. Left to its own devices, her naturally wavy hair would dry in a confusion of curls, waves and ringlets. Today of all days she didn't want to resemble a French poodle with a topknot. She plugged in her hair dryer, sat at the dressing table and began to tease her curls out into long straight tresses.

When she'd finished and turned her attention to her nails, she heard someone returning to the farmhouse. By the sounds coming from the kitchen she guessed it was Liza, making a pot of tea. Quietly, she opened her bedroom door and paused for a moment, listening until she was certain that whoever it was in the kitchen was alone. She made her way cautiously down the stairs.

Liza smiled as Sally popped her head round the kitchen door and immediately reached for another mug, waving Sally to sit down at the kitchen table. Sally could see that Liza's usually wayward hair had been tamed into a very smart coiffure. Privately, Sally thought it didn't suit her at all but nevertheless, mindful of good manners, she enthused politely at the smartness of the new look.

'Aye, but nae doubt within an hour or so it will be back the way it always is. It's got a mind of its own,' responded Liza. 'Where's Dougie? Have you seen the girls at all?' Liza asked as she poured the tea.

'Doug went out to give Iain and Hamish a hand and I haven't seen the others. I hope it was all right to have a bath? And I washed and dried my hair and gave myself a manicure,' Sally told her.

Liza guessed that having come back to find the farmhouse empty, Sally had found it preferable to stay close to the confines of her own bedroom rather than run the risk of an encounter with Moira.

'We'll all need to start getting ready shortly and there'll be a queue for the bathroom. It's as well you had the sense to bathe early.'

Liza smiled as she looked across at Sally. The poor lass had suffered quite a bit, being no match for Moira's sharp tongue and withering sarcasm, and this afternoon had wisely stayed out of harm's way. It was such a shame, Liza thought, for these two girls to have met in such circumstances. Liza blamed Moira's parents for spoiling her and encouraging her to expect to have everything she wanted. Liza knew that Moira had set her cap at Doug and she'd not been blind to what had gone on under her nose last summer. What a fool that son of hers had been to encourage Moira. And from the way she had seen Moira behave and the things that she had heard about her, Liza couldn't really blame her son for taking advantage. Liza was certain that Moira was no innocent and suspected she had made all the running; her behaviour now was nothing more than the temper tantrums of her younger days. Pouting, sulking and being generally unpleasant to everyone around, until eventually, to keep the peace, somebody, usually her parents, would give in to her; or, worse, buy her something to help her get over her 'disappointment'. Liza had made it clear to her from the start that that sort of behaviour was not acceptable at the farm and, until now, Moira had been careful to moderate her behaviour in Liza's presence.

Now Doug had brought home this well-mannered, beautiful young lass, who was rapidly winning all their hearts. Well, he had created this uncomfortable situation and now he would have to put things right. Liza knew that Moira had not yet given up and, as her eyes met Sally's over the rim of their mugs, she silently prayed that this lovely young girl would still be here when Moira's fury had blown itself out. Just then, they heard the sound of laughter and men's voices and the noise of the outer porch door slamming shut, heralding the arrival of Hamish and the boys.

'That's good – the boys helping Hamish means he's finished nice and early,' said Liza, getting up from the table to make a fresh pot of tea. 'Now all we have to do is get them all cleaned up and smelling sweet.'

Doug was first through into the kitchen, looking happy and relaxed. Behind his mother's back, he swiftly pecked Sally on the cheek as he passed by her on his way to the teapot.

'You girls not getting yourselves fancied up yet? You've only got two hours,' he teased them. His mother flicked the tea towel at him, laughing, as he dodged away out of her reach. Iain and Hamish had followed Doug into the kitchen and over to the range and the teapot.

'Well, are we all set for tonight, ladies?' Hamish enquired. 'I can see Liza has been to the sheep shearer. Mind, I have to say he's done a good job with the clippers; the cut looks very bonny and suits you well. Takes years off ye,' he said, chuckling.

'Away with you, Hamish, and wash the perfume from the sheep off yourself!' Liza laughingly chided him. Having collected a mug of tea from Liza, Hamish sat down to join Sally at the table.

'Would you like more tea?' Doug called over to Sally as he held the teapot aloft, and she took her empty mug over to him. Liza saw the look that passed between them. He was her elder son and she wouldn't have stood between him and any girl that he chose, knowing that in doing so she risked losing him. She hoped that when he finally made his choice, it would be someone like Sally, or even Sally herself. For she could think of no other reason why he had brought this girl home to meet them all, if not for that very purpose.

When the tea was drunk, the men began to make their way upstairs and Sally stayed just long enough to help Liza clear away the mugs, before she made her way back up to her bedroom. Not a moment too soon, for just as she left the kitchen she heard Moira's voice raised excitedly as she came in from the yard with Fiona.

Apart from her underwear, Sally's clothes for the evening were still laid out on the bed where she had left them. Sally took off the trousers and top that she had put on after her bath and, opening a drawer, lifted out a pale blue bra, panties and suspender belt set. Changing quickly into the new silk undies, she carefully slipped on a pair of sheer nylons and attached them to the suspender belt. She reached for the blouse and thrust her arms into the sleeves before struggling to do up the tiny pearl buttons hidden among the lace that decorated the front. Then, carefully, she dropped the tartan skirt over her head and buttoned it at the waist. Glancing in the long mirror on the wardrobe door, she reassured herself that it hung perfectly, without drawing attention to her hips. She sat at the dressing table and scrutinised herself in the mirror. The blouse's white lace frill stood up all around the base of her neck before lying against her skin as it plunged into a modest 'v' which came to a point just above her bosom. She rummaged among her bag of hair ornaments and found a black velvet ribbon. Pulling her shining hair back from her face, she used an elastic band to secure it in a loose ponytail at the nape of her neck and expertly folded the ribbon over the band to conceal it, finishing with a neat bow. Make-up had never been her strong point, but spurred on by the thought of Moira's immaculate grooming, she set about making an extra effort. With the mascara making her big blue eyes look even larger, she aimed a dab of pink lipstick at her lips and decided that that would do!

Carefully she reached for the pendant. The clasp was so tiny that it took several attempts, making her arms ache as she reached continually behind her neck trying to do it up. Finally she gave up and flipped the pendant round to the back to bring the clasp to the front and see what she was doing. The chain sat perfectly around the neck of her blouse and the pendant nestled among the lace just where the 'v' came to an end. Shyly she peeped at the mirror for one final look and allowed herself a smile – for once she quite liked what she saw. Slipping her feet into a pair of black patent sling backs, she was satisfied that she could do no more.

Taking a deep breath, she made her way down into the large sitting room where it had been agreed the family would gather for a 'wee dram' before they set off for the party.

Sally had assumed that Doug would be wearing a suit, but there he was in full highland dress. He looked up at her as she stood admiring him from the doorway.

'Kitten, you look fabulous,' he said, rising to meet her as she came across the room towards him. Grateful to find him alone, Sally caught her breath – he looked so devastatingly handsome. His height and physique set off to perfection the highland dress he wore so nonchalantly. The black velvet jacket, with a froth of white lace at his throat, suited his colouring and his newly-washed hair was as black as his jacket. She gazed at him adoringly as he held her at arm's length. In return, she could see the love and affection for her in his eyes.

'Just let me look at you ...' he whispered. Then, as he was about to lean forward to kiss her, the door opened again and Iain and Hamish, also wearing the MacDonald tartan, joined them. Hamish cocked a quizzical eye at Doug when he saw Sally was wearing the family tartan, but said nothing. Instead he went straight to the sideboard and began to fill glasses with whisky from the crystal decanter and hand them round.

'Well, Dougie, that's a rare woman ye have there. Not only a bobby-dazzler, but can get herself ready on time. I expect your mother will be last down as usual. I've no' changed her in twenty-five years and I doubt it's worth trying now!'

They were laughing at his comment when the door opened and in came Fiona and Moira. The latter swept into the room looking radiant, confident and very sophisticated. Her hair and make-up were immaculate and she had chosen to wear a long black dress: velvet, figure-hugging and nipped at the waist. Around her tiny waist she wore a red leather belt which matched the leather clutch bag she carried. As she entered, Sally caught a glimpse of scarlet petticoat and red patent-leather shoes peeping out from beneath her dress. Enviously, she watched as Moira skilfully tossed her head, making her hair swing back and forth like a silky black curtain. The sight of it made Sally wish she had made more effort with her own hair instead of just tying it back with an elastic band and a black velvet ribbon. Vivid red lipstick made Moira's teeth look whiter than ever and Sally noticed that even her red-painted nails exactly matched her accessories. She had to admit it, Moira looked stunning and the very epitome of sophistication.

Fiona wore a cream lace blouse that suited her complexion and complemented the rich auburn hair that framed her sweet face and gentle expression. The blouse was beautifully teamed with a full-length silk skirt which at first Sally thought was black, but as Fiona moved across the room and the light caught it, she could see was actually a deep, rich emerald green.

'More bonny lasses! Here we are, ladies,' Hamish handed each of them a glass of whisky. 'Ah! Here's my Liza! Last as usual, but not least. Looking a picture and not a day older than the day I married her.'

'Away with you, Hamish,' Liza retorted, giggling like a schoolgirl at her husband's compliment. The fire and passion that she had uncovered 25 years previously still burned strong between them. She loved him now as much as she did on their wedding day. Liza made her way over to Hamish, putting a hand lovingly up to his cheek as he bent to swiftly plant a kiss on her lips.

Sally thought they made a handsome couple; Hamish in his MacDonald tartan kilt and Liza wearing a sash of the same tartan draped over her shoulder. The sash was held in place by a beautiful silver brooch depicting a handsome stag with a magnificent set of antlers, his head thrown back in a call. Around her neck was a silver chain with an emerald-green pendant that Hamish had given her earlier that day.

'A keepsake to remember our special day,' he'd said and he'd kissed her. Now he gazed lovingly down at his Liza, who looked markedly different to the harassed farmer's wife in charge of a kitchen with three hungry men to feed. Liza wore a long black velvet skirt teamed with a silver satin blouse and the MacDonald tartan sash that Hamish had given her years ago; he felt a proud and happy man.

Once his mother had been handed her glass, Doug let go of Sally's hand and stepped forward.

'As the eldest, I feel it falls to me to make the first toast of the evening. Please raise your glasses to a champion mother and father,' he glanced towards Iain and Fiona, 'and may we follow their fine example by making the same wise choice in our partners for life.'

'Hear! Hear!' chorused Iain and Fiona.

'To mother and father!' Doug raised his glass and his gaze fell meaningfully on Sally as they exchanged smiles. The rest of the family, busy toasting Hamish and Liza, hadn't seen the look that had passed between them, but Moira had and inwardly she seethed. To her, the look was a blatant declaration of Doug's true feelings for Sally. Coupled with his choice of words, she was in no doubt as to where this was leading.

Suddenly, a cacophony of frantic yelping and barking erupted from the hall as Cloud and Skip announced the arrival of the two taxis to take them all to the hotel.

'Come along, folks! It's party time!' Hamish said, putting his glass down and ushering everyone out towards the waiting cars.

Chapter Sixteen

By the time they arrived at the hotel, relatives had been gathering for some while and there was quite a crowd waiting in the reception hall to welcome the anniversary couple. The hotel manager was on the steps to greet the main party and he stepped forward to open the door of the first taxi. Taking charge of the couple and using his arms as a gentle barrier to fend off the many well- wishers, he manoeuvred the immediate family through the throng to the ballroom. Proudly, the manager showed them the tables laid out in readiness for the celebratory dinner before guiding them to the top table, where a large white cake with silver decorations was placed as the centrepiece. Liza was thrilled with it all. Having checked that everything was to their satisfaction, the manager suggested that perhaps Mr and Mrs MacDonald, together with their children, might like to stand in the doorway to welcome each of their guests as they filed into the ballroom.

As the manager had led Liza and Hamish to their table, Sally had paused at the entrance to the ballroom. She turned and realised that Doug and Iain had been swept away into the arms of their relatives. Keen to hear all the news, Fiona, too, had disappeared into the throng of waiting guests and, to her dismay, Sally found herself standing next to Moira in the doorway to the ballroom. Moira saw the look on Sally's face as she realised she had been left with just herself for company.

'Why would a Sassenach want to wear the tartan?' Moira sneered, looking down her nose at Sally's skirt.

'Doug bought it for me this morning in Edinburgh,' Sally mumbled, frantically casting her eyes about in search of Doug.

'Oh, did he, indeed?' Moira's eyes flew wide open, but just as quickly she smiled, ever so sweetly, catching Sally unawares. 'How canny of him to buy you one as well.' Sally was about to excuse herself politely and move away, but she hesitated.

'He likes his ladies in uniform –"tartan for his tarts"! It's a bit of joke, you know – marks you out as one of his conquests.' Seeing Sally's eyes widen, she knew she had hit her mark. 'Oh? Did you think you're the only one he's bought the family tartan for? Sorry to be the one to disappoint you.' Moira smiled at the look of shock on Sally's face. 'I've got one myself somewhere at the back of my wardrobe,' Moira lied, enjoying Sally's obvious discomfort.

The truth was very different. When she had walked into the sitting room earlier that evening and seen Sally standing there in a skirt of the family tartan that looked as though it had been made for her, she could have screamed. She had hinted to Doug all through last summer how she would be willing to show him her 'appreciation', were he to buy her something in the family tartan. For a time she had been tempted to buy something in the MacDonald tartan herself, but decided it would be more meaningful to persuade Doug to purchase it for her. She had been looking forward to renewing her efforts, but now she knew it was highly unlikely that he would ever do so. She was jealous, more jealous and angry than she had ever felt about anything.

Sally stood like a statue, trying to absorb the impact of what Moira had said about the wearing of a tartan skirt. Was it true? 'Tartan for his tarts.' It couldn't be! Could it? Oh, where was Doug? Would everybody be laughing at her? Would he do that to her? No, he wouldn't, he couldn't. Frantically she looked round, still trying to find him. Once again, Sally was about to make her excuses and move away.

'Still, like father, like son, they say. I expect the old man has had his hand on your backside a few times already? No?' Moira let loose a peel of laughter. 'Why ever did you think he wanted to take you riding?'

As Sally opened her mouth to explain, Moira ruthlessly continued, 'Well, whatever his pathetic excuse was, let me assure you his motives would have been far from honourable!' Moira saw Sally's eyebrows draw together in a frown as a puzzled look came over her face and quickly added, 'This is all a bloody sham! Tonight! This celebration of their love! Hah! Hamish has tried every which way to get me into his bed, but I was having none of it, my dear Sal! If he hasn't tried you out yet, believe me, he soon will! I could tell you things about these MacDonalds that would curl even that lifeless mop on your head.'

Sally had noticed that Hamish was always in a bad mood whenever Moira had been around during these last couple of days. Would that explain the reason? Hamish? No, surely not! The phrase Moira had used rang alarm bells in her head: like father, like son.

'As for Doug, well, let me tell you, Sally, he'll never marry you; he'll fuck you until you bore him and then he'll be off looking for something a bit more exciting. Believe me, look how he treated me! A vague promise of marriage, up in the hay barn and he was off, away down south.' Sally stood in silence rooted to the spot. She wanted to walk away but she couldn't make herself leave.

'You make him feel safe, you see – you're "South of the Border" and he'll have to start flat-hunting soon. So in your case, he'll be away up here, "North of the Border",' Moira laughed. 'You did know that, didn't you? That he's coming back up here, to Edinburgh, with his job?' Moira was enjoying this one-sided conversation. 'Did you know that, Sal?' she repeated the question. Even in the dim light of the hall Moira could see that Sally was as white as a sheet, and she grinned maliciously.

'Well, if you didn't know that yet, then I'm sorry to be the one to tell you, but maybe that skirt is his way of saying "Thank you and farewell".' Moira casually lit a cigarette and as the smoke drifted across Sally's face, it caught in her throat, making her cough. It brought her out of the numbness that had taken hold of her senses; her thoughts were racing around inside her head with all the things that Moira had divulged. Surely none of it was true? Doug had already told her he was moving back to Edinburgh, so yes, she did know that, but the tartan skirt? Hamish? She wanted to ask Moira more about his vague promise of marriage; was Doug being vague when he had asked her too? No, surely not. Just then, she heard Hamish calling her name. He was making his way over to them; while Liza had continued to be engrossed in conversation with the ingratiating manager, Hamish could see from across the ballroom what was happening in the doorway. Where was that son of his? What was he about, leaving Sally alone with Moira like that? Well, whatever it was that the little minx was up to, he would put a spike in that malicious tongue of hers. 'Sally!' he called to her across the room. 'Will ye come over here a while, please?'

Mechanically, Sally obeyed, relieved to have an excuse to walk away from Moira. Struggling to make sense of it all, she walked stiffly over to join Hamish. Her head was filled with the many possible reasons why Hamish had been kind to her, ones which would certainly explain his evident dislike of Moira. Was that it? she wondered. Had she really been so blind? So stupid? Naïve! That was the word. And here he was again; was it kindness or was there some hidden agenda? As she approached Hamish, he held out a hand to her and Sally, carefully studying his face, could read nothing but concern under those bushy grey eyebrows.

'I want ye to stand in the line next to Dougie – he'll be back presently,' Hamish said, giving her hand a squeeze as she reached his side.

Moira was livid at the interference but, not to be outdone and for the benefit of anyone who was watching, she wandered nonchalantly along in Sally's wake. Just at that moment, Doug, Iain and Fiona came in search of their parents, and quickly Liza and the manager informed them of the plan to form a reception line. Doug was delighted to see that Sally was included and took his place next to her, unaware that Hamish had just rescued her from the clutches of Moira.

Too late, Moira realised her dilemma. For, having taken up a position just behind Sally, it was obvious to her that she was to be excluded from the family line-up. Hamish saw her standing there but pointedly ignored her. Moira felt trapped and a little foolish. She wanted to leave and join the rest of the waiting guests, many of whom were old friends, but she stayed where she was, a little to one side of the family group. Her own parents had rushed to the sick bed of an elderly relative she had never met and they seldom saw but, as they stood to inherit his fortune to add to the one they had already amassed, their priority as always had been personal gain over friendship. The guests began to file in and, amid the kissing and congratulations for the anniversary couple, Moira's mounting frustration reached new heights when she heard Sally constantly being introduced to family and friends as 'Dougie's young lady'. She moved away, making a beeline towards the waiters standing nearby with trays of drinks ready to offer to the guests.

Among the tall glasses of orange juice and dainty little glasses of sherry she spotted the tumblers used for a 'wee dram of whisky'. Swiftly, she snatched a whisky from the tray and, throwing her head back, downed it in one gulp. She quickly replaced the empty glass on the tray and helped herself to another, before she wandered away to mingle with her friends.

The four-course dinner was soon over and the toasts began. Sally noticed that, without any prompting, individual guests would suddenly stand up to propose a toast and the longer it went on, the more hilarious the toasts became. The food, wine and gentle good humour that surrounded the occasion had a calming effect on Sally's jangled nerves. Happy and relaxed, she laughed along with everyone else, even though, with the Scottish accents liberally laced with alcohol, she could barely understand a word. Eventually, Hamish got to his feet among the ribald laughter and it seemed to take an age before everyone was sufficiently hushed to allow him to speak. Holding his glass aloft, he looked down at his wife.

'Liza, it seems like only yesterday that we made our vows, but I don't recall reading anything in the small print about having to raise those two young rams!' He smiled, giving a cursory nod in the general direction of Doug and Iain, and a ripple of laughter circled around the room, with several heads nodding in agreement at this apt description of his two sons. 'But you did a good job on that pretty little filly of ours, Fiona,' and he raised his glass towards his daughter, who blushed to find herself the centre of attention. 'However, there's one advantage to having a couple of strapping lads on a farm ...' he paused as more laughter rippled around the room, 'apart from the obvious one of a couple of extra workers. And that is, that they bring home such pretty girls between them – and none prettier than Sally there, sitting beside our eldest.' Hamish smiled across at Sally. Like Fiona a few moments before, Sally turned bright red with embarrassment at having been singled out. But it wasn't just the compliment that Hamish had paid her that had made her blush. As she looked up and across the room, her eyes locked with Moira's and Moira mouthed one word: 'See?'

Quickly, Sally averted her gaze and turned her attention back to Hamish, but Moira couldn't believe her luck! It would be so easy from now on, she thought, to convince Sally that what she had said about Hamish was true.

Sally's heart was pounding against her chest and she lowered her eyes to her lap. What if Moira had been speaking the truth? Could Hamish really be that deceitful? Like father, like son – what did that mean? Doug had spoken about 'willing women'. Had he learnt that from his father? Sally wondered. And the MacDonald tartan – was that, in fact, a message to everyone to tell them that she had been seduced by Doug and was soon to be discarded? After all, she thought, wasn't that exactly what he had done to Moira? Oh, it couldn't be true! Sally didn't know what to think. For goodness sake, Sally Phillips, she said to herself. All those years at an all-girls convent school, watching and listening to all that bitching and backbiting. Isn't that just what they used to do – stir up trouble and upset with their lies and snide remarks? Could that be what Moira was doing now? Why am I struggling to believe that Moira could be just as wicked? 'Now ...' Hamish cleared his throat. 'I dinnae want to speak out of turn, but I've a feeling Sally there might just be the one to clip our Dougie's wings for him.' At this several of Doug's male cousins and friends began to wolf whistle, banging the table; under the influence of the best malt whisky, lewd comments could be heard about Doug's past record and success with the ladies.

Hamish held his hand up. 'No, no ... joking apart ... it must be a serious situation, you see ... he's already bought her the MacDonald tartan.' There were further whoops and shouts from the around the room and when it died down Hamish continued. 'Aye, and in our family that's just one step away from the ring.' The room exploded in a thunderous uproar of applause, whistles, stamping of feet and banging on the tables.

Sally's head shot up at the mention of her skirt. What Hamish had just said was exactly what Doug had said to her: 'Now that you're almost a MacDonald, I fancy you should own a skirt in the family tartan'. Doug reached out to her and squeezed her hand, and Sally turned towards him. Of course Moira was lying, she was sure of it now, and she smiled happily at Doug.

'Aye, but she'll need a ring to put through his nose like the bull that he is!' she heard someone shout, and someone else called out, 'Or else she'll no ken where he is aw' the time!' It was the signal for more light-hearted ribaldry. Waiting until it quietened down, Hamish raised his glass high and there were calls for hush.

'Thank you for everything you've given me, Liza, and here's to the next twenty-five years, my darling. And to all our kith and kin, ladies and gentlemen, we wish to thank you for coming here tonight to join with us in our celebration of this special occasion. And now, will you all be upstanding to toast the best wife and family a man could ever wish for!'

It was the final toast of the evening and when it was over the waiters began whisking away the remnants of the meal. The tables were quickly moved to one side of the ballroom and the band struck up The Anniversary Waltz. Hamish, to cheers and applause, made a grand flourish in his kilt as he whirled Liza out onto the dance floor to begin the evening's dancing. After leaving them in the limelight for a minute or so, Doug took Sally's hand and joined his parents, and before any of the young bucks could claim her, Iain led Fiona out for the first dance of the evening to complete the family set.

Through a haze of smoke and alcohol, Moira watched Doug's arm encircle Sally as he led her in the waltz, jealousy oozing out of her every pore. It should be me out there – the stupid man, he was blind with infatuation. Well, she decided, the night was young yet, plenty of time to point out a few things to him about his precious Sally. Suddenly, a firm hand grabbed hers and before she could prevent it she found herself whisked onto the dance floor, nearly losing her balance in the process. It was Duncan, an old school friend of Doug's, a giant of a man, powerfully built and with a shock of red hair. Moira detested him but she was in danger of falling over, as she'd had quite a few whiskies, so she had little choice but to cling desperately to him while he hurled her around the dance floor at an alarming pace. Misinterpreting her need to cling to him as desire, Duncan was delighted! He had always fancied his chances with Moira; those pretty lips and that figure of hers! Although she had always spurned his advances, he was too vain to take it seriously – after all, didn't girls say nay, when they really meant aye? Tonight he hadn't given her a chance to refuse to dance with him and it had worked. For here she was in his arms – and hadn't she just flung her arms around his neck? More than that, she was still hanging there and pressing herself close to him. Man, she was hot! No resistance now, he thought, as he grinned and pulled her closer. When the waltz ended, he tried to kiss her but Moira wriggled out of his grasp and hurried away. As she left him standing there in the middle of the floor, he threw his head back and howled like a wolf. As far as Duncan was concerned, the chase had only just begun!

Doug escorted Sally off the floor and led her towards to a group of his friends but Liza, keen for kinsfolk to know Sally better, intercepted them. She took Sally by the hand, saying she would like to introduce her to some relatives. Not wanting to be quizzed by his aunts, Doug reluctantly let her go and settled down at a table with Duncan and some other friends. Seizing her chance, Moira made her way to his table. Duncan jumped to his feet, convinced that she was heading in his direction. After the way that she had clung to him throughout their dance he was certain that Moira must have felt his all-too-evident desire for her beneath his sporran. He stepped forward, grinning. 'Ye cannae resist me, eh?' He leered at her wolfishly, opening his arms wide, ready to scoop her up into them. Finding her path to Doug blocked by the red-headed buffoon, Moira pushed him aside as she laughed in his face. 'Not you – him!' she said, pointing to Doug. 'Come on, Dougie – it's my turn.' A chorus of cheers went up. Doug shuffled uncomfortably. Egged on by his friends and suspecting that Moira had had far more than her fair share of drink – increasing the risk of a scene if she didn't get her way – he acquiesced. Grinning sheepishly at his friends, he got to his feet. Taking Moira's outstretched hand, he allowed her to lead him back onto the dance floor. She draped her arms around his neck, pressed close and sighed contentedly as she felt his hands move to her trim waist, steadying her as she swayed in time to the music.

'Mmmm ...' Moira murmured appreciatively. 'Just like old times, isn't it, Doug? Before that blonde tart turned your head.' Her head rested against his chest and, as he looked round at the sea of faces, he was aware that his friends were looking on in amusement and making lewd gestures. He suspected that they were probably taking bets as to who he would end up with by the end of the night.

'Sally is not a tart,' he hissed back at her through clenched teeth.

'Don't be so blind – you only have to look at her to see it.'

'To see what?'

'To see her for what she is! A blonde floozy! All legs and no brains. My, she's really fooled you, hasn't she? Blinded you to the obvious, she has.'

Doug tried to block out Moira's snide comments, but she persisted.

'I don't doubt she's been around the block a few times. Is that it? Is that why you like her?' Moira looked up at Doug.

'Sally is not a "floozy", neither has she been "round the block", as you so eloquently put it.'

They danced on in silence and Doug began to think that this had not been a good idea. He'd consumed a fair quantity of wine and champagne as well as a couple of whiskies, and now the closeness of Moira's voluptuous body pressed up against his and her familiar seductive perfume was making his head spin. It was as if she were casting a spell on him, pulling him back to a certain time last summer, attempting to reignite something of the spark they had shared.

Moira, sensing a change in him, knew she was getting the reaction that she had been hoping for. Pulling herself still closer to him, she raised herself on tiptoes to whisper in his ear.

'Tell me, is she better in the hay than me?' and she brushed her lips seductively against his earlobe in the process.

Doug straightened up. He had automatically lowered his head as they had swayed together in time to the music but now he took up a more formal pose with her, holding her firmly away from his body. He didn't trust himself to answer her and his eyes began searching the room for Sally, his mother, any excuse to leave the dance floor safely without a scene and end this dangerous situation.

Despite her large intake of alcohol, Moira was still in sufficient control to choose her words for maximum effect, and she played him like a fish on a line. 'Come along now, you didnae fall for the one about you being only the second person she's slept with, did ye?' she whispered in honey-sweet tones like a mother soothing a troubled child.

'No!' Doug jerked her closer to himself. 'I was not the second!' he whispered fiercely in her ear. 'And, to answer your previous question, even lacking your wide and varied experience, yes – she is better in the hay than you!' he hissed at her through clenched teeth. Angry with himself, angry with Moira, angry with the situation that he found himself in, his temper was almost out of control.

Moira threw her head back and laughed, knowing that as she did so it would expose more of her cleavage, and hoping that Doug would be unable to resist the desire to renew his acquaintance with her ample bosom.

'Are you telling me that you were her first? I don't believe it. A virgin! You got yourself a virgin? Oh, Dougie! Sweetheart! I'm sorry, but did you really believe that? Is that what she told you? That you were the first?'

'She was telling the truth. I know she was. It wouldn't have mattered! I love her anyway, so she had no reason to lie.'

'You love her! What do you mean, you love her? You've hardly known her five minutes!' She tried to sound amused, but Doug's open admission of his feelings had shocked her. Love was a word that she had never heard him use before.

'I know her well enough to know that she is the one I want, so please don't spoil my parents' evening by carrying on this way. You and I can still be friends Moira, if you will.'

'Friends!' Moira spat the word out. 'Friends? I want more than friendship. Besides, everyone knows that one woman alone will never keep Dougie MacDonald satisfied.' She pressed herself against his groin to cover the hand she had insinuated behind his sporran. She could feel the hard swelling through the thickness of the kilt material. 'Ah yes! Just as I thought, the Beastie stirs! I know you well, Douglas MacDonald – I've known you a long time and I know you'll be back.'

Doug grabbed her wrist and towed her off the dance floor, wishing with all his heart that he had done so before the nearness of her had aroused him, and before she had made him lose his temper and divulge personal confidences.

In his fury, he had told her things that were nobody else's business but his and Sally's. Doug left her standing on the edge of the dance floor.

Emerging from the cloakrooms a few moments earlier, Sally had scanned the room for Doug as she threaded her way through the crowd, nodding and smiling politely to his relatives, making her way back towards the family table. None of the family members were at the table and, as Sally sat down, to her dismay she saw Doug dancing with Moira. Watching them together, she noticed how closely Moira clung to him and her heart missed a beat when she saw the determined way in which he tugged Moira off the dance floor. For a moment she lost sight of them both until, with relief, she saw Doug striding purposefully towards her.

'Are you okay?' she asked him as he flung himself down in the chair next to her, his face still flushed with anger.

'Aye!' was all he could say, in response both to her concern and to a passing waitress who was offering him a drink.

Clearly he was angry and Sally didn't know what to say. For a few moments they sat in silence, watching the couples twirl around the floor. Then, as the band struck up a Highland Reel, Doug, now more in control of his feelings, leaned towards Sally and placed his hand on hers.

'If you're coming up to Scotland to live, we'll have to get you started on some Scottish country dancing. D'you fancy giving it a go?'

'I know a few of the dances already,' Sally smiled at him.

'Don't tell me yon nuns were country dancers as well!' Doug hooted with laughter.

'No, we had a Dance Mistress; she was a very sophisticated French lady. Our first lesson with her was hilarious. We were in the large Assembly Hall and although we all had to wear soft indoor shoes so as not to damage the parquet flooring, she still made us take our shoes off before she would instruct us in Scottish Dancing! One or two girls had smelly feet and she wrinkled her nose and held both hands up: 'Geerls! Geerls! Dis odoure! It ees most unbecoming!'

'Nuns! You were taught by nuns?' They had been so engrossed in each other that neither of them had noticed Moira eavesdropping from the other side of the table. Knowing that she'd ruffled his feathers and that what she'd said about one woman not being enough to satisfy him was not so far from the truth, Moira had followed Doug back to the table. Listening to Sally talk about her time at a convent school fuelled Moira's vindictiveness. She knew that Doug had an unparalleled reputation with women and was confident that a simpering virgin wouldn't hold his attention for long – she'd put money on it. Now she saw another opportunity to taunt him and, in the process, jaundice Sally's view of her lover boy! She moved in closer, choosing the chair next to Sally, who flinched as though she had been struck. Moira smiled sweetly at her, then leaned across to speak to Doug, ignoring Sally as though she wasn't there. 'Of course! I see it now! A convent schoolgirl!' Between her fingers, she held an unlit cigarette and she waved it at him as she spoke. 'Remind me now, Doug. Wasn't that one of your sexual fantasies – to find yourself a repressed, virginal convent girl and unleash her?'

Doug's father, briefly returning to the table in search of Liza, overheard Moira's crude jibe and bent over to whisper in her ear.

'That's enough of that kind of talk, Moira! I think you need to go outside for some fresh air for a wee while and sober up.'

'No thank you, Hamish. I'm enjoying myself well enough right here,' she replied without turning round. 'Besides, I want to know what Doug meant when he said she ...' – Moira jerked her head in Sally's direction – 'would be coming up to Scotland to live. Well, Doug?'

'It's none of your business, Moira, and you'd be wise to leave the subject be.' This was news to Hamish, too, and he glanced sharply at Doug. So he had plans, did he? Sally, moving up to Scotland? Well, what the devil was the boy about, letting Moira know? Hamish tut-tutted under his breath. Aye, for all his cleverness, at times like this he was putty in the hands of this scheming minx.

Hamish realised that if he stayed he would be in the middle of a brewing row and, to avoid a scene, he wandered away to find Liza.

Moira was undeterred. Waiting until Hamish was out of earshot, she continued with her cross-examination.

'Are you planning on moving her ...' – again she jerked her head in Sally's direction – 'in with you when you come back here?'

'As you seem so interested in our arrangements, I'll tell you and perhaps you'll have the decency to leave us be! Yes – Sally and I will be living together!' Doug said, quickly averting his eyes from Moira's bosom, which was threatening to spill out of the front of her low-cut dress.

Sally felt tears stinging her eyes and hurriedly blinked them away. How could they talk like this in front of her as if she were invisible? As much as she wanted to respond to Moira's jibes, she knew that she hadn't the courage to cause a scene. The ballroom was dimly lit but Sally's face was burning so hotly that she was sure Moira would notice, would see how much her remarks were hurting and humiliating her. All she could do was sit there silently, allowing it to happen. Sally caught the combined whiff of perfume, cigarette smoke and whisky emanating from Moira. It made her feel physically sick and she turned her head away to gaze across the ballroom. As if in a dream, she saw the happy faces and listened to the sound of their laughter and wished that she were a million miles away.

'Hah! You'll be lucky! Convent school virgins don't do that living in sin thing. Oh no! Tut ... how silly of me! I remember now – you're a fast worker, so she'll hardly be a virgin for very long after you've had your hands on her.'

'Moira! Will you leave it now – it's none of your business.'

'Ah! But of course! I was forgetting – she's been in the hayloft! You've already had her!' And Moira threw her head back with a harsh laugh.

'I've asked Sally to marry me, and with her parents' approval we'll marry in the spring. So it won't be a case of living in sin, as you so crudely put it!'

Abruptly he stood up and strode purposefully over to where his parents were chatting with friends at another table, their backs to the dance floor. Moira and Sally, startled by Doug's sudden departure, stared after him as he strode away. They saw him place a hand gently on each of his parents' shoulders as he came up behind them, and bend down to speak to them. They spun round – his mother grasped him in a hug and his father shook his hand vigorously, clapping Doug across the shoulder. Sally and Moira watched, trance-like, as Doug then walked over to speak to the bandleader, who immediately signalled the band to stop playing.

'Family, friends, ladies and gentlemen, could I have your attention for a brief moment? I'd like to take this opportunity, while we're all gathered together, to make an announcement. Sally, would you come over here, please?'

Sally wanted the ground to open up and swallow her, but she made herself get to her feet. 'Remember, girls, when walking across a crowded room, do not slouch! Head up, shoulders back and smile as you glide gracefully across the room ...' She could hear Sister Mary's voice, loud and clear. It gave her the courage to make her way across the crowded ballroom but she couldn't raise the requisite smile. Conscious that all eyes were on her, she kept her own eyes firmly fixed on Doug's, relieved when she could finally grasp the hand he was holding out to her.

Moira sat as if cast in stone, lips slightly parted and eyes unblinking. 'Ladies and gentlemen,' Doug began again as he took Sally's hand. 'There's not much that gets past my father and he was quite correct tonight when he said he'd thought I'd had my wings clipped. This very morning, in Princes Street Gardens no less, I asked Sally if she would marry me and I am very happy to be able to tell you that she accepted my request to be my partner for life. So, without further ado, could I ask you to raise your glasses once more and give a warm highland welcome to my fiancée, Sally?'

The room exploded into a tumult of applause, whistles, foot stamping and shouts of congratulations.

Moira stood up. She wanted to scream, but pride kept her silent and instead she fled unnoticed into the cloakrooms.

Realising what an ordeal this was for Sally, Doug put his arm around her and held her close through the cheers and shouts. When the band struck up again, he led her back on to the dance floor. Sally's emotions had been on a roller coaster throughout the evening and suddenly she felt exhausted. Doug had been watching her closely and saw the colour drain from her face.

'If all this excitement has made you tired,' he said, holding her at arm's length and grinning cheekily at her, 'might I suggest we call up our taxi and go home? The others will have to stay until the end, but we don't,' he finished in a whisper.

'Are you making improper suggestions?' she whispered back to him, her spirits reviving a little as he had spoken. Throughout the evening she had felt under scrutiny from his relatives and friends, and under threat that at any moment Moira might launch another bombardment of taunting slights, so the thought of leaving the party and being alone with Doug, safe in his strong arms, was very tempting.

'Aye – I am,' he whispered, nuzzling her neck.

Sally chuckled. 'Well ... I've always been very curious to know what a Scotsman wears under his kilt,' she whispered back.

He hugged her and they laughed together. Sally might be shy in public, but she was confident and naughty with him in private, and he loved her for it. Moira was so wrong. Sally would be more than enough. She would always be all he ever wanted.

'We'd better go round and say goodnight to a few of the clan, then leave with a little decorum. Better not raise too many eyebrows by just sneaking off.'

Chapter Seventeen

Cloud was fast asleep by the kitchen range and completely deaf to their early return, but Skip was up on his feet and waiting at the door to welcome them.

'Hello, Skip. Sorry we woke you up from your sleep, boy. Away back to your bed now, there's a good dog.' Doug patted the collie's head. 'As for you, my lady, up those stairs you go.'

'No, you go first,' Sally giggled, 'then there's a chance I can take a look up your kilt.'

'Brazen hussy! You don't have to go to all that trouble. I'm more than happy to show you,' he said, pulling her by the hand up the stairs. They fell, laughing, through her bedroom door and on to the brass bed.

'Oh! I love you so much, Sal!'

That night, driven on by his encounter with Moira on the dance floor, there was a hunger in Doug's kisses and he was possessive and demanding when he made love to her. He held her tight and spoke very little, and Sally sensed the tension in him. She enjoyed the strength of the restrained anger within him; strangely it excited her. They fell asleep in each other's arms, sated and exhausted.

Dawn was breaking when a foul smell and a wet tongue awakened Doug. He opened one eye to a close-up view of Cloud's yellowed teeth and a pair of milky soulful eyes staring into his.

'Oh! Shit!' he muttered under his breath and, as he leapt out of Sally's bed, Cloud promptly took his place.

'Thanks, pal,' Doug patted the dog's head. He had not intended to stay the whole night in Sally's bed and, despite the halitosis that lingered in his nostrils, was grateful that Cloud had woken him before anyone else had. Swiftly gathering up his kilt, sporran and the rest of his clothes from where he had carelessly dropped them the previous night, he gently kissed Sally's hand where it lay on the pillow and quietly slipped out of the room, leaving Sally deep in sleep. As he crept naked along the hallway towards his own room, he heard noises in the kitchen – somebody was up and about. Swiftly, he dumped his clothes and ruffled his bed, before climbing into it with every intention of getting a few more hours of sleep. But after a few moments he got up again, dressed and went down to the kitchen instead.

'Cup of tea, son?' Hamish didn't look round from filling his own mug, but reached up and took another off the hooks above the range. He was smiling and chuckling to himself as he did so.

'I think that cunning old dog has crept up to your lass's room again. Did you see him at all?' Hamish asked, feigning an innocent air.

'Briefly,' Doug mumbled, suspicious of his father's chuckles and well aware of the loaded question.

'Aye, he might be getting on a bit, but he's still useful for rounding up the odd stray.' Hamish winked at his son as they sat down at the table. He had looked in on Doug before coming downstairs and, seeing his room empty, had guessed where he was. He didn't blame the boy, but Liza would have something to say if she found out and Hamish, not wanting any more upsets in his house, had positively encouraged the old dog up the stairs. Seeing the door to Sally's room firmly shut, he had quietly turned the handle just enough to nudge it off the catch, and Cloud had done the rest. Hamish had hastily made his way back down the stairs, reaching the kitchen just in time to rattle the cups Doug had heard as he crept along the landing.

'Thanks, Dad.' Doug smiled gratefully at him across the table. 'Where's Mum? She's usually first down. When I heard noises down here I thought it would be her.'

'Aye, an' ye thought ye were for the high jump, eh? Dinnae worry about your mother, son, she won't be down for a wee while yet.' He paused as a grin spread from ear to ear across his face and he murmured, half to himself, 'I think it was all the dancing and celebrating ... it err ... made her tired'.

Doug looked across the table at his father, who wore a smile like the Cheshire Cat. Well, the randy old devil, thought Doug as realisation dawned that his parents had been having their own private celebrations. When they finished their tea, Hamish got up and walked to the back door.

'I expect you could do with a hand this morning, Dad? I'll come out with you now, if you like,' Doug said, getting up and following him out.

'Aye, making your escape before your mother gets down. Can't say I blame ye – she'll be wanting to start arrangements for yon wedding.' They laughed as they stepped out into the early morning sunshine.

It had been well past midnight before Liza and Hamish had finally said goodbye to the last of their guests at the hotel and in consequence it was gone nine by the time Liza came down to the kitchen. She liked to be up early with Hamish in the mornings and she felt a little flustered to think that she had slept so late – and with guests in the house. In the kitchen she immediately started preparations for breakfast and realised that Cloud was nowhere to be seen. 'The old devil's got up there again,' she muttered to herself. 'Oh well, I expect Sally's ready for a cup of tea.'

Tapping lightly on the bedroom door, Liza popped her head round to find Sally just waking up and smiling sleepily up at her.

'Come in. That's a welcome sight.' Sally was naked and, as she sat up, she hastily gathered the sheet and blankets around her, hoping that Liza would not notice. Taking the cup and saucer from Liza, she reached over to place them on the bedside table and as she did she saw that Doug's watch was by the reading lamp. Quickly she put the cup and saucer down in front of the watch, hoping to hide it from Liza. It was too late – Liza's hawk-like eyes had spotted it. Having noticed that Sally wasn't wearing her nightdress, she had a fair idea what had been going on. Looking at the guilty smile on Sally's face, she said nothing, but she would have a few words to say to that boy of hers when she caught up with him.

As she got dressed it seemed to Sally that the week had flown by, and now they only had this one day left. Early the next morning they would have to start back down south, and Sally realised with a pang that she would miss the countryside. Doug's family had taken her in and treated her as if she was already one of their number. Apart from Moira, she thought, the week had been a blissfully happy one, and Sally couldn't entirely blame Moira for not liking her. It did seem as though Doug had ditched Moira for her, even though he had steadfastly maintained that Moira was never a serious girlfriend.

By the time the men came back for a mid-morning break, Sally was helping Liza with the preparations for dinner that evening. Doug was first through into the kitchen and he made straight for her to kiss her cheek.

'It's our last day to enjoy some freedom before we are on the road again and back to work. Do you fancy another ride, Sal?' he asked. 'The grass is a getting a bit thin on the upper fields. I told Dad I'd help him out a bit by taking some sheep over to Uncle Bob's – they need to be turned out on to the lower slopes. I could use a good outrider.'

'I'd love to!' Sally said as she smiled up at him. 'I'll just finish peeling the spuds for tonight.'

'Where are my lazy sister and Moira? Can they not lend a hand in the kitchen?' he called over to Liza.

'Now, Doug, don't go stirring things up in that department,' his mother answered without turning round. 'They'll be down presently and can finish off helping me, so you and Sally get along.'

'I'll just go and change.' Sally smiled her thanks and, wiping her hands, hurried out of the kitchen.

'Father seems a bit weary this morning, Mum. I expect it was all that celebrating last night that has caught up with him?' he said, grinning at her, but Liza caught the suggestive implication in her son's voice and refused to make eye contact with him. She was well aware that when he put his mind to it he could charm birds out of the trees. Well, she thought, he needn't think he's getting away without a telling off just because he thinks he knows a little more than he should. Liza turned to face her son and the smile faded from his lips.

'I hope you're taking care, son.' Liza had a way of lowering her head, like a bull about to lock horns, and Doug knew he was at his mother's mercy.

'Sorry, Mum? Taking care of what?' he brazened it out.

'Aye, ye ken full well! It seems to me you're pretty careless where you leave your possessions!' Doug fell silent and looked uncomfortable. Of course he knew what his mother was referring to – he had remembered his watch when he was across the fields with his father, but by then it was too late to do anything about it. He knew his mother had eyes like a hawk and could only hope that Sally had woken up and discovered his watch before anyone else saw it. He looked sheepishly at his mother and shrugged his shoulders.

'I just hope you're not leaving other things where you shouldnae!'

'It's okay, Mum, really.' Grown man that he was, she could always reduce him to a nervous child with a guilty conscience. He looked away, withered by his mother's intense gaze.

'Aye, it'd better be "okay"! She's very young! It's up to you to be the responsible one! And she's a bonny lass! Just make sure you treat her right, or you'll have me to answer to!'

'I will, Mum, I will ... I promise.'

Just then, Sally reappeared, suitably dressed for riding in the hills, and Liza turned away to continue with her preparations. Doug ushered Sally out before his mother could detain them any longer.

As they rode abreast, Doug brought their conversation round to the wedding. He wanted to discuss a few of the arrangements before they left Scotland and out here, with no one else to disturb them, was an ideal opportunity.

'Do you have any preferences for the wedding – any dreams you've been harbouring for your big day? he asked.

'I think it should be a small family wedding,' Sally suggested, and was content to leave it at that. She had been daydreaming, drinking in the view all around her and thinking how she would never tire of the spectacular scenery.

'Virtually impossible!' Doug laughed out loud. 'You only met half my relatives last night, and that's six busloads before we start! When mother gets round to contacting the others and they know there's a family wedding in the offing, you'll get the full turnout. What do you think your parents are going to say about getting engaged and married?'

'Oh, I expect they'll be glad to get rid of me! Lottie will be, that's for sure,' she joked. In truth, the way she felt at that moment, she really didn't care what her parents said; she was determined to be with Doug, but the question brought her back down to earth.

'We haven't even mentioned this to my parents yet, and here we are making wedding plans,' Sally said. 'I know I joked about them wanting to get rid of me but, Doug, what if they refuse their permission?'

'I doubt that they will. I expect you were quite correct when you said that your mum and dad couldn't wait to get you off their hands. A fiery piece like you must be an awful worry to them,' he teased.

'Doug MacDonald, that's not fair! What about your poor mother? From what I hear she's suffered more sleepless nights over you than my mother ever has over me.'

'I don't doubt that, Sal. But I promise you my wandering days are over now.' Doug hesitated. 'We do have another problem, though. Most of my relatives are farmers and for them to leave the livestock and get down south for a few days would be nigh on impossible. Would it be a problem for us to marry up here in Scotland? We have what is almost a family kirk nearby where it all happens. As our auld preacher always says, he hatches, matches and dispatches most of the folk around here.'

Sally laughed. A wedding in Scotland was fine by her –she was prepared to go to the ends of the earth to marry Doug, but the thought of how her parents might react to this news was a sobering one. Doug was not a Catholic, so that was yet another hurdle to overcome. Mixed marriages were conducted within the Catholic Church as long as the non-Catholic agreed to a list of rules and regulations. At the top of that list was a promise that any children would be brought up in the Catholic faith. Sally looked across at Doug, wondering how he would feel about that. Why, oh why, were so many obstacles rearing up in front of them? Not only did she have to gain her parents' permission to marry, but she also had to persuade them to let her get married away from her hometown! And if that wasn't bad enough, not even married by a priest in a Catholic Church but by a preacher in a Scottish kirk!

'Doug ... marrying in Scotland is fine by me. But ... I'm not sure what my parents will say.'

"Don't worry, kitten – I'll have a serious talk with your father and see if there's some middle ground. I'm not taking no for an answer. I want you for my wife.' With a twitch of the rein, he leaned over in the saddle and stretched out his hand to her. For a few strides, the ponies fell into step and she took his hand, gripping it tightly before Molly tossed her head and their clasp was broken.

'What about your Jack Russell?' he suddenly asked.

'Caroline? I think she'll be pleased. I don't think she really dislikes you at all. She even wanted to know if you had a brother.'

Doug laughed. 'Poor Iain! Should we introduce them, or should I save him from a fate worse than death?'

'Doug, that's not fair. I love Caroline. She's my best friend and she's really loyal.'

'Oh, aye. She might be nice enough to you but ... well, she scares the life out of me.'

And she would have scared the life out of Moira too, thought Sally. More than anything, Sally wished Caroline had been with her at the party last night. She certainly would have known how to deal with the likes of Moira. Wistfully, Sally began to think about how different her life would be from now on, with Doug to take care of her. It would be painful parting from Caroline and all her other friends, but then she glanced across at Doug's handsome profile and her heart missed a beat. It'll be worth it, she thought. I love him so very much.

'We're nearly there. Uncle Bob's place is just around the next bend in the valley. It's a bit remote, but in a wonderful spot with the most amazing views. You can reach it from the lane too, so we can go back home that way.' Looking up, he scanned the sky. 'Looks like we've had the best of the weather – it's clouding over fast and the lane will be a much shorter way back.'

Bob was Hamish's elder brother and Sally had been introduced to him at the party, where they had taken an instant liking to each other. In answer to Sally's polite enquiries about his family, he had told her that he had never married but that this was not a conscious decision on his part – he had just drifted into his fifties and not got around to it. He had begun to tell her how he had stayed on at the family farm with his elderly parents when Hamish had interrupted, telling her that it was because Bob was too comfortable at his mother's fireside with her cooking. Bob's good-humoured response had been that it was because the right girl had never come along, but that he was still in the market should she come by. Sally had enjoyed the fraternal exchange but sensed that Bob was quieter and more placid than his younger brother, and she was looking forward to getting to know him a little more.

When he saw the sheep and the riders coming down off the hill into his top fields, Bob parked his old Land Rover by a drystone wall and jumped out. Walking over to a wooden five-bar gate, he opened it and stood off to one side with his sheepdog bitch, Lass, sitting obediently beside him. Doug whistled and Skip moved from his position at the rear of the flock to be at Doug's side. Seeing the fresh green pasture ahead, all the sheep filed obligingly through into the middle of the meadow while Skip and Lass remained alert and ready to round up any stragglers that broke away from the flock. As the last sheep trotted by, Bob closed the gate behind them. With their work done, Lass and Skip began to chase each other around like pups, and Sally laughed at their antics.

'That's Skip's mum – they're always very pleased to see each other,' Doug explained.

'She's beautiful. What an unusual colour coat – and I love her eyes,' Sally said, admiring the silver-grey and black-flecked coat and the bright blue eyes of the collie bitch.

'That's what they call a blue merle,' Bob called out to her as he walked over to where the young couple sat on their sturdy ponies. 'Well, this is a nice surprise. Hello, Sally,' he said, reaching up to shake her hand. 'I wasn't expecting to see you up and about so early this morning.'

'Well, you surely won't see any of the others – the three of them were still abed when we left!' Doug said. 'And I'm afraid you won't be seeing us for a wee while after today. Sally and I are making the most of the fresh air before we head back down south early the morrow.'

'Och, there's a pity you have to be going back so soon. Never mind, we'll hopefully be seeing more of both of you in the New Year,' he said, beaming up at the pair of them.

'Aye, I hope so, Uncle Bob. But we'd better be getting back now. I don't want to keep Sally out too long. We've been lucky with the weather so far but I don't like the look of that sky.'

'Eih, it does speak of rain, and I can feel it in my old rheumatic knee.'

Sally automatically looked down in puzzlement at his legs. Seeing the look, he explained: 'It's a farmer's knee, you see. They say it's from always jumping out of the Land Rover and off the tractor from the same side and landing on the same leg.'

'Oh, I see. I'm sorry.

'Don't worry yourself, lass – it's an occupational hazard,' Bob smiled reassuringly up at her. 'Well, I'll bid you both a safe journey and look forward to seeing you back soon.'

'Bye, Uncle Bob,' Sally called out to him, and waved as she turned Molly round to follow Doug across the field to the gate leading into the lane.

They rode at a brisk trot, Sally hardly able to tear her eyes away from the heather that dressed the far side of the valley. 'It's such a wonderful colour, like a carpet of pink, lilac and blue that someone has thrown over the hillside,' she murmured to herself but Doug heard and smiled across at her. He would never tire of gazing at her loveliness.

'You'll be part of it soon. Mind, I might need three strapping sons to help run the place!' he said with a knowing grin on his face.

She grinned back at him. 'Oh? And what if you get three strapping daughters?'

'That'll do fine, if they can work as hard as you do,' and they dissolved into laughter as they rode along.

Arriving back at the house, they received a warning look from Liza as they entered the kitchen. They could sense that the atmosphere was electric with emotion and it wasn't long before they realised the cause – Moira was sitting at the kitchen table nursing a record-breaking hangover. Lifting bloodshot eyes to gaze at them as they entered, she got up and pointedly ignored them as she walked out of the kitchen.

Sally and Doug, unperturbed by her theatrical exit, sat down at the table and began chatting to Liza, telling her of the plans they had discussed during their ride.

'I don't know where the time has gone this week,' Liza sighed, 'but I dare say you'll be back up soon looking for somewhere to rent in the city.'

'Aye, and we'll have to make a very early start tomorrow,' Doug said, pouring out two cups of tea from the fresh brew in the teapot. 'I've asked agents to send me details of houses to rent and I've got a week off at the end of October. We can arrange to pop up and view a few places then.'

'Aye, well, you've quite a lot of arrangements to make, young man. There will need to be a wedding before yon lass joins you.'

'Right enough, Mother! But I must speak to Sally's parents first. Sally and I have talked about it and we both like the idea of using the kirk. It would be nice keeping to family traditions, but we have to make it right with Sally's parents. There's a religious issue that has to be talked through. We were thinking that maybe we could get married in early April?'

'That would be just grand! Your father and I would love that, if Sally and her parents are okay with the idea. I'll not interfere but if you want any help with the arrangements, just ask.'

'Ha! Won't interfere!' Hamish snorted as he came into the kitchen and overheard what his wife had just said. 'Just try and stop her. She's been on the phone to your Auntie Mary already. They're only away to Edinburgh next week to buy their hats,' he said, chuckling with glee.

'Hamish! Behave yourself now!' Liza said, trying to keep a straight face; but as she hastily got up from the table and busied herself at the range, they could all see the happiness in her eyes.

First Love

Chapter Eighteen

As soon as she arrived home Sally told her parents that Doug had proposed to her and a few days later he called round to see them. Forewarned as to the reason for his visit, her father had time to consider this turn of events, and he had some serious reservations about his daughter's ability to settle down and become a wife. In his estimation, committing herself to the first serious man that came along seemed to be a huge gamble, even though Rose told him that Sally could not have picked a better candidate as his future son-in-law.

Sally also had time to warn them both that the wedding would take place in Doug's local church. Her mother offered no resistance to the marriage, but was unhappy that the wedding was not to be local, thus proving Doug quite correct in his assessment of his future mother-in-law's attitude. This was not to say that Rose did not love her elder daughter, but Sally had become a constant worry to her and she had never quite understood her. Thanking God in her prayers that night for sending Doug, she was more than happy to hand over the responsibility for her daughter's happiness and welfare to a nice young man with a good job.

Conveniently, Lottie was out at a friend's birthday party the afternoon that Doug came round to talk to her parents. As the four of them stood awkwardly in the hall for a few moments, her father hastily suggested that they talk a few things over, 'man to man'. They disappeared into the sitting room and Rose ushered Sally down the hall and into the kitchen.

Once they were alone, Joe coughed nervously and cleared his throat. 'Well, now, let's not beat about the bush,' he started, and paused as he began to clean his pipe. 'Sally's told us that you've proposed marriage, but I have to say, Doug ...' and he paused again as he filled the pipe, 'Sally's still very young ... and ... this is all very sudden ...' He lit the pipe and began to draw on it. He blew the smoke up to the ceiling before looking sternly across at Doug, fervently hoping that this young man was not about to inform him that he was doing the 'honourable thing', having impregnated his daughter. It was happening all around him these days and he didn't want that, not for his Sally.

Reading his thoughts, Doug spoke quietly. 'Yes, I agree she's young in years, but she's quite mature in many ways. I wouldn't have rushed the situation, but there's a reason for the haste.'

Joe took a deep breath and sighed, removing the pipe from his mouth. Here it comes, he thought.

'You see, I've been offered promotion, but it means that I'd have to relocate to Edinburgh and I don't want to leave Sally behind. I want to take her up there with me, but I want to marry her first so that everything is done properly. May we have your blessing, Sir?'

'Oh! Oh, I see ...' Joe tried to disguise his relief. So it wasn't to be a shotgun wedding after all. Perhaps he had jumped too quickly to the wrong conclusion but, even so, Sally was still very young. He closed his eyes for a moment and thought about all the upset that would follow if he said no. He knew that Rose considered Doug the answer to all her prayers and the trouble was, if Sally had made her mind up that she was going up north, Joe knew from experience it would be very difficult to stop her. He seemed a fine young man, good job, wanted to do right by his Sally, and maybe he had been wrong to have doubted his intentions. The house would be quiet without his Sally and he knew he would miss her. Though maybe ... He left his thoughts unfinished and sucked on his pipe while he tried to direct them down another path. Choosing his words carefully, he answered Doug's question.

'Well now, Doug, you have my blessing but, believe me, if you're marrying Sally, then at times you'll also need my sympathy.' He chuckled to himself, and Doug's eyes shone as he grinned with relief.

'Now if I can't dissuade you from tying yourself to my daughter for life, how about a celebratory nip out of that bottle you kindly brought me back from Scotland?'

In the kitchen, Sally and her mother were anxiously waiting, hardly a word passing between them.

'Why are they taking so long?' Sally was nervous and impatient.

'Well, your father's not keen, you know. He says you're far too young. But he also knows you'll probably run off if he doesn't give his consent, so you have him over a barrel, really. Better to have a respectable wedding, even if it is in some godforsaken part of the country, than an elopement, with the neighbours whispering behind closed doors. At least I'll have a photograph to put on the sideboard, showing it was done properly. We have to live here after you've gone, you know.'

Sally was not remotely surprised at her mother's priorities. All her life, she had lived with her mother's 'What will the neighbours think?' mantra. Finally, after what seemed an age to them both, the sitting room door opened and Joe came out, followed by a smiling Doug.

'Your father says I've to take you away, as far as possible and as soon as possible,' he joked. 'So I'll pick you up on Saturday and we can start by going into town and choosing an engagement ring.'

Sally thought her heart would burst with happiness.

Over tea, they got the calendar out and, after much discussion, heart-searching and head scratching, the wedding date was set for 10th April, a couple of weeks after Sally's eighteenth birthday. It was to be in Scotland, at Doug's family kirk. Rose tried to voice her concerns about Sally marrying outside the Catholic Church, but Sally was adamant that she was prepared to face God's anger rather than arrange a wedding in her hometown. She knew that Doug wanted as many members of his family present as possible, and that would be out of the question if they had to travel south. Besides, the way in which Liza and Hamish had made her feel so very welcome, she already felt that they were her family too, and Sally wanted to be with them.

Not being a Catholic, Joe had never shared his wife's religious fervour and was indifferent to the venue, immediately appreciating the difficulties for Doug's family if they had to travel south for the nuptials. Joe had promised to bring his children up in the Catholic faith and he had kept that promise. He had done his best with Sally, always ensuring that she went to confession and attended Mass on a Sunday, but he doubted that his daughter had any real commitment to the Catholic faith other than that based on fear and guilt instilled in her by the nuns. Rose remembered the dreadful arguments she'd had with her parents when she and Joe had wanted to marry. They had finally given in and allowed her to take part in what they referred to as a 'mixed marriage' in the Catholic Church's 'abridged' version of the marriage ceremony. As years went by, everyone had got over it so now, reasoning that it was far enough away for the neighbours not to know and the priest not to find out, Rose consented to Sally marrying in Scotland.

Caroline was genuinely delighted when Sally told her of the engagement and assumed she had misread Doug. She vowed to do everything to make the wedding day a happy one for her friend and, as Sally had asked her to be Chief Bridesmaid, she was committed to making sure that nothing would spoil the day. Sally thought it would be lovely if her bridesmaids wore pink until she saw the look of horror on her friend's face. They agreed to search the shops together until they could find a colour that Caroline would agree to wear and that would suit Fiona's colouring as well.

During October, Sally and Doug returned to the farm and were kept busy. Every day they drove into Edinburgh looking at properties to rent and it was not long before they found a suitable three-bedroom semi in a quiet road just on the outskirts of the city. Although Doug was due to take up his new post at the end of November, it was part of her parents' agreement to the marriage that Sally would not move up to Scotland until just before the wedding in April. She would spend Christmas with her parents and go by train to join Doug and his family in Scotland for the New Year celebrations.

When the festive season arrived the weather had other ideas. Across the country, snow began to fall on Christmas Eve in large white flakes and what started as a winter wonderland soon turned into a nightmare for Sally. It snowed and thawed, and snowed again, and the roads became icy and in many places impassable. If it was bad in the south, it was ten times worse north of the border. Even the snowploughs were having difficulty keeping the country roads accessible. Sally was heartbroken but could see the wisdom of cancelling her plans to join Doug for Hogmanay.

It was some small consolation to Sally that her parents had installed a telephone that autumn, so at least she was able to speak to Doug on Christmas Day, but New Year's Eve found her still at home with her parents. In the last few years she had celebrated New Year with Caroline, whose parents always had a huge party, and Sally would be allowed to spend the night at her friend's house. But Caroline had gone to London for a party and Sally found herself with just her parents and Lottie, who had been allowed to stay up. Just after midnight, Sally hovered in the hall watching the telephone, wondering if Doug would call her. Lottie, who was now tired and irritable, started teasing her about her vigil and inevitably a row had followed. Shortly afterwards, they had all gone to bed.

On New Year's Day the phone didn't ring at all and by the evening Sally decided to telephone Doug, reasoning that they had all had time to get over their Hogmanay excesses. At seven o'clock, leaving the warmth of the sitting room and its open fire, Sally settled herself on a chair in the draughty hallway and dialled the number. Her heart fluttered with excitement at the thought of hearing Doug's voice again. She listened to the distant purr-purr of the ring tone, then her call was answered. Sally's heart sank as she recognised the voice. 'Hello, Moira, may I speak to Doug, please?' She was pleased that she had managed to keep her voice calm, giving no hint of her dismay that Moira was there.

'Oh! ... Hellooo! A Happy New Year to you ...' Moira purred down the phone. 'Of course you may speak to him ... he's right here beside me.' She heard Moira call, 'Dougie! Your wee virgin is on the phone and wants to speak with you.' Moira giggled and Sally froze. She heard what sounded like a scuffle at the end of the line and Doug's voice say, 'Hello? Hello? Sally? Are you there?' She could hear the concern in his voice as he called down the phone.

'Yes, I'm here.' Her heart felt like lead as she answered him. 'The line isn't too good but I can hear you.' Unable to stop herself and before even wishing Doug a Happy New Year, she blurted, 'I didn't know Moira was going to be at the farm for New Year'.

'She wasn't supposed to be! She came for a short visit beforehand to see Fiona but then couldn't get home what with all the blizzards, so we're stuck with her. But not for long! When I put this phone down, I assure you I'm going to murder her!'

This was some reassurance to Sally and they chatted on for a while. Doug was in mid-sentence, telling her how much he had been missing her, when there was a crackle and the line went dead.

'Hello ...? Hello ...?' Sally called down the phone, hoping in vain for a response. Giving up, slowly she placed the handset on the cradle and shivered as a cold draught from the front door swirled around her ankles.

'It's probably the snow, brought down some lines I expect,' her father offered by way of consolation. As he had stepped into the hallway, he had heard her and had guessed what had happened. Sally was close to tears; he put his arm around her and encouraged her to return to the warm sitting room.

A few days later, Doug rang and confirmed what her father had suspected – the weight of the snow on the lines had taken down a critical cable and all the phones in the area had been cut off. It had taken the engineers until now to get through the snow to fix it. He told her that he had moved into their house, so that he could still get to work should they have more heavy snow.

Happier now, having heard Doug's voice, Sally set about the arrangements for the wedding. She had a shopping trip planned with Caroline to buy her wedding dress and to find a bridesmaid's dress for her friend, and a matching one for Fiona to be sent north for final fittings and any necessary adjustments. She had bowed to her mother's wish to make Lottie's bridesmaid dress.

With Doug now living and working in Edinburgh, Sally had plenty of spare time to get things done and she spoke on the telephone regularly with Liza, who reassured her that they were well on the way with preparations at the Scottish end. Sally knew that Caroline was dating her first serious boyfriend but she had been so busy with her wedding arrangements that she'd hardly had time to find out anything about him, other than that his name was Alex. When she had asked Caroline if she wanted to invite Alex to the wedding, Caroline had surprised her by shaking her head.

'No, if Alex is there, well ... besides, this is your day.' Infuriatingly, she had left it at that. Eventually Sally managed to establish that Alex was a friend of Caroline's elder brother, and this told her that he must be several years older than Caroline.

After yet another day hunting for dresses and trying on wedding outfits, the friends retired to their favourite coffee bar for a well-earned rest. Looking across the table, Sally realised just how much they had both changed in the past couple of months. Caroline had dyed her hair blonde at Christmas and often swept it up into a neat chignon that made her look every inch the suave, sophisticated secretary – unless of course, Sally mused, Caroline was trying to look older for the new boyfriend.

'So come on, tell me about Alex, this friend of your brother's? I can't seem to put a face to the name.' Sally had spent so much time at Caroline's house when they were growing up that she thought she knew all her brothers' friends. 'And the real reason why you don't want him invited to the wedding?'

'Sal, you must remember who he is – he came to my brother's graduation party and knocked a glass of red wine all over my mother's spanking new outfit!'

'Oh! That one! Tall, skinny, light brown hair and glasses?'

'He's not skinny any more. Grown into quite a hunk.'

'Wasn't he the one with all the answers – the swot?' It was all coming back to Sally now. Of course she remembered Alex! Sally remembered being shocked when, as a very young child, she heard Caroline calling him a 'smart arse'. Unfortunately for Caroline, her mother heard it too and she'd been soundly smacked and sent to bed with no tea, loudly protesting that that was only what everyone else called him. After that, Caroline was careful to modify her language but settled for calling him 'Smarty Pants' to his face, making sure that she was well out of her mother's hearing. Secretly, Sally agreed with her, because Alex was one of those smug older boys who, infuriatingly, always had an answer to everything. Sally always tried to avoid him if they met at Caroline's house but it seemed to her that Caroline enjoyed taunting him, always trying unsuccessfully to outsmart him.

'You had a crush on him when we were still in junior school and he was in the senior scouts.'

'Yes, all right, Miss Know-it-All!' Caroline was laughing as she blushed, embarrassed to be reminded of her childhood fantasies.

'Went to Cambridge with Chris?'

'No he went to Oxford, got a First in Languages and joined the Foreign Office. I hadn't seen him since Chris's graduation – when he threw that wine all over mother, she vowed never to let him anywhere near her again!'

'So come on then, tell all – when, where and how did you meet up with him again?'

'It was really weird. In London – I literally collided with him when we both dived for the same taxi. Didn't recognise him at first. Of course, he's been abroad a lot and he's filled out. He was wearing a pinstripe suit and bowler hat. Real city gent, very smart and very ... um...' She was going to say 'sexy' but, as she hesitated, Sally asked, 'So at what point did you recognise each other?'

Caroline laughed loudly. 'Apparently it was my green eyes blazing with fury at him for trying to steal my cab.' She paused as she remembered the soft brown eyes that had laughed at her from behind his black-rimmed glasses.

'And ...?'

'Oh ... and we ended up sharing the taxi, chatting about this and that. We exchanged addresses. He said he would call me, though I never thought he would. Anyway, he did and now we're dating,' she finished in rather a rush. Had Sally not been quite so preoccupied with the arrangements for her own big day, she would have wondered why Caroline was glossing over the details. Part of Sally's mind was elsewhere but suddenly she asked, 'So was it him you went with to that New Year's Eve bash in London somewhere?'

'Oh, Sally, it was a fabulous do, some big place in Knightsbridge. When it was over, he took me back to my auntie's in Wimbledon. I should have been in by one but we didn't get back until gone two in the morning! I was expecting a lecture but, unlike Mum and Dad, they were fine about it, still partying themselves. The whole place was heaving with people! We all carried on partying and dancing 'til dawn, and Renee cooked breakfast for everyone. They're so different to my parents that it's hard to believe that Fred is Mum's brother. I got on really well with them – in fact, they've invited me to stay with them, so I might be moving up to London soon.'

'D'you think your parents will let you do that?'

'As long as I don't tell them why,' Caroline said with a twinkle in her eyes.

'Oh ... and why?'

'Why do you think?'

Sally thought for a moment, 'In case they ask too many questions?'

'Yep! You got it!' and they both burst out laughing. 'Besides,' Caroline continued, 'you'll be moving up to Scotland after the wedding and London is where I work and where it's all happening at the moment and ... well, it would be convenient.' She grinned across the table at her friend.

'And I suppose Alex has a flat in London?' Sally added. Caroline nodded and they laughed again. 'Well,' Sally said, looking at her watch, 'Sounds like fate to me.'

The numerous other things that had to be sorted out before her wedding began to crowd her mind again. 'This is not getting anything done – we'd better get on. If you don't make up your mind about your dress soon, Caro, I'll ask my mother to make it for you.'

'Oh God! Please, no! I don't suit yards of tulle in powder blue or rose pink. Anyway, what about you and your dress?'

'Well, you've been warned ...' Sally laughed, ushering her friend out into the High Street to continue their hunt for the dress. Finally, Caroline settled for a maroon Empire-line dress, which would also complement Fiona's colouring and figure and be a good contrast against the pink of Lottie's dress. In the same bridal shop Sally spotted a full-length white lace wedding dress. The body of the dress was fitted, the sleeves were long and the neckline had a modest scoop. She slipped it on and the fit was perfect. The assistant then showed them a selection of headdresses and veils and, with Caroline's help, Sally chose a floral headdress of mock orange blossom and teamed it with a short lace-edged veil. Meanwhile, Rose was in a sewing frenzy most of the time and thus in her element. The dining room table was strewn with baby-pink satin and matching net for the under petticoats, satin ribbons, bows and rosebuds and it didn't take much to imagine what Lottie would look like on the day. As well as designing a bridesmaid's dress for Lottie, Rose was going to make her own outfit. Navy blue material was folded neatly on the sideboard waiting for its conversion into 'something tasteful in navy to be worn with white accessories'. No surprise there, thought Sally, as she'd politely admired her mother's purchases.

While they were apart, Doug wrote tender love letters and telephoned twice a week. He promised to get down to see her for a few days during February and Sally couldn't wait to see him again.

Mid-February could not come soon enough and on the day that Doug was due back Sally caught the bus straight after work and headed across town to Pete's flat. She was deliriously happy, knowing that Pete was away for a few days and that they would have the flat to themselves. Sitting on the bus, she realised that the next time she would be hurrying to meet Doug would be just before their wedding day, and her heart skipped a beat.

Doug had been watching out for her from the large bay window in the sitting room and was waiting at the top of the stairs as she ran up them two at a time.

She fell into his arms and they kissed, clinging tightly to each other. She loved everything about him and realised how she had missed even the little things like the smell of his aftershave and the roughness of his tweed jacket against her cheek. He hugged her in silence and held her for a while. Then he gently whispered to her, 'Come on in, Sal, we have to talk,' and, taking his hand, she followed him into the sitting room.

'Talk? Do we have to talk now?' She was so excited to see him again. 'I've missed you so much. All I want is lots of kisses and cuddles and all those other things that go with it,' she flirted, offering her lips for another kiss. 'Do you know, I've been positively drowning in my mother's arrangements for the wedding?' She chatted away, hardly able to contain her happiness. 'I've got the dress – can't we just run off and get married and tell them all afterwards?' She giggled as she wrapped her arms round his waist, inviting him to hold her close. Instead, he steered her towards the old settee and Sally fleetingly wondered if he wanted to recapture that time on the settee when he had first awakened in her a response to feelings she never even knew she possessed.

'Sal, please sit down. I have to talk to you.' It had been dark in the hallway and now, for the first time since she arrived, she could see Doug's face. He was very pale and his eyes red-rimmed. The smile that was never far from the corners of his mouth was gone and the light she always saw in his eyes when he looked into hers was missing. Something was wrong – she sensed an overwhelming sadness.

'Doug, what is it? It's not your parents, is it? Iain? Fiona ...?'

'No, it's nothing like that, they're all fine.'

'Well, what's wrong?' As she put her arms around him, to her horror and shock, she saw his eyes were filled with tears. He gently disentangled himself from her embrace and took hold of both her hands. She could barely hear his words as he looked down and began to speak, unable to look at her, to watch her face or meet her eyes.

'Sal, there is no easy way to say this. I've let you down. Very badly.'

She was about to interrupt him, to tell him that there was nothing that he could possibly have done to warrant this degree of unhappiness, but he shook his head and the words died on her lips.

'Just listen to what I have to say, please. Hear me out before you say anything.' He took a deep breath and continued. 'On New Year's Eve, I did something stupid that I will regret all my life.' He took another deep breath to enable himself to utter the words that he knew would crush Sally.

'I slept with Moira.' He looked up and saw the utter disbelief on her face.

Sally, completely unprepared for this, could only sit rigidly in front of him, staring at him uncomprehendingly.

'I feel so ... so ... very ... bad about it, my darling. But ... but ... it's too late, it's done.' Doug remained quiet while Sally took in the enormity of what he had just said. When she said nothing, he continued, 'I could hide behind the fact that there had been a lot of drinking. It was, after all, Hogmanay. I could be ungallant and say that Moira stage-managed the whole incident, but, even so ... I ... I should have been able, with the strength of my love for you, to ... to walk away. But ... but ... I didn't ...'

Sally sat in silence as the tale unfolded. Her hands had fallen away from Doug's grasp and now they lay, lifeless, in her lap. It was her turn to lower her eyes, trying to take in all that Doug was telling her and trying to make some sense of it all. Where did she go from here? She would forgive him, of course, but could she ever trust him again? No, the trust was gone, probably for ever, but did she still love him? Yes, she had to admit that, whatever he did, now or in the future, she would always love him.

Doug's voice was nothing more than a strangled whisper as he looked imploringly at her. 'Sally, say something, please.'

'I don't know what to say,' she said, choking on her tears as she looked at his ashen face. 'I just wish you hadn't told me. I love you so much and I still want to marry you, but how can I ever trust you? Why did you have to tell me? Why did you have to spoil everything by telling me?' Her face crumbled and she leaned forward to slide her arms around his neck. Perhaps if Doug took her to bed it would erase the pictures that were playing over and over in her mind; Doug entwined with Moira.

Doug could not respond to her advances, not even when she placed her lips on his. He didn't trust himself, and tenderly he removed her arms from around his neck and held her at arm's length.

'Sally, my darling ... there's a reason I had to tell you ... and I have no choice but to tell you.'

'Doug, it's not an insurmountable problem,' she interrupted. 'I'm sure we can get over it and ... and ... in time I can forget all about it. You'll see ... we'll be ...'

Doug interrupted her desperate attempts to make things right. 'Sal, it is a big problem and it's not going to go away. Moira's pregnant.'

'No!' Sally gasped, and the colour drained from her face.

'I don't know how I could have been so stupid!' Tears were running down Doug's cheeks, and it was his turn to reach for her, to hold her, to stop the pain that he knew she was feeling. 'Oh, Sally! I am so sorry!' He sobbed into her neck.

Sally sat unmoving, unresponsive. This could not be happening– she would wake up in a minute and find it was all just a very bad dream. Doug was speaking again and she felt her world finally come crashing in on her as he whispered, 'It's you I love and will always love, Sally ... but it's Moira I'll have to marry.'

Chapter Nineteen

Sally sat in the departure lounge at Heathrow airport waiting for the announcement to board her flight to Al Khaleej. She was excited, but nervous too – she had never flown before. In 24 hours' time it should have been her and Doug's first wedding anniversary and she'd decided that she just wanted to be somewhere else on that day, somewhere as far away as possible.

Sally had no memory of getting home the night Doug broke the news to her that the wedding was off. Numbed with grief, all she could focus on was the pain, the hurt, and the overwhelming sadness on her father's face as he had struggled to find the words to comfort his distraught daughter. She remembered trying to brazen it out: 'It's all right, Dad, really, I'm fine,' she heard herself saying. Caroline had been her greatest support in the weeks that followed. Her bridesmaid dress chosen, and thinking that her closest friend was well on the way to the altar, Caroline had persuaded her parents to let her leave home to stay with her childless aunt and uncle in Wimbledon. Keeping in touch by phone, the girls had spoken to each other two or three times a week but, when Caroline's mother called her one evening to tell her that the wedding was off and that rumours were flying round town about what could have happened, she was on the first train back home. Her one thought was to get Sally away from the small-minded busybodies in the town they had both grown up in, to get her to Wimbledon and look after her.

Sally remembered the taxi ride to the station, getting on and off the train, the awfulness of the crowds on the Underground. Throughout it all, Caroline had kept up a constant stream of chatter, forcing Sally's mind to concentrate on the very things that she least wanted to think about. Caroline had talked excitedly about London, the shops, restaurants and theatres, her aunt and uncle and how she would help Sally find a job – and, throughout it all, Sally tried to shut out the sound of her friend's voice. She wasn't interested in such trivial things. Masochistically, her mind kept returning again and again to the happiness that she had felt with Doug and the fact that he was gone now. Time and again, she relived the happier times she had spent with him in Scotland before tormenting herself as she thought of Doug and Moira getting married, living together and starting a family. Caroline's constant chatter kept interrupting her self-pity and she would turn vacant, red-rimmed eyes brimming with tears on her friend, wishing that she were a million miles away.

Arriving at the big old semi in the leafy suburb of London, her inbred good manners took over. Sally went through the motions, smiling politely and saying the right thing, but wanting only to crawl away and be left alone. On hearing the whole sordid story from Sally, Caroline was angry but not surprised. What Caroline was more concerned about was its impact on Sally, and she vowed that if she ever came across Douglas MacDonald again, she would tear him limb from limb.

If Caroline's aunt and uncle knew what had happened, they never let on, and Doug's name was never mentioned in the house. Caroline was right; her middle-aged aunt and uncle were only too happy to have another youngster staying with them in their spacious house. Sally had found her freedom in Scotland but Caroline had found hers in London. It was such a contrast from the small town they had grown up in. Caroline felt so free and anonymous in London and she loved it all - the theatres, the restaurants, the parties, the shops – but most of all the way her aunt and uncle encouraged her to go out and enjoy herself. More liberal-minded than her own parents, it had been a revelation to Caroline to realise that she could come and go as she pleased with no one to 'just mention' to her parents that they had seen her with so-and-so or in such- and-such a place.

In contrast, Sally had hated London, the crowds, the traffic and the fumes and, most of all, the Underground. But she found a secretarial job and stayed on, not knowing quite what else to do or where else to go. Caroline had been right – she could lose herself here in this city; there was nothing and no one to remind her of Scotland or Doug. For weeks Sally felt like a spectator of the life that was going on all around her, as if she was no longer part of it. As if from a distance, she watched herself mechanically going through the motions of meeting, greeting, talking and socialising, all the time longing for the solitude of her own bedroom where she could be alone with her thoughts, torturing herself with images of Doug, and Doug with Moira.

As the weeks passed, the pain in her heart became easier to live with. In the depths of her grief, it had filtered through to Sally that it would be the height of bad manners to inflict all her unhappiness on everyone around her and gradually her life began to resume some semblance of normality. Day by day, her general sense of weariness with life began to lift.

It was like old times that summer - the pair of them were never short of invitations to parties and outings, most of which were arranged by Alex, who introduced Sally to any number of his old university chums and work colleagues. They were charming, flirtatious and funny and the lead weight around her heart began to lighten.

'Sal, you can't carry a torch for Doug for ever, you know. You'll have to let it go one day,' Caroline taxed her friend as she and Sally were having a picnic lunch break. It was late summer and they lay stretched out on the grass in St James's Park.

'I can't help it, Caroline. Besides, I don't think it's a torch for Doug so much as being unable to trust another man. It's easier not to get involved; then there's no chance of getting hurt or being let down.'

'Let down! Brought crashing back to earth without a bloody parachute, more like!' Caroline, to her credit, had never once said 'I told you so'.

Caroline and Alex had become inseparable and Caroline had finally confessed to Sally that he had proposed to her. Sally was delighted for her but was aware that Caroline was trying her best to avoid talking about the wedding arrangements in front of her. It was difficult. Caroline and Alex were to be married back home, two weeks before Christmas, and it was rapidly becoming the local wedding of the year. The Foreign Office were sending Alex off to the Middle East, to a place called Al Khaleej, just before Christmas and, as his wife, Caroline would be entitled to go with him.

The news of her friend's wedding had aroused no deeper feelings in Sally than the hope that Caroline would not have to go through the heartache that she had endured. Sally was surprised that she felt so calm about it but thought that this was a good sign, a sign that at long last she was getting over Doug.

On her wedding day, Caroline looked radiant in a full-length cream lace coat over a dress of the palest cream silk. Sally, wearing a silk bridesmaid's dress of dark blue, spent most of the day fighting off the amorous attentions of Alex's best man. To cap it all, the star-struck fool attempted to help Sally catch the bride's bouquet when Caroline had pointedly hurled it straight at her best friend. Caroline and Alex left for a short honeymoon and flew out to the Middle East just three days before Christmas.

Sally then spent the most miserable Christmas of her life at home with her parents and Lottie. Although she hated London, being back home with her parents seemed worse. There were too many people in her hometown asking her too many questions to which she either did not have or did not want to give an answer. At the earliest opportunity, she returned to London and work. Caroline's aunt and uncle welcomed her back like their own, but the house was eerily empty without the laughter that always accompanied the two girls when they were together.

That winter was damp, dark and dismal and seemed never-ending to Sally as she trod the pavements on her way to work each morning, weaving between the dark, imposing buildings in the heart of London's Square Mile. By the middle of March, the weather forecast was still predicting more rain, with freezing temperatures at night. It would soon be her birthday and she was trying hard to forget the date. It was too near the date that her wedding should have taken place the previous year. Rose wanted her to come home for her birthday but Sally refused, preferring to stay on in Wimbledon. Renee and Fred invited a few friends over for a little 'celebration supper party' on the night and Sally was surprised to find she quite enjoyed the day after all.

By the end of March, there was still no sign of spring. When she heard the sleet and hail hitting the bedroom window, Sally would snuggle back down under the sheets and blankets and indulge in an extra few minutes of warmth before stepping out onto the cold lino to get ready for work.

One morning, as she was about to leave for the office, gloomy at the thought of yet another Underground journey with all the other strap-hanging commuters, she bent to pick up the mail that lay on the doormat. There were several letters for Renee and Fred and, as she placed them on the hall table, she smiled to see there was one for her from Caroline. It always gave her spirits a lift when she recognised Caroline's handwriting on an airmail envelope bearing a colourful foreign stamp. She had long ago given up looking for any communication from Doug, who had, it seemed, wisely decided on a clean break, and Sally had made no attempt to contact him. What was the point? The baby must be at least six months old by now. Stuffing the letter into her handbag, she set off for the Tube, looking forward to reading it over a cup of coffee later that morning.

Caroline's letters were always full of her exciting new life in the Middle East: Embassy parties, dinner parties at friends' houses, the beach and shopping in a place called the souk. Sally wasn't too sure what 'shopping in the souk' involved, but it all sounded very exotic. Caroline's letter ended with yet another plea to Sally to visit and stay with her for a while. Reading between the lines, it seemed to Sally that, as much as her friend enjoyed living in the Middle East, some days she was desperately homesick. As Sally folded the letter and slid it back into her handbag, she glanced out of her office window into the street below. A cold, howling gale was bending the bare branches of the trees into unnatural shapes and driving flurries of rain against the window. Why not, she thought? The fact that she had never flown before did not deter her from walking into the travel agents during her lunch break and booking a return flight to Al Khaleej. On her way home that evening, she posted a hastily- scribbled letter to Caroline to say she would soon be on her way.

Now here she was, being escorted to a window seat by a smartly-uniformed air hostess, listening to the captain as he outlined their route. He welcomed the passengers aboard, informing them that their aircraft was known as a Britannia and that there would be one refuelling stop, and then gave some statistics about altitudes and speed. Well, thought Sally, he sounded reassuringly in control and the aircraft very patriotic, but as it hurtled down the runway with its engines screaming and every part of the plane seeming to shake, some of her courage began to evaporate. In her flight bag she'd packed several books but for quite a while Sally stared out at the whirling propellers in a daydream until darkness fell. The air hostess brought refreshments and meals throughout the twelve-hour flight and at some point Sally fell asleep. She awoke as dawn was breaking and watched in wonderment from the porthole window as the rising sun painted the sky gold and pink outside. In the early morning light, the plane began its descent, descending at such a rate that it made her ears ache. Finally, when she was completely deaf from the pressurisation, the pilot muttered something inaudible over the intercom and lined the plane up for its approach to the airport. As they circled, she could see below clear, turquoise water and palm trees edging what seemed to be an extremely short runway, at either end of which was the sea. The Britannia's wheels hit the runway with a thud, the pilot applied the brakes and the plane shuddered, slowed and taxied slowly across the tarmac towards a small group of huts, where it finally stopped.

Pleased to be leaving the confines of the aeroplane, Sally thanked the air hostess and clambered down the rickety steps that had been pushed up against the open door. She assumed that the blast of heat that hit her as she disembarked was coming from the four engines that worked so hard during the long flight. But, as she followed the rest of the passengers across the tarmac towards a Nissen hut bearing the sign 'This way please – Arrivals Area and Customs – Welcome', she was shocked to realise that the heat was less to do with the engines and more to do with the climate!

As requested by an official in a khaki uniform at the entrance to the hut, Sally produced her passport and was disconcerted when he took it and turned to a swarthy man standing behind him, who promptly disappeared, taking her passport with him. Inside the arrivals lounge, ceiling fans rotated noisily at alarming speeds and angles, driving hot air and a variety of smells, most of them unpleasant, back down onto the people below. Sally was just beginning to wonder what, if anything, she was supposed to do next, when the swarthy man reappeared at her side. To her surprise, he was holding her suitcase.

'This cases for you, yes?' He placed the suitcase on the floor in front of her when Sally nodded. He then asked if she had anything to declare and, fairly certain that she hadn't, Sally smiled at him and shook her head.

'Okay. This way, please, follow me.' He picked up her suitcase and led her through the crowds to where, just beyond large swinging doors, to her relief, she could see Caroline and Alex. The customs officer shook hands with Alex, who thanked him for his help, while Sally and Caroline hugged, kissed, cried and tried to talk all at the same time.

Alex seemed genuinely delighted to see her and gave her a brief hug before saying, 'Come on, you two, save all that until we get home. You need to know, Sally, that such open displays of affection are frowned upon here.' Picking up Sally's suitcase, he began to make his way to the car.

Caroline laughed out loud and called after him, 'That's rich! We live in a country where the men hold hands and kiss each other whenever they meet!'

'That's their culture, and not quite the same thing at all,' Alex said, without looking round as he strode purposefully ahead.

Ever defiant, Caroline promptly linked arms with Sally and they began to giggle like schoolgirls as they followed him.

As they drove along, Sally peered out of the car window at the strange, sandy-coloured world she had arrived in. They drove past bungalows and flat-roofed, two-storey houses and through small villages where the homes were mud huts with roofs made from palm fronds. Finally, the car came to a halt outside a block of flats, three storeys high with a flat roof, which was home to Caroline and Alex. In the spacious ground-floor apartment supplied by the Foreign Office, Caroline showed Sally to the guest bedroom.

'The shower works well, so if you want to freshen up, please do. I'll put the coffee on and get some breakfast on the go.'

Although it was early morning, it was already very warm in the apartment and Sally gratefully stood under the shower, allowing the cool water to wash away the grime and sweat of the long flight.

The girls talked non-stop over breakfast and soon Alex excused himself to head off to the relative peace and quiet of his office at the Embassy. He would grab a sandwich for lunch and settle down in his office for a siesta, leaving the coast clear for the girls to catch up on the gossip or whatever it was that women talked about.

At lunchtime, the two friends ate a light salad outside on the terrace under a shady umbrella and Sally was surprised when Caroline produced a bottle of chilled white wine.

'I didn't think alcohol was allowed,' Sally mused out loud as she raised a glass to her lips.

'As expatriates, we have a licence to collect a certain amount each month from the bonded warehouse on the quayside,' Caroline explained. 'Would you like to look around the garden? We've got quite a large patch of our own and we can get to it down those stairs.' She nodded to the corner of the stone terrace where a set of wooden steps dropped down to the gardens below.

'They don't feel very safe,' laughed Sally, catching hold of the handrail and following Caroline down the wobbly steps. They strolled across the sparse lawn of coarse grass edged with flowerbeds, from which sprouted purple-headed flowers that neither Sally nor Caroline could identify. Several tall palm trees cast welcome shade over everything. The long journey combined with the heat and the wine were beginning to take effect and, when Caroline suggested that they have a little siesta, Sally readily agreed.

Waking a few hours later, Sally was relieved to find that it was a little cooler. Enjoying the feel of the marbled floor under her bare feet, she wandered into the sitting room and through to the kitchen, where Caroline was preparing an evening meal.

'Oh, good, you're awake. I've just made some tea.' In the more comfortable temperatures of the late afternoon, they sat drinking tea in the sitting room. Caroline was doing her best to ignore the fact that today Sally should have been celebrating her first wedding anniversary and, as if she'd read her thoughts, Sally suddenly said, 'It's all right, Caroline. I know what the date is. I just had to get away. All last year I kept wondering if he would write, then for a while I got out of the habit of looking for a letter from him. But in February, you know, around the anniversary of when I last saw him, I began to think about him again and, during these past few weeks, the nearer it got to April, the more I kept expecting to hear something from him. But I don't suppose I ever will now. It just all seemed so sudden – at the time.' Sally stopped as the memories came flooding back, and hastily blinked away a few tears.

Stop it, she told herself. It's been over a year now and you've got to get over it! Best forgotten and put aside as a lesson learned the hard way. 'You're so lucky with Alex. He obviously thinks the world of you. I bet he would never be unfaithful.' Sally fell silent again. 'I suppose with Doug I should have seen it coming. There were so many little tell-tale warning signs that I chose to ignore. I was so head-over-heels in love with him. I kidded myself I might be the one who could change him and I really believed him when he said I was different from all the others. That I was special.'

Caroline sat quietly listening to her friend pour her heart out. When she stopped she said, 'Sally, if it's any consolation, I think you were special to him.'

'Huh!' snorted Sally. 'But not special enough for him to keep someone else out of his bed.'

'You don't know that. From what you said about Moira, it may have been her not being able to keep out of his bed. If it was offered to him on a plate, I doubt any man would find it easy to refuse.'

It was after five-thirty and Sally slowly got to her feet and strolled out on to the terrace to watch the colours in the sky as the sun began to set on her first day in the Middle East. Just then, a loud wailing reverberated from an ornate tower in the distance. 'Caroline, what is that? I thought I heard it earlier today as well.'

'It's the muezzin. You'll see minarets and mosques all over the town and in all the villages. At sunrise and sunset and a couple of other times during the day, they call the faithful to prayer,' Caroline explained.

'It's so beautiful!' Sally stood for several minutes listening to the muezzin's call, entranced by its haunting quality.

By the end of her first week in Al Khaleej, Sally's fascination with her new surroundings had grown in intensity. She loved the warmth of the place, the certainty that the sun would shine – it was all so different to London and England and she found herself dreading the thought of returning to that cold, wet climate.

To satisfy her curiosity about the souk, Caroline took her there the very next day and Sally instantly fell in love with the busy, colourful, thriving market where it seemed that one could buy practically anything. It reminded her, just a little, of Petticoat Lane on a Sunday morning, but here there was no litter or empty cardboard boxes being blown hither and thither down streets and alleyways by cold, biting winds. Everything seemed much brighter and everywhere in this land of sunshine there were smiling faces. The market was full of exotic food, fruits, spices, fabrics and jewellery, as well as clothes and trinkets. Sally, who had never encountered anything like it, thought it was wonderful and found herself smiling back in response to the friendly greetings that were directed towards them as they made their way about the market.

The children were particularly entertaining and Sally loved chatting to them, enjoying their attempts to improve their English and in the process teaching her some basic Arabic. The shops were invariably family businesses, and stepping into any of them in the souk was like walking into someone's sitting room. Most had an elderly grandmother shrouded in black or a grinning toothless grandfather bouncing the latest arrival on his knee. Children could be seen helping out by sweeping the floors or weighing vegetables and spices. In the fabric part of the souk, children delighted in folding lengths of colourful cloth to put into the boxes of remnants.

The morning after the souk visit, Caroline drove away from their apartment in a different direction and after a short while they arrived at a local beach, where they took off their sandals and strolled along the water's edge. Sally loved the clean and uncluttered expanse of sand, which in places had been swept up into miniature sand dunes, and was enchanted by the natural setting of the palm trees that grew along the shoreline, right up to the water's edge in places. It reminded her of a picture she had seen as a child in one of her storybooks; was it Treasure Island? Or maybe it was Robinson Crusoe, she thought. The calm blue waters looked inviting but, when she asked about swimming, Caroline told her that it was not allowed unless one wanted to wear an old-fashioned Victorian-style bathing suit. In this part of the world, it was considered immoral for women to show too much flesh in public and the penalties for doing so were harsh. If one wanted to swim, Caroline told her, they had to hire a boat and swim offshore. Alternatively, there were private swimming pools such as the one in the grounds of the Embassy, where they went the next day.

The British Embassy was a very imposing colonial-era building, a sweeping driveway leading to a grand entrance with a long flight of stone steps, which in turn led to the marble-colonnaded frontage. Through the wrought-iron fencing and a pair of huge wrought-iron gates, Sally could see lush green gardens. A single white barrier was set across the gateway to prevent anyone from casually driving in and to one side of the barrier was a small sentry box occupied by a policeman in a white uniform.

'Crikey! Is this where Alex works?'

'Yeah, but if you think this is anything special, you should see the American Embassy! Luckily Alex's office is on the first floor, around the side, but the pool is at the far end of the grounds. Just as well – wouldn't do for him to know how many times a week or how long I spend lazing round the pool.'

'Do you? Spend a lot of time lazing round the pool?'

'No, not really. I like to swim, and usually just have a quick one most days to cool down, but once I've dried off in the sun, I leave. During the week, it tends to be just the women who have time to use the pool, and all-female groups have never really been my thing. It's a hotbed of gossip, too – reminds me of school too much, and you know what that was like! Most of them are only interested in finding out little bits of tittle-tattle and what they don't know they tend to make up,' Caroline said with sigh, and Sally could empathise. Both of them had been tomboys and as a result neither had really enjoyed the all- female environment of their convent school.

Caroline drove on a little way past the main entrance, the metal fencing giving way to a six-foot high wall, and turned in through a smaller gateway. Here, too, was a barrier with a policeman in a box. As Caroline slowed down he stepped out and, recognising her car, hurried to lift the barrier and wave her through.

Sally was impressed that they had been allowed to enter without any further checks, until Caroline told her that she had told Alex of their intention to swim at the Embassy today, so that he could inform security.

'Do you have to do that every time you want to come here for a swim?' Sally was incredulous.

'Oh no, only if I want to bring a guest, and of course they already have all your details.'

Sally wondered what kind of details they had and wasn't sure she liked the idea of Alex, of all people, getting hold of 'details' about her. Still, there was nothing she could do about it and in any case, in this heat, the idea of a swim to cool off was still just as inviting.

They entered a short driveway lined with palm trees and Sally could see cars parked in the shade they created. It was a short walk to the pool through some shrubbery, up some steps and out onto a large stone terrace on which tables, chairs and comfortable loungers were laid out underneath large sun brollies. Formally- attired servants were on hand to serve food or drinks to the wives and friends of the officials or visitors staying at the Embassy. As they mounted the steps to the terrace, Sally could see that the gardens surrounding the pool were made up of English-style herbaceous borders, tall bushes and plants that were constantly being watered with sprinklers. The vegetation provided a natural shield, avoiding the risk of causing offence to visiting local dignitaries and preventing bathers being seen by any casual observer looking out of the Embassy windows. Paths shaded by palm trees meandered in and out of the neatly-trimmed hedges and bushes. As they reached the terrace, Sally caught a glimpse of the rear of the Embassy, which looked just as imposing as the front. But she also thought that the quintessentially English gardens with their immaculate lawns were somewhat at odds with the palm trees and seemed out of place here in Al Khaleej. They made their way over to a couple of vacant sun loungers, Caroline nodding a greeting to some of the women they passed without introduction, explaining to Sally in a whisper that she didn't really know any of them. When Sally expressed surprise, Caroline explained that they were probably the wives, girlfriends, sisters or possibly even an odd maiden aunt or two of Embassy officials, or visiting dignitaries staying with the Ambassador. Sally wasn't surprised that Caroline had felt homesick if the motley collection of staid middle-aged women seated around the pool that morning were the only people Caroline had to socialise with.

The following day, they set off in yet another direction, this time taking a busy coastal road into a local town. Large trucks competed with donkey carts and people on their bicycles, dangerously weaving in and out of the traffic. Sally could see the vibrant blue of the sea and, as they drove along, she caught a glimpse of a pretty, little fishing harbour nestled in a small bay. As they approached the town, Sally was disappointed to see that it resembled a vast building site. Flats, town houses and shops were being hastily erected to meet the demands of the increase in trade that had followed the discovery of oil in the region. Caroline drove her down to the bonded warehouse by the side of a busy port, where she collected a couple of cases of wine for Alex. Looking round, Sally saw that a crane was unloading cargo from an enormous container ship moored alongside one of the quays.

'Are those battleships over there? What on earth are they doing here?' she suddenly exclaimed, pointing at three sombre grey ships.

'Oh, Alex says it's because of the Russkies and the Americans trying to get in on the act with all the oil. That's why we have to be here too. Look over there – British frigates!'

Sally followed Caroline's pointing finger and saw more grim- looking warships, and thought what a pity it was that this peaceful, faraway country was now the focus of the world's attention.

Having collected the wine, Caroline took her to a smart, British-owned restaurant on the quayside for lunch. From their table, they watched the bustle of activity in the port. Sally could hear that it was all very cosmopolitan – there must be natives of almost every country on the planet settling here, she thought, as she recognised accents from Germany, France, America and a whole host of other places. With the influx of so many foreigners and all the building work that was going on to accommodate them, Sally felt Al Khaleej was in danger of losing its identity, together with many of its local customs. To Sally, it looked as though the area was being reshaped to take on a more westernised look and she felt the urge to learn more about the history of the place before it all was buried beneath the concrete.

One morning, just as the sun was rising, Sally lay in bed listening again to the muezzin calling the faithful to prayer. Suddenly, her eyes began to fill with tears at the thought that she must soon leave and return home. What, she wondered, was she going home to? She couldn't lodge with Renee and Fred for ever. She would have to move out sooner or later – then what? She certainly didn't feel that she could return to her parents' house, not having tasted freedom. The muezzin's call was haunting, thrilling even, and bizarrely, she felt, for someone brought up in the suburbs of Middlesex, it aroused a sense of belonging within her. It didn't make any sense but, prompted by the panic she felt about returning to London, she spoke to Caroline and Alex about her feelings over breakfast. Caroline urged her to stay on with them for a bit longer, pointing out that her visa was for six months and it would be a shame to waste it.

'But if you're serious about staying, I imagine you'll want somewhere of your own to stay, of course?' Alex suggested. He smiled as he said it, but Sally caught the implication that it was a foregone conclusion that she would want to be independent.

Pleased though he was for Caroline's sake that her friend wanted to stay on, Alex was not so sure that he wanted a permanent houseguest playing gooseberry! He needn't have worried. Sally was only too willing to move out – she had been as embarrassed as they were when, on a couple of occasions, she had walked into the kitchen or the sitting room only to realise that they had swiftly drawn apart from what had obviously been a passionate embrace! As welcome as they had made her feel, she was keenly aware of their attempts to be discreet and had begun to feel awkward about her continued presence.

Taking the hint, Sally said, 'Oh yes, of course, Alex, I would love a place of my own. Do you think that would be possible?' She added, 'But I'll also need a job'.

'Well, I'm sure we can find you somewhere to live without too much trouble, and there's plenty of work around. If you're sure you want to stay, leave it to me – I'll see what I can do,' Alex said, grinning with relief that, if Sally was staying, she wouldn't object to moving into her own place.

It was part of his job to be aware of the comings and goings of all Britons in the area, and a few days later he arrived home with the news that there was a vacancy at the offices of an airfreight company. The young woman whose job it had been was returning to England and Alex was confident she wouldn't be coming back. Sally successfully interviewed for the position of English-speaking secretary.

One afternoon, before starting her new job – and what she hoped would be a new start in life – she sat and wrote to her parents, telling them how happy she was. She told them not to worry because, even though she was miles from home in a strange country, Caroline was looking after her. Fortunately, Sally would never know the effect this last statement had on her mother. Having Caroline looking after her daughter in a country thousands of miles away and full of foreigners meant that Sally was back at the top of her prayer list every night.

Sally also wrote letters to Doris, to Renee and Fred and to her employer in England, tendering her resignation and apologising for her hasty departure. With the rate of new construction in Al Khaleej, it was not difficult to find accommodation. Caroline drove Sally round and together they viewed several properties before choosing a ground-floor apartment in a block of six that had just been completed. The terrace doors opened into a private garden and this swung the decision for Sally, even though the 'garden' was still a bare patch of sand. The road up to the apartments was of compacted sand and, though rutted, was fairly accessible.

The rented apartment was fully furnished, so within a week Sally was able to move in. She had barely unpacked her suitcase when there was a knock at the door.

'Hello, I garden, I make grass come,' said the swarthy little man in a long tablecloth wrap and grey shirt. Just over his shoulder Sally could see a donkey and cart, with what looked like gardening implements.

'Oh, right, but I haven't got a garden, really – just sand.' She received a blank expression in response to her reply, and tried to explain. Hell, she thought, what's Arabic for 'no garden'? She remembered that greens or grass was hasheesh, and stumbled on. Adopting the pose that she'd seen used to denote a problem, she raised her shoulders, held her arms forward, and turned her palms up. 'Mafee hasheesh,' she said, and waited for a reaction.

'I make hasheesh,' the man said, pointing at his chest.

Stumped by this response, and hoping that they were both on the same wavelength as to exactly what she did want growing in her garden, Sally walked round to the back of the apartments with her new employee. Without any word of encouragement, the donkey fell in behind his master and followed them to the back garden gate, the large wooden wheels on the cart rattling on the rutted road.

After a quick survey of the plot the gardener put forward his ideas. Sally wondered if he was also looking after Caroline's garden, as he seemed to favour a square of grass and purple flowers round the edges. The quote for grass seed and plants duly given and a price agreed for his time, the man left happily and promised to be back early the next morning to make a start.

Chapter Twenty

Early morning starts were the norm in this part of the world and, arriving for work at six-thirty, Sally had easily found a parking space for her rusting Frogeye Sprite. Her complete ignorance of the mechanical workings of the motorcar was a blessing and meant that travelling to work was an unalloyed pleasure. Once she had struggled into the driving seat, she could imagine her little car was something more than fading yellow paint and rust balanced on four treacherous tyres.

She had gained her driving licence in Al Khaleej by taking a couple of lessons with Afi, a local driving instructor, and presenting herself at the Police Station for a mandatory driving test. Afi had warned her that the test would be carried out by the police and that it was usual for two policemen to accompany learner drivers. But when Sally arrived, four smiling policemen in white uniforms had squeezed into her instructor's car to assess her motoring skills. Most of the roads in Al Khaleej were not overly busy and Sally set off with confidence, following the directions of the policeman in the passenger seat next to her. She had learned very quickly how to drive forwards and reverse, indicate, turn left and right, and stop and start reasonably smoothly. There had been a faint murmur of what sounded like approval from all four policemen at her clutch control as she'd pulled away from the police station. However, they were totally unprepared for the emergency stop as Sally rounded a corner in one of the villages to find a mother hen and several chicks pecking the dirt in the middle of the road.

Having recovered from being launched forward from their seats, they were amazed to see Sally leaning out of the window and shouting to the hapless mother hen, 'Take your babies off the road, what sort of mother are you?' Ignoring her, the hen continued to peck at the dirt road. Sally, remembering to put the car into neutral and pull on the hand brake, leapt from the driver's seat and set about shooing the indignant hen and her brood of cute chicks to the relative safety of the roadside. Returning to the car and ignoring the grinning faces, Sally studiously looked in the rear-view mirror, indicated and set off once more. They had hardly gone a mile further down the road when three goats with their kids strolled out in front of the car, and once more Sally swiftly applied the brakes. This time the policemen were half-prepared for the emergency stop and were holding on to their seats and each other.

The whole test progressed in this manner, with Sally repeatedly hitting the brakes and leaping out of the car to clear the road of ungrateful suicidal livestock. Once they'd got used to her frequent and frantic use of the brakes, the policemen could enjoy watching Sally and admired her lissom figure and long slender legs as she chased the animals off the road. Within half an hour they had all agreed that she easily qualified for a driving licence. To Sally, this unanimous decision seemed to be based on her ability to avoid knocking down any of the baby goats, donkeys and chickens aimlessly wandering the unmade roads where the test had taken place. Completely unaware that her success was, in part, due to the policemen being totally mesmerised by the pretty blue-eyed blonde behind the wheel, she thanked her examiners and couldn't believe how easy it had been.

In comparison to Afi's new Hillman Hunter that she'd used for her driving lessons and test, her own little yellow car was somewhat dilapidated and nowadays remained permanently convertible, its smart black hood having long since disintegrated. It had been given to her by a friend of a friend who had returned to Britain on completion of his contract. The car's mechanical condition was undoubtedly a danger to the driver and a threat to all other road users, but it had been freely given. However, as with most 'free' gifts, there had been a catch. Written into the small print of the deal was custody of the dog! In the fullness of time, it became apparent to Sally that it would have been cheaper to pay for a car – but she was flat broke, grateful for transport to get her to work and, besides all that, she had always wanted a dog.

Bouncy had been delivered to her apartment along with the car. Thirty kilos of canine testosterone, the end product its mother's numerous love affairs with the indigenous packs of pi-dogs. In his shape there was just a hint of saluki, the Arabian hunting hound, pointing to a possible royal connection, but in the main Bouncy was just a common, loveable mutt. His coat had the texture of thick coconut matting and with its wiry tufts of tawny hair it was perfect for harbouring ticks and fleas. His ears stuck out at right angles from his head before folding over at the tips. His large, soulful eyes brought a startled yet somewhat vacant expression to his whiskery face. No doubt as a small pup abandoned on the roadside he had been cute and in need of rescuing, but now it seemed his aim in life was to get back on the road and procreate. To keep Bouncy safe, Sally had asked the gardener to raise the height of the boundary by adding three feet of chain-link fencing to the top of the garden wall, thereby fulfilling her promise to his previous owner to take good care of him. In his frustration at being confined, Bouncy repaid her concern for his welfare by regularly emptying dustbins, eating the furniture and, in the early hours of the morning, howling until he was allowed into the bedroom to sleep at the foot of her bed.

Despite the early morning start, her journey to work was always a pleasure. It was in sharp contrast to commuting in England, where she might be squeezed into a seat next to a red-nosed sneezing stranger trying to empty the contents of his nasal passages into a hankie, or sandwiched between strap-hangers with her nose embedded in a smelly armpit. Here, there were clear blue skies every morning and warmth in the early morning sun. Taking a deep breath, filling her lungs with the fresh sea air, she decided that her life had certainly taken a turn for the better.

The last haunting wail of the muezzin drifted over Sally as she carefully picked her way across the patch of uneven waste ground used by many as an unofficial car park. She reached the narrow pathway that would lead eventually to the tarmac road, at the far end of which was the office block where she now worked as PA to the manager of First Class Air Freight. A grand title, but her job largely consisted of producing endless cups of coffee strong enough to counteract the excess of alcohol her boss had imbibed the night before. The airline offices stood one block back from the seashore and, as Sally walked along, she caught glimpses of the vivid turquoise waters of the Gulf between the small, flat-roofed houses that lined the shore. Early morning sea mist hovered in swirling candyfloss patches over the calm waters and a flotilla of colourful wooden dhows could be seen heading back towards the harbour with their night's catch.

The design of the Arab dhow had remained unchanged since biblical times as the skills and secrets of traditional boatbuilding were passed down the centuries from father to son. In Al Khaleej they were constructed by families who lived all along the seashore in rustic houses made from wood and palms.

Ever since Sally had arrived in Al Khaleej, she'd wanted to learn about the country's history, culture and people. Late one afternoon, on her day off, she'd walked from her apartment through the town and down to the seashore. The fierce rays of the midday sun had abated but, wanting to escape the heat still trapped in the town, Sally sought the cooling breezes that could always be found by the sea. Seeing the boatbuilders at work along the shoreline, she made her way along the narrow sandy beach to where several partially-built dhows sat just above the water's edge. From a distance, they hadn't looked very big but as she got closer the skeletal wooden structures, held upright by poles propped against the main struts, towered above her. An old man with a wrinkled, nut-brown weather-beaten face was working on one of the boats, and called out to her in English and waved.

'Hello, yes, welcome.'

Sally returned the wave and called back, 'Salaam'.

The boatbuilders were friendly, keen to show their skills and willing to share their time with her. Sally had noticed that time was often freely given in this land of warmth and sunshine, where nothing was so important that it couldn't wait until tomorrow. Conscious that boatbuilding was their livelihood and thus not wanting to hold up their work, Sally settled herself on an old wooden crate nearby and quietly watched their progress. The old man strolled across to her, holding out some of the ancient handmade tools of his trade for her to see, using mime to show her how they worked.

That afternoon, she learned that everything was crafted by hand, including the specialised tools needed for the job. She watched with amusement while a young boy haphazardly nailed together a makeshift ladder from offcuts of wood. He wore a long, grubby shirt with the back hem pulled through between his legs and tucked into a belt, creating the impression that he was wearing a pair of baggy shorts. When he'd placed the homemade ladder against the side of the boat and scurried confidently to the top rung, high above the ground, she feared for his life. Laughing, he waved to her as he balanced on one of the lopsided rungs of the ladder that now leaned precariously against the hull of the boat.

The lazy swish of the Gulf's gentle waves tipping onto the shore provided perfect background music to the hammering and sawing, constant chatter and frequent laughter. Despite the noise of labour, Sally found the seashore peaceful and she stayed until the setting sun turned the sky on the horizon a deep orange. Against the glow of sunset, the dhow's wooden skeleton resembled the ribcage of a giant animal picked clean by scavengers. When the sun had all but disappeared, she thanked the family and promised to return and follow the progress of the craft they were building. The old man was quite insistent, using a combination of sign language and broken English, that Sally should come back when they 'make the boat go in the bahr'. The rest of his family crowded round her, nodding and grinning enthusiastically, reinforcing the invitation. In case she hadn't understood, he hurried back to the unfinished boat, put his bony shoulder to the front of the hull and pretended to push. There was much laughter when several of his younger relatives, also communicating by sign language and laboured English, joked about it sinking straight away, but the elderly boatbuilder took the leg-pulling with a grin. Sally promised to keep an eye on the boat's progress and be there for the launch and managed to ask politely, in her scant Arabic, when this might be. As an understanding of what she was asking dawned on him, the old man held up one hand and said, 'Khamsa'. Sally had learned her numbers and knew that this meant five, but as she bid goodbye to all her new-found friends, she wasn't sure if the old man meant five weeks, five months or five years.

That morning, as she walked the final few yards to her office she glanced towards the sea, watching as the majority of dhows were silently and expertly guided into the harbour under sail. As was the way in this country, most of them seemed to be in no hurry but, as Sally heard the noisy chug-chug of the diesel motors with which some of them were now fitted, she sighed. No doubt a couple of the returning fishermen were anxious to land their catch before the others and Sally thought it a shame that a manmade noise should disturb the natural peace and serenity of her surroundings.

Walking on past several open-topped rusty oil drums serving as dustbins, she was deep in thought, her brows drawn together in a frown as she wondered what the day ahead might hold for her. The world of freight airlines and cargo was still quite new to her and, although she had learned a lot in the past few weeks since she'd started working, she knew that she still had much to learn. Suddenly, two skinny cats leapt vertically out over the rim of the nearest oil drum and fled past her in a blur of ginger and black. The indigenous cats were long and sleek with small heads, almond-shaped eyes and large, pointed ears, similar to the ones she had seen in history books on Ancient Egypt. The speed with which the scavenging felines had appeared from the bottom of the oil drum startled Sally – for a fleeting moment, she'd feared they might be rats.

Grinning with relief, she continued to pick her way along the narrow, uneven and in places non-existent pavement until she reached the road. From behind her, Sally heard the fast clip-clop of hooves and turned to see a donkey cart laden with locally-grown vegetables heading straight towards her. The driver applied his accelerator – a short piece of hosepipe – to the long-suffering donkey, and Sally winced as she heard the 'thwack' as it hit the donkey's bony rump. The driver was in a hurry to get his fare to the local market. Sally waited for the weary donkey to pass before crossing the road.

Arriving at work, she returned the cheerful Arabic greeting from the doorman and climbed the stairs to the first floor, where she popped in to the communications room to collect the overnight telexes.

'Good morning, Amiri. How are you today?' Sally liked Amiri. He smiled regardless of his difficulties, of which, it seemed, he had many. Being in charge of modern communications in a land where all errors or successes were attributed to the will of God was a difficult enough job, but Amiri was also a martyr to his wives.

When Sally had first taken the job, Amiri possessed only two wives but was negotiating for a third. Now that he had purchased the third wife, he was beginning to realise his folly. The first two wives, while happy to share Amiri between them, objected strongly to the arrival of a third contender for his affections. Amiri had tried to please them all by providing each wife with a home of her own. Unfortunately, they were all housed within the same three-storey apartment block which he had recently inherited, and his plan for a wife on each floor was proving to be a bad idea. Problems seemingly arose because the walls were thin and the floors not insulated, so that sound travelled easily between the flats, allowing each wife to know Amiri's whereabouts and, more worryingly, what he was doing. This morning, Amiri looked particularly pale for an Arab, but attempted to mask his worries with his usual welcoming smile.

'Are you well, Amiri?' Sally asked. 'You look very pale and tired.'

He waved his hands in the air in a gesture of despair. For some reason, Amiri always spoke openly to Sally about his marital relations and this morning he launched straight into the latest episode.

'Too many problems with my wife, Sally. I do not know what I can do. If I make love with one wife I know the other two for sure they are listening, then they want me to go to be with them also. If I make love to my new wife, maybe for a long time,' Amiri gave a coy smile, 'my other wives they want the same. How can I? It is possible? I not so young now. Believe me, Sally, sometimes I am so weak I cannot climb up the stairs to my first wife on the third floor, but I have to because if I am hungry she is the best for cooking.' He shrugged his shoulders in despair.

The pecking order seemed to be wife number one on the top floor, wife number two in the middle and the new young wife, number three, on the ground floor. Sally tried to smother a grin as she realised that the disruption to his domestic bliss was caused because Amiri, still enamoured of his new wife, seemed incapable of getting off the ground floor! He explained to Sally that when he got home to his new wife, his first wife would immediately leave her top-floor apartment and run downstairs to visit his second wife in the middle apartment. Anticipating what was likely to go on below them, they would sit together drinking coffee and gossiping; they would bang on the floor and shriek with laughter, thus upsetting the third wife.

'What can I do, Sally? I must divorce one, but not the first one. She old now and looks after me very nice, her food good. Not the second, she is the mother of my two sons.'

'Well, what about the system some companies use in Britain?' Sally offered.

'
What is that?' Amiri looked hopeful at the possibility of a simple solution to his problem.

'If somebody joins a company and that company has to reduce its staff, they sometimes use a "last in, first out" policy.'

Amiri thought for a while. Then, realising the implication of this arrangement, he said, 'Oh no! Not my new wife! She cannot go! She is too good for ...' Amiri hesitated, searching for a polite description of his latest wife's attributes. 'She is good for bedroom,' he finally offered, this confession causing the colour to creep back into his pale cheeks.

Amiri quickly turned to face the rows of pigeonholes behind him, reached for a handful of telexes that were stuffed in the slot marked for the attention of her boss and handed them to her. Shrugging her shoulders, Sally grinned at Amiri and promised to have coffee with him later if she was not too busy.

Climbing the final flight of stairs, Sally unlocked the door to her office, sighing as she sat down at her desk. Thinking of her conversation with Amiri, she felt that she was not much use to him as an agony aunt but she was a good listener. He wasn't to know that Sally's whole reason for being in the Middle East was to rebuild her own life after her first and only attempt at forming a serious relationship with the opposite sex. From this distance in miles and time, she could see that possibly she had mistaken infatuation for love, but she'd had no experience of either emotion at the time; whatever it was she had felt for Doug, it still hurt a lot when she thought about it. Despite her best efforts to put it behind her, occasionally her thoughts drifted back and she caught herself rummaging through that parcel of memories marked 'best forgotten'.

She gave herself a mental shake as she put the handful of telexes on her desk. The memories were still very painful and sometimes her emotions threatened to overwhelm her, just as they had done during those first few months after Doug's shattering revelations about Moira. She made herself some coffee, sat down at her desk and settled her mind to the business of sifting through the telexes to identify what, if any, custom clearances were needed to allow the day's imports into the region.

First Love

Chapter Twenty-One

The Al Khaleej branch of First Class Air Freight that Sally worked for consisted only of the manager, Hishaam, and herself. Part of her job involved liaising with airport customs and checking what they required for clearance to release any imported goods. It was pretty dull, straightforward stuff – flight numbers and arrival times, lists of boxes detailing their contents, weights and measurements. The imported cargo mainly consisted of engine parts for the big oil company in the region or components for the equally large construction industry that had started up in recent years. Sometimes there were spare parts for cars imported from Europe and at others it was crates of personal effects belonging to recent arrivals from around the world.

The imports side of the business was easy for Sally, as the freight costs and delivery times had already been worked out at the airport of origin. If she had any problems, she knew that she had a reliable ally at the airport customs office. Exports, however, were quite another matter. Sally found that filling up the cargo planes to make their journeys more economically viable was quite a responsibility and had involved a steep learning curve for her. Hishaam could easily work out on the back of his cigarette packet how much space was left on each plane, and how many cubic feet would be required to fill it and still remain within the weight allowance. But at times, like now, when she was on her own in the office, she dreaded anyone phoning for an instant quotation as she had yet to master the mathematical formulae for working these out. All she knew was that the final price would depend on whichever was the greater, volume or weight. Sally would struggle along, trying to run the office until her boss put in an appearance, which was becoming later and later in the day as he began to feel confident that he could rely on her. After only a month in the business, the world of imports and exports was still very new to Sally and her boss's increasingly frequent late starts put her under pressure to cope with whatever turned up on her desk.

In Al Khaleej, most of the population kept out of the sun during the hottest part of day and took a siesta. Sally's office hours were from 7 am to 12 pm and from 4 pm to 6 pm, in line with other local businesses. All the shops would close at noon and open again at four– many shopkeepers would then stay open until almost midnight to catch the last few nocturnal shoppers or insomniacs.

The afternoon siestas meant that nobody went to bed very early at night. The higher the sun rose, the fewer people were out and about. At first Sally found it strange to see the deserted streets filling up as the sun set and people began to emerge from their homes, spilling out into the tiny alleyways of the town and the local markets to shop or just to take a walk in the cool night air. During the intense heat of the summer months most sensible people took advantage of these late hours and did their shopping after dark, when it was cooler.

As the morning ticked slowly by, Sally hoped her boss would soon arrive. He suffered terrible bouts of headaches, which at first she'd charitably put down to migraine, only later discovering that most of his 'headaches' were in fact hangovers. It was against his religion to consume alcohol but Hishaam had long since lost the battle between his belief, his conscience and his addiction. Alcohol could only legally be purchased on licence in this part of the world but in his line of work and with his many contacts in the import business, Hishaam could lay his hands on most things. For all his failings and weaknesses he was a kind-hearted boss and her pay packet was generous.

Hishaam being of Egyptian origin, Sally had supposed he would have been used to the heat, but he wasn't. She had quickly learned that when he did finally arrive in the mornings, his coffee had to be hot but the office had to be cold. In Sally's office the air-conditioning unit was set rather precariously into a hole made in an outer wall. At the flick of a switch it noisily whirred and rattled and sucked in the humid moisture-laden air from the room, exhaling an icy cold blast in its place. With its mesh front and row of knobs it looked like a giant old-fashioned radio. Sally constantly worried that the heavy contraption would one day rattle itself out of the wall and drop into the street below onto some poor unsuspecting pedestrian. Never knowing when to expect the arrival of Hishaam, Sally kept the coffee pot primed and ready to go at the touch of a switch.

Seated at her desk reading through the telexes, she wished she had remembered to bring a cardigan as she began to shiver in the rapidly chilling office. In the telexes that morning, among the usual lists of boxes, weights and measurements, something caught Sally's eye – 'One pallet: Eng. TBs.'

'Eng. TBs?' she asked herself out loud and, being an equine enthusiast, her immediate definition of 'TBs' was Thoroughbred horses.

'English Thoroughbred horses?' she asked herself again. Surely not! But what else could it be? Boxes, not horses, came on pallets, thought Sally as she tried to visualise a terrified horse balancing on a flat wooden pallet. No, it can't be, she thought, because how would they keep a horse in place when its natural response to any stressful situation would be to run as fast and as far as possible in the opposite direction? Anyway, why would anyone want to import English horses to the desert? Surely they had much more suitable animals already here, indigenous horses bred to survive in the heat – although she was yet to see one.

She decided she had jumped to the wrong conclusion, but her curiosity was aroused and, combined with her passion for horses, she just couldn't leave it at that. Picking up the phone, she called Tewfik, her reliable ally at the customs office who was always willing to help and every time sounded so genuinely pleased to speak to her.

Whenever he answered the phone he launched into the traditional Arabic custom of enquiring after her health, her state of happiness, her well-being and, because he knew she was not married and had no children, the health of Bouncy, her dog.

Sally reciprocated, so that several minutes would pass before they got down to the real reason for the call. Sally had learnt that in this part of the world, before any business was mentioned or conducted, good manners required people to respond to a greeting with more than just a straightforward reply. Sally loved these gracious little exchanges but sometimes she became so engrossed in them that shed couldn't remember what she had telephoned Tewfik about in the first place.

'Everything is fine and I am very well, thank you,' Sally would respond and ask Tewfik, 'How are you, Tewfik? And how is your wife, and is your son better now? How are all your other children?' Tewfik, in turn, answered each of her polite enquiries with 'Alhumdulallah,' the traditional Arab reply which credited God with keeping him and his family well and out of harm. This time, though, there was no chance of Sally struggling to remember the reason why she had called him. As soon as the formalities were over she asked him if he would kindly go through the freight 'Inwards' list with her.

'Oh yes. Plenty of work for you, Miss Sally, many, many, many things.'

'Tewfik, I know this might be a funny question, but is there any livestock for us to collect?'

'No, nothing liverstock, but there is coming two horses,' he replied, 'for the Sheikh. Two horses from Ingerland.'

'So where it says "Eng. TBs" on the telexes, they are horses?'

'I do not know what his name but he is horses, two horses for the Sheikh,' Tewfik repeated.

'Tewfik, it says they are on a pallet? Tell me, how can you put horses on a pallet?'

'No, no! Horses not on pallet! Horses in box and box on pallet ... or he be run away!' Tewfik was laughing when he put the phone down. How sweet this English girl was, but how could she possibly think a horse would stand on a pallet? He shook his head as he turned back to carry on with the mountain of paperwork in front of him.

Replacing the receiver on its cradle, Sally was excited. This was the first time since she had started working for Hishaam that they had flown in any livestock, and suddenly her job seemed that much more interesting. Then she realised that, because it was the first time, she was unsure of the correct procedure for customs clearance and she should have asked Tewfik what she needed to do while she had been speaking to him. Uncomfortable about imposing on him again, Sally was confident that Hishaam would know and decided to wait for him to arrive. It was still early yet and she did not expect to see him until 10 am. When it got to 11 am and he had still not appeared, Sally was increasingly worried that she had not done whatever it was that should have been done to arrange clearance for the importation of the horses. Any minute now, she was convinced, the phone would ring and somebody would ask her whether or not the horses could be collected or delivered or whatever other arrangement had to be made for them.

Although Hishaam had made it quite clear that he did not like to be called at home, she took a deep breath and dialled his home number, and waited while the phone rang and rang and rang. 'Naam ...?' It was more of a groan than a recognisable response when Hishaam's sleepy voice finally answered.

'Hishaam? It's me, Sally.'

'What do you want?' he croaked in a husky voice. 'Can't you hear? I am sick! Very, very sick. I will see you later.'

'Hishaam! Please don't hang up! Listen! There are two horses coming in on today's flight. Tewfik said they are for the Sheikh, but what clearance do they need and who do I contact?'

There was a long silence, making Sally wonder if Hishaam had fallen asleep again. 'Hishaam ...?'

'Sheikh ...' she heard him mumble almost to himself, 'which Sheikh? This place is full of sheikhs. Some are important ... others not,' groaned Hishaam.

'I'm sorry, I don't know which Sheikh. Tewfik just said "the Sheikh",' Sally said in an effort to be helpful. When no answer was forthcoming, she asked again, 'What do I need to do about customs?'

'Oh ... my ... God!' she heard him whisper reverently on the other end of the phone. Ignoring her question, suddenly he became more alert. He yelled,

'He actually said "The" Sheikh? Are you sure he said "The" Sheikh?'

'Well, yes. What he actually said was that the two horses were for the Sheikh, but Hishaam ...'

'Oh, my God!' Hishaam said again, shouting down the phone. Sally winced and held the phone away from her ear.

'That can only be one person! Okay! ... Okay! ... Don't panic! I am coming in now! Make my coffee. Quickly!' And the line went dead.

Sally was more amused than panic-stricken as she tried to visualise a sheikhly Pecking Order, wondering how far up or down the line was the sheikh that these horses were destined for. But at least Sally now had the reassurance of knowing that Hishaam was on his way to the office.

Ten minutes later, she pressed the switch on the kettle. Twenty minutes after that, Hishaam arrived, sweating profusely, his face a peculiar shade of yellowish-green. When he removed his sunglasses, Sally could see that his eyes were bloodshot.

'Coffee, Sally! Please bring me black coffee, quickly,' he said brusquely as he snatched the telexes from her, before slumping down in the leather swivel armchair behind his desk. No sooner had he drained his first cup than he held it out to Sally in an agitated gesture for her to refill it. He slurped at his coffee, quickly glancing through all the telexes, then picked up the phone and called the airport. Sally could tell from the shrill pitch and squeak of his voice that Hishaam was becoming increasingly upset by the conversation he was having with the airport authorities. Vigorously nodding or shaking his head, he raised his eyes to heaven and mouthed silent pleas and prayers in response to the information he was receiving. He swiftly downed several more cups of coffee in quick succession while he was talking, each time draining his cup, then holding it out to Sally to refill. Eventually he slammed the phone down. If he had looked unwell when he had first arrived at the office, Sally was convinced that he was now about to have a seizure. While he had been on the phone, even the yellow in his face had drained away, and was now replaced with a deathly pale hue which made the dark shadows beneath his bloodshot eyes even more noticeable than before. For a moment longer he sat at his desk, agitatedly wringing his hands before pulling out a handkerchief to wipe the nervous sweat from his palms. Then he mopped the sweat from his face, his bloodshot eyes staring straight ahead of him.

'Big problem. Very big problem,' he muttered, shaking his head. Then, as if in a trance, speaking very slowly in English, he repeated to himself the information that he had been given over the phone. He had always found that when he translated his thoughts into English, it gave his brain time to think – to get his thoughts into some sort of order, rather than the jumbled mess that his alcohol-infused brain seemed to be in these days.

'There are horses coming. For the Sheikh. They have diverted en route. Minor engine problems with the plane. They will be delayed. At least ten hours. Maybe more,' he said. At last he looked up at Sally, who had remained standing by his desk, coffee pot in hand. Oh, it was perfect, he thought. The answer was staring him in the face.

'Somebody has to go to the offices and tell them.'

'Which offices?' Sally innocently asked, as she poured him more coffee.

'The Palace offices for the Sheikh. They must be told, reassured that the horses are well. But tell them not to send the horse transport to the airport until very early tomorrow morning. I cannot rely on these people answering the phone in the Palace offices. Or to deliver important messages correctly. Somebody from here must go in person. As you can see, I am not well. I cannot drive. So you must go.'

Sally had not been paying too much attention to Hishaam's murmuring. He often talked quietly to himself, muttering as he worked out the various problems that confronted him, and she had assumed that was what he was doing now. But as she turned away from his desk to refill the coffee pot, she wondered where it was that she was going.

'Go where?' she asked.

'Don't you listen to anything?' Hishaam suddenly screamed at her, as she walked away from his desk. 'You must go to the Palace offices! Now! Immediately!'

Sally turned, staring open-mouthed at Hishaam as his voice reached its highest octave. She had never seen him in such a state and, with the sound of his scream still ringing in her ears, she anxiously glanced towards the windows wondering if the panes of glass were in danger of shattering. She was about to remonstrate with him for screaming at her, but realised that Hishaam was genuinely frightened and was close to becoming hysterical. Well, if the delay of a couple of horses could put Hishaam into such a state of nervous agitation, then this Sheikh must be at the upper end of the pecking order, she surmised.

'But Hishaam,' Sally said calmly as she put down the coffee pot and turned to face him. 'I am not dressed to go to any Palace offices. Surely I should put on something more suitable if I am to go?'

But Hishaam was in no mood for any arguments. 'You are perfectly okay like that! There is no time!'

Sally had put on a blouse and short skirt for work that morning; not exactly a miniskirt, despite the fact that they were the height of fashion back in Britain – since arriving, Sally had not worn a miniskirt in public. Alex had warned her that in a Muslim country, out of respect for local customs and religion, she should dress modestly. Nonetheless, during her first visit to a local hairdressing salon, it had been a revelation to her to discover that beneath their all-enveloping black abayas, Arab girls wore the shortest, most fashionable miniskirts she had ever seen! Even so, Sally was adamant that she would not go to a 'palace' dressed merely in a skirt and blouse. If Hishaam thought that the delay of the horses was so important that someone had to go in person to the Palace to inform them, then Sally felt that, if she was the one to go, the least she could do was to dress as smartly and as modestly as possible. And that meant, at the very least, as far as she was concerned, changing into a dress.

Hishaam was equally adamant that she should leave immediately and was in danger of becoming even more hysterical, mopping his face and yelling at Sally that the Palace had to be told right away, or at least as soon as she could get there. He then launched into a diatribe about her driving in general and his doubts about her ability to even find the Palace offices. Sally retaliated that if that was what he really thought and if it was so important, then perhaps Hishaam should go in person. Hishaam broke into a cold sweat as he imagined the reception he would receive if he dared to go the Palace in his present state, and yelled back at her.

'You must go! Now! It is only a twenty-minute drive! But in that beat-up junk of old iron you call a car, it will probably take you the rest of the day to get there! No! You must leave, Now! Immediately!

It wasn't until Sally pointed out to him that it was already 11.45 that he began to calm down. They both realised that, even if she left immediately, the Palace offices would be shut by the time she had driven there. Changing tack, he decided that Sally should go home. Now - even though it was early. But he made it clear that she would need to leave her flat earlier than usual that afternoon, to be sure of arriving promptly at the Palace offices by 4 pm.

'Give yourself plenty of time!' He then gave her detailed – and Sally thought somewhat confusing – directions to the Palace and made her repeat several times the very apologetic message she was to deliver.

When Sally finally stepped out of the office, for once she welcomed the searing heat of the midday sun, glad to be away from Hishaam's all-pervading state of hysteria. She had promised him, for the umpteenth time, that she would go home, change and be at the Palace offices as soon as they reopened at 4 pm.

Phew! What a lot of fuss, she thought as she hurried to the shady spot where she had left her car. With all the innocence and arrogance of youth, Sally just could not imagine why anyone would get so upset about a plane being delayed! Despite all Hishaam's attempts to instil in her a degree of urgency and panic about the whole affair, Sally had remained unmoved. The plane had developed a fault – it was not Hishaam's fault, so what was there to panic about?

Chapter Twenty-Two

When Sally arrived home slightly earlier than usual, Bouncy was ecstatic to see her and, to illustrate his delight, performed several high-speed pirouettes while holding on to the end of his tail. He then took off around the sitting room at breakneck speed, clearing the coffee table in one leap and running along the back of the settee during each circuit. As soon as he had calmed down, Sally phoned Caroline to tell her the news about the horses. While she chatted to her friend, Bouncy stood patiently by the coffee table, gently wagging his tail, with each sweep of which another book or magazine would be swept off the table to the floor. With his ears erect and his head held appealingly on one side, he listened to the conversation, waiting to hear the magic word 'walk'.

'Yes, isn't it exciting? I hope Hishaam will let me help with the collection and customs clearance. I haven't seen a horse for months.' Just then she caught sight of Bouncy and, with a guilty start, realised that he was expecting her to take him out.

'I'll have to hang up, Caro. Bouncy is giving me the look that says, "Walk me or you'll have a nasty surprise when you get home"!'

He was a clever dog and easily picked up the words 'Bouncy' and 'walk'. As soon as he heard them, he took off again, doing the 'wall of death' around Sally's sitting room, making her laugh at his antics.

'Bouncy, you're bananas!' She giggled. As soon as she had hung up, she realised that she hadn't told her friend the other bit of news about having to go to the Palace offices. Oh well, she thought, I'll catch up with her later about that.

Later that afternoon, while Sally showered and dried her hair, Bouncy snoozed happily on the settee. Sally had been delighted to find that such luxury items as silk blouses, skirts and dresses were relatively inexpensive compared to back home. Having made the decision to stay on in Al Khaleej, she had quickly replenished her wardrobe with as many of them as she felt she could afford. So today, knowing that silk would not crease as much as her cotton or linen dresses did in this heat, Sally changed into a knee-length pale blue silk dress, with short sleeves covering the upper part of her arms. Glancing at herself in the mirror, she was reasonably confident that she was suitably dressed for the job in hand.

She did, however, have one pressing problem. The parking facilities at the

Palace offices were an unknown factor. Her car was so old and the hinges so rusty that the doors had been welded shut to stop them falling off. The only way to get in was to clamber over the driver's door. Being a convertible, it was reasonably low to the ground so it wasn't too difficult when she was wearing trousers, but in a dress? The technique, if not executed swiftly and discreetly, could be ungainly and thoroughly unladylike. The manoeuvre involved hitching her skirts up high enough to get her long legs over the door and slither into the seat. If nothing else, she was mindful of Alex's lecture about trousers: that they were only to be worn when she socialised among the expat community, as they were deemed far too revealing for a woman to wear in public in Al Khaleej! As much as she would have liked to, she felt she certainly could not wear trousers on her 'business trip' to the Palace offices. For the sake of decency and decorum, she always tried to park in a discreet corner when wearing skirts or dresses. Oh well, she thought, I just hope there's a 'discreet corner' at the Palace offices – though what she would do if there wasn't one, she hadn't quite fathomed.

In the privacy of her garage, Sally hitched up her dress, slid easily behind the wheel and dropped her large fashionable sunglasses from the top of her head onto her nose. Tying a blue headscarf securely under her chin, she pulled away from her apartment in a cloud of grey smoke, leaving behind the usual puddle of oil. Once the engine of her jalopy had warmed up, it settled into its top speed of thirty miles per hour and Sally imagined herself as Grace Kelly, cruising along the French Riviera in her open-topped convertible – even if the film star had the added luxury of being able to put the hood up when it rained. After a 20-minute drive she arrived at the outskirts of Jazeera. In spite of the convoluted directions Hishaam had squeaked and shrieked at her, she found her way without difficulty. She turned into the narrow private road that led up to the Palace, delighted to find that it was lined either side with bushes of sweet- smelling pink and white oleanders. Breathing in their scent, she drove slowly towards ornate gold-and-white gates in the distance. She saw two gardeners holding a large pipe that gushed water from a rusty old bowser into narrow irrigation ditches running parallel with the road. Driving in Al Khaleej in an open car was a far cry from the Riviera. All the roads were permanently dusted with a fine covering of sand blown in from the desert. Even in the larger towns it was impossible to forget that, just a little way off, the desert lay waiting to reclaim the land lost to concrete. The slightest breeze was enough to send clouds of swirling sand onto the roads and into the streets and alleyways. The sand would find its way through any open window, coating everything and everyone in seconds, making her appreciate the cool oasis she was now driving through.

Sally pulled up in front of the large, elaborately-decorated gates and a smartly-dressed guard, gun on arm, stepped out of his sentry box and held up his hand. Remembering Hishaam's hysterical state, Sally suddenly felt nervous but smiled bravely and waited while he slung the gun over his shoulder and walked the few steps to her car.

'Hello? Yes?' He queried, beaming down at her with a broad smile.

'Salaam,' Sally grinned nervously up at him. 'I need directions to the Sheikh's offices. Can you help me, please?'

'Sure.' The guard pointed through the gates and towards a large wooden door under an archway. 'Office that way. Okay? But please, you leave your car there,' he pointed to the left of the big gates. As Sally turned her head, she saw rows of shiny and expensive-looking cars parked under shady lean-to shelters made of dried palm fronds held aloft by wooden poles.

'You can park there from the backside,' the guard added helpfully and pointed to the far side of the car park.

Sally was only too happy to obey his order in the hope that, by parking at the 'backside,' she would be far enough out of sight for no one to see her as she clambered out of her car. Driving slowly the length of the first row, she saw that the cars were mainly Cadillacs, Mercedes-Benz and Rolls-Royces, along with a few very sleek beasts she couldn't identify. Daunted by their quality, Sally parked her little Sprite at the end of an especially long row of these top-of- the-range models. Quickly glancing round to make sure no one was watching, she executed a reasonably modest escape from the confines of her car. Before setting off back across the car park, she ran her hand down the front of her dress, brushing off the dust and smoothing it out at the same time. She tossed her headscarf carelessly onto the front seat and pushed her sunglasses on top of her head. She made her way through the gates, smiling at the guard as she went, and crossed the forecourt to the entrance of the Palace offices.

Sally stood at the wooden door that had been pointed out to her as the entrance to the offices, and politely knocked on it, oblivious of the guard's amusement. She knocked again, and still getting no reply, pushed at the door. She was startled when it opened. Expecting to find herself in an office and bracing herself to apologise for intruding, Sally was amazed when the open door revealed behind it not, as she had supposed, an office but a large, open courtyard.

Feeling just a little foolish, she hastily stepped into the quadrangle, the walls of which were lined with beautiful stained-glass windows. There were several wooden doors leading off the square at regular intervals, each one intricately carved and shaped, and Sally noticed that these too were set well back into the walls, under symmetrical arches. What a clever idea, she thought, to design offices around a square, thus providing plenty of daylight as well as protection from the fierce heat of the desert sun.

Not sure of which way to go, Sally hesitated for a moment before tapping lightly on the nearest door, and jumped when immediately there was a response from the other side. 'Aiwa dahell.'

Hoping that this roughly translated as 'Come in,' Sally peeped round the edge of the door. Seated behind a desk by the window was a plump middle-aged Arab wearing a spotless white thobe and a white ghutra on his head, held in place by a black rope agaal.

'Please come in, sit down. How can I help you?' His voice was gentle, almost fatherly, as his hand indicated the chair in front of his desk. Sally saw a flash of gold among his white teeth as he smiled up at her. She cautiously sat down on the edge of the chair to explain the purpose of her visit.

'Well, you see ...' she began, then hesitated. Gently, the man sitting opposite her put down the pen he had been using and folded his hands together on top of the desk as he waited patiently for her to continue.

'Well, you see ...' she paused again. Was this the Sheikh? she wondered. Why would Hishaam be so scared of such a kindly old man? Crikey, she thought, I don't even know how to address a sheikh! At school, they had been taught how to address the Queen, Peers, Archbishops and the like (not that she ever really imagined that she was likely to bump into Her Majesty), but not a sheikh! She decided to play safe and assume that he was the Sheikh. 'Sir ... I am working with First Class Air Freight. Two horses were due to arrive for you today but, unfortunately, the plane had a problem and they are going to be delayed by ten hours. I am to tell you that the horses are in good condition and will be at the airport in the morning. So, if you wouldn't mind, please could you rearrange transport to collect them tomorrow? We are so sorry for the inconvenience and ...'

Suddenly the large black telephone that sat between them on the desk cut short her apologies as it sprang to life.

'Excuse me,' the Arab said, smiling apologetically at her. Before answering the phone, he expertly flicked one side of his brilliant-white ghutra up on to the top of his head, where it balanced precariously like a large white meringue.

The Arab spoke quietly to the caller for a few moments, before replacing the receiver. In one smooth movement he rose from his seat behind the desk while rearranging his headdress. Sally, assuming that this was the signal for her to leave, jumped to her feet.

'Please, can you come with me?' he said with a smile. Although it sounded like a question, he did not wait for her reply as he turned and walked towards a door on the far side of the room. Obediently, Sally followed. An overpowering aroma of aftershave or even, she thought, perfume wafted over her in his wake like a scented cloud as they walked along a corridor. Momentarily, he paused outside a pair of intricately-carved wooden doors; then, pushing both doors open, he stood to one side, indicating with his hand for Sally to go through. The room was more luxurious and cooler than the office they had just left.

'Please take a seat,' the Arab smiled reassuringly at her as he pointed towards a large armchair covered in deep red brocade, and as Sally sat down she heard the doors quietly closing behind her. Twisting round, Sally realised that he had left her alone. Now what? she wondered.

It was enough to disconcert anyone, but Sally felt no alarm. Rather, she was intrigued and fascinated by her surroundings. There were no windows in the room and her eyes were drawn to the wall behind the huge desk in front of her. It was panelled in dark wood from floor to ceiling, each panel exquisitely carved with desert hunting scenes. Leaning back in the chair, she gazed round the room, noting how quiet it was; no sunlight could penetrate the rich red damask hangings covering the walls on three sides of the room. No wonder it was so peaceful, she thought – the thickness of the walls and those damask hangings would absorb any intrusive sounds from outside. The room was softly lit and Sally gasped as she glanced up and saw hanging from the high vaulted ceiling above her an enormous crystal chandelier sparkling with hundreds of tiny lights, each one encased in its own magnificent crystal.

The minutes ticked by. She was trying not to worry about why she had been left there. She had delivered her message – surely she could now leave? The mahogany desk in front of her was the biggest, most highly-polished desk she had ever seen and on it was a collection of silver- and gilt-framed photographs, some so old they were in sepia. Leaning forward, she craned her neck to look closer at them. Many of them were of Arab men standing next to horses or camels; some were on horseback with a falcon perched on their arm, surrounded by regal-looking salukis. Sally's eyes moved across the desk taking in more photos, these taken at sea and depicting more Arab men aboard dhows, obviously enjoying fishing trips. Sally was fascinated by the pictorial history of it all and was immersed in studying the photos when a door suddenly opened. She jumped, feeling guilty as if she had been caught in the act of prying into someone else's life.

'Sorry, I didn't mean to startle you," said a voice. My name is Abdullah.

Welcome.'

The owner of the voice smiled as he entered and walked towards her, holding out his hand. Taking the proffered hand, Sally looked up into a pair of sparkling eyes so dark that they were almost black. Long thick eyelashes fringed the ebony irises, creating the illusion that he wore eyeliner. He was dressed in full traditional Arab robes similar to the man in the outer office, only this one was younger, slimmer, taller – and devastatingly handsome. He smiled down at her and a row of perfect white teeth lit up his face, causing her stomach to somersault as it hadn't done in a long time.

'And you are?' he asked, still holding on to her hand. His voice was soft and gentle, and he tilted his head to encourage her to speak.

'Er ... my ... my ... name is Sally,' she stammered, and smiled nervously as her eyes fleetingly locked with his. She felt herself blushing and this caused her to blush even more, unaware that her blushes were in some part disguised by the suntan that she had acquired since arriving in Al Khaleej.

'I am pleased to meet you, Sally.' Releasing her hand, he walked back round the desk and sat in the dark leather chair behind it.

Allah be praised! She was even lovelier close up. Her complexion was clear and fresh without a trace of make-up, her face was perfectly framed by her blonde, shoulder-length hair and her eyes were as blue as any sky he had ever seen.

Sally didn't know it, but His Highness Sheikh Abdullah, only son and Heir Apparent to His Highness the Amir of Al Khaleej, thought that he had never seen anything quite so attractive as the young woman who'd walked across his office compound a few minutes earlier. Nor had he ever met a girl as pretty as the one that now sat opposite him in his office. Seeing her close up and noticing the sprinkling of freckles on her nose that gave away her youth, he realised that she was probably younger than he had first thought. Now that she was here, sitting opposite him, his heart was beating so fast he wondered if she could hear it. Suddenly remembering his manners, he stopped staring at her and composed himself to speak.

'Now, Sally, I understand there is a problem with some horses.'

Sally found herself wondering if this man was 'The' Sheikh. Apart from telling her his name was Abdullah, he hadn't said who he was, but Sally thought he looked rather young to be the all-powerful Ruler of Al Khaleej and guessed he was only about 30 years old.

Once again, she found herself delivering her well- rehearsed speech, this time throwing in a couple of extra 'Sirs' for good measure. Sally outlined the problem, careful to reassure this man, whoever he might be, that the horses were in good condition, and reiterating that, although their arrival would be ten hours later than originally expected, this was, of course, no fault of either the airline or the freight offices. Hishaam had made her learn her lines well.

When she had finished speaking, she could feel her heart thumping against her ribcage and in the silence that descended on the room she was convinced that the loud beating of her heart could be heard. It had taken her less than a minute to deliver her carefully-rehearsed speech but during that time she had found it difficult to maintain eye contact with this very handsome man sitting opposite her. As she spoke, he had sat quietly with his hands resting on the desk in front of him and not for a second had he taken his eyes off her. Conscious of the fact that he was watching her intently as she spoke, Sally had gazed first at the wood panels just to one side of his face and then at the photos on the desk, and as she finished speaking she lowered her eyes to her hands in her lap.

After a moment she looked up to see if he was still watching her and as their eyes met once more it was like an electric shock – her heart gave one furious bump in her chest, leaving her breathless. The feeling was completely alien to her. Sally quickly lowered her gaze again, conscious now of having difficulty breathing. What was happening to her? Was it fear? Yes, Sally decided, it was. She was afraid, more afraid than she had ever been in her life. But her fear had nothing to do with the graphic descriptions that Hishaam had painted of punishments that might be meted out in this part of the world to anyone unfortunate enough to incur the displeasure of those in charge.

Abdullah was experiencing much the same reaction but, seeing her blush and quickly look away, he realised that he had been staring at her. He had been waiting for her to look at him again, waiting to see those blue, blue eyes and when, finally she had looked directly at him, his heart missed a beat. What, he wondered, could he say to her, to detain her, here in his office, for just a while longer? For truly this was the most captivating young girl he had ever met.

He sighed. So many beautiful young women that he had met were vain – was this girl vain? Had Hishaam sent this beauty to placate him for any upset or blame as a result of failing to make sure that his horses arrived on time? Was that it? Was this girl being offered to him as compensation, and was she complicit in the arrangement?

More likely, he thought, Hishaam had been too drunk to deliver the message in person and Abdullah knew that he would not dare present himself at the Palace reeking of alcohol. If he valued his business Hishaam would know that such an apology should have been delivered in person, not by his secretary sent along to do it for him. But Abdullah had to admit that Hishaam obviously knew all about his weaknesses for young beautiful women. Hmm, yes, well, all right, he thought, I will accept Hishaam's apology, but where did he find such a lovely young girl as this? Who is she? She is English, but what is she doing here in Al Khaleej? How long has she been here? So many questions – I must find the answers. Good manners dictated that he should not embarrass this young girl, but for once he found himself lost for words.

'Do you like horses?' he gently asked her, not knowing what else to say and not realising that fate had played into his hands.

'Oh yes! I love horses!' Sally exclaimed, pleased to find herself on familiar ground. 'To tell the truth, I thought Arabia would be full of them, but I've only seen donkeys so far.' She ended this admission with a nervous giggle, adding 'Very nice donkeys and very hard-working donkeys but still ...' As she finished with a slight shrug of her shoulders, Abdullah found himself grinning back at her.

'Well, we cannot have you thinking that my homeland is full of just donkeys.' He saw how her demeanour had changed at the mention of horses and as he continued to grin at her across the vast desk, Sally found herself smiling back at him, happy to talk about her favourite subject.

Glancing quickly at his watch, he asked her 'Have you time to come with me? I have horses. I will show you some Arabian horses.' He stood up, and reached for the black bisht edged with gold that lay draped over a chair nearby. Sally stood up and waited while he swung the cloak over his shoulders, covering his long white robe. He then straightened the black cord of the agaal that held his red-and-white checked ghutra in place and, turning round, opened a concealed door in the panelling.

'Come with me, this way.' He indicated for Sally to follow him. Fleetingly Sally hesitated, wondering where on earth she was being invited to go. It seemed to her that she was being drawn further and further into the depths of the Palace compound and her sense of direction, albeit unreliable, told her that the exit from the Palace was behind her. Suddenly she felt unsure and wondered if she ought to make her excuses and leave.

'Do not worry. I am not going to kidnap you for the Sheikh's harem,' Abdullah joked, noting her hesitation. 'Believe me, it is just a convenient short cut,' and without waiting for her reaction he stepped through the doorway and into the corridor beyond.

Sally had not been aware that her nervousness was so obvious or her thoughts quite so transparent. It would be silly, she argued with herself, to turn down the opportunity to see some real Arabian horses, if that was indeed all that this devastatingly handsome man was inviting her to do. Quickly making up her mind, she followed him out of the room and down the corridor. Walking closely behind, Sally jumped when two armed guards snapped smartly to attention as Abdullah swept past them and out into the sunlit courtyard. Sally thought that, although he might not be a sheikh, he must be fairly high up in the Sheikh's employment to have that effect on the guards that lined their route. They quickly crossed the compound and out through a smaller door. He had been telling the truth about a short cut, for they had emerged from the compound right into the car park. They walked side by side down two steps and headed towards the parked cars.

'Yours?' Abdullah grinned boyishly as he nodded towards her little yellow and rust-coloured car standing at the end of the line, next to a brand spanking new limousine. Sally wanted to drop through the floor with embarrassment.

'I'm afraid so,' she smiled weakly. It was the first car she had ever owned and, although it might not look too good, it had given her some independence and a sense of freedom. Relying on it more and more, she had set about exploring her new environment and it had never let her down.

'It's actually very reliable and, downhill with the wind behind, I can get up to and occasionally over 30 miles an hour,' she added in defence of her little car.

'I think you are very brave to go over ten miles per hour in it. I will take my own car and you can follow,' he chuckled as they walked towards the car.

Sally assumed that he would go straight to his own car, but instead he carried on walking until he had reached hers. With gentlemanly good manners, he reached for the door handle, giving it several tugs as he attempted to open the door for her.

'Er ... sorry about that, but the doors don't open. They're permanently stuck ...' Sally mumbled, embarrassed again.

He stopped tugging at the door and turned to her, laughing out loud, 'Well, how can you possibly get in?'

'I can get in easily, over the top.'

'May I help you?' He solemnly held out his hand to her; she really was quite delightful, he thought.

'No! No. Thank you, Sir, but no ... it's ... a ... a bit difficult in a dress,' Sally added, flustered and dismayed to think that he might remain there in close proximity as she clambered, unladylike, into her car.

'Ah!' He was stunned. This was a new experience for him – having his offer of help turned down! He couldn't remember a time when he had offered his hand to help a young lady and been turned down and, just for a moment, he was lost for words. Quickly recovering from his surprise, he smiled at her.

'Okay! I will be a gentleman and turn the other way while you climb in,' and gallantly he turned his back on her. Sally quickly hitched up her dress and leapt hurriedly over the door and into the driving seat.

'Are you in? May I turn round now?'

'Yes, thank you, I'm ready,' she called out to him, hastily rearranging her dress over the tops of her knees. He turned and gazed down on her, willing her to look up at him, desperate for another glimpse of those blue eyes. But Sally kept her face turned away as she pretended to settle herself behind the wheel, dropping her sunglasses back onto her nose as she did so. He was tempted to leap in beside her but knew that protocol dictated that he could not do that. Heir Apparent he might be, but even he was bound by the strict protocols of his own homeland. He dallied by the car, trying to think of something to say that would make her turn her head and look up at him.

'Will it start on its own? Or must I push?' he offered, teasing her again. Whoever he was and no matter how polite he'd been, Sally was becoming mildly irritated by his attitude.

'It has never needed a push, but thank you, Sir. It usually starts first time,' she replied coolly.

'I wish I had your faith,' he chuckled as he wandered away to his own car, shaking his head. Never, never before, had anyone dared to take such a haughty manner with him, and he loved it! Either she was being deliberately provocative or – it suddenly struck him – perhaps she really did not know who he was? He hoped with all his heart that if she did not know who he was, she would never find out. He was relishing the novel experience of anonymity and being treated like any other man. Sighing, he remembered that, despite their archaic communications, news travelled fast in his country, purely by word of mouth. If she really did not know who he was, it wouldn't be long before she found out. Would she then still dare to speak to him in that manner? He accepted that he would only have a short time to enjoy his anonymity before she became like all the rest: 'Yes, your Highness,' 'No, your Highness,' he mimicked in his mind! How he longed for an honest answer instead of everyone just saying what they thought would please him. Always he had to weigh up whether or not those around him were being truthful with him. Never mind, he would enjoy his brief encounter with this lovely young girl while he could.

Chapter Twenty-Three

As Abdullah reversed his dark blue Mercedes out of the line, Sally turned the key in her little car and pressed the starter button, praying it would not let her down.

'Come on, ol' thing,' she coaxed and the car answered her as it backfired, discharging a cloud of blue-black smoke, before roaring into life. 'Oh, well done, ol' girl!' Sally muttered under her breath as she followed the Mercedes back down the lane and out onto the main road.

The engine barely had time to warm up before, a few hundred yards down the main road, they turned left into another private road. Ahead of her, the Mercedes drove through an archway, then slowed down and stopped in front of a tall white wall. Sally pulled her little car up on the right of Abdullah's car. She had quickly worked out that as the driver sat on the left, Abdullah would turn to his left to get out of his car. This enabled Sally to swiftly step up onto the passenger seat and launch herself nimbly over the tightly welded door, relatively unseen. Getting out was marginally easier than getting in, but nevertheless she did not want him to see her ungainly exit. Landing safely on both feet, Sally walked quickly around to stand at Abdullah's side.

'Ah, you managed to escape,' Abdullah said, grinning at her.

Through a nearby gap in the wall by the cars, Sally could just see the top of palm-frond roofs and guessed that the stables and horses were somewhere behind the wall. Oh, what a lovely smell! The unmistakable familiar whiff of horses assailed her nostrils, bringing back happy memories of the riding stables back home.

The yard, which had been empty when they had first driven in, was rapidly filling with men, young and old, who were appearing from the doorways of the buildings to their left and from behind the wall in front of them. As Sally watched she saw others, who had been pushing wheelbarrows, hurriedly abandon them to join the throng, all eager to welcome and acknowledge Abdullah, who smiled benevolently at them all, speaking to each and every one in turn, exchanging the traditional greetings as he received their effusive salaams.

'They are offering us a drink, Sally. Would you like some Arab coffee? I can recommend it.'

'I've never tasted it, but I would love to try it. I've seen men sitting drinking coffee outside shops in the souk but so far have never got round to asking them about it. My boss only drinks gallons of percolated coffee, and everywhere else I go it's the dreaded Nescafe.'

'Then now is your opportunity to put that right.' Abdullah nodded acceptance.

Sally could see that running along part of the stone wall was a wide ledge covered with richly-coloured carpets in a Persian design. As she walked with Abdullah towards the carpeted ledge, some of the men raced ahead, placing colourful cushions on top of the carpets.

'Please, sit,' he indicated to Sally. 'It is quite comfortable.'

Sally sat down, fascinated by the enthusiastic welcome that Abdullah had received and wondering what was coming next. She didn't have to wait long. Hurrying towards them was an elderly man clutching a large, gold-coloured coffee pot in one hand and what looked like a stack of china eggcups in the other. The servant poured a small amount of a clear, pale green liquid into the top cup in the stack and held it forward to Abdullah.

'Sally, please you take that one.' She reached forward. The tiny cup was hot and she held it gingerly by the rim.

Abdullah took the next one being proffered. Seeing Sally put the cup cautiously to her lips, he warned her, 'It is not to everyone's taste'.

The hot liquid had a strong but pleasant spicy aroma and, although the taste was unusual, Sally quite liked it.

'That was very nice, thank you,' Sally said, handing the cup back to the servant who stood waiting in front of them. To her surprise, he immediately refilled it and handed it back to her. Sally wasn't sure that she wanted another quite so soon but, fearful of giving offence, she accepted the cup again. Abdullah could tell that she had not expected this to happen.

'How long have you been in Arabia?'

'About six weeks,' she replied, smiling at him over the top of the cup before quickly averting her eyes. He smiled back, reassured to know that such a beautiful young girl had not been so very long in his country without his knowledge.

'Well, let me advise you, otherwise you are going to be awash with Arab coffee. When you have had enough, just shake the cup as you hand it back. If you do not, that man will keep refilling it and handing it back to you until you do.' Leaning closer, he lowered his voice. 'A word of warning, the strong taste in the coffee is cardamom, and in this part of the world it is considered an aphrodisiac.' He was grinning at her, waiting to see what her reaction would be.

'What! ...Oh!' she choked on the last sip and shook the cup vigorously as she held it out towards the coffee bearer. Abdullah was charmed by her reaction. There was no attempt to flirt with him, which was the usual reaction from European women when told the aphrodisiacal properties of the coffee. Nor, Abdullah noticed, did she display a false coyness – unless she was a very good actress, and her years indicated that she would hardly have had the time to perfect the craft. No, what he had just seen was genuine shock and embarrassment.

'I am sorry – I have embarrassed you,' Abdullah whispered. He couldn't ever remember being so enchanted by a young woman. At that moment they heard the sound of horses' hooves and Sally was grateful for the interruption before this wickedly charming man could embarrass her any more.

High-pitched screams and deep, throaty roars, followed by a lot of snorting and blowing, accompanied the clatter of hooves – the sounds thrilled Sally to the core. This was not the indifferent friendly whinnying with which she was familiar at the riding school back home. Eagerly, she twisted her head this way and that, trying to guess where the horses were coming from – for although she could hear them, she couldn't see them.

'Ah! I can hear that the horses are ready. I have asked for three stallions to be brought out to show you,' Abdullah said and raised his hand. A man standing facing the gap at the end of the wall also raised his hand. Immediately, from behind the wall, three grooms came into view, each leading a horse. One was a magnificent dark bay, followed by a snow-white stallion and the third was a beautiful red bay. Abdullah always felt his heart swell with love and pride at the sight of his horses, but now he turned to watch Sally's reaction. He was not disappointed. He saw her eyes widen with appreciation and heard the intake of breath as she stared at the magnificent animals. So it is true, he thought, she really does love horses.

Wearing traditional Arabian head collars made of brightly-coloured wool decorated with amber and turquoise beads and shiny seashells, the horses were brought before her. But instead of standing quietly, they continued to prance excitedly on the spot, as if they had springs in their hooves. Sally was enthralled and so enchanted that she could hardly draw breath as she watched them arching their necks and blowing short sharp blasts of air noisily through their flaring nostrils. Their nosebands were made of silver chain and hung with charms, crescent moons, stars and such like. The charms gently clinked against each other when the stallions shook their heads. How wonderful they were! She had only ever seen horses like these in books and paintings – they were the horses her dreams were made of ! The desert sun had dropped low in the sky by now, but its dying rays held enough light to illuminate the coats of the two bay horses, turning them to molten copper. Where the skin stretched taut over their rippling muscles it reminded her of the iridescent metallic colours on a pigeon's breast. But it was to the white horse that her eyes were continually drawn. The sheen on his coat gave off a hint of blue and, combined with the soft blue-grey mane that lay against his neck, there was an ethereal look to him that fascinated her.

'Look at his eyes,' she whispered in hushed tones, leaning slightly towards Abdullah. 'Aren't they beautiful? They're enormous!'

The stallion's large, inquisitive eyes stared at her from behind a forelock so long that it reached down between his nostrils. Sally gazed in admiration at all three horses in turn but her eyes were repeatedly drawn back towards that white stallion. Ruefully, Abdullah grinned. It was usually he who was the centre of such frank and open admiration and he would have given anything to receive such a look from her, directed at him and him alone. Sally remained seated on her cushion as Abdullah got to his feet and walked over to the stallion.

'In this part of the world,' he said, turning to look back at her, 'we believe that you should be able to look into a horse's eyes and see straight into his heart. Believe me,' he said, laying his hand on the stallion's neck, 'this horse has the kindest of hearts.'

He continued to caress the horse's neck without taking his eyes off Sally, who sat entranced gazing across at all three horses. He realised that she was totally oblivious to him, her eyes focused solely on his horses. Smiling to himself, he continued to stroke them lovingly, talking softly in Arabic until he gradually calmed them. They ceased their prancing and vying for his attention and eventually all three stood quietly and patiently before their master. His love for his horses was obvious to Sally and clearly shown in his handling of them. In his presence, they stood quietly and patiently, demonstrating in return their love and respect for him.

'Come closer, Sally,' he beckoned her. 'They will not hurt you.' Sally needed no further encouragement and had to resist the temptation to leap up from where she had been sitting. Eager as she was to reach out to touch these wonderful creatures, she did not want to startle them, so she slowly and calmly made her way towards them.

'They are, all three of them, stallions – passionate and by nature noisy, but they are also very gentle,' Abdullah continued as Sally came closer. 'My ancestors traditionally and wisely chose to go to war on mares; they are much quieter. You see, attacking the enemy in the open spaces of the desert where there was little cover, they needed the advantage of surprise. You heard these noisy boys just now. In the wild, a stallion has to call to warn his herd or maybe to scream in response to threats from other stallions who might challenge him to try to steal his mares. He will also use his voice to seduce his mares. It is in the nature of a stallion to be more vocal than a mare. In battle, therefore, one must ride a mare. She is less likely to call and warn the enemy that you are close by.'

In awe, Sally stood between two of the stallions, running her hand over the satin coat of the white horse, spellbound by her surroundings. The Arab among his desert horses, standing there in the dying rays of the sun: it was like a scene from ancient history – it was from another age! She felt as if she had been transported back in time to another century. Watching her, Abdullah saw that she was totally fascinated by the horses.

Realising that he had finished talking, Sally whispered, 'Do you know, I think I'm dreaming?' She was lovingly rubbing the stallion's ears and stroking his coat, enjoying the feel beneath her fingers. 'Their coats are so fine they feel like silk. I have never seen horses like these. They are incredibly beautiful.' She was shaking her head in disbelief. 'I must learn more about them, their history, this culture. I find it all so fascinating,' she said almost to herself, not wanting to break the spell and bring the magic of this moment to an end.

Abdullah could see her honest admiration for the white stallion as she pressed her cheek trustingly against the horse's soft muzzle.

'Believe me, you are not dreaming. He is real.' Abdullah also spoke quietly. But I could be dreaming, he thought, standing here with you beside me, so lovingly caressing my horses. Ah, my lovely boys, it is as well that you do not know how I envy you this moment of her undivided attention. Suddenly and on an impulse, he offered, 'Would you like to ride him?'

'Oh! Yes please, Sir! Could I?' Her response was immediate and she turned to look at him as she answered with no hint of shyness or hesitation. Sally could not believe what she was being offered! For a moment, all her earlier feelings of shyness in the presence of this handsome Arab man were forgotten in the sudden rush of excitement at his invitation. Abdullah smiled at her, pleased to have found the key to seeing more of this lovely young woman. Aywa, he thought, I have found her weakness!

'I will make arrangements. Somebody will telephone you.' But still he could not bring himself to end these precious moments in Sally's company. Another idea occurred to him, and he glanced quickly at his watch. 'Come. I have just time to show you some of my mares, then sadly duty calls and I must go back to work.'

Reluctantly, Sally left the stallions and followed Abdullah across the yard. As he led the way between two of the buildings and under an archway, Sally would have liked to ask him what position he held in the Sheikh's employment. Obviously, from what she had seen, his duties must include being in charge of these horses and she wondered if he was 'Master of the Horse' or the Stable Manager, or did he have some other grand title? she wondered.

They walked under a second archway into a large sandy paddock. Circular concrete feeding troughs dotted the enclosure; each trough had an umbrella-shaped shade over it, made from palm fronds that fanned out and were held aloft by a single pole that rose out of the centre of the trough. Sally counted ten mares, standing quietly by the troughs, picking at bunches of bright green alfalfa – but it was the gambolling and prancing young foals that held her attention. As she watched, they played 'chase' like excited children around their mothers.

Sally thought her heart would melt at the sight of them. They were so delightful that she found herself putting a hand to her mouth to stop herself crying out in wonder at the sight of them. She had never seen a foal close up before and was amazed by the long-legged babies. The foals, sensing their presence, suddenly stopped their game of chase to stare at them.

Abdullah whispered to Sally, 'Stand quietly – they are naturally very curious and will come to you. Even better, if you make yourself small, near the ground like this ...' – slowly he lowered his body until he was squatting low down in the sand – 'they will not feel threatened and they will come to you.'

Sally squatted on her haunches beside Abdullah and immediately one of the older foals lifted his head high and sniffed the air. Keeping his eyes firmly fixed on Sally, he cautiously made his way towards her. Sally remained very still, holding her breath in case the slightest movement scared him away, but the brave foal inched forward and got close enough to inspect her hair, eventually relaxing enough to rummage through it with his nostrils. Then he stood four-square in front of her and, without moving her head, Sally cast her eyes down, noting how tiny and perfectly-shaped each of his hooves were. Then the foal dropped his head very low, almost as if he was trying to look straight into her eyes. Sally felt she was being evaluated in some way, as if this young horse was carefully weighing her up before making up his mind about her. He was only a baby but Sally felt it was important to win his approval and, for a moment, nothing and no one else existed for her. For several minutes they both remained motionless; then, after what seemed an age, he gently blew warm breath onto her face from his tiny nostrils and the spell was broken. Sally knew that she had just won his trust and instinctively responded by blowing softly on to his nose, then very gently rubbing her hand against his forehead.

Soon his fellow playmates were crowding round her and eventually even the smallest and youngest baby, gaining courage from the others, came over to her. Trustingly, Sally remained squatting in the sand allowing the foals to nuzzle her and returning their affection by blowing softly back at them and gently kissing their inquisitive noses. In danger of being nudged over into the sand by the number of foals that now surrounded her, Sally slowly stood up. The foals had become increasingly confident and remained close by her side, unafraid as they nibbled at her clothes and licked her bare arms, making her laugh out loud. Abdullah had also remained motionless, watching her, mesmerised.

Never before had he brought a European woman into this compound and there was an ache in his heart, a longing to remain. How he would have loved to exchange places with these foals who, like him, were captivated by her. This girl had seduced him from the moment he had set eyes on her when she had arrived at the Palace offices. There and then, he had made a hurried phone call to his secretary to make sure that, whoever she was, she did not leave before he had had the chance to speak with her. Now he tried to analyse why his feelings were different – he felt strangely protective towards her. What he felt for this young girl was not the usual lustful urges that were so familiar to him at the sight of a pretty young woman. Abdullah continued to squat in the sand, looking up at Sally as the foals surrounded her demanding attention, and knew he wanted to spend more time with her, to get to know her. But today was not the day.

Glancing at his watch again, he sighed, realising that he had already spent far too long away from his duties. A slave to the clock, he knew he must return to his offices – at any moment his prolonged absence would begin to alarm Khalid, his secretary. If it got to the point where they had to send someone out here to find him, he knew he would face days of accusing looks from Khalid, followed by many visits from his uncles. There would be recriminations as they reminded him of the weight of filial responsibility to his beloved but ailing father. He knew he would find it impossible to explain to them that he just wanted to escape for a few moments, to take pleasure in the company of a lovely young girl. He could hear them now – did he not, they would ask, have access to many lovely young women? Was not enough time already set aside for his pleasures? Was he finding his duties too onerous? Then they might wonder who was the lovely young girl that had tempted him to steal away from his duties.

He was the only son, with no siblings – his father, possibly due to his frail state of health, had only taken one wife and she had only borne him the one child.

There were many eager young cousins only too willing to help him and at times, like now, he would gladly have shared some of his responsibilities. Undoubtedly, as his father and Khalid had so wisely counselled him in the past, such a move would only arouse petty jealousies and squabbles among all his relatives. If he left now, he could be back at his office without causing alarm. Reluctantly, Abdullah rose from where he was still hunkered down in the sand. Immediately the foals took flight, rapidly cantering back to their mothers, bucking and shaking their heads in mock anger at having their new game spoiled. Abdullah laughed out loud.

'It seems they clearly prefer you to me. Just look at their little tempers showing.' Then he turned to Sally, who was still grinning broadly at the antics of the foals. 'I am sorry to spoil their good time and yours with it, but I have to leave now.' Sally tore her eyes away from the foals to look at him as he spoke. The sheer delight on her face and the sparkle in her eyes took his breath away and momentarily he hesitated. Abruptly, before he changed his mind, he turned on his heels and headed out of the paddock and back towards the cars.

Sally was equally reluctant to leave the friendly foals but she hurried after him, noticing as they walked back across the yard that there was no sign now of the stallions that she had met a few moments before. Walking directly to his own car, Abdullah quickly turned to her as he opened the door.

'Now you have seen Arabian horses and I must go. Goodbye, Sally,' he said, formally shaking her hand.

'Goodbye, and thank you for taking the time to show me the horses. I have never seen such beautiful animals in my life.'

He nodded his appreciation at her compliment, then got into his car and drove out of the stable yard, the tyres throwing up clouds of dust as it sped back down the private road. Not sure how to interpret the suddenness of his departure, Sally stood for a moment, staring wistfully after the quickly-disappearing car.

Sighing, she turned towards her car and was surprised to see a row of faces watching her. The grooms and stable hands who had lined up for their arrival were now lined up for their departure. She smiled at her audience and gave a dismissive wave as she stood waiting to clamber into her little car, hoping that they would return to their duties, but they just returned her wave and stood watching her. She realised with a sinking heart that they were obviously not going to leave until she too had left. Damn! This must be some sort of local etiquette, she thought, as she was treated to a row of smiles – some displaying white and gold teeth, some with black stumps and others completely toothless. Clinging to the hem of her dress, she climbed into her car with all the modesty that she could muster.

Sally was acutely aware, as she turned the key and pressed the starter button, that her departure was not going to be anywhere near as flamboyant as Abdullah's. The little car started first time, but a cloud of black smoke from the exhaust enveloped the closest bystanders. Ignoring the sound of coughing and choking behind her, Sally waved graciously as she pulled out of the stable yard. The sun was sinking quickly on the horizon and, glancing at her watch, she was surprised to see that it was nearly six o'clock! She had arrived at the Palace offices promptly at four as she had promised Hishaam, and nearly two hours had flown by! Deciding that it was not worth going back to the office, Sally headed straight for her flat, grateful to have some time to herself to reflect on her encounter with the devilishly handsome Arab and those wonderful horses!

First Love

Chapter Twenty-Four

When Sally arrived in her office the following morning, much to her surprise Hishaam was already behind his desk.

'Hishaam! You're very early – couldn't you sleep?' she joked.

'Sleep? Sleep?' he squeaked. 'No, I couldn't sleep! Of course I couldn't sleep! Where were you? I expected you back by five o'clock last night to tell me that all was well! Did you even find the offices? Who did you see? What did they say?' Hishaam's voice was hitting its highest octave, and once again Sally felt that there was every danger of the office windows shattering.

Shortly after Sally had left the previous day, Hishaam had begun to have second thoughts about the wisdom of sending his secretary, a mere girl, to do what he knew he should have done himself. As he had sobered up, his levels of anxiety had fluctuated. One moment he felt brave as he prepared the speech he anticipated he would soon find himself making to explain why he had sent his secretary to apologise instead of going in person. The next he cringed and cried, wringing his hands until the need for Dutch courage overtook him. Then he hid under his desk, fearful that he was already being watched as he took a swig of the forbidden liquid from the hip flask which he kept hidden in his drawer. This was medicine, he convinced himself, and, as the drink took effect, he would feel brave again, emerge from under his desk and start rehearsing his speech all over again; and so the cycle repeated itself throughout the afternoon and well into the evening.

He had remained at his desk until late, expecting that at any moment he would be summoned to appear before the Sheikh. Where was Sally? Why hadn't she come back to the office? Had she even gone to the Palace in the first place? Finally, at around midnight, he had gone home, where he had showered, shaved and changed in readiness to leave at a moment's notice. He promised Allah that he would never touch another drop if only he could hear that all was well and that he was not about to be blamed for not delivering the horses on time. Nervously, he had paced up and down the sitting room of his apartment, not daring to succumb to the alcohol that would bring blessed oblivion to his senses and temporary relief to all his worries. At dawn, he had showered, shaved and changed again and hurriedly made his way back to the office. And now here was Sally, calmly strolling into his office, making jokes at his expense.

Didn't the stupid girl realise that he hadn't slept all night? Didn't she know that he had been worried about her? The phone on his desk began to ring, breaking through his tirade of questions.

'First Class Air Freight office!' he shrieked down the phone. After a short pause, he abruptly stood up, nodding his head in silent response to the person on the other end of the phone and rolling his eyes heavenwards. Then he sat down and began to shake his head. Seconds later, he jumped to his feet and stood almost to attention, vigorously nodding his head. Then he stood stock still and stared at Sally across his desk. In disbelief, he held out the phone to her. 'It's for you,' he said hoarsely. His voice turned to a high-pitched squeak as he added, 'It's the Palace offices.'

Sally took the receiver with a puzzled look and Hishaam slumped back in his chair, nervously mopping his face with a handkerchief

'Hello, can I help you?' Sally said into the phone.

'Good morning, Miss Sally.' She recognised the fatherly voice of the Arab she had met in the outer office at the Palace the previous afternoon. 'I have to make arrangements for you to ride some horses. Will it be convenient for you to come tomorrow afternoon, at about four o'clock?'

Sally's heart missed a beat. He had said that someone would telephone. He had said that he would make arrangements, and it was already happening! Sally had found the pace of life out here in Al Khaleej so much slower than back home in Britain, that when Abdullah had said those things, Sally thought it would be weeks before she heard anything. Overnight, she had convinced herself that in all probability she would never hear another word about riding those fabulous horses. But he had done it, and so quickly that her heart began to race.

'Thank you. That would have been very nice, but I'm sorry I have to work tomorrow until six.' He then surprised her by asking for Hishaam to be put back on the phone.

'Yes ... okay ...' Sally held out the phone to Hishaam and with her hand over the mouthpiece she whispered, 'He wants to speak to you again.'

Hishaam stood up as he took the phone from Sally's hand.

'Naam, aywa, aywa ...' Once again Hishaam nodded his head vigorously as beads of perspiration broke out on his forehead. His voice returned to a high-pitched squeak until, abruptly, he stopped and handed the phone back to Sally.

'Miss Sally, it is all agreed,' the fatherly tones continued. 'Please, if you can come to the same place as yesterday, by the stables, at four o'clock, everything is arranged. Can you remember how to get there?'

'I'm sure I can find the place again. Thank you, I will look forward to that.'

Sally heard a click as the phone went dead at the other end. Breathless with excitement and with her heart furiously thumping in her chest, she wanted to shout for joy, but instead she turned away to put the coffee pot on, doing her best to hide her elation from Hishaam who had slumped back down in his chair.

Mopping his brow again with a hankie, Hishaam spoke quietly – he was exhausted by lack of sleep and the stress of the telephone call. 'Okay, okay, tell me everything that happened yesterday. What is going on? Don't say "nothing", because the Sheikh's First Secretary is not in the habit of personally telephoning me!' He jabbed himself several times in the chest with his index finger as he spoke.

'The Sheikh's First Secretary, eh? Is that important, being a First Secretary?' Sally's happiness was bubbling up inside her and she couldn't help teasing Hishaam just a little bit.

'Yes, yes! It is! He is! Okay, now tell me quickly before my heart attacks me from all this stress.' Sally was about to make the coffee, but Hishaam interrupted her, telling her to come and sit down and tell him exactly what had happened at the Palace offices.

Sally recounted her afternoon to him, ending with a brief description of the elegant Arab gentleman, who introduced himself as Abdullah, and who had taken her to see some Arabian horses.

'Abdullah? Some Arabian horses? No, no, no!' Hishaam groaned, as realisation dawned on him. 'Not "some" Arabian horses, Sally, not "some", they were his!' he whispered hoarsely at her in awed tones across the desk.

Hishaam was still perspiring profusely, and approaching borderline hysteria again. He took the small flask from his desk. Raising it to his lips, he threw his head back and took a long swig, confident now that there would be no summons for him to attend the Palace.

'His?' Sally asked somewhat apprehensively, as the significance of what Hishaam was saying began to dawn on her.

'Is he one of your big sheikhs? Or a little sheikh, or possibly "The" Sheikh?'

Hishaam's hysteria was rubbing off on Sally, but for very different reasons.

Hishaam couldn't bring himself to answer immediately. He waited until he could feel the liquid begin to course through his veins, calming his nerves. Sally tried again.

'Okay, when you say "his", is he "The" Sheikh? You know, like when you said "Theeee Sheikh"?'

Regaining some measure of control, Hishaam jumped to his feet and pocketed the flask, as he began to make his way hurriedly out of the office.

'Come! Come with me, let us be quite sure about this.'

Her breath coming in short gasps that matched the rapidly increasing beat of her heart, Sally followed the departing Hishaam down a corridor and up a flight of stairs to the offices of Bacher and Johansson, Silk Merchants. There, with a flourish, he threw open a door marked 'Boardroom'. Stepping inside, he walked smartly over to the far wall where a gallery of portraits hung. He planted his feet squarely on the floor, putting his hands on his hips to steady himself as he looked up at the portraits high above him on the wall.

'Look, Sally, up there on the wall. Tell me. Is he there, this Abdullah?' Sally studied the carefully-posed portraits of the four Arabs staring down at her and immediately recognised him.

'That's the one!' she said, pointing to Abdullah's handsome smiling face. 'He showed me the horses.'

Hishaam groaned. His worst suspicions were confirmed. 'Are you sure?' he asked resignedly, though in his heart he knew that it was true. No one could forget that handsome face.

'Of course I'm sure. Why? What's wrong?'

'Nothing is wrong, Sally. That sheikh, he is a very good man.' He could say that now after the complimentary phone call that he had just received from the First Secretary. 'But, believe me, Sally, he is also a very powerful man.'

In a very small voice that was barely a whisper, she heard herself say, 'He only invited me to ride the horses. I may never see him again.'

Her heart sank and she felt embarrassed, remembering how she had assumed that he was an employee at the Palace. She could feel herself blushing as she recalled some of the things that he had said to her. Certainly, she had thought that he must be a high-ranking employee, but Abdullah's hasty departure from the stables last night now made sense to her and she concluded that he had been kind to her and that was all.

Having confirmed that it was indeed the Sheikh who had shown Sally the horses, common sense told Hishaam that he should go in person to the airport to oversee the arrival of the Sheikh's property. He was still suspicious about the flattering comments that had been showered upon him by the First Secretary, but one thing was certain – he very much suspected that, for the foreseeable future, he could no longer operate comfortably under the all-seeing radar of the Sheikh's network of informants. The First Secretary had reassured Hishaam that, of course there was no problem about the delay of the Sheikh's horses!

After all, the Sheikh was confident that if there had been a serious problem, then naturally Hishaam would have gone in person to the Palace to inform His Highness. But His Highness Sheikh Abdullah had been most impressed with his efficient and prompt handling of the situation. The First Secretary had been asked to call Hishaam personally to thank him for showing such delicate consideration in this matter. In fact, such lavish praise did the First Secretary heap upon Hishaam that he had begun to wonder if, like a scorpion, there was going to be a sting in the tail. But it really seemed that, after all his worries and fears the day before and his sleepless night, all was well and that he, Hishaam, had been personally thanked for his efforts in this matter. At first, he could not believe what he was hearing, but – Allah be praised! – it seemed that everything really was going to be all right.

He looked at the slip of a girl he had taken on as his secretary and was pleased with his decision to send her to the Palace in his place. Whatever she had said or done, it seemed to have worked and the fact that she had managed to personally meet the Sheikh was a bonus. Well, for him anyway. He would not allow the recesses of his conscious mind to allow him to feel guilty in any way about the obvious impact that Sally had had on the Sheikh and what he knew would be the inevitable consequences of their meeting. Leaving Sally to man the office, he set off for the airport.

Sally was disappointed that she was not invited to go with him to see the horses arriving, but the planned treat for the following day more than made up for it. Tomorrow she was going to ride one of the beautiful horses that she had met yesterday. Tomorrow still seemed a long way off and she was eager for the hours until then to pass quickly. Heaving a sigh, she decided to make herself as busy as possible in the hope that the time would pass more quickly.

Sally daydreamed as she worked. So Abdullah was a sheikh, and an important sheikh, according to Hishaam. How did one find out who did what in this land of essentially zero communications? There were no local newspapers and the television was only on four hours each day – and even then it was mostly an old gentleman reading the Koran, or American films which were entertaining purely for the way they had been censored. All the love scenes would be cut, so the lingering, smouldering looks of love and the slow sensuous coming together of lips would stop short of actual contact and result in the lovers suddenly leaping backwards, the actual kiss having been removed. Her only real communication with the outside world was her attempts to tune in to the BBC World Service. Some evenings it was barely audible and others interspersed with so much interference in the way of shrieks, hums and tweets

263

that it sounded as if they were broadcasting from a clearing in a jungle. The only way to know what was going on was word of mouth; her hairdresser was useful in that respect and so was Caroline, with her connections in the Embassy.

She sighed once more. Hishaam's filing system was non-existent and Sally had set herself a Herculean task in just sorting out the obsolete correspondence from the current stuff. It would take months to put in place a proper system and she hadn't yet worked for him long enough to be able to make order of the chaos. Sally wondered how on earth his previous secretary had coped with it all. Hishaam worked from several untidy piles of paperwork placed on the floor around his desk. He had no diary and relied on his alcohol-fuddled brain or people reminding him of appointments. Abusive phone calls about missed meetings meant they would be rescheduled, only to be forgotten again at a later date. Occasionally, he dictated replies to his letters on tape for Sally to transcribe but, thankfully, his attempts at this were few and far between. Hishaam had never quite mastered the tape recorder and was at best disjointed, and at worst completely incoherent. On the odd occasion when Sally did manage to type a letter to the end, he would invariably want a sentence inserted into the second paragraph and Sally had to retype the whole thing again. It didn't help matters that the old black typewriter was long overdue for retirement. Sally had cleaned the typebars with an old toothbrush and oiled them, but still letters ended up on the page crooked, unevenly spaced and not necessarily in the right order. The letters 'o' and 'e' continually jammed together in an upright position, causing a major pile-up of the other keys as Sally's fingers flew over them. By the time Sally managed to prise the keys apart, her hands would be covered in ink, which would inevitably find its way on to her nose or chin. It was all very frustrating. Happily there was no typing to be done today, so she set about tackling the piles of papers strewn around Hishaam's desk to see if she could get them into some sort of order.

'Can I smell coffee?' came a softly-spoken request from a familiar face peeping round her office door.

'Hello, Ahmed. Please, come in.' Sally enthusiastically welcomed the kindly old Arab, who not only owned the large office block where First Class Air Freight rented their offices but was also landlord of a number of other properties in the area. He had a ritual of calling on some of his tenants for coffee most mornings, which meant he could both keep an eye on his property and an ear open for gossip, one of the few remaining favourite pastimes that he could still indulge. If only he were forty years younger, he thought as he greeted Sally, lowering his bulky frame onto the office settee before interrogating her for any gossip while she made the coffee.

A coffee table, settees and comfortable armchairs were commonplace in offices in this land where nobody was in a hurry. Sitting down to drink coffee provided the opportunity to exchange pleasantries before business transactions, always carried out in a most courteous and cordial manner, got underway.

The only business transactions that Ahmed involved himself in these days was the collection of his rent, although the subject was rarely mentioned when he popped in to see his tenants. The frequent visits and the fact that he maintained friendly relations with all his tenants was usually enough to secure the payments on time.

Sally liked Ahmed. He'd been born at the beginning of the 20th century and like many Arabs was an excellent storyteller. She loved to hear his vibrantly descriptive stories of a time lost forever to Arabia – about the years long before the motorcar, when it was still a land of camels, donkeys and horses. He would describe for her the desert battles fought on horseback and retell tales of brave men and horses that had passed into Arab folklore. As a young boy, he'd sit close to the campfire in the evenings when the men sat down to eat, relax and smoke their shisha pipes. They would talk long into the night and young Ahmed would listen to every word, soaking up their knowledge, learning about his culture, traditions and his ancestors. He told Sally how he had ridden with his father and uncles bareback across the desert, leaping on and off their horses with the same ease that a gazelle leaves the ground. His words brought to life the hunting with falcons and salukis and Sally could see that, in the telling, he was reliving his treasured youth.

Sally was fascinated by Ahmed's tales. She tried to imagine him as a young man, thinking how sad it was that now he could barely pull himself to his feet from the depths of the couch, let alone spring onto a horse like an acrobat. Age and excess had made him heavy and she could tell that he yearned for the carefree days of his youth. He had obviously prospered as a businessman and, although prosperity had brought its own rewards, sadly not all of them had been beneficial. He enjoyed such luxuries as air-conditioned cars, entertaining lavishly and accepting the reciprocal hospitality from his friends, but it had taken its toll on both his waistline and his agility.

As Sally busied herself making fresh coffee, he asked her, 'Where is Hishaam?'

'He had to go to the airport. We have two horses arriving. They should have come yesterday but there was a problem, so they are arriving this morning instead. Hishaam was very worried because they are for somebody important.'

Sally had learnt not to divulge too much detail about the goods that were being imported and exported or who was doing the exporting and importing.

'Ah yes, they are for Sheikh Abdullah,' Ahmed said. 'English horses.'

'Oh, you know about them?' Somehow Sally was not really surprised. It seemed that in this friendly land everyone knew his neighbour's business. It was a small community, similar to a village in rural England where everyone seemed to know everyone else or was related either by blood or marriage.

'Tell me, Ahmed, why does he want horses from England, when his own are so beautiful?' Sally asked innocently, as she sat down next to him on the settee. Ahmed, surprised by her question, asked one of his own.

'What do you know about Sheikh Abdullah's horses?'

'He showed them to me yesterday when I had to go to the Palace offices.'

'You went to the Palace offices?' He was incredulous and when Sally nodded, he asked, 'On your own?' Sally nodded again and he shook his head from side to side, muttering, 'Ay yi! A lamb into the lion's cage!'

'Pardon?'

'Nothing, nothing at all.' Ahmed quickly schooled his features, aware he had already shown too much concern. 'I am just surprised Hishaam sent you.'

'Hishaam thought that it was very important to let the Palace offices know as quickly as possible about the delay.'

'If it was so important why did he not go himself?'

'He had a headache, so he sent me instead.'

'Ah yes, I know. A headache that is coming from inside the bottle, eh?' Ahmed stuck his thumb in his mouth pretending to raise an imaginary bottle, and they both laughed. But Ahmed knew that Hishaam was playing a dangerous game and that one day he would go too far.

'So why does Sheikh Abdullah want English horses?' Sally repeated her question.

'Oh, he wants them for racing. He likes speed and he has heard that the English racehorses are very fast.' He sipped at his coffee before continuing. 'Do you know what they say about Arab men in the West nowadays, Sally? They joke about us. I heard this when I was in London. They say we like three things above everything else: fast horses, fast cars, and – please excuse me for being rude – fast women.'

Sally blushed and they both laughed again.

'Do you know it was not so long ago that we were a dignified people of the desert, following ancient traditions and living our own way of life? A hard life but a good life. Now look, with all this oil coming up from the ground our world is changing far too quickly. Now the poor donkey she has to jump out of the way of the motorcars. Once upon a time only birds and clouds made shadows from the sky on to the desert sands, now strangers arrive from all over the world in big aeroplanes. Our world is changing so fast, believe me, it makes me dizzy even to think about it.'

'I don't think you can stop progress, Ahmed – besides, I wouldn't be here if somebody hadn't invented the aeroplane.'

'Then, Sally, we would all have been poorer, because you have always a smile on your lovely face and you make such good coffee.' Sally took the hint and got up to refill the coffee pot.

'You are young to be away from your home. Do you miss your homeland, Sally?' Ahmed asked. So young, so innocent, he thought, and far too beautiful to spend her time here, particularly with the likes of Hishaam for a boss.

'No, not really. Well, maybe one or two things,' she corrected herself as she brought the replenished coffee pot back and poured a fresh cup.

'Tell me. What do you miss?' He had a mischievous twinkle in his eye, which Sally couldn't resist.

He's fishing for gossip, she thought, not realising that she had already provided plenty of it. She smiled at him. 'I miss the flowers. By now the gardens in England will be full of flowers and you can buy them in the shops. I saw flowers growing when I went up to the Palace offices, and that made me feel a little bit homesick.'

'There are plenty of flowers here, Sally, but they are grown in private gardens for their owners' pleasure. It is difficult because we have to add things to the earth to make it fertile, provide shade from the sun by planting trees and bring sweet water from under the ground to irrigate. I have a garden; you must come there one day. I grow many, many roses and carnations for the smell. You shall have some flowers. You must not be unhappy in my country.'

'Thank you, Ahmed, that would be lovely, you are very kind.'

Ahmed hauled his bulky frame up on to his sandaled feet. He enjoyed his chats with Sally; Hishaam did not deserve to have such beauty and charm gracing his often drunken, sometimes shady dealings. She was loyal too, he noticed, for no matter how much Ahmed pumped her for information, she always managed politely to sidestep his attempts to glean any really juicy titbits about what Hishaam was up to. But today he would not go away empty-handed. This young girl had caught the attention of the most powerful man in the land and, what's more, Ahmed had learnt that he'd even taken time out from his busy schedule to personally show her his horses. He was puzzled. His Highness

Sheikh Abdullah usually kept the two greatest loves of his life, his horses and his women, very firmly apart. He smiled as he shook Sally's hand formally.

'Thank you for the coffee, Sally. Now I must go and do some work,' and he wandered away down the corridor, pondering over the change in his beloved Sheikh's behaviour.

Sally returned to the tedious task of sorting out Hishaam's paperwork, without making much progress. Her concentration was interrupted by a very handsome face that insisted on grinning back at her from among the piles of paper on the floor. As if that wasn't disruptive enough, her mind continually returned to the beautiful horses that she had seen. Time and again, she found herself remembering the magic of the bold little foal, his warm soft muzzle pressing against her cheek. Then she would recall the dark brown eyes fringed with long lashes that had watched her, and her heart would begin to beat faster. She persevered until noon, when she locked up and went home.

After taking Bouncy for a run, she ate a light lunch and lay stretched out on a pile of cushions on the floor while she chatted away to Caroline on the phone. Caroline was grateful that Sally had responded to her pleas to come and stay with her in Al Khaleej and, now that Sally had made a decision to remain, she wanted to make sure that she was never left on her own for too long. Fearful that Sally might return home to England if she became lonely or homesick, Caroline ensured that the constant flood of invitations she and Alex received were extended to include Sally. Determined to help her friend regain the happy-go-lucky, spontaneous and carefree approach to life that she'd had before her encounter with Doug, Caroline made no secret of the fact that she had appointed herself as Sally's 'matchmaker'. She was still furious with Doug and rued the legacy of mistrust he had left in her childhood friend. But Caroline remained confident that Sally's naturally sunny nature would soon resurface, if only she could move on and put the past behind her.

Sally was always amused and sometimes bemused by the social niceties of the 'dress code' instructions that accompanied every invitation from Caroline. There was yet another party that evening.

'It's casual and round the pool, so don't overdress – but you're also going to be outnumbered by about fifty to one as the only single female within a hundred miles, so don't show too much flesh either,' Caroline chuckled. 'You could get crushed in the rush.'

Sally sighed, 'You're not setting me up with someone again, are you? I've told you, Caro, I'm actually enjoying my freedom.'

'Setting you up? I don't need to do that, Sal. This place is like a sweetie shop. You can nibble for weeks on unattached men until you find one to your taste.'

'Thanks, but I don't think I've quite got my appetite back,' she said, trying to sound nonchalant yet knowing full well that a certain pair of brown eyes had already reactivated her taste buds!

'Come on, Sal, it's been well over a year now – cut loose. Just have fun. You don't have to get serious.'

Sally changed the subject by asking Caroline what she was going to wear to the party. While they chatted, Sally wondered if she should mention her forthcoming visit to the stables and her meeting with Abdullah, but thought better of it. Alex had mentioned that 'fraternising' too closely with the locals was frowned upon by the expat community and could cause 'problems,' but had infuriatingly refrained from elaborating on what, exactly, those 'problems' might be! Now Sally realised that, actually, she wasn't too sure what 'fraternising' meant either, and whether or not her invitation to ride one of the Sheikh's horses constituted 'fraternisation,' which would turn out to be one of those 'problems'. What she did know was that nothing would induce her to do or say anything to jeopardise the opportunity to ride one of those fabulous creatures tomorrow – and there was just a remote possibility that she might meet up with 'him' again. A little alarm bell in her head told her that to say anything now about her latest adventure would result in a whole host of questions she would prefer not to answer. The more she thought about it, the more she was grateful to whatever hand of fate had guided her to say nothing to Caroline about her trip to the Palace. Caroline, she was sure, would have told Alex and that in itself would be enough to create 'a problem', as it would start him off on one of his famous lectures about 'appropriate behaviour'. So, in the end, as much as she wanted to share the thrill of her forthcoming treat with Caroline, she decided to keep mum about it.

'Gotta go, Caro. I have to be back at work at four. See you tonight.'

'Okay, Sal, we'll pick you up about eight.'

First Love

Chapter Twenty-Five

Back at work later that afternoon, she went along to see if there were any telexes for her to collect from Amiri's office.

'How are you this afternoon, Sally?' Amiri beamed at her.

'I am very well, thank you. And are you okay, Amiri?'

'Yes, everything okay. Inshallah, today all my wife, she veeeery, very happy.' He held up three fingers in case Sally had forgotten the extent of his happiness.

'Any telexes for me, Amiri?'

'Too late. Mr Hishaam, he already here and he take the telexes.' It was the second time that day that Hishaam had been in before her and Sally was surprised at this sudden change in his habits.

Approaching her office, she could see that the door was wide open and from within Hishaam could be heard sneezing and swearing simultaneously. Once inside, Sally saw to her amazement that there were vases all around the office filled with sweet-smelling roses and carnations! There were four vases on her desk, four more on the coffee table and three on each of the windowsills. So overwhelmed was she that she just stood there for a second, breathing in the heavenly perfume of fresh flowers. Stunned by the sight and smell, she failed to register at first that the phone was ringing.

'Quick! Quick! Answer the phone!' Hishaam fought to control paroxysms of sneezing as he shrieked at her through his sodden handkerchief.

Sally hurried over to his desk and picked up the receiver.

'Sally? Now you are happy, yes? Every day I will send some fresh flowers for your office from my gardens.'

'Ahmed, that would be wonderful, they are beautiful, thank you so much.' And she heard him chuckling to himself as he said goodbye. Ahmed had been as good as his word and Sally gazed around the garden that the office had become. Between bouts of sneezing, Hishaam wanted to know who had phoned.

'It was only Ahmed, to see if I liked the flowers.'

'That crazy old fool! He is trying to kill me!' gasped Hishaam. 'Take them quickly! Out! Out!' he spluttered, before another bout of frenetic sneezing overwhelmed him.

Sally picked up a couple of the vases. 'Take them ... but ... but where?' she asked hesitantly.

'I don't care! Just take them out! Out! ' he screamed at her, bent double. 'I am ... aller ... aller ... allergic! Can't you see?' Once more Hishaam's face contorted as another explosion of sneezes took hold of him. His red-rimmed eyes were streaming as he held his handkerchief to his nose, trying in vain to stop the pollen attacking his sinuses.

Sally managed to pick up another couple of the vases and fled with them in her arms, running back along the corridor.

'Amiri! Please help me! My office is full of flowers and Hishaam is allergic to them.'

'What you mean he hallergic? What this hallergic?'

'No time to explain! You'll see, come on!' Leaving the first vases in his office, they ran back along the corridor and Amiri, taking one look at Hishaam's face, quickly helped Sally to grab the remaining containers and together they raced with them back to the telex office. By the time they got there, they both had tears of laughter streaming down their faces.

'Poor, poor Mr Hishaam. Miskin, his face, like big red tomato!' Amiri spluttered as he held his sides, laughing. They continued to giggle until Sally suddenly remembered that Ahmed had said he would send flowers every day.

'I'd better go and telephone Ahmed to explain that I don't think Hishaam will be able to survive a daily delivery of carnations and roses,' she said, chortling as she sauntered back to her office.

While Hishaam disappeared outside to try to clear his head, Sally quickly phoned Ahmed. She could tell he was trying to suppress his laughter as she described Hishaam's plight. He was, nevertheless, very understanding and promised to have flowers delivered direct to her apartment and they agreed that, instead of every day, once a week would be ideal.

Ahmed arranged for all the vases of flowers that had been taken from Amiri's office to be placed in Sally's car. Driving home that evening in a cocoon of flowers, and enveloped in a cloud of fragrance, Sally felt happier and more relaxed than she had for a long time. Her little car resembled a carnival float. Drivers and pedestrians turned their heads as she drove past and, when she slowed down at a crossroads, a passing donkey hastily grabbed a mouthful of carnations, much to the amusement of everyone watching.

Bouncy began to sulk as soon as he realised that Sally was going out that evening. He could always tell the difference between her routines when she came home – whether she was staying in or going out. And he definitely preferred it when she stayed in with him, stretched out on the sofa, reading. He would curl up next to her, snoozing and snoring happily as Sally would casually reach out, between turning the pages of her book, to stroke him or rub his tummy. This blissful state would be interrupted only by the occasional need for a lazy scratch when one of the passengers hidden in the depths of his forest of fur moved. Every now and then, he would stand, stretch and yawn. Before settling down again, he would investigate his private parts, nosily licking them until he was satisfied that everything was in order. He had to be careful because sometimes when he was engaged in this activity he would break wind; he had quickly learnt that this was unacceptable and resulted in banishment for the rest of the evening in the kitchen on his own. Now, on the rare occasion when he lost control, he would leap to his feet and slope off in all innocence to the bedroom, hoping that his mistress hadn't noticed.

Caroline and Alex arrived promptly at eight to collect her for the pool party, which was just as Caroline had said it would be. Sally had put on a swimming costume underneath a long wrap-around skirt and a loose cheesecloth top, knotted at her waist; throughout the whole evening she was never short of male company. The party had ended at midnight with everyone who was not already in the pool jumping in. Among the general shrieks of laughter, Sally was convinced that there were more than just a few 'harmless pranks' taking place!

It was just as well that Hishaam had magnanimously given her the whole of the next day off. The pool party had been fun and, despite the many amorous approaches from handsome young bucks who wanted her to 'slip away with them to gaze at the stars', Sally left the party as she had arrived – chaperoned by Caroline and Alex. When she reached home she slid gratefully into her bed, excited thoughts about her forthcoming ride and the possibility of meeting Abdullah again keeping her awake until nearly dawn. Finally, as the sky began to lighten, she fell asleep with Bouncy snoring happily alongside her on the bed; and as his bladder control was excellent, neither of them stirred until gone ten.

After lunch, she showered and ironed a blue cotton shirt ready to wear with the jodhpurs she had brought from England. Caroline had let her know about a riding establishment near the Embassy where horses could be hired and Sally had treated herself to a new pair. Since making the decision to stay in Al Khaleej, she had been busy finding somewhere to live and then starting work, and there had been little spare time between that and all the social engagements to meet up with Caroline for a ride. Her creamy-beige jodhpurs were still brand new and Sally was glad to have something suitable. She had bought them from a very smart establishment in London and, unlike her old baggy ones which flared at the hip and were made of cavalry twill, these were skin-tight stretch material for comfort when mounted. Mindful that trousers were considered too revealing, she wondered about the figure-hugging jodhpurs and hastily decided to discard the tucked-in blue shirt in favour of her longest, loosest shirt over the top of them. Next, she pulled out the leather riding boots from her suitcase, where they had lain untouched, and gave them a quick polish. Then, grabbing her sunglasses, she was ready.

Arriving promptly at the stables at four o'clock, she pulled up in the yard beside a big, shiny American car parked in front of the wall. Beside it, waiting patiently, stood a slim elderly man in traditional Arab dress. As Sally climbed out of her car, he came towards her with a smile, which creased his walnut-coloured face into even more wrinkles; some would call it a 'lived-in' face. She smiled back at him, thinking that his face was very much a 'lived in the desert for a long time' face.

'I am Tariq. For the Sheikh's horses. I take you for riding. Today, just small way in desert,' he said, holding out his hand as he introduced himself. To Sally's discomfort, he continued to hold onto her hand while he called out orders in Arabic. A groom led two horses into the yard; one of them was the white stallion Abdullah had shown her and the other was a bay mare. 'Which one you like to ride?' Tariq asked, still clasping her hand in his and pointing with his free hand towards the horses.

Sally knew instantly which one she wanted to ride, but had reservations. 'The stallion is lovely, but I've never ridden a stallion before,' she explained to Tariq.

'He is same as mare. Very, very quiet,' Tariq said, nonchalantly shrugging his shoulders. 'You want him, you take him.' He couldn't see what the problem was, mare or stallion? A horse was a horse in his eyes. Finally releasing her hand, he turned and signalled to the groom, who led the stallion to them.

Both horses wore ornate bridles but no saddles, and while Sally was wondering when the saddles would be put on, her question was answered as Tariq bent down, offering her a leg up on to stallion's back. Sally gathered the reins in one hand and placed the other on the horse's withers; she bent her knee in readiness. Grabbing her raised ankle, Tariq launched her high up into the air and she expertly threw her free leg over the stallion, landing gently on his wide, soft back. Beneath her, the horse instantly arched his neck and started forward at a smooth trot. Sally gently reined him back while maintaining her balance and the stallion stood waiting impatiently, champing at this bit and salivating in the process. Tariq quickly walked over to his horse, pulled his thobe up under his arms, revealing long white cotton trousers, and vaulted on to the bay mare's back. Seeing the manoeuvre from the corner of her eye, Sally was amazed at the old man's agility and, as he quickly drew alongside her, she threw him a look of admiration. Looking straight ahead, Tariq did not acknowledge it and they trotted side by side in silence for a few moments until Sally, wanting to break the ice between them, looked over at him.

'I've never ridden a horse without a saddle. It feels quite strange,' she confessed, smiling at Tariq. She had the vaguest suspicion that he disapproved of her but, to her relief, he smiled back at her.

'Look, make like this,' Tariq said, as he leaned slightly back with his legs hanging loosely against the horse's sides, his feet slightly forwards. 'You can hold his hair in your hand.' He took a handful of mane to show her and Sally, following his instructions, soon began to relax, and in a very short time the feeling of being precariously perched on the horse's back left her and she found herself easily able to keep her balance. Astride the stallion's flat, comfortable back she began to feel quite safe and before long even forgot about grabbing handfuls of mane to secure her sense of balance. As they trotted on in silence, her eyes scanned the desert ahead of her, but the only visible landmarks were a few large rocks and sand dunes on the skyline. After a few more minutes, she realised that distances in the desert were deceptive – some things that looked far away were not, while others that looked close by seemed always just out of reach. Suddenly, she felt a stab of immense sadness as she remembered the night she and Doug had shared fantasies and he had teased her about her fantasy of riding across the desert with a sheikh. Her memories, it seemed, were like the spaces in the desert – confused by distance and time. It felt a lifetime ago that Doug had held her close and proposed to her, yet it was barely eighteen months.

Sally's perception that Tariq disapproved of her was not so very far from the truth. Jameel was the Sheikh's favourite horse and he had been shocked to learn that he was offering this English woman a chance to ride him. Of course, he would not dare to question his Sheikh, but it was with serious misgivings and a heavy heart that he had waited for the girl to arrive at the stables that afternoon. But as he'd carefully watched her, he reluctantly had to admit that his boss had chosen wisely – she handled Jameel well. Discreetly, he continued to watch both horse and rider carefully for any sign of unease about this new experience and as he did so, he saw the flicker of sadness move across her face. 'Are you unhappy? Do you like to go back?'

Looking across at Tariq's wizened and sun-lined face, Sally regained her irrepressible sense of humour. Nice as he was, he was hardly the sheikh in her fantasy and she grinned. 'Tariq, I am very, very happy! Can we go a little further?'

Tariq checked his watch. 'Okay, we can go there,' he pointed ahead to some sand dunes. 'Then we must return. You like to make canter now? You feel safe?'

'How do I make him canter?' The horse was so responsive that she was sure she did not need to dig her heels into his ribs, as she had been taught to do at the riding school in England.

'You must leave this go free –' having no idea what they were called in English, Tariq rattled the reins, to show her what he was referring to, '– and talk his name, Jameel. Tell him what you want.'

'Come on, Jameel!' Sally dropped the reins and the horse leapt forward into a rocking-horse canter – his back hardly seemed to move and Sally felt as if she was sitting on a big white cloud. 'Oh, Tariq!' she cried out, laughing spontaneously and with sheer delight. 'He's wonderful! I've never ridden a horse like this before!'

After a few hundred yards at this pace, it seemed to Tariq that she was as well balanced as any rider and by the time they had reached a flat piece of the desert, he judged her to be safe enough on Jameel's back.

'Would you like to make small races?'

'Oh! Could we? Yes, please!'

'To go fast you must say, 'Yallah, yallah'. Make him little excited.' To his surprise he had hardly finished speaking when Sally called out 'Yallah, Jameel! Yallah!'

Slackening the reins, she threaded her hands deep into his mane and then they were flying across the desert, the speed whipping her hair back from her face. Hooves beat into the desert as the horses raced across the sand for several minutes until Tariq called out in Arabic to Jameel. With no signal from his rider, the stallion began to slow down underneath her, gradually dropping back to the smooth canter, then a trot, gently decreasing his speed until he was walking. Sally was breathless and exhilarated by the whole experience and it showed on her flushed cheeks and in eyes that shone with the sheer thrill of the gallop. It was as well Jameel responded to voice control, because the gallop and the heat had caused him to sweat, especially where she sat. Sally's jodhpurs were wet with the horse's sweat and when she applied pressure to his sides with her legs, she began to slide about on his back – he was as slippery as a bar of soap.

They turned for home and all too soon the ride was over and they were back at the yard. As Sally threw her leg over his quarters and slid to the ground, Jameel turned towards her and rubbed his head against her shirt to relieve the itchiness of his face and ears caused by the sweat under his bridle. When Sally caressed the horse's ears, he held his head low to get the full benefit of her attention.

'Thank you, Jameel. That was the most unbelievable ride. You're a fantastic horse,' she told him as the strong head rubbed against her, almost knocking her off balance. Engrossed in the mutual grooming ritual taking place between horse and rider, Sally was unaware of the consternation around her as a groom ran over to Tariq, whispering something to him. Tariq nodded and the groom ran to where Jameel and Sally were virtually locked in an embrace. Without a word he took the reins from Sally and led the horse away before she could finish saying her goodbyes.

'Quickly! Sheikh waiting!' Tariq called over to her before she had time to realise what was happening. He beckoned her to follow him, then quickly turned and sped away from her. Hurrying after him, Sally's heart began to beat wildly. She followed Tariq into a smaller courtyard where cushioned seats had been set out around a long, low coffee table. There was Abdullah, dressed in such a brilliant white robe and ghutra that in the bright sunlight it was almost too painful to the eye to look at him.

'Welcome, Sally,' he said, holding out his hand to greet her. Sally was aware how strong, cool and smooth his hand felt in comparison to her own, which was greasy with sweat and still covered in fine grains of sand. Abdullah turned to Tariq and Sally noticed the genuine affection between the two men as they kissed each other on the cheek several times while exchanging traditional greetings. They talked together in Arabic for a few moments and then, turning back to Sally, Abdullah smiled at her.

'Would you like a cold drink?' She was even more beautiful than he remembered.

'Yes please, that would be lovely. I think I swallowed quite a bit of desert this afternoon.'

Abdullah laughed, 'Come, please sit down,' he said, pointing to a chair.

'I'd better not,' she replied looking ruefully at the beautiful cushions that adorned the chairs. She would not have dared to sit down on her mother's cushions, having just come in from the stables. 'I'm covered in horse sweat.'

'Believe me, that is not a problem. Please, sit,' and Abdullah settled himself in a chair opposite. 'I hear you chose Jameel. He is quite an old man now, but still one of the best horses in the place to ride. Do you know how old he is?'

Sally shook her head.

'My father gave Jameel to me when he was a colt just weaned from his mother and I was a small boy. Tariq taught the horse to obey his voice. So even if I wanted him to gallop, Jameel would always have one ear listening to Tariq for permission. You know how small boys love speed and danger? Well, Tariq was Jameel's brakes.' Abdullah was laughing as he reminisced.

Sally, comfortable now that the big, brown, suggestive eyes were screened by his sunglasses, watched his handsome face as he talked. The previous day, she had guessed that he was probably about 30, but now she thought he could be younger.

'Do small boys ever grow out of their fascination with speed and danger?' Sally asked.

'Well, some of us, of course, move on to even more dangerous hobbies,' Abdullah said quietly, teasing her.

Sally walked straight into the trap. 'What's more dangerous than fast horses?' She thought for a moment. 'I know – fast cars?' she offered.

'Even more dangerous than fast cars?' chuckled Abdullah; leaning forward he said, 'Fast women!'

Too late, Sally remembered the third element of Ahmed's joke and, blushing furiously, she reached for the tall glass of cold lemonade that had been placed in front of her and sipped at it. Abdullah was delighted by her reaction – this young girl was so refreshingly innocent. He noticed the defensive lift of her chin and realised that here was a woman who would not just laugh politely at his jokes – and he loved it. Still smiling, he spoke in Arabic to Tariq, who nodded his head in response, his face breaking into a wreath of smiles in return.

'I am sorry, Sally,' Abdullah turned back to face Sally again as he explained, 'that was very rude of me, but Tariq's English is not so good. He is well over 70 and now is not the time to insist he perfects another language.'

Sally had guessed that Tariq was no youngster but was still amazed that at that age he could vault onto the mare's back with the ease of a teenage gymnast!

'Please don't apologise. I am trying very hard to learn Arabic and it is easier if I can listen to it. I could understand some of your conversation, but not enough to make any sense of it. I expect I will improve if I get out and mingle a bit more,' Sally replied, still feeling embarrassed as she assumed that he had repeated his little joke on her to Tariq.

'In that case, I will have to be careful what I say in future, but I was just asking Tariq whether you are a good enough rider to trust with my horses,' he explained. 'You have obviously made a conquest because he was very flattering about you. So please feel free to ride them any time. It is better in the evenings when the sun has lost some of its ferocity. Of course, in the winter the weather is kinder and you can ride at any time of the day.'

For a moment Sally was speechless, totally overwhelmed by the generosity of his offer.

'Thank you! I ... I would love to!' she stammered before she found her voice. 'I will only be able to ride on my days off, of course, as by the time I finish work it's dark. Though it would be wonderful if I could ride at weekends – it will give me something to look forward to during the week. As for the winter, well ... my visa is only for six months ... I may not even be here.' Involuntarily, she shivered and the smile on her face disappeared as she thought about having to return to the damp and cold of an English winter.

Abdullah noticed the change of her demeanour and wanted to sweep this girl into his arms and make her promise never to leave this land. Instead, he leant towards her, saying gently, 'There will be no problem renewing your visa, I can assure you.'

Sally would not allow herself the luxury of planning that far ahead. She had made plans before and they had come to nothing. Better to just take each day as it came; that way there was less risk of disappointment. Briefly, she smiled an acknowledgement at Abdullah before taking another sip of her cold drink.

'Look, on Fridays we race the horses on a small track in the desert just north of here. You must come and watch. It starts at about three-thirty. You will see the cars parked in the desert, so you will know where to go.'

Sally was about to decline, but then remembered that Thursdays and Fridays were the weekend – not Saturdays and Sundays as they were back home. Again, she shivered, remembering the long, lonely weekends she had endured until she had made the decision to come out to Al Khaleej.

Abdullah saw her shiver and sensed that a dark shadow had descended on her, a deep sadness threatening to overwhelm her, and it aroused his curiosity about her even more.

'Racing horses is a very old tradition of ours,' he continued. He tapped the inside of his wrist and added, 'It runs through the very blood in our veins. We race horses and camels and we love to fly falcons. Nothing can match the speed of a falcon when it dives from the sky to strike its prey. Although many Arabs drive fast cars, fly their own aeroplanes and are falling under the spell of modern technology, the desert ways are still very strong.' Abdullah had been turning a circle of coral beads through his fingers as he spoke, winding and unwinding them. Seeing her attention drawn to them, he leaned forward and handed them to Sally.

'We call them worry beads.'

'Worry beads?' Sally repeated as she took the beads from him and in turn began to run the circlet of beads through her fingers.

'Yes, you will see most Arab men have the need for these but, strangely, rarely our women. But you are welcome to keep them in case you need to relieve any worries in your life. I would hope that none will cloud your happiness.' It was perfect. Unobtrusively, he had been able to hand to her this small token. Sally was touched by the gesture and, smiling her thanks to him, knew that she would never part with them.

'It is almost time for the horses to have their evening feed. Would you like to see?' Abdullah asked as he stood up.

'Oh, yes please!' Sally eagerly replied, and pocketed the beads as she followed him out into the main yard, where grooms were pushing wheelbarrows piled high with horse feed. Almost every wheelbarrow gave off a high-pitched squeak, making the place sound as if it was full of frightened mice.

'Listen to them,' said Abdullah stopping for a moment. 'We are awash with oil but not enough, apparently, to spare a drop for the wheelbarrows.' Once again he repeated this in Arabic to Tariq, who laughed and responded in Arabic.

'Ah-ha! Tariq thinks they don't want to oil the wheelbarrows as it makes them go too quickly and then they would have to work faster.' Abdullah was laughing as he translated for Sally's benefit and was about to move on.

'But that doesn't make any sense,' Sally said, as she could immediately see a flaw in his logic.

Abdullah had begun to walk on but he stopped and turned to face her. He could not believe what he had just heard her say! He wasn't used to people answering back, particularly after he had just recounted a funny story – certainly no one had ever told him, not directly, that what he had just said did not make sense. Once more, this delightful creature was treating him like any other – he suspected she now knew who he was and yet still she spoke her mind. Instead of laughing politely at his comments, as others would have done in her place, keeping their thoughts to themselves, Sally had challenged him. He looked enquiringly at her and Sally continued.

'Well, if they oiled their wheelbarrows, it would be to their advantage, as the wheelbarrows would become silent.'

It was obvious to Sally but Abdullah looked slightly bemused.

'Don't you see? You couldn't hear how fast or slow they were working if the wheelbarrows didn't squeak. The speed of the squeak gives the game away.' As she stood there grinning, Abdullah felt laughter welling up inside him. She was right! How wonderful! Not only a beauty but one with brains and who dared to correct at him. He laughed back, slowly at first, but gradually the laughter gathered momentum until tears streamed down his face.

'Oh! Sally! That is so funny! But it is true!' He wanted to wrap his arms around her. Sally watched in astonishment as, between irrepressible bouts of laughter, he translated for Tariq. Then Tariq and Abdullah began to mimic the squeaks of the wheelbarrow, to the bewilderment of the grooms.

'Hey!' Abdullah called out to one of them, 'your barrow is not squeaking fast enough. It is only going s-q-u-e-a-k ... s-q-u-e-a-k ... s-q-u-e-a-k. It should be going: Squeak! Squeak! Squeak!' And Abdullah wrapped his arms around Tariq's neck as together they bent double with uncontrollable laughter.

The grooms, hesitating in their work, smiled nervously in their direction and then at each other. They had never before known their boss to laugh so openly or behave this way in front of them. Not sure what their reaction should be to this uncharacteristic behaviour, they began to push their wheelbarrows faster, causing the noise of the squeaks to speed up! This had the effect of making both men laugh even harder until they were holding their sides as tears rolled down their cheeks. After several moments, Abdullah gradually began to compose himself and turned to Sally.

'Oh Sally! You are so amusing, such good medicine. I will never be able to hear a wheelbarrow squeak again, without checking to see that the speed is correct.'

Sally was not sure that what she had just said had been that funny, and felt a bit sorry for the grooms who had unwittingly got caught up in it all. Slightly embarrassed, she turned away and strolled over to take a look at the contents of the wheelbarrows. It was full of a strange, sweet-smelling mixture. Still chuckling quietly, Abdullah walked over to her.

'It is whole barley soaked with dates for twelve hours, then we add a little bran for dryness,' Abdullah told her. 'Later, they will bring milk from the camels for the young horses, those that have just left their mothers. We also feed them a green food we call jet, but you probably know it by the name alfalfa. It is grown in the plantations under palm trees for shade. We cut it, but within three weeks it grows back and then it can be cut again.'

'What about the stones inside the dates?' Sally had squeezed one of the dates and had been surprised when a stone peeped out from the soft flesh.

'If you look in their mangers afterwards you will see the stones placed carefully to one side. The horses have learned to remove the date stones as they eat,' Abdullah explained. 'Come! We have time for coffee before I have to go.'

Together with Tariq, they walked back to the table and sat down again. By now, Sally felt that the pungent smell of dry horse sweat she was wearing must be a fair match even for Abdullah's perfume. A servant quickly appeared with a coffee pot and small cups and Sally found that she was looking forward to tasting again the slightly bitter but very refreshing drink. This time she knew to shake the cup when handing it back to the servant. Abdullah checked his watch and promptly stood up.

'Sorry, I must go.' Sally was about to stand but Abdullah held up a hand, signalling for her to stay. 'Please, you are most welcome to stay and enjoy more coffee. Please do come again, any time you wish. Do not forget the racing on Friday.'

'Thank you for lending me your horse today – he was wonderful,' she said, smiling gratefully up at him as he held his hand out to her.

Leaning slightly over her he said quietly, 'I am sure the pleasure was all his, to have someone so attractive on his back'. There, he had done it, he had paid her a compliment. There was so much more that he wished to say but this was neither the time nor the place. Quickly straightening up, he grinned at her. 'He usually has to carry Tariq.' Letting go of Sally's hand, he patted his old friend on the back, strode over to his car, and was gone.

Driving home, Sally could smell Abdullah's perfume on her hand – the sensual combination of rose and musk lingered in her senses

.

Chapter Twenty-Six

Sally had told Caroline very little about her week, mentioning merely that she had been given the opportunity to go riding and had taken it. Naturally, Caroline was curious but Sally had done a good job of being as vague as possible about where exactly it was that she had gone, when and with whom.

They had always shared their adventures but, from the moment Sally met Doug, she had got into the habit of not disclosing too much detail about what she was getting up to with him, and since his betrayal of her trust in him, she had clammed up even more. The year she had spent in London with Caroline's aunt and uncle had allowed her more freedom than she had ever experienced in her life. It had felt strange at first, not having to explain where she was going or what time she would be in – except to Caroline, of course, but somehow that didn't count. Renee and Fred only asked that she take care and let them know if she was staying out all night – not that she ever did. They had given her a front door key and she found she could come and go as she pleased without the interminable questions her mother would have asked. Meals had no set time in Renee's place, unlike her mother's inflexible routines, so there was never any pressure to be home in time for dinner or tea. If she was late, she could just cook herself something or find something in the fridge, and in Renee's fridge there was always plenty to choose from! There was no nagging about missing breakfast if she chose to sleep in and, as time went on, Sally gradually began to appreciate the freedom of being unattached and not answerable to anyone but herself.

Sally was slowly coming to terms with the fact that she had 'loved and lost', and had promised herself that never again would she be so quickly taken in by a handsome face and a winning smile. Until her encounter with Abdullah, that is. Her reaction when first meeting Doug paled into insignificance compared to when she had first stared up into Abdullah's beautiful brown eyes. But, this time, she was armed with the knowledge that comes from experience. She knew that the outcome of such an attraction to a member of the opposite sex came with a price tag and the fear she had felt there in Abdullah's office was the fear of paying that price all over again. The danger signals were all there and she was trying so very hard to ignore them. She certainly could not share it with Caroline, who would no doubt find a hundred reasons why she should not ignore the danger signals, and all that Sally knew was that she didn't want to hear them!

Since arriving in the exotic and beautiful country of Al Khaleej, Sally began to feel as if she was waking up from a long hibernation. The minute she had arrived in this land of warm sunshine and friendly faces, she had begun to take a fresh look at the world around her – this was a new place; a new beginning; a new Sally.

The new Sally, she felt, was older and wiser. During her first few weeks in Al Khaleej, when she'd stayed with Caroline and Alex, she had been a spectator to the relationship between the two. Caroline told her husband everything and, as she had watched them, she hadn't been able to work out if it was because that's what husbands and wives did or if it was because Alex was a very subtle interrogator. Unfailingly affectionate towards his wife, he always sounded genuinely interested in what Caroline had been up to while he had been at work. Always so reasonable, always with just a hint of a smile, but always persistent in wanting to know just where Caroline had been and with whom. Watching her friend, she could tell that Caroline adored him but Sally, still bruised from her first encounter with love, remained unsure about the wisdom of telling another person – whoever it was – quite so much about one's activities or what one was planning to do next.

Never again would she go public with her feelings, nor be so quick to tell a man of her love, for fear of the humiliation of rejection. Never again did she want to see the look of sadness, concern and pity in the eyes of either her father or her best friend. She would show them all that she could cope, and she would cope by keeping her thoughts and feelings to herself. Sally was getting to like her new persona. For a start, it allowed her to be private with her thoughts and she recognised immediately that being vague and a little non-specific about what she was planning to do or had done also gave her some room for manoeuvrability in her own plans.

Without really knowing the basis for it, Sally suspected the reason Alex was always so interested in his wife's activities had more to do with his career ambitions than his concern for Caroline. Promotion within the Foreign Office was vital to him. It occurred to Sally that if he knew what Caroline was up to at all times he would be in a position to nip in the bud anything she might do to cause him embarrassment. Well, whatever his motives were, it was his business, but she was determined to ensure that Alex did not interfere with hers. She had left home over a year ago and was now living abroad; she was independent, she had a job and her own flat and was no longer controlled or restricted by her parents – and she certainly had no intention of allowing anyone else to dictate how she should lead her life!

Sally had fully intended taking up Abdullah's invitation to go riding the following weekend, as long as she could put her friend off the scent of where she was going. Unfortunately fate, in the shape of Caroline's birthday and a surprise party being organised by Alex, prevented her from carrying out her plans.

On the Thursday morning, instead of heading for the stables she found herself in her kitchen making a birthday cake. The party went on into the early hours of Friday. Having surfaced late on Friday morning, Sally had taken Bouncy for a walk and, after lunch, was about to set off on her own to find where in the desert the horse racing took place when, once more, she was thwarted, this time by a phone call from Caroline. Alex was going to play golf and Caroline asked if she could come over for a girlie session. Caught unawares, Sally couldn't think up a plausible reason for refusing without arousing Caroline's suspicions and having to face a whole series of questions which Sally did not want to have to answer.

The doorbell rang and Bouncy's deep bark announced Caroline's arrival. In anticipation, Sally had opened a bottle of white wine and placed it in a cooler next to two wineglasses. Now she filled them both and handed one to Caroline, who sank into the nearest armchair, studiously avoiding the settee.

Bouncy had the habit of leaping onto the settee to befriend Sally's guests when they sat on it. Settling himself next to them, he would gaze adoringly and forlornly up at whoever it was. It rarely failed and was not long before they would be rubbing his tummy or his ears in those places that were hard for a dog to reach himself. Caroline liked dogs and had been happy to oblige on the first few occasions – until she saw something move in his fur, and was horrified when she got back to her apartment to realise that the 'something' had bitten her. What with that and Bouncy's tendency to break wind and slurp noisily at his genitals every few minutes, Caroline preferred to distance herself from his affections.

As well as having a girlie catch-up session, Caroline had called round for a reason and wasted no time in coming out with it.

'Sal, there's an official reception at the Embassy coming up, for the Queen's Birthday – you know what they're like, any excuse for a party. Will you come along as our guest? Please say you'll come, then we can hit the town and have one of our shopping expeditions in search of the right outfit.' Caroline loved parties and, as the wife of a Foreign Office diplomat, had thrown herself wholeheartedly into the endless round of social events and gatherings that were laid on in Al Khaleej.

'I'll certainly come along, but I think we might be stuck for choice in our search for "the right outfit".' Sally grimaced as she named the only three shops in town that she knew sold a limited range of dated, unfashionable European womenswear.

One of the delights for Caroline while living in Wimbledon had been the ease of access to the West End and its shops. Now she made no secret of the fact that she missed the shops in London and, in particular, Oxford Street. After Alex had proposed, he had surprised her by providing a very generous 'dress allowance', explaining to Caroline that, as his future wife, she would be expected to attend formal functions, particularly when they were living abroad. At first Caroline had refused to accept such a generous allowance, but Alex had insisted. He explained that she would need to stock up with evening gowns to take out to the Middle East as fashionable dress shops might be difficult to find there. Alex had been right. Dress shops were few and far between and Caroline had been grateful that she had brought several evening gowns with her.

Now there was yet another 'do' in the offing and she was seriously in need of something different to wear, having worn all her gowns at least once. Caroline had been mortified when she had overheard one of the Embassy wives, barely concealing her sarcasm, comment loudly that she had 'admired the dress that Caroline was wearing, the first time she wore it!'

Caroline sighed. 'I wonder what the Arab ladies do around here when they want something really special?'

'I've no idea, but I've just thought of somebody who may be able to help. I'll ask him in the morning,' Sally offered, as she reached over and topped up Caroline's wineglass.

'Him?' Caroline queried. 'Well, if you think he can help, by all means ask and tomorrow evening we can go hunting for dresses. Now tell me about this riding that you've managed to do. What are the nags like? Where are they? Whose are they?'

Sally couldn't help wondering if her friend had been prompted by Alex to ask at least one of those questions.

'They were fabulous horses, Arabians. They belong to somebody I met through work,' Sally responded, ignoring all the other questions and concentrating on describing the horses. By the time she had finished describing the most fabulous animals that she had ever met, Caroline's eyes were aglow with the pictures that Sally had painted.

'That's some job you've got there.' Caroline raised her eyebrows as she surveyed the vases of fresh flowers adorning Sally's sitting room.

'Is the admirer who sent the flowers the same chap who owns the horses?'

'Ahmed isn't an admirer, he's just a friend. An old Arab gentleman,' Sally answered, again neatly side-stepping the question about who owned the horses.

'Yeah, right! Alex says the old Arab gentleman not only happens to be the landlord of the office building where you work, but also owns a chunk of the city as well! Own up, Sal, you've got yourself a sugar daddy in tow, haven't you?'

Any lingering doubt that Sally might have had as to the range of Alex's ever-watchful eye went out of the window with that remark! It seemed that not only did he watch his wife and her friends, but the friends of the friends too. 'Caroline, that's not true. You've got me worried now. You don't really think Ahmed fancies me, do you?'

'Well ... what do you think?' Caroline asked, raising her eyebrows and leaving them there until her friend responded.

'I didn't actually think anything about it at all until you brought the subject up! He pops into the office most mornings and chats to Hishaam, and I make them both some coffee.'

'Oh yeah! And when Hishaam isn't there – which according to you seems to be most of the time?' Caroline prompted, laughing at her friend.

'I still make Ahmed coffee and we sit and talk.'

'Sit and talk?'

'Yes, we sit and talk ...'

'Uh-huh! So what's with all the flowers?'

'Look! It's all very innocent! Last time he popped in, Ahmed asked me if there was anything that I missed about living in the Middle East and I told him the truth. I miss seeing fresh flowers!'

Caroline let out a most unladylike snort.

'I do!' Sally continued. 'There're no flower shops in Al Khaleej! The gardener here at the apartments tells me he's growing zinnias in that sandy flowerbed that he optimistically dug round the edge of the sparse lawn, but nothing has appeared yet.'

'Getting a little defensive, aren't we?'

'No! We are not!' But Sally was becoming exasperated with the questioning.

'So, let me get this straight. You tell him you're homesick for flowers and he fills the place with flowers for you? Hmm ... could be useful! Next time be sure to tell him you miss driving that little sporty number you left back home and see what turns up in your garage,' Caroline said, grinning mischievously.

'I couldn't do that!' Sally was shocked at the suggestion. 'And in any case, I didn't have a car back home. You know full well that I've only just got my driving licence.'

'Sally, wise up!' Caroline held her glass up for more wine and Sally obligingly refilled both their glasses. 'If he wants to spoil you and make you happy ... with no strings ....?'

'Caroline! Oh, shut up!' Sally was shocked. Women who took advantage of men in that way appalled her and the thought of using dear old Ahmed for personal gain horrified her. It went against everything she had been brought up to be. By nature, Sally was a giver, not a taker.

She's not safe to be let out alone, Caroline thought and found it incredible that Sally still didn't seem to realise the effect that she had on men. If she chose to, Caroline felt certain that Sally could ask for anything from any man and, if it was within his power, he would get it for her. She tried to think what she would do if she were in her friend's shoes – tall and blonde with those blue eyes, and men falling over themselves to get near her. Fortunately, Alex was very generous, and always teasing her that she was 'cheap to keep'. She was aware of the ploys that some wives used to get their husbands to spend more money on them. No, she decided, even if she had been lucky enough to have her friend's good looks, she had too much pride to use guile for gain.

'Keep your hair on, Sal! Just teasing!' Caroline said with a wicked smile, and chucked a nearby cushion at her friend.

With their wineglasses refilled and the bottle now emptied, they lounged in contentment – Caroline because she really appreciated having the company of her childhood friend again, and Sally because of her increasing sense of well-being since meeting the Sheikh and riding his horses.

The open windows and doors allowed a breath of early evening breeze to circle around them. As they sat in companionable silence with their own thoughts, an enthusiastic muezzin began calling the faithful to the final prayer of the day. The tall minaret of the mosque overlooked Sally's apartment and the voice through the loudspeakers made it almost impossible for them to continue their conversation for several minutes.

When the final wail resonated around the sitting room Caroline grinned at Sally. 'Do you still find that as "haunting and romantic" as that first time you heard it at our place?'

'Even more so,' Sally replied without hesitation. 'But I was a bit disillusioned the other day when I discovered that sometimes they use a record of the prayer rigged up to a microphone. The record got stuck and we had twenty minutes of continuous Allah Akbar before anyone noticed and moved it on,' Sally said, laughing out loud. 'That's progress, I suppose.'

By nine o'clock, after a supper of sandwiches and crisps, Caroline decided it was time to leave. As she stood up, Bouncy launched himself from the settee into the vacated armchair.

'I don't know why you keep that fleabag in the house! I bet he's got ticks as well as God-only-knows-what crawling all over him,' complained Caroline.

'He's the only man I really trust,' Sally said as she bent over the dog, fondly ruffling the frizzy hair between his ears. Bouncy rolled over onto his back in appreciation, placing his genitals on full view in the process. Caroline hiccupped and giggled irrepressibly.

'Well, don't go stroking old Ahmed like that, will you? It might have the same effect! Then he'll be upside down on that settee in your office showing you his crown jewels before you know it.' The friends giggled helplessly as the image of Ahmed lying on his back formed in their minds. After a while, Sally began to feel a bit guilty about a joke at the expense of the kindly Ahmed's dignity, and the laughter slowly subsided.

'Oh, shut up, Caroline and go home!' she said, but she was still laughing as she closed the front door behind her friend.

Chapter Twenty-Seven

Arriving home from work the following evening, Sally took a quick shower, changed and grabbed a leg of cold chicken before Caroline collected her at six-thirty just as it was getting dark. Darkness descended suddenly in the Middle East and, in Al Khaleej, one minute the sun would be a fireball high in the sky, and the next it would plummet to the horizon, becoming a giant ball of fiery orange. Then it rapidly slid out of sight, taking the heat with it and, in the blink of an eye, day would turn into night.

By seven o'clock, total darkness had descended; window shutters were opened or raised to let in the cool night air and in the little streets and alleyways of the souk, shop lights blazed out in the darkness as the town came to life.

The two women strolled along the narrow streets. Everywhere they went their senses were assailed by the delicious aromas of fresh spices hanging on the warm evening air, creating a very exotic ambience. Behind plate glass windows in Gold Street, there were yards upon yards of gold bangles on display, having been threaded on what appeared to be horizontal broom handles. In the front window of one shop, gem-encrusted sets of matching necklaces, bracelets and earrings lay on red velvet cushions. In another, subtle Gulf pearls and locally-crafted gold jewellery nestled beside the more vulgar imported diamonds that sparkled under the lights. Inside many of the shops sat an Arab with his worry beads, his family and a set of scales. In others, only the men sat drinking coffee with their customers or friends, as they weighed the gold or jewellery and haggled for a good price.

Sally had asked Amiri's advice about dresses, and had been told that anything his wives required for a special occasion was always tailor-made by his cousin. He had given Sally directions and helpfully suggested to her that she should first go to the material shops in the souk and choose her fabric, then take it along to his cousin's shop. Of course, his cousin was the 'best tailor in town' and if she went to him she could sit and look through the latest styles in the imported magazines he ordered specially for his customers. Amiri assured her that his cousin could make up any material into anything Sally chose from the magazines or even, if she preferred, from her own designs.

When Sally explained it all to Caroline, they both became excited by the creative possibilities now open to them – if, as Caroline pointed out, it was true.

Not being very adventurous, she only visited the souk with Alex and that never included browsing around the material shops and dressmakers. The expats she had befriended arranged for dresses to be flown out from the UK but the prospect of asking her mother to shop for her and choose her dresses didn't bear thinking about. Hence she had resorted to wearing dresses twice and sometimes three times over, rather than risk asking for her mother's help and having dresses arrive that her mother thought suitable.

The two friends turned into a maze of alleyways just off the main road where the material souk had been situated for centuries. These alleyways were barely the width of a donkey cart and immediately they found themselves under a rainbow canopy of fabrics as the colourful materials hung high up outside the shops on each side met in the centre to create a ceiling of riotous colour. There were silks from India, cottons from Egypt, brocades from China, damask, lace, velvets, cashmere; the choice was endless and the rich colours came in every shade imaginable.

One shop displayed luxuriant brocades in different shades of red and vibrant turquoises, and they went in to examine them more closely.

'I think this might be a bit over the top for the Embassy, don't you?' Caroline held a cherry-red brocade against herself as she glanced in a nearby mirror.

'Absolutely not ... I think it's sensational! Go for it, Caro! Just have a straight shift, let the material do the rest. It's detailed enough.' But Caroline still wasn't sure that such a bright red suited her complexion.

'If you don't want it, I'll have it!' Sally thought the colour was wonderful and both of them could see immediately, when she draped it across her, that it would suit Sally's lighter skin tone. 'Then again, if somebody makes me blush you won't know where the dress ends and I begin,' Sally joked.

'Now you come to mention it,' Caroline said, chuckling, 'we're hoping to have somebody there who will make you blush. So I'd go for the blue, if I were you.'

'Oh no,' Sally sighed, 'not more matchmaking! When will you ever give up?'

Noting the exasperation in her friend's voice, Caroline realised that some fast talking was necessary.

'I promise you, you'll like Matt. He's a real sweetie and, of course, no obligations. He's just your dinner partner for the evening. He's on our table, you see. We needed him to balance the numbers. He's only just arrived and he's at a bit of a loss.'

'So you think if you give me a homesick puppy, I'll take him under my wing?' Sally cast her eyes up to heaven.

'Well ... it has been known.'

Continuing to examine different fabrics, pushing some aside and drifting on to others, they found themselves at the back of the shop. Turning to make their way back out, they realised that the enthusiastic shopkeeper, encouraged by their obvious interest in brocades, had barricaded them into a corner with virtually every roll of that material in his shop! He had even arranged for more rolls in the colours that he didn't have in his own shop to be rapidly ferried across from the shop opposite, in anticipation of making a sale! The girls looked at each other and then back at all the materials and then grinned as they realised that it would be impossible now not to buy something from him.

'Look, I don't think we should both go clad in brocade, but I'm buying some of the turquoise and a couple of yards of the red, for future use,' Sally said.

'Oh good, you're still coming, then. I quite like this mulberry colour and that green matches my eyes,' Caroline said, unravelling a few turns of each and holding them up against herself.

'Yes. This very nice colour for you, lady,' the shopkeeper enthused, energetically nodding his head and grinning. They selected their colours and then watched, fascinated, as the shopkeeper skilfully threw the bolts along the length of the glass-topped counter so that they rolled and unfurled. Reaching under the counter, he brought out a wooden stick that he used to measure the required lengths of material, cut and folded the brocade and then made two neat brown paper parcels tied up with string so that they could easily be carried. Neither of the girls felt confident enough to negotiate, so they paid the shopkeeper what he declared was the 'best price' and made their way out of the shop.

The evening was still very warm as they stepped out of the shop and into the narrow confines of the alleyway. Each shop had its own exotic smell, some from incense and others from the fabric on the rolls of material that lined the walls from ceiling to floor.

Strolling towards the area where all the tailors were situated, the two friends would stop occasionally to point up to a length of material, which would immediately be floated down within their reach by a hopeful shopkeeper, with the aid of a hook attached to a long pole. As they continued through the labyrinth of streets under the multicoloured fabrics, the heady cocktail of perfumes, eastern spices, burning incense and exotic cooking that hung in the air somehow rekindled in Sally the need for romance. Without quite knowing why, Sally began to think how lovely it would be to stroll through here with someone special. Someone who would hold my hand, she thought, someone to share a secret whisper with. Suddenly, she had an overwhelming longing to feel a strong pair of arms around her. In her mind, she could see again a pair of brown eyes smiling at her from a very handsome face and she felt her heart give one furious bump in her chest. In a rush to hide her thoughts from Caroline, she pointed to some very beautiful lace. The lace was proffered for closer examination and Caroline became absorbed in looking at the wide selection of colours available.

At every shop, friendly greetings were exchanged and they had been offered hot or cold drinks whether they purchased anything or not, but, with the reserve of the British, Sally and Caroline were at first reluctant to accept. Once reassured that, even if they did not see anything they wanted to purchase, on this occasion, they were still welcome to a drink, they eventually accepted the hospitality so generously offered.

'Inshallah, next time,' the shopkeepers would say if they failed to make a sale, happy, with a smile and a wobble of the head, to rely on the will of God to generate sales. By the time they reached the end of the kaleidoscopic canopy, Sally and Caroline each had several brown paper packages containing lengths of silk, brocade and lace and were awash with sugary black tea. Having made a lot of new friends, they set off in search of Amiri's cousin's shop.

They threaded their way up and down unnamed alleyways, still brightly lit but less crowded. Characteristically, it was Caroline who pointed out that they were straying into seriously unknown territory and Sally who remained totally unperturbed. She was once again enjoying the feeling of being transported back in time. The narrow alleyways were like the streets portrayed in biblical times and Sally wondered how old some of the buildings actually were. The more inquisitive Sally became about 'let's just see what's round the next corner', the more anxious Caroline became as they strayed further and further from the hubbub of the main souk. Sally strode ahead, calm and confident with no sense of any danger, while Caroline kept a watchful eye on every shadow in every doorway, convinced that at any minute they might be pounced upon. Other women they passed were veiled or wearing all-enveloping black abayas and Caroline felt thoroughly conspicuous as they wandered about in their skirts and blouses.

'I'm sure he said it was down this end of town,' Sally reassured her, as they continued to head away from the bright lights of the main souk. As they turned the corner into the street where the majority of the tailors' shops were situated, they realised that they need not have worried – Amiri's cousin knew that very few Europeans found their way into this part of town and had positioned himself in his shop doorway. As soon as they turned the corner he had immediately recognised Sally from his cousin's description of her: 'a very beautiful, tall, blonde English lady'. He waved and smiled as they approached his shop and came towards them to usher them into his premises before they were canvassed by another tailor.

'Hello. Welcome. My name is Saeed. Cousin for Amiri. Yes. Please, come. Come inside. Please take a seat. What would you like to drink?'

He guided them towards the obligatory settee and coffee table – in this instance strategically placed in the shop window, no doubt believing that the shop looking full and busy would encourage more trade. Saeed left them there and hurried away towards the rear of the shop, disappearing behind some curtains and calling out to someone as he went.

They made themselves comfortable on the settee. Sally glanced around the inside of the shop and, hearing the familiar whirr of not just one but several sewing machines coming from somewhere in the back of the shop, she was immediately reminded of her mother. Spying a large, old-fashioned cheval mirror standing in one corner of the shop, she had an uncomfortable feeling that maybe this had been a mistake. To her horror, she saw posters on the walls of just the sort of dresses that her mother loved to make! The heads and shoulders of dewy-eyed models emerged from a froth of pale pink, lemon or powder-blue net and tulle. Their bright red lipstick and tightly-permed hair made Sally shudder. Caroline had also spotted the dated appearance of Saeed's shop and she too had begun to wonder if this had been such a good idea. They glanced at each other, feeling rather foolish sitting there with their brown paper parcels.

'Oh Lord!' Sally groaned in a whisper. 'Look at the styles! My mother would love it here. You don't think he's stuck in the 1950s too, do you?'

'If he makes dresses like the ones your mother turns out, then I'm definitely out of here!' Caroline whispered back.

'I'm so sorry, Caro, we'll just have a chat and then we can say we'll think about it and make our escape.' Sally was mortified that she had dragged her friend along, wishing that she had checked it out first before involving Caroline.

'Ssssh ... he's coming back with the coffee.' Caroline dug Sally in the ribs and they both smiled sweetly at Saeed, who was hurrying back towards them wearing a very big smile. However it wasn't coffee that Saeed was carrying, but two large mail order catalogues, little more than a year old, and several copies of more recent fashionable ladies' magazines from France, America and Britain.

He handed each of them a catalogue and laid the magazines and a book of dress patterns on the coffee table in front of them.

'Now, please, you choose and then I make measurement for you. Now I fetch coffee.'

Hesitantly at first, they turned the pages until they found the section containing cocktail dresses and long evening gowns. Caroline picked up the French magazine and her eyes opened in amazement at the wonderful array of styles and colours. She nudged Sally.

'Can he really make any of these?' she whispered in awed tones.

'Wow, won't it just be fantastic if he can?' Sally whispered back in relief.

Just then, Saeed came hurrying back to them with their drinks, still beaming from ear to ear.

Caroline was still a bit suspicious, but Saeed knew his trade well and it wasn't long before both girls realised it. As he offered help and advice about the different styles and colours that would suit them, his expertise became obvious. For Sally, he asked her if she wanted to accentuate her height and suggested styles that, even with his broken English, Sally quickly understood would help her look tall and slim. Alternatively, there were other styles that would make her look 'not so tall'. He examined the materials they had brought with them and showed them how the cut and colour of each could accentuate a feature or subdue it.

To Caroline, he made suggestions that she could easily see would make her seem taller, if she wished, and others that would make her appear petite. He told them why some of their fabrics could be used for certain styles and not others. He explained to them how some of the styles that they were interested in required the softness of, for example, silk, in order to achieve the soft folds and fall required. He advised lining some of the silk fabrics with an additional layer of plain silk, maybe in a different or complementary colour to achieve that certain chicness. He showed them styles that would be best for them and other styles that would be more suited for the silks and laces, and so on. He was easy to talk to, and so obviously loved and knew his craft, that it wasn't long before both girls were totally enamoured of him. Finally, when they had both made up their minds what they would like to do with their chosen fabrics, he announced, 'Okay, now I take all measurements. After two days you come for fitting and next day after, then I finish.' He held three fingers up to illustrate the days in case they hadn't understood.

'Come, come with me,' he said, leading them to the rear of the shop and through the curtains to one of the fitting rooms, where he pulled his old tape measure from around his neck. He measured them both using a technique that he had perfected over the years to avoid close bodily contact. Where the tape met he held it well away from the body, then deducted the extra six inches that he had left for a 'safety zone'. A smiling Filipina girl stood close by, recording the figures in a little book along with the instructions he called out to her.

'Now, please, you don't get more big or more small,' he joked. 'I have your measurements near name in book. If you want anything, just bring material and you can bring picture of dress, shirt, or choose from book. Two days everything ready for fitting. One day after that, all done,' he reiterated.

As the girls drove home after a very successful evening's shopping, they couldn't help marvelling at such a find – to have such fashionable clothes made to measure and done so quickly, too.

Two days later, the girls discovered that Saeed's expertise meant that there was very little to alter in the dresses and were delighted to find that their three dresses each were all taking shape exactly as they had hoped they would.

When they returned on the third day the fit of them all was perfect. Sally was particularly thrilled with the vibrant, turquoise brocade evening dress which, encouraged by Saeed, she had designed herself. Even from her abysmal sketch, true to his word, the workmanship and end result was superb! She had wanted it plain at the front, but the back daringly low, and explained to Saeed that she did not want to wear any undergarments 'around here', waving her hands generally in the direction of her bust. Beaming from ear to ear, he had nodded and suggested that he put a lining of dark blue silk under the brocade. In the fitting room, Sally slipped out of her bra and stepped into the dress.

Her breasts were young and firm so that even without support they didn't sag and spoil the line of the material. Full length, it allowed the splendour of the rich brocade to be displayed to its best and follow the contours of her body perfectly. The 'v' shape plunged daringly to a point just a few inches above the curve of her bottom. For ease of movement, Sally had included a split at the back that reached to just above her knees and when she tried it out in the fitting room, she was thrilled to find that it worked; she could sit and walk without any restriction at all. She loved the dress. It made her feel glamorous, sexy and sophisticated and she couldn't wait to wear it! The finished article was exactly what she'd had in mind. And, from the squeals of delight coming from the fitting room next door, she could tell that Caroline was as thrilled with her own finished creations as Sally was with hers.

After collecting the finished garments, they sat in Sally's flat drinking coffee and talking about the horse racing that Sally had told Caroline she 'had heard about', which took place on a Friday afternoon. Reluctantly and tentatively, she had asked Caroline if she and Alex would like to go with her. Having been unable to visit the stables or attend the racing the previous weekend, Sally, unusually for her, was feeling shy about suddenly turning up on her own and unannounced. Now she wished more than ever that she had been able to go to the stables the weekend following the invitation from Abdullah to ride whenever she wanted to.

'No, Alex won't budge on that one. I haven't been able to persuade him to take me. He's never been terribly keen on horses, as you know,' Caroline grimaced as she remembered when they were in Wimbledon, being torn between wanting to go riding with Sally or go out for the day with Alex. Alex liked his golf, tennis and fishing, was a good swimmer and had rowed for Oxford – though they had lost the year that he taken part. Animals, however, had not featured large in his life and he saw no good purpose for them other than as food.

'But he should make the effort to attend, Caroline – it's part of the culture out here, horse and camel racing.'

'Yeah, right! Horseracing is also part of the Great British culture back home in good ol' Blighty – the Sport of Kings and all that – but Alex never went to it there either! Besides, he says the horses here are reasonably okay but the camels are, and I quote, "fucking dangerous". Apparently when they try to race the camels they tend to gallop off, totally out of control, in four different directions. On one occasion, a camel ran straight into the car park and left a series of dents across the bonnets of several of the cars parked in the front row. Could you imagine his reaction if a camel dared to put a dent in that beloved Mercedes of his?' Caroline said, rolling her eyes in mock horror at the very thought.

'I'd love to see that!'

'No, you wouldn't! Neither would I, come to think of it! A grown man crying! Ugh!' Caroline shuddered. 'It's just too horrible!'

'I didn't mean that,' Sally managed to say between bouts of laughter. 'I meant I'd love to see the camels taking off in four different directions!'

'Oh, well, yes that might be fun, I suppose.'

'Why don't you and I go, if Alex doesn't mind?'

'No, I don't think he'll mind. I expect he'll be quite happy to go and play a round of golf or go fishing or something. Then he'll think what a wonderful wife I am, encouraging him to go out to play with his friends. Yes, okay, but we'll go in my car. That way I can be sure that we will both get there and back again in one piece.'

Bouncy chose that moment to sit up and begin a frantic scratching of his ribs with a hind leg, dribbling with ecstasy as he moved his tormentors around. Seeing Sally's fond glance at her dog, Caroline hastily added, 'And by the way, we're not taking your flea factory with us!'

'Ah, poor Bouncy. Sorry about that – he's overdue for a bath. Bouncy! Stop that!' Sally threw her sandal in the dog's direction. Bouncy dutifully stopped what he was doing while he sniffed at the sandal, before deciding that it was nothing very interesting. Getting up, he walked twice round in a circle before settling himself down again to snuffle loudly at his genitals.

'That's it! I'm definitely off!' Caroline stood up. 'See you Friday, about three. I don't suppose they'll start on time, nothing seems to round here. So that gives us plenty of time to get there and find somewhere to park, well away from the notorious front row!'

First Love

Chapter Twenty-Eight

There was a warm breeze blowing in through the open windows as Caroline turned the car off the main road and onto the rough track that led to the level sand used for the races.

'I think we'll park over there,' Caroline said as they bumped across a patch of stony ground towards the rows of cars furthest from the track. 'Alex will never let me hear the end of it if I go home with a camel's hoof print on the bonnet.'

'Foot,' Sally corrected.

'Pardon?'

'Foot. It would be a footprint. Camels don't have hooves.'

'Whatever it's called, for the continuation of marital harmony, we don't want one. Can you imagine Alex's reaction?' Caroline pulled up and parked the dark blue Alfa Romeo in the back row.

Insisting that she had a driving licence before taking her to live abroad, Alex had paid for her to have driving lessons in Wimbledon and, at the third attempt, she had passed her test a week before they got married. The status of the car her husband had bought her went straight over Caroline's head. It was a tin box with four wheels and, as long as the damned thing got her from A to B and back again, that was all that mattered to her. But Alex would insist on inspecting it every weekend, checking the radiator, the tyres and the oil, refilling the windscreen washer reservoir and then the petrol tank. Caroline teased him, saying that he paid more attention to the car then he did to her. That was a mistake, because he had then proceeded to explain to her, in great detail, the damage that could develop in this hot climate if these things were not regularly checked, 'and a damaged car is a dangerous car, Caro'. He was right, of course, he always was! He was still a smart arse!

The racetrack car park held a large selection of cars new and old, from top-of-the-range Mercedes and Chevrolets to complete rust buckets. There were ancient, wood-framed coaches, some garishly hand-painted, many with wire chicken cages strapped to the roof racks. The squawks and clucks of the closely-packed chickens, with their heads stuck out through the wire mesh and their bright red combs flapping in the breeze, could be heard above the general hubbub of the crowd. Although the chickens had the best view at the venue,

Sally couldn't help feeling a little sorry for them. Confined in their cages, she wondered how far and for how long they had travelled on top of the coaches exposed to the sun. Several pickups, with ornate wrought-ironwork sides, held long-haired, floppy-eared goats chewing happily on bundles of greens, unperturbed by their surroundings. Sally had a mind to take a peep inside to see if any water had been left for them, but Caroline pulled her away, not wanting a scene in the event that the welfare of the goats did not meet with Sally's approval.

Both girls carried floppy sun hats for, although the meeting was taking place late in the afternoon, the dying rays of the sun could still be quite fierce.

Wondering if Abdullah would be at the races, Sally had put on a colourful blue- and-white skirt with a matching blue shirt and white pumps. Caroline, dressed all in khaki, was wearing her desert boots, fearful of being bitten by any of the many insects that always seemed to scurry around on the ground

They walked across the sand to where the crowds of eager racegoers were gathering. Sally could feel the warmth from the sun lightly toasting her face, no doubt encouraging more freckles to bloom on her nose in the process. Enviously, she looked across at her friend, realising that she would never achieve a golden, even tan like her. Instead she settled for replacing her British winter pallor with a peachy sheen, having no idea that in doing so her skin had become the epitome of 'English peaches and cream' – the envy of many, including Caroline.

There was a huge crowd, mostly locals, but Sally noticed a sprinkling of other Europeans, mainly men. All the local women were heavily veiled or covered from head to toe in their abayas, and stood about in small groups. Numerous young children ran playfully around them, reminding Sally of the young foals at the Sheikh's stables. The smaller children were carried aloft on their fathers' shoulders for a better view, obscuring everyone else's in the process.

As Sally and Caroline made their way towards the flimsy, white wooden rails that marked out the racetrack, they could see ten camels with their riders already mounted. The riders made futile attempts to form a line for the start of the first race, and the crowd pressed eagerly against the rails. A few of the riders, in an attempt to keep their mounts calm, were trotting up and down while the camels protested loudly with deep guttural groans. Green saliva drooled from their mouths. Occasionally they would spit and, if they were passing near the rails at the time, unlucky onlookers would be spattered in the foul-smelling, green spittle.

Looking closely at the nearest camel Sally could see that, as well as wearing a rope head collar with reins attached, the camel had a ring through its nose. Attached to the nose ring was a single piece of rope, which the rider was futilely pulling in his attempt to control the animal and curb its enthusiasm. It looked so cruel, but Sally noticed that the technique had little or no effect on this or any of the other camels, whose riders were doing the same.

The more skilled riders quietly circled their camels and were pointing in the right direction when the starter called 'Go!' But the not-so-skilled and those with the less biddable mounts kept going round in ever-decreasing circles and were still at the starting post long after the others set off. When they realised that most of their friends had gone, the remaining camels bolted in whichever direction they happened to be facing. At least two were seen heading inland, destined for a night in the desert, while another was on course for a trip to the coast. And, just as Alex had predicted, a couple of the camels stayed closer to home and were definitely heading for the parked cars!

'Bugger,' said Caroline laughing. 'Will you just look at that, Sal! Alex is right again! He's going to be so smug when I tell him.'

'Well, you know the answer to that, then, don't you? Don't tell him,' laughed Sally, dropping a broad hint that Caro didn't have to tell her husband everything.

The racing camels stirred up a huge sand cloud, making the girls turn their heads away, using their hats to cover their mouths in an effort to avoid breathing the sand and dust into their lungs. A roar down the track signified that the race was over, and they stood with their backs to the rails, idly gazing round. Sally noticed a large white concrete stand, to the right of where they were standing. Even from this distance, she could see that it was bedecked with colourful carpets and cushions and covered with an awning to protect it from the sun's fierce rays. It was empty at the moment and Sally supposed this must be where dignitaries sat when they came to the races. Just then a cheer went up, and many in the crowd surged towards the stand, where Sally could make out several large limousines pulling up alongside it. Her heart began to beat a little faster at the thought that Abdullah might be among them, but from this distance she couldn't be sure. All she could she was a group of Arabs climbing the steps to the stand and taking their seats to watch the racing in comfort.

She turned her attention back to Caroline and they agreed that, although the camels were highly entertaining, they were eager to see the horses. Sally suggested making their way across to where the horses were standing patiently waiting for the racing to begin. She had an ulterior motive: their path would take them past the front of the stand. Sally hoped that if Abdullah was among the recently-arrived VIPs, he might just spot her in the crowd. There weren't that many tall blondes around, if any, and he would know if he saw her that she had not ignored his invitation.

Having been unable to go to the stables the previous week, she now felt shy about going there again. Two weeks had passed since he had issued the open invitation but she couldn't face the awkwardness of turning up at the stables, not knowing whether or not they were expecting her. As they made their way towards the horses, Sally glanced up at the stand, certain that she recognised Abdullah. Of course he would be here, she thought – he was enthusiastic about the racing and doubtless many of the horses racing were his. Her heart missed a beat. Had she done the right thing in coming here today? she wondered.

Like Sally, Caroline was enchanted with the horses. Compared to the hunters and hacks she had ridden in England, these Arabian horses looked small – she reckoned they were on average around 15 hands. She was amazed to see that the jockeys seemed to range in age from 5 to 65 and in size anything between 5 and 15 stone. Caroline thought it was preposterous!

'Sal. How on earth can the race be fair when some of the horses are carrying skinny little boys and others have grown men on their backs? Do they put extra weight in the saddles to even it up?'

Sally grinned at her. 'There's no weighing in or out with your saddle here, Caro – mainly because there are no saddles!'

'What! Are you serious?' Caroline was stunned but, before she could say any more, they were interrupted by someone calling out to Sally. It was Tariq, running towards her, his face beaming.

'Sally! Hello, Sally, welcome!'

Abdullah never failed to attend the racing on a Friday afternoon; it was one of his few pleasures and his busy schedule was kept free to allow him to indulge it. The previous week he had eagerly and expectantly scanned the crowds, hoping to see that Sally had taken up his invitation. He was more disappointed than he cared to admit that she had not come to ride his horses the previous day. He had made time for a trip to the stables hoping to see her again, convinced that she would come, but when darkness fell, he had finally given up and left, unable to find a reason to linger there any longer. He had then convinced himself he would see her the next day at the races and had eagerly taken his seat in the stand, his eyes searching the crowds for a head of blonde hair. One of his sharp-eyed cousins, noting his interest in the crowd, had asked Abdullah who he was looking for, so he had had to stop searching so obviously for her. When she didn't come, he was forced to cope with the unfamiliar feeling of 'personal disappointment'.

Throughout the following few days, Abdullah was puzzled. He just could not believe that he had been mistaken in either the pleasure that she had shown at the sight of his horses nor the meaning behind the brief looks that had passed between them. Unusually for him, he became irritable and when had Khalid asked him most solicitously if he was unwell he pleaded a mild headache. He had smiled at his secretary and apologised for being so ill-tempered. He found himself making excuses for Sally; perhaps she had already been committed to doing something else. Maybe, even, she had been unwell. He could not bring himself to believe that she did not want to come, and convinced himself that something momentous had prevented her from taking up his offer.

Yesterday, he had again visited his stables late in the afternoon, hoping to see Sally. Once again, when there had been no sign of her, he was beside himself with angry frustration. Never, never before had anyone dared to flout his personal invitation and he came close to lashing out at the grooms on the slightest pretext when once again darkness fell and Sally had not come.

Perhaps, after all, it was just an act that she had put on that day? But no, he argued with himself, according to Tariq, she had really enjoyed riding and had been so happy while on Jameel's back. She might have had a prior engagement that first weekend, but surely, if she had been so keen, she would have come this weekend? He couldn't understand it. It was all he could do to prevent himself from having Hishaam dragged before him to demand an explanation of Sally's whereabouts. He remembered the look on that lovely face as she had gazed at his horses – how the foals had all gathered around her ... and it calmed him. He thought that he'd seen something else in her eyes too, so if not for just the horses, he had hoped that she might want to see him again. Perhaps she was shy – but again no, that didn't seem right, as he remembered that she had not been shy about the wheelbarrows. And so the arguments went round and round in his head, his worry beads keeping time with his thoughts as he constantly threaded them to and fro between his fingers.

Bah! He gave up! Did she not know the honour that he had shown her by personally inviting her to ride his horses? Had he not paid her a compliment? Had he not given her a small personal token? Usually good humoured and benevolent, he would have been mortified had he known to what lengths those closest to him had gone to be extra-diligent in their duties. Khalid had worked very hard in the past week to ensure that every little thing was just as Abdullah required it to be. Aware of his Sheikh's dark mood, the First Secretary had shielded him from the more mundane problems and trivial issues. Speculation began to grow about the worried frown on Abdullah's face and rumours began to spread about the effect the workload he carried was having on his health.

Arriving at the races today, Khalid continued covertly to watch his master closely, ready to intercept any trifling annoyance.

It was with a heavy heart that Abdullah had set out to the races with several of his uncles and cousins, knowing that he could not be seen to be searching the crowds for that one face that would make his heart beat faster. Alighting from his car, he made his way through the crowd and took his seat. Refreshments were offered and, just as he was about to take a sip of coffee, he glanced up and spotted a flash of blonde hair moving through the crowds. His hands shook and his coffee spilled, as he strained every muscle in his body to prevent himself from leaping up from his seat. Seeing the coffee spill on the Royal thobe, the servant bowed lower, fearful that he had done something wrong.

She had come! She was here! Abdullah, much to the relief and confusion of everyone around him, found himself grinning. Noticing the sudden smile that had spread across his face, Khalid had quickly followed the direction of his master's gaze; he knew now, without a doubt, the cause of the sudden and unusual bout of bad humour that had fallen upon His Highness during the past week. He had known Abdullah since the day he'd been born and understood that he was struggling between his duty and personal desire. His Highness must not be allowed to leave the stand to go chasing after his current heart's desire – that would only fuel further speculation in the family about his dedication to duty.

Inclining his head towards Abdullah, he spoke quietly. 'Your Highness, a guest that we entertained at the Palace a short while ago is here, with a friend. With your permission, may I send Tariq to offer some refreshment?'

It was not unusual for Abdullah to send out refreshments to foreign visitors among the crowds, particularly if they had previously been guests at the Palace. Abdullah looked sharply at Khalid, and knew from his expression that his Secretary was referring to Sally. He should have known that he could hide nothing from his beloved Khalid. But what did he mean by 'with a friend'? Of course! He understood now – how stupid of him not to realise! Such a beauty would not be without her admirers and he realised that she could hardly come to such an event as this on her own. But who was she with? He couldn't see from where he was sitting, but clearly Khalid had seen that she was not alone.

'Who is the friend?' Abdullah asked impatiently, before quickly turning his head away to respond briefly to one of his cousins. Seeing Tariq standing nearby, Khalid signalled for him to come closer and Tariq brought his ear very low to receive his instructions before setting off to do his master's bidding.

Tariq had no difficulty in finding Sally, and she turned as he called out to her. She noticed he was smartly dressed in a long cream thobe covered by a thin brown muslin bisht trimmed with gold braid. In the desert wind the soft fabrics wrapped themselves around his gaunt frame as he hurried towards them. His white ghutra was wrapped several times around his head, turban style, to hold it in place in the tugging breezes. Sally smiled at him, thinking he looked every inch a man of the desert.

'Hello, Tariq, are you well?' Sally held her hand out to him.

'Yes, thank you, Sally. And this is your friend?' Tariq beamed at Caroline as he stood holding on to Sally's hand.

Caroline was taken aback at Tariq's effusive welcome and wondered when he would release her friend's hand. Alex discouraged too much fraternising with the locals and Caroline's acquaintances were mostly confined to the Embassy wives and other Western nationals living in Al Khaleej. Rarely did she meet, let alone socialise with, the Arabs and Caroline had advised Sally not to, either. It had fallen on deaf ears.

Sally had been in the Middle East nearly two months now and was feeling completely at home. She loved the place and the people and was beginning to learn the language and as much as she could about the region's history. History had been her worst subject at school – all those dates of long-dead kings and queens – but here she was fascinated by the culture and ancient traditions still evident in much of the day-to-day activities taking place around her. It was 'living history' and she felt a part of it.

'Tariq, this is my friend, Caroline. We were at school together. Caroline is the person who invited me to come here for a holiday and now I don't want to leave.'

Despite her reservations, Caroline's manners, courtesy of the same convent school education as Sally, were polished and she stretched out her hand with a pleasant smile.

'How do you do?' she said in her best English accent.

'I am do good,' Tariq smiled. He released Sally's hand to clasp Caroline's and, much to her relief, let go of it immediately.

'Now you must excuse. Enjoy the races – you see many, many beautiful horses today.' Tariq headed off back towards the stand to report to Khalid the name of the English woman who was with Sally. He hadn't been too sure how he was going to find out 'who is the friend' but Sally had made it easy for him by introducing her straight away. He grinned as he ran back; he would be able to make a full report to Khalid.

'What a funny chap. How do you come to know him?'

'Oh, he's just the man that took me riding last week, my guide,' Sally replied, then quickly added before Caroline could ask another question: 'Hasn't he got a fascinating face? Have you ever seen such a lined face before? Wonder how old he is? And did you see all those gold teeth?' Sally's heart was beating faster, for if Tariq had recognised her, surely that might mean that Abdullah would also know that she was here? Eagerly her eyes scanned the stand. Yes, she could clearly see him, sitting there, right in the centre.

Fortunately, just then Caroline lost all interest in Tariq, as seven magnificent Arabian stallions bounced out onto the track.

'Let's get back to a place on the rails so that we can see,' Caroline said, and quickly they made their way back to the railings to watch the race.

The horses were taut with excitement and anticipation, every muscle visibly straining beneath their fine silken coats as they arched their necks. They set off down to the start, several of the stallions cantering sideways in their attempt to get away from their jockeys' grip and begin their race with a flying start. Above the noise of the crowd they heard one of the stallions emit a full-throated scream as it challenged its rivals. It was answered immediately by several of the others, with snorting and high-pitched neighing. The atmosphere among the crowd was electrifying but, no matter how excited their mounts became, the riders sat relaxed and upright, with their legs swinging loosely against their horses' sides. They made their way round to the starting post on the far side of the track, the riders laughing, calling and teasing each other. By the time they reached the start most of the stallions were excitedly prancing on the spot, just waiting to feel the slackening of the reins.

Suddenly there was a shout and the crowd surged forward as the horses set off, their tails held vertical to their bodies so that they streamed out like banners behind their thundering haunches. A huge cloud of sand was thrown up behind the front runners, enveloping the stragglers and the crowd as they thundered by.

The roar of the spectators drowned out everything else as the horses came round the bend for the final time and into the straight. The excited throng leaned forward against the creaking rail and the girls thought that it would collapse with such a weight pressing against it. Some spectators seemed oblivious to danger as they ducked under the rails and stepped out onto the track to get a better view of the leaders coming towards them up the final straight. Most quickly dived back under the rail, but one or two lingered until the last possible moment, making both girls scream in unison: 'Get out of the way!' – covering their eyes as they shouted, as neither wanted to see anyone crushed to death by the several tons of horseflesh bearing down towards the finishing line! The ground shook under their feet as the horses thundered past the winning post, three of them matched stride-for-stride for first place. Gradually, the horses slowed and finally were pulled up, their sides heaving and their coats glistening with sweat. Their nostrils flared wide to draw in the extra air needed to fill their lungs in that final, all-out effort to win; veins stood out on their fine coats and their eyes were wild and wide open, alive with the thrill of the race – and Sally was captivated!

With excitement in her eyes, she turned to her friend. 'I'd love to have a go at that, wouldn't you?'

'Are you mad? Anyway it's only for men! Women aren't allowed to do things like that, especially out here,' Caroline said, betraying a hint of envy. All her life she had been plagued by the fact that she was a 'girl' and not allowed to do half the things that her brothers could, no matter how much she tried to join in with them. She had wanted to play football, but only boys were allowed to play; she was good at cricket, and could throw a ball so accurately that her skill was admired by her brothers, who let her join in games with their friends. For a time, she had wanted to join the police force until, much to her parents' relief, she found out that only men were allowed to ride or handle the dogs. Huh! Her parents and teachers had encouraged her to think about nursing ... yuk! She had settled for secretarial work until she could make up her mind, and for a while it had been exciting working in London. Then she had met Alex again ... 'Besides, what with no saddles and no crash hats, that could be bloody dangerous!'

There was certainly something thrilling about the horses but, as ever, Caroline could only see the dangerous side of it, and it made her wish she was as brave and gutsy as Sally. Their friendship was grounded in a mutual love of horses and dogs, but it was also a case of opposites being attracted by each other. Although they had both enjoyed pony riding when they were younger, it was Sally who had given Caroline the courage to mount her first horse. At ten years old, Sally was eager to progress from riding ponies to horses but, with some of the riding school horses over 16 hands high, to Caroline their backs had seemed an awfully long way up from the ground! Equally, it was Caroline, wiser than her years at times, who had given Sally very good reasons for not jumping every hedgerow, fence or gate that they had come across.

Soon there was another thrilling and noisy stallion race. Once they had raced past and the dust had settled, there was a short pause before ten beautiful Arabian mares trotted soundlessly and effortlessly onto the track. They didn't scream out challenges and show off like the stallions had, but pranced silently with tails curled elegantly over their backs. They were as light on their feet as ballet dancers up on points – only the hint of sweat on their necks showed that they were as excited and as keen to race as the stallions. Their silence and demeanour illustrated perfectly to Sally what Abdullah had tried to explain, and she could see for herself why Arabs went to war on mares.

'Oh, I like these, Sal. They're different from that first lot, more elegant, quieter. Are they a different breed or something?'

'Same breed, no balls!' Sally whispered in her ear, quietly giggling.

'I beg your pardon!'

'Take a look, Caro. Notice anything missing? These are mares.' 'Do you mean to say that the others were ... were ... all stallions?'

'Yep.'

'Not geldings?'

'Nope!'

'My God! That's amazing! No wonder they were making all that racket! I've never seen a stallion, let alone seven all together at the same time!' Caroline continued to watch the mares, unable to take her eyes off them. As they too thundered round the racetrack to the finishing line, Tariq was once more running towards them.

'Please, Sally, you and your friend you like coffee or cold drink?'

They both accepted his offer and thanked him as he led them towards the rear of the VIP stand. Several servants were waiting next to a row of the tallest coffee pots Sally had ever seen. Sally's tummy was doing somersaults as they had approached the stand, half hoping that she would see and meet Abdullah again and half wondering how the hell she was going to explain to Caroline that she already knew him.

'Coffee?' Tariq asked.

'I would love coffee, thank you, Tariq. What about you, Caroline? Have you tried Arab coffee? It's not like the usual coffee, but you might like it.'

'Yes, please. I'd like to try some, thank you.'

Sally and Caroline downed two cups of the tasty refreshing liquid and, following Sally's lead, Caroline shook her empty cup as she handed it back.

'You enjoy to see horses races?' Tariq directed his question at Caroline. 'Oh, yes I did – it was very exciting. In England we have horse racing but it seems tame by comparison and I've just realised what is missing here. At the racetracks in England we also have bookies,' she responded.

'What is bookies?' Tariq queried.

'People place bets; they give money to someone we call a "bookie",' Caroline explained. 'They gamble money on their favourite horse to win.'

'For making bets? Yes, with money. Yes, I know this. This not allowed in our country. Please excuse.' Tariq flashed his golden smile at them before quickly making his way off towards the horses. His sudden departure surprised both of them, Caroline in particular.

'Oh Lord! Didn't offend him, did I? You know what I'm like. Always putting my foot in it.'

'Shouldn't think so,' Sally reassured her, although she had also been surprised at Tariq's disappearance, but assumed it was because he was busy with the Sheikh's horses. 'He didn't look offended.'

Not knowing quite what they were supposed to do, they decided to make their way back towards the racetrack.

'So ... er ... this Tariq, the man you went riding with? How come he can help himself to the VIPs' coffee on race day?' Caroline was fishing, curious now to discover how her friend was on such good terms with a member of the Royal Household that she could be offered refreshments.

'Oh, you know what it's like around here, Caro – the coffee bearer is probably his cousin,' Sally replied, deliberately keeping her eyes straight ahead and avoiding her friend's suspicious look. She was busy trying to work out if it was just Tariq being hospitable, or had the offer of refreshments come from Abdullah? Hopefully, Abdullah had seen her in the crowd and it was his way of letting her know that he knew she was here. If it was, she was grateful that he had done nothing to expose their previous encounter with each other. Knowing how much Alex disapproved of Caroline getting too friendly with the locals, Sally was anxious that Caroline did not find out the truth about exactly where she had gone riding.

Caroline felt responsible, having invited her friend out to stay in this foreign land in the first place. Now that Sally had got herself a job and her own apartment, Caroline felt it was her duty to make sure that Sally did not expose herself to hidden dangers lying in wait for an innocent visitor in these parts. Caroline's mother-hen protectiveness made Sally suspect that many of the questions were prompted by Alex, and it was beginning to irritate her. It was worrying enough that Abdullah was a powerful man – she didn't need Caroline's lectures and warnings as well. When the final race was over, Sally gave one last look towards the stand and saw that the VIPs were getting ready to depart. She wasn't sure if she was relieved or disappointed that she hadn't met Abdullah but, on balance, thought that maybe it was for the best.

'That was the last race. Shall we get going?'

'Yes, okay,' Caroline agreed, looking round at the slowly departing crowd. 'Let's head for home. I've swallowed enough sand for one day.'

Walking back to the parking area, Caroline commented on the odd taste of the coffee, remarking, 'Not sure I liked it – and what was all that cup-shaking about? I assumed it was good manners or part of some local ritual, so I went along with it.'

'Good job you did, or we would still be sitting there now, drinking coffee. Shaking the cup is a sign that you've had enough and don't want your cup refilled. By the way, that odd taste was cardamom and it's reckoned to be an aphrodisiac.'

'What!' Caroline stood still for a moment and, after a short pause, muttered, 'Well I wonder if that explains it?'

'Explains what, Caro?'

'Oh! Well,' she looked at her friend and for a moment Sally thought she saw her blush. 'It wouldn't surprise me to learn that Alex has been overdosing on it at his meetings with the locals – he's all over me like a rash since we arrived out here,' Caroline giggled nervously. 'I can't keep up with him, Sal,' she said shyly glancing up at her friend.

Sally roared with laughter. 'Well then, that's a bit of local knowledge that might come in useful for you two honeymooners,' and they were both still chuckling as they jumped into Caroline's car and slammed the doors.

'I hope the side effects of the coffee last until Sunday for you.' Caroline had regained her composure and seized the opportunity to bring up the subject of Matt, Sally's dinner partner for the forthcoming do at the Embassy.

'Honestly, Sal, Matt is a real sweetheart. Promise you'll be nice to him.'

'I'm always nice, but don't expect me to fall in love with him. I told you, I don't want to get involved,' Sally said and turned to look out of the window. She really wasn't interested in men but had to admit to herself that the handsome young Sheikh had aroused a spark of something within her. But, as he was obviously unattainable, she felt safe to fantasise – he had, after all, only invited her to ride his horses. More than ever, she wished that she had gone riding that first weekend, and made up her mind that, come hell or high water, she was definitely going at the next opportunity.

She found herself thinking about Doug, and involuntarily she shivered. With Doug she had been so sure of a future together – was she really ready for another romance yet? With someone as important as the Sheikh, it would be doomed from the start. And then there was Caroline, partnering her up with some 'nice' unsuspecting friend of Alex's. A sweetie shop, her friend had said, but Sally wasn't sure that she was ready to indulge herself again, not yet.

Caroline bumped the car back over the rough ground, manoeuvring in and out of the heavy traffic heading away from the racetrack in all directions, a bit like the camel race. In spite of the wipers working overtime, she could barely see through the clouds of dust and sand being thrown up. At last, they pulled onto the main road and Caroline glanced at Sally and saw the sad, faraway look on her face. She guessed the cause of it, and thought it might help her to talk.

'Do you still think about Doug, Sal? Does it still hurt as much as it did?' It was something she had avoided directly asking up until now and she kept her eyes studiously on the busy road ahead.

Caroline's question brought the memories flooding back. 'I don't know what I feel. It was all just so final and it all ended so quickly. I don't think I hate him but, yes, it still hurts. I thought for a while he might have written a letter, to explain a little more, but he didn't. I suppose I respect him for standing by Moira, but despise his weakness that got him into that situation.'

Caroline was relieved that Sally was as least beginning to articulate her feelings, so cautiously she continued.

'Sally, it's been more than a year now since that all happened and you had hardly known him that long ...' Caroline talked on for a while, trying to help Sally accept that, while it had been a terrible thing, it was nevertheless a very short interlude in her life which was now fading into the past.

'That's true, Caro, but I grew up so much in just those few months. He made me happier than I'd ever been in my whole life. You know, I'd never felt so wanted or so loved before? That's how he made me feel. Doug made me feel important, that I mattered – he made me laugh and he was kind and gentle. He taught me so much and I can't just forget that. I wanted to feel that way forever and that's how long I expected it to last ... forever ...' Sally's voice trailed off with a stifled sob at the memory of that last painful meeting with Doug. Caroline drove on in silence for a while until she was sure her friend had finished pouring her heart out.

'I'm sorry. I shouldn't have pushed the point. I guessed you might still be harbouring feelings for him. It won't help, though, if you keep it all bottled up inside you all the time. And it has been over a year now, Sal. I think you've got to accept that he is never going to be part of your life anymore.'

Feeling that progress had been made, and when she felt Sally had regained her composure, Caroline changed the subject to direct Sally's thoughts towards something more cheerful.

'Which Saeed creation have you decided to wear for the Embassy party?' Sally sat quietly for a while, still lost in thought.

'I've almost decided on the turquoise brocade. Do you think that will be suitable? How about you, what are you going to wear?'

'Wow! Absolutely! That turquoise will really show off your blue eyes! If you're in brocade, I'll go for the beige silk-and-lace creation, just to ring the changes.'

When they arrived back at her apartment, Caroline left the engine running, indicating that she did not intend stopping, much to Sally's relief. After their conversation, Sally needed to be alone for a while.

'See you on Sunday evening. Be ready at about six-thirty? Will you be able to get away from work early? It is an important do. I'm sure Hishaam will understand.'

'I'll have to ask him, but isn't that a bit early for a party?'

'Apparently there are some local VIPs coming to give official birthday wishes for the Queen and we have to line up and shake hands, etcetera, which all takes time. After the formalities are over, the loyal toast will be drunk, in orange juice, no doubt, if there are locals present. Then, when the VIPs leave, we can break out the Bolly and have a proper birthday party for her.'

Chapter Twenty-Nine

The next day, Sally asked Hishaam if she could have the following afternoon off. After a lot of moaning and mumbling he agreed and, on her way home from work, Sally called into the hairdressing salon to make an appointment for the following day.

Michael, the salon owner, was charming – a Lebanese cocktail of French and Arab blood and, from the way he minced around the salon, it was obvious that his hormones were a bit of a mixture too.

The back-combed beehive of a high bouffant glued together with pints of sticky lacquer so popular in the West hadn't reached the Middle East. During a previous visit Sally had watched Michael working on the Arab girls' hair to produce luxuriant shiny locks. She envied their beautiful hair and now she shyly mentioned to Michael that she would love her hair to look the same as theirs.

'No problem my dearest honey-bun,' he cooed at her. 'It can be done. Your hair is very similar in texture to my Arab ladies. You've got good thick hair, plenty of volume daaarling,' he said, running his expert fingers through her hair. 'If you want me to treat it the same, I can do that quite easily.'

Sally booked an appointment for four o'clock the following afternoon, when the salon reopened, but on hearing that she had to be ready to leave her flat at six-thirty, Michael rolled his eyes.

'My dear, if you come at four you won't be getting out of here until six-thirty at the earliest!' He was horrified at Sally's crestfallen expression. Such a sweet young girl, he didn't like to see her with such a sad face.

'Never mind, sugarplum, for you, as it is a special occasion, Queenie's birthday and all that, I will open at two-thirty. Yes, you get yourself here for then, sweetie, and I will make sure that you leave here in time to get home and change.'

The salon still looked closed when Sally arrived, but when she pushed the door it opened and Michael swooped down on her.

'Good afternoon, Sally, my sweetheart,' he said, planting a brotherly kiss on each of her cheeks. 'Come along, darling, and sit down in this cubicle, because first we have to remove your dead ends. Can't have dead ends, can we, my dear?' Today he was going to take off the dry ends of her hair and give it some extra conditioning; then he would blow-dry it gently in a free-flowing style. The cubicle resembled a chapel, with tall candles burning brightly in holders on a trolley. As she sat down in front of the mirror, he whisked a protective covering around her shoulders and, smiling at her in the mirror, he asked, 'Have you seen this done before, Sally? Removing the dead ends with candles?'

'No, I haven't. Why do you need candles?'

'All will be revealed,' he answered theatrically.

'Now, relax. Believe me, this is where we begin to give you beautiful Arabian hair. But, perleese, my darling, we must keep the English colour. Do not even think of asking me to dye it black because I will refuse. Right now!' He pretended to stamp his foot in temper. Sally laughed and shook her head. With her complexion she couldn't imagine herself ever having black hair.

Sally watched in the mirror, fascinated as Michael used a tail comb to separate a small section of her long hair, combing it through, then twisting it round several times until it was rolled tightly together. As he held the twist of hair between his thumb and fingers, Sally could see all her dry dead ends sticking out from the tight roll. Holding her breath, she watched as Michael expertly flicked the lighted candle along the twist, burning off the dead ends. After he had completed this process over her whole head, he spent several minutes drenching every single strand of hair in coconut oil and then wrapped her hair in several hot towels.

'I smell like an exotic ice cream,' Sally told him as her senses took in the aroma of coconut and transported her back to days out at a local funfair where she and Caroline always chose coconut ice cream.

'Mmm ...! And I'm sure there will be plenty of men who will want to lick you! Lucky you! Want to swap places, dearie?' he joked. 'But, my darling, tonight ...' – Michael raised his hands and his eyes to heaven as he sought the words to describe what he wanted to create for this beauty – 'tonight you will look like an exotic flower, and not a dollop of ice cream!' He then piled stacks of reading matter within her reach, ordered the salon junior to supply her with tea or coffee, and glided away. It would take at least an hour of hot towels before the coconut oil and the other ingredients could be rinsed off.

It was after five by the time Michael had finished and her hair hung to her shoulders in a silk curtain. Sally sat with a big grin on her face and her blue eyes shining with delight at the result, as Michael leaned over her shoulder to admire his work with her. Reaching for a hand mirror, he stepped back, holding it so that Sally could see the back of her head.

'Shake your head, sweetie, let me see.' He twittered with delight as the satin hair rippled like a slow-moving river of soft, molten gold. Sally was thrilled to bits – it was exactly how she had wanted it to look.

'Perfect, just perfect! Off you go, my lovely child,' he said as he whisked away the protective wrap from her shoulders, 'and have a wonderful time!'

Just before six-thirty, Sally was ready. In under an hour she had managed to shower without getting her hair wet, apply a little make-up and step into her turquoise dress. It fitted her perfectly. She slipped on gold sling-back shoes to give herself a couple more inches of height. Cautiously, she ran a brush lightly over her hair and then shook her head as Michael had shown her. Standing in front of the mirror, she studied her image – the tall, elegantly-dressed female that stared back at her was almost a stranger. Doug had changed her in so many ways – he had taken a shy naïve teenager and, having shown her how to love and given her a degree of self-confidence, he had hit her with the cruellest blow imaginable to her self-esteem! Sally had fought hard to regain it and here in this friendly country, miles away from him, she felt she was making progress. It would have been easy to allow herself to wallow in self-pity but, instead, she chose to keep fighting the waves of hurt and loneliness that washed over her every now and again. The constant struggle to keep those feelings from engulfing her was now, after all this time, becoming easier and she felt she was coming out of her grief a stronger person.

The doorbell brought her thoughts back to the present. Grabbing her evening bag and silk shawl, she patted Bouncy on the head and walked out to the car.

'Fantastic!' Alex said appreciatively, eyeing her up and down over the rim of his spectacles as held open the car door for her. 'You're going to get crushed in the rush tonight, Sal. You look a million dollars!'

She grinned at him. 'Thanks, Alex. You look dishy, too, in your DJ.'

Caroline immediately fell in love with the way her friend had had her hair done. 'Wow! Love the hair, Sal! You've had it done differently.'

In the beige silk-and-lace creation with her hair swept up in a chignon, Sally thought her friend was a picture of elegance. Since arriving in Al Khaleej, Caroline no longer needed to bleach her hair to lift the colour from the mousy brown that nature had bestowed on her. The highlighting was now done naturally by the sun – with her sun-kissed hair and golden tan, Caroline looked quite different. Sally suddenly felt her own outfit was loud and flamboyant – even brash – in comparison, but it was too late to change now.

'We're meeting Matt at the Embassy,' Caroline explained.

'What does this Matt do at the Embassy?'

'Assistant Naval Attaché,' Alex replied.

'Which means he goes to sea sometimes but has an office as well,' Caroline chipped in as she looked over her shoulder to grin at Sally.

'Which means,' Alex corrected, 'that although he is in the Royal Navy, he is, for the moment, shore-based at the Embassy, attached to the Diplomatic Corps.'

'Oh? And ... um ... does that ever work the other way round?' Caroline asked innocently.

'Does what ever work the other way round? What are you wittering on about now, child?' he asked her, throwing her a sardonic look.

He had known Caroline when she was a child– she'd been an argumentative tomboy, wilful, naughty, mischievous and adorable, even then. He hadn't see her seen her since her brother's graduation some nine years earlier when they had had their little contretemps over the taxi in London, and at first he had not recognised the feisty young woman who was challenging him for possession of the cab. When he finally recognised her, he marvelled at the transformation from tomboy to engaging, vivacious young woman.

His job had taken him all over the world and he had enjoyed dalliances with women across several continents, in the process becoming thoroughly disillusioned with the wiles of the fairer sex – for him, it had definitely been a case of familiarity breeding contempt! Thirty years old, he considered himself a confirmed bachelor until Caroline had bounced back into his life, tossing his orderly existence and his emotions into a state of chaos. She would always remain 'a child' in his eyes and, in return, she affectionately called him her 'Old Man'.

'Well, do diplomats ever go to sea on attachment to the Royal Navy?'

'Not really. It doesn't work quite like that. Why? Want me out of the way so that you can "nibble in the sweetie shop"?'

'Alex! Really! Have you been listening in to my private conversations, Old Man?'

'But of course!' Alex grinned at her.

Sally hadn't been far wrong in her assessment of Alex's avid interest in what his wife got up to while he was at work all day. Caroline's fiery temper and her tendency to let fly at any hint of injustice could, if not checked in time, create a serious breach of protocol and would inevitably have a knock-on effect on Alex's career. Worldly and wise beyond her years at times, it was easy to forget how young she was when he had first brought her out to the Middle East. Having taken her away from her home, her large family and all her friends to live in a completely different culture, he knew how homesick she had become.

One of his fears had been that if she didn't settle down he would have to make a request to be relocated back to England, something that he would prefer not to have to do. Another fear was the danger of boredom setting in, and he was only too well aware of what bored wives got up to in these foreign parts! When Sally agreed to come out for a holiday and had then announced that she wanted to stay on in Al Khaleej, he was delighted. Caroline not only had someone of her own age to talk to but he knew she now had a 'mission'.

Caroline was pouting, pretending to be shocked by his admission of listening in on her phone calls, though she knew full well that Alex had been in the room when she had used the phrase on the phone to Sally.

'So, come on then, tell me why this request, "does that ever work the other way round"? Plotting to get rid of me? Or maybe you're plotting to trade me in for a younger model, eh?'

'Me? Of course not,' she said, feigning innocence, but, turning to Sally with an irrepressible grin, she mouthed, 'Just a night off would do!'

When both girls burst out laughing, Alex, trying hard to keep a straight face as he caught the gist, took one hand off the steering wheel and placed it provocatively on Caroline's knee.

'Not a chance, Missus! Not tonight, tomorrow night or any other night!'

'Alex, you're embarrassing me!' Caroline shrieked as he squeezed her knee. Witnessing this exchange of flirtatious banter and the loving looks that passed between them, Sally felt a sharp pain in her chest and tears begin to prick the back of her eyes. It reminded her of the little private jokes between Doug and herself – the language of love, she guessed. It was those moments of intimacy she had shared with Doug that she missed the most.

Walking into the reception area at the Embassy with her friends, Sally saw a tall young man in naval dress whites coming towards them. Slim, blue-eyed and blond, the handsome young officer was clutching his cap nervously as he shook hands with Alex and kissed Caroline on the cheek.

'Hello, Matt. Good to see you again. Sally, may I introduce Matt?' Caroline said as she turned to her friend.

Here we go again, thought Sally as she stepped forward and held out her hand to him, saying with a friendly smile, 'Hello, Matt.' '

Hello ... Sally ... I ... er ...um, pleased to meet you,' Matt stuttered.

Sally noticed a blush spreading from his cheeks, turning his ears bright pink. Recognising a fellow blusher, Sally immediately felt sorry for him. She suspected he had been cajoled into partnering her for the evening by an overzealous Caroline.

'Pleased to meet you too, Matthew,' Sally replied and smiled up at him again, anxious to put him at his ease.

'May I get everyone a drink?' Alex asked. 'We seem to be short on waiters tonight. We have to wait for the VIPs before we can go through to the main function rooms, but we can have a quickie in the other bar.'

Caroline asked for a Martini, but Sally thought she would stick to fresh orange juice for the moment. They squeezed into the crowded bar, nodding and greeting acquaintances along the way, and when Matt spied an empty table in the far corner, Caroline said, 'You two go ahead – we'll join you in a minute.' Sally followed Matt over to the table and they sat down with their drinks.

After a few moments, Sally broke the uncomfortable silence. 'Sorry, Matt, you were probably press-ganged into partnering me this evening by Caroline, weren't you?'

'Well ... actually ... yes ... I was,' he said hesitantly, leaning forward in his chair. 'But I don't mind ... honestly ... especially now that I've met you! Oh! Er ... sorry, that sounds so rude.' He blushed and quickly leaned back again. 'S-s-sorry ... no ... that sounds wrong ... s-s-s-orry. Look, what I meant was ... I had no idea what you looked like ... Ah ... no ...' He leaned forward in his chair again. 'That sounds even worse. What I mean is ... well ... it's just that you don't look like ...' As he stumbled to a halt, Sally started to giggle.

'Matthew, the advice to someone digging themselves deeper and deeper into a hole is to stop digging!' She smiled at him. 'I suggest you stop digging. But first, do tell, what did you imagine I would look like?'

Matthew hesitated. He had never met such a beautiful girl and was completely out of his depth. He looked straight at her with innocent eyes, not sure how much to confess, but she was smiling at him and he found himself smiling back.

'Well, here goes,' he said, with more composure. 'Caroline said you were tall, liked horses and collected stray animals. I thought you would be more like one of those loud horsey types, you know, County Set ilk. But you're not. You're ... you're ...' He wanted to say how beautiful he thought she was, but guessed that she had probably heard it all before.

'You mean pleated skirts, twinsets, heaving bosoms and hairy legs!' Sally said, coming to his rescue.

'Hey! Steady on, old girl!' Matthew said, taken aback at her blunt approach, but he began laughing with her.

Sally asked him how he liked being based at the Embassy and whether he missed being at sea. As Matt began to tell her how being ashore was a wonderful opportunity for him, Sally was pleased to see him visibly beginning to relax. He was in the middle of recounting an amusing story about something that Alex had told him the first day he had arrived at the Embassy, when Caroline and Alex joined them at the table and he stopped, mid-sentence.

'Well, you two seem to be getting along famously. Would you like to share the joke?' Caroline said, grinning at the pair of them.

'I'd rather not, if it's all the same with you,' Matthew said, blushing. He didn't know Alex well enough to know whether or not he would appreciate his witty observations on life in Al Khaleej being retold to his wife's friend.

'What do you say, Sally?'

Sally saw the blush and, although she didn't understand the reason for it, she wanted to put him at his ease and replied, 'I agree with you, Matt. Private joke, and I think we should change the subject.'

'The VIPs arrived a few moments ago and everyone is starting to file in,' Alex announced, 'so we'll have to drink up a bit sharpish, otherwise we'll miss the line-up. That would never do.'

'Come along,' Caroline bestowed a motherly smile on them both, rather pleased with herself that they seemed to be getting along so well at such an early stage in the evening.

They joined the end of a long procession that snaked along the corridor and through the double doors into the ballroom. Alex and Caroline were just ahead of her and Sally recognised the Ambassador and his wife heading the official line-up. Ranked alongside were various other personages Sally vaguely recognised from previous social gatherings she had attended with Alex and Caroline. Further down the line, Sally could just make out the visiting local dignitaries. Reaching the start of the line-up, she was asked her name by a smartly-dressed gentleman.

'Miss Phillips!' The official called her name out in a stentorian voice and Sally felt a moment of panic; then, behind her, she heard Matthew announced: 'Lieutenant Commander Rawlinson!' As she made her way down the line, shaking hands, she began to feel a bit easier. Ahead of her, out of the corner of her eye she saw Caroline give a slight curtsy and wondered if there was a member of the Royal Family in the line-up. Then she froze. Suddenly she was shaking hands with the man she now knew to be the Sheikh's First Secretary. His duty was to repeat the names and present the guests to the man at his side. Sally felt her stomach somersault as she looked up, straight into a pair of familiar, laughing brown eyes. His Secretary made the formal introductions. 'Your Highness, may I present Miss Phillips?'

Abdullah smiled and held out his hand. 'Good evening, Sally. How are you?' He held on to her hand a moment longer than was necessary.

'Your ... Highness ...?' Sally replied as she bobbed a little curtsy. Her face was a picture of confusion and Abdullah's smile widened as he inclined his head towards her. She heard Matthew being presented, and Abdullah let go of her hand and moved on to shake hands with him.

Sally's mind was in turmoil! Abdullah was not just one of the many important sheikhs in Al Khaleej, but carried the extra title of 'His Highness'! Now she understood why Hishaam had been so agitated, but even he had never mentioned the 'Highness' bit! He had merely said that the Sheikh was a very powerful man. The First Secretary had given no hint of it when she had first met him. And from the way Abdullah himself had behaved, Sally at first thought he was just an important employee at the Palace. She found herself blushing all over again as she recalled some of the things that he had said to her. And now she wondered what on earth he'd thought of the things that she had said to him! Shaken, breathless and with her heart beating furiously, she continued to shake hands, until thankfully she reached the end of the line.

Alex and Caroline were standing a little way off to one side talking to acquaintances, and Sally saw Caroline make her excuses and hurry over towards her, with a look of suspicion on her face.

What Sally really needed was a stiff drink! The sight of Abdullah had unnerved her, but she knew she would have to keep her wits about her to allay Caroline's suspicions. Thank goodness only fruit juice was being served at the moment. Add a drop of alcohol and there was no knowing what she might come out with!

Just at that moment, Matt arrived at her side and she smiled sweetly up at him. 'Oh Matt, we'll need some orange juice for the toast. Would you ...?'

'Right-oh! Two glasses of orange juice coming up,' he said, and headed off in search of refreshments just as Caroline reached her.

'Sal! Sally! Did I hear right? Did the Sheikh call you "Sally"?' Caroline hissed in a stage whisper.

'What? Oh... no ... no ... I don't think so ...' Sally replied airily, as she studiously avoided looking at Caroline and tried not to think about the lie that would bring on a tell-tale blush. Adopting a nonchalant pose, she began to gaze around the room, conscious that her friend's eyes were fixed on her.

'I could have sworn he knew your name,' Caroline said, eying her friend suspiciously, 'and he smiled at you.'

'Oh? It seemed to me that he smiled at everyone.'

'Well, I got the distinct impression that he knew you.'

'Oh, look ... I think Alex is trying to attract your attention.'

Caroline turned and saw that Alex was indeed indicating for her to re-join him, and she wandered back to the little group she had been chatting with a moment earlier.

Matthew arrived back with the drinks, and a silence fell over the assembled guests while the Ambassador made a short speech, welcoming their Royal guest, His Highness Sheikh Abdullah. Abdullah responded with his thanks for their hospitality and his good wishes for the health of Her Majesty Queen Elizabeth.

The loyal toast was drunk and, with the formalities over, people began to circulate or form little cliques. Sally and Matthew went to join Alex and Caroline and, from where she stood, Sally could see Abdullah and his entourage talking and laughing with the Ambassador and other Embassy officials as he slowly made his way round the room.

Dinner was to be served once the visiting VIPs had retired and Alex had managed to secure one of the prime tables on the terrace for his party. It wasn't long before the little group of people Sally was with decided to move outside, into the coolness of the night air, to find their table and sit in comfort. With her thoughts in chaos and wishing she felt as sophisticated as she looked, she allowed herself to be guided out onto the terrace by Matt.

Chapter Thirty

While Abdullah and his entourage had been circulating round the room, shaking hands and making polite conversation, his eyes searched for a stunning turquoise dress. He couldn't believe it! She was here! He was overjoyed to see her again, and so soon after the races. She had been as surprised as he was when she had been introduced to him and he smiled inwardly, recalling her reaction when she had been made aware of his title.

From the minute of his birth it was expected that one day he would serve his people as their Ruler, but all his life his father had suffered ill health, so at a young age Abdullah had willingly accepted great responsibility to ease the pressure on his father. At 16 years of age, he had been married to a suitable wife, chosen for him by his parents and uncles, as was the tradition. The marriage had been fruitful; he had four beautiful daughters, but no sons. Now, aged 33, some days he felt so tired, so weary, so old. Most of his time was spent listening to problems and finding solutions, surrounded by yes-men and advisors. The affairs of state had created a heavy burden for his young shoulders and, while he never complained, sometimes he wished his life could have been different.

He had his pleasure palace for recreation, but the girls there bored him – brainless and brazen, they gave themselves freely to him and his friends in exchange for baubles and money. He knew he had a reputation with the ladies, but most of it was greatly exaggerated.

That first evening at the stables, Sally had lifted his spirits with her easy manner. The laughter that they had shared over the squeaking wheelbarrows had made him feel young and carefree again. Surely she must have known the effect she'd had on him – he hoped that he'd had a similar effect on her.

Suddenly, he caught sight of her out on the terrace and, turning, he spoke quickly and quietly to his Secretary. Slowly, they began to thread their way towards the open doors and out onto the terrace, knowing it would not cause comment. The young Sheikh was known for his gracious good manners and showed a genuine interest in meeting and speaking to as many people as possible when he attended these functions at embassies.

As the Sheikh's entourage approached their table, Matthew jumped to his feet, his long legs knocking the table and spilling the contents of several glasses in the process. Alex, Caroline and everyone else also stood up. Recognising Alex, Abdullah made his way towards him and they shook hands again, while exchanging a lengthy greeting in Arabic. As they spoke, Abdullah positioned himself so that he could watch Sally but, realising that everyone was still standing, he graciously addressed them all: 'Please, be seated. I did not mean to disturb you.' He smiled round at everyone before turning back to Alex to enquire about recent proposals to further British trade in the area.

Sally's heart had missed a dozen beats when she had first seen him stepping out onto the terrace and she was grateful that everyone's attention was focused either on the Sheikh or on preventing their glasses being knocked flying by Matt. At first she found herself dreading the possibility that he would make his way over to her in front of everyone else. Then, rather confusingly, she realised that she was disappointed when he had made straight for Alex.

Meanwhile, Khalid had positioned himself beside Sally and quietly he asked her, 'Please, may I speak with you on a private matter?'

'Oh, yes of course,' she answered, surprised to find him standing at her elbow. Realising that everyone's attention was still firmly focused on the Sheikh, Sally stepped to the side, well out of everyone else's earshot – particularly Caroline's! Caroline had been presented to Abdullah on a couple of occasions previously and knew how devastatingly charming he was. She could not deny that he was handsome – particularly his eyes, which she thought were almost mesmeric. But she also knew that he was a shocking flirt. Having seen the way women threw themselves at him, she was not surprised he was such an accomplished ladies' man.

It never occurred to Caroline to flirt or flatter any man's vanity with open displays of admiration. Having so many older brothers made her totally at ease in any male company and she responded to them in the same way as she did to her brothers. Her green eyes were often full of infectious laughter and her general sense of ease in their company meant men were often charmed by Caroline, enjoying her frankness and sense of fun. Now, standing next to her husband, she felt inordinately proud of him, talking and laughing with His Highness as if they were old friends, so she did not at first notice her friend slip away from the table. Matt was dumbfounded as Sally stepped to one side with the First Secretary, and he couldn't take his eyes off her as she wandered away along the terrace, deep in conversation with him. Crikey, he thought as he watched her, Sally consorts with the First Secretary and the Sheikh seemed to come over here especially to talk to Alex! He was slightly overwhelmed to be in such company.

As they moved away, Khalid asked her in that same fatherly tone that he had used when she first met him, 'His Highness wishes to know when you will come again to ride?'

Sally was thrilled to hear the question, for it meant that the invitation was still open.

'Well, I'll have to wait until next weekend now. As it is, I have had to ask Hishaam for time off in order to be here this evening, so I don't think I can ask him for any more time off this week.' Khalid's face was a mask as Sally joked, 'Sadly it seems that my employment is seriously hampering my social life'.

'His Highness thought you might say this and requested me to ask you to resign from this job and work for him at the Royal stables.'

Sally was taken aback. 'Resign from my job? Are you serious?'

Khalid raised his shoulders and smiled at her. He himself had been shocked when Abdullah had suggested it to him, just a few moments before. Such decisions should not be made in haste and he wasn't sure that he approved of the idea. He was only relaying the message word for word as His Highness had given it to him. He had no answers to any questions. There had been no time to think through such a proposal properly.

Sally, realising from the expression on his face that she would get no further explanation, continued, 'Well ... I'll consider the offer ... but only if I can oil the wheelbarrows so that he doesn't hear how slowly I work!' she joked. She needed time to think. How could she give up her job? What would she say to Caroline? How the hell would she explain this sudden turn of events? But she also thought how wonderful it would be if she could spend her days working with horses - it had always been her dream!

'Ah, yes, His Highness told everyone about the wheelbarrows and your joke - it amused him greatly. But it is not his intention that you will push this wheelbarrow. He wishes you to train his horses, exercise them, teach them jumping like English horses. You will come?'

In her excitement, Sally was becoming breathless, her heart beating rapidly at the thought of the opportunity that was being offered to her. Her mind raced - things were very different out here and much of what she knew about horses and riding would be of no use at all. In the desert there was no need to know the correct length of one's stirrup, when to use a martingale, how to rise to the trot, or any of the other things that she had learned in England. At the end of the day, she was only a recreational rider and certainly she had had no formal training in how to train a horse. She was very flattered, of course, but she wondered ... could she really do the job? How difficult could it be? She certainly knew how to take a horse over a jump and she would love to have a go, but ...

She decided to be honest with Khalid. 'First Secretary, I am not an expert, I have no proper horse training expertise ...' she began.

'Please, call me Khalid. But you will come, please, Miss Sally?' he persisted. He couldn't go back to the Sheikh without an answer and he needed the right answer to take back.

After a pause Sally said, 'Okay ... I'll think about it.' Maybe there was a way, but first she would have to prepare the ground very carefully with Caroline and Alex.

'Think about it?' Khalid almost choked on the words. Having reached the end of the terrace, he stood still and looked straight at the girl. 'Think about it?' he repeated. 'I am not sure that you appreciate the situation. To refuse a request from His Highness is not good. He does not make this offer lightly and, if I may advise you, when one receives a request from His Highness, it is not wise to turn him down.' Khalid's tone was still paternal but his look held meaning. Her heart began beating wildly in her breast as she studied his face for moment.

'He ... he is ordering me?' Sally was shocked to think that he could do such a thing!

Khalid might not approve of the Sheikh's desire to have this young girl at his stables, but whatever His Highness wanted, if it was in Khalid's power to do so, he would obtain for him.

'Can he do that?' Sally asked, beginning to feel vulnerable – but also irritated that Abdullah thought that she could be ordered about in this way.

Once more the shoulders were raised and a look of resignation passed over Khalid's face. What was the matter with her? So many people would give anything to be the future Ruler's favourite, even for just five minutes. It had not gone unnoticed that she had already brought him much laughter and for a few moments had touched his life with happiness. Khalid knew that Abdullah felt her presence at his stables would lighten his days. Why didn't this girl behave like everyone else? Why didn't she rush to serve his master? Then it occurred to him that if she had displayed this indifference towards Abdullah when he had first met her, this would be the very reason he had been so taken with her. Ah, yes. He began to understand.

Sally continued to stare at him, then glanced across to where Abdullah remained talking to Alex, and for a moment their eyes met. Quickly, she looked away as she felt her cheeks flaming with confusion and embarrassment.

Yes, she would love to work at his stables, but on her terms, not his! She looked back at Khalid, then began walking slowly back towards the table. She wasn't prepared to commit herself one way or the other, not yet.

Khalid fell into step beside her, believing that he understood what she was thinking. He realised he had used the wrong approach, but he had seen the look that had passed between them. She would come. Of that he was certain and that is what he would tell His Highness.

'Think carefully about this offer to come and work with the horses. His Highness says you are like a bird in a cage at the place where you are employed. He does not like your employer. We know that he drinks alcohol, too much. This is not good.'

Sally came to a halt again in surprise. 'How do you know that?'

'From where I sit it is easy to know most things. There are always those who will happily keep me informed. We have a saying – if I can translate, we say, "Gossip and bad news always run around on faster legs than good news". Sadly, it seems it is in human nature to enjoy the discomfort of others more than their joy.'

Without a word, Sally moved on once more and Khalid quickly changed the subject. 'We also heard that Old Ahmed nearly killed your employer by filling the office with flowers for you. We laughed so much when he described to us how everybody was running with vases of flowers to take them away before Hishaam went to meet his maker!'

Sally smiled at the memory. 'It was funny. Poor Hishaam – he sneezed so much I thought he would blow his brains out, and his face puffed up like a huge red tomato! Do you know Ahmed?'

'Of course! His Highness and I have known him since we were small boys. He is a very a good friend to both our fathers.'

'I like Ahmed.'

'Good. He will be pleased to know that, because he also likes you and I believe he wants to marry you.' Despite not receiving the answer he needed, Khalid was becoming more jovial as their conversation progressed.

Sally burst out laughing. 'What!' She couldn't believe that he was serious. 'Don't worry. He is a very rich man,' he teased, 'and will pay your father a good price for you. You will be very, very wealthy. Lots of servants and Ahmed is an old man these days. He will not be very demanding in the bedroom.' It was his turn to burst out laughing at the horrified expression on Sally's face.

'We do that in our culture, you know? Arrange marriages; purchase a wife. It's not really buying a wife, it is, how you say, a dowry? So you will put my friend Ahmed out of his misery and let me have your father's address?'

'I will not!' Sally replied, smiling up at Khalid, certain now that he was teasing her. They had slowly made their way over to where Alex was now presenting Caroline.

'Sir, my wife, Caroline.'

'Ah yes, Caroline,' Abdullah extended his hand to her and Caroline took a step forward, giving a slight curtsy as she shook hands with him again.

'Your Highness.'

'I believe I saw you on Friday with Sally at the races. Did you enjoy your afternoon?'

'Yes, I enjoyed it very much, thank you, Your Highness. I like horses. Sally and I have ridden together since we were children.'

So! The Sheikh did indeed know Sally before they had met tonight! The little minx, she never said a word! What has she been up to? wondered Caroline.

At the races, Khalid had recognised Caroline as the wife of Alex Buchanan, one of the diplomats at the British Embassy. Officials at the Palace liked and respected Alex, recognising in him a skilled negotiator who understood and respected their customs. Unlike some of his colleagues, Alex did not push himself forward, seeking to use his position purely for self-advancement.

'Then she must bring you one day to my stables, when she rides again,' Abdullah generously invited her. He was taking no chances and would not take no for an answer, although he was yet to hear Sally's response to the question his First Secretary had been despatched to ask her. By inviting her friend to ride, she was compelled to return to his stables at least one more time.

Oh Lord! thought Sally. That's torn it! Her eyes flew to Caroline's face.

'Oh yes, indeed she must! Thank you, Sir,' Caroline smiled sweetly up at him before directing a fixed smile at Sally, the significance of which was, luckily, lost on Abdullah.

'Tell me, Sally, did you also enjoy the races last Friday?'

'Absolutely, Sir! It was an unforgettable sight. Those magnificent horses in that lovely desert setting – I certainly did enjoy it, Your Highness.'

Abdullah chuckled, catching the slight inflection as she used his formal title. He suspected that she was cross with him again, just as she had been when he had teased her about her car. Ah, what a breath of fresh air she was! Even here she was sending out a challenge. Her very presence brought fun and laughter into his heart.

'Unfortunately, that was the last meeting until November. The days will get too hot now to be able train the horses and expect them to race.' There, he had also informed her that the only chance to see the horses again would be if she came to his stables. He turned back to Alex, who had been highly amused by the whole of this little charade. Even before tonight, he'd begun to put two and two together about the owner of those 'fabulous horses'. After all, there were not so many to choose from in the immediate vicinity. Alex had been as curious as Caroline to find out where Sally was riding and for a while considered making enquiries through official channels. But he also knew that would have led to certain questions being asked about his wife's friend and, knowing the speed with which rumours sped about in this place, he had decided against it.

Since Sally's arrival in Al Khaleej, Caroline had been happier than at any time since coming to the Middle East. Alex could imagine how upset she would be if her friend became the latest target for gossip – and if she ever found out that the gossip had begun because of his enquiries, well, the consequences didn't bear thinking about! It had not escaped his notice that, while the Sheikh had been making small talk with him, he had barely taken his eyes off Sally, and he was glad now that he had said nothing to anyone at the Embassy. The Sheikh had obligingly just confirmed the riding venue and the owner of those 'fabulous creatures' Sally had told his wife all about. Hmm ... there are going to be some interesting times ahead, he chuckled to himself, wondering what his wife would make of it all!

'I must pay my respects to your Ambassador and take my leave,' Abdullah was saying as he shook hands with Alex. Everyone at the table stood up again. 'Now you may all relax and begin your party, I think,' he said, beaming at them, before he made his way down the steps and back into the ballroom.

As everyone else began to seat themselves again, Caroline pounced. 'Excuse us a moment, chaps,' she said to Alex and Matt and, grabbing Sally by the arm, hissed 'Sally! Ladies room! Right now!'

Unable to delay the inevitable any longer, Sally meekly followed her.

'Well?' Caroline confronted her. 'I think you have some explaining to do, Miss Phillips, so come on, out with it!' In the sumptuous Embassy loo with its wall-to-wall gilded mirrors and deep-pile carpet, they sat on stools in front of the make-up mirrors and Sally explained briefly to Caroline how she had met Abdullah.

'Do you know who he actually is?' Caroline was stunned.

'I do now, after tonight. But I didn't before. When we were laughing and joking at the stables I just thought he was probably the Stable Manager or something similar, someone employed at the Palace offices. When Hishaam showed me his photo and warned me that he was a powerful man, I assumed he was just a little Sheikh and possibly the boss at the Palace office.'

'Oh, he is certainly the boss at the Palace – and in every direction, for as far as the eye can see!' Caroline had opened her powder compact and was vigorously dabbing at her nose while she listened to Sally's explanation.

'You were having a long chat with the First Secretary. What was all that about, then?'

Sally tried to look vague. 'Oh, that ...?' She began to laugh as she explained that Ahmed, being a friend of the First Secretary, had shared with him the effect of his floral gifts on Sally's employer. The First Secretary, Sally casually explained, was merely making polite conversation with her about this event. She simply couldn't tell her about the offer to work at the Sheikh's stables and breathed a sigh of relief when it seemed that Caroline's curiosity was satisfied.

They walked back out to the terrace, and although Caroline sensed Sally was still holding something back she knew she would get nothing more out of her tonight. She wondered what Alex would have to say about it all and looked forward to having a post mortem with him later. To Sally's relief, Abdullah's comments about riding at his stables were not mentioned again and it seemed that, apart from Alex and Caroline, no one had overheard them.

When the dinner was finally over, Matt, fortified by several glasses of wine, summoned up the courage to ask Sally for a dance. When he led her onto the floor, it became apparent that he was an accomplished dancer and Sally enjoyed putting into practice the ballroom steps she had learnt at school. Unfortunately, being one of the tallest girls in the class, she had always had to take the part of the male. The long-term effect of this was that Sally had got so used to going forwards and taking the lead that she found herself forcefully manoeuvring Matthew, instead of allowing him to lead her. When Sally once again expertly swung him round he cheekily whispered to her, 'Sally, I think you're on the wrong side of the bed again,' making her giggle.

'Sorry, it's habit. I can't help it – just shove me round to the correct side when you feel me taking over,' she whispered back. The band stepped up the tempo and from the waltz and foxtrot couples drifted apart to attempt the twist, while the keen ones attempted to 'rock an' roll'. The sight of grown men in dinner suits and women in full-skirted ball gowns trying to rock an' roll amused Sally and she was glad of the split that she had incorporated into the design of her straight shift dress.

The band ended the medley of fast tunes and slowed the tempo back down with a rendition of Distant Drums. Matthew caught hold of Sally, eager to hold her in the circle of his arms. As he did so, the memories flooded back to Sally of the last time she had heard this tune and her heart began to crumble. With her eyes closed and her head resting against Matthew's shoulder, she gently swayed in time to the music that had first taken her into Doug's arms. It had played that very first night they'd met at the party that Caroline had dragged her along to; the memory of Doug was so clear it seemed like only yesterday. When the music ended, Matthew escorted her back to their table. Caroline had not said anything to him about Sally's past, but he was perceptive enough to notice a change in her mood while they had been dancing close to each other.

'May I get you another drink, Sally?' Matt asked gently as she sat down. When she looked up at him, he was tortured to see that her beautiful eyes were wet with unshed tears.

Sally had stuck to orange juice throughout the meal, wanting to keep a clear head to fend off any further questions that might arise about how well she knew the Sheikh. Alex had ordered a jug of freshly-squeezed orange juice for her while everyone else round the table had polished off several bottles of wine. Now both the jug and all the wine bottles were empty – most of the men were caressing snifters of cognac in their hands and the women were sipping at little glasses of liqueurs, the Sheikh's visit to their table long forgotten. Sally badly needed a drink. 'Yes please, Matthew, but this time please may I have a glass of white wine? It's time I got into the spirit of this party.'

'One large glass of white wine coming up. Caroline, Alex, may I get you another?'

Alex declined and Caroline, giving a very good impression of someone who'd already had more than enough to drink giggled, 'No thank you, Matthew. Unlike Sally I've already been well into most of the spirits at this party.'

But when Matthew had disappeared towards the bar, Caroline leaned over towards Sally, enquiring in a concerned way that held no trace of inebriation, 'Are you all right, Sal? You've gone very quiet.'

'Yes, I'm fine,' she smiled at Caroline, who could see she was very far from being 'fine' and that her eyes were glistening with unshed tears. Caroline patted her hand.

'Buck up, ol' thing. What's happened? You seemed to be having a good time with Matthew. He's not upset you, has he?'

Sally averted her eyes and shook her head. When she could trust herself to speak again, she looked at Caroline, swallowed hard and answered, 'It's just that some songs bring back such vivid memories. I'm cross with myself for letting Doug back into my thoughts, especially as Matt is being so kind.' Heaving a big sigh, she went on, 'You were right, Caro, maybe it's time to try to shelve the past and loosen up a little'.

'I see. Hence the request for wine?' Sally nodded. 'Good idea – you can try and catch up with the rest of us. I think Matt is smitten. Do you like him? Even just a little bit? Please say you do.'

'Ssssh. He's coming back.' Sally nodded towards the terrace doors.

Matt reappeared carrying a large tray holding a bottle of champagne and four tulip glasses, and carefully placed it on the table.

'Now, I know you two declined the offer of a drink but I thought you wouldn't mind sharing some of this with Sal and me. Hope you don't mind bubbly – it's just that the white wine didn't look very special. Who-oops, sorry – I seem to have spilt some,' Matthew said as he mopped at the tray with a linen napkin. 'Not sure how that happened. The ship must've rolled.'

Sally and Caroline exchanged glances and started to giggle.

'That's got to be good stuff,' Alex nodded to where Caroline and Sally sat. 'It's got the two of them giggling and it's not out of the bottle yet!'

Sally drank a glass of the chilled champagne and began to feel much better. If only she could learn to let go of the past completely and move on, to enjoy herself and begin a new life. The second glass had the desired effect. This time, when she danced with Matthew and he drew her in close, she rested her head on his shoulder and was happy to be in his arms without the shadow of Doug between them.

'Sally, may I take you out? Do you sail?'

'I've never been sailing, but I couldn't think of a better person to start with, Captain, Sir,' she playfully murmured.

'Thank you for the promotion, but I'm a long way from being a Captain. I'm a lowly Lieutenant Commander.' Sally looked up at him and smiled.

Boldly he planted a quick kiss on her lips, something that he had been longing to do all evening, and he pulled her closer, wrapping his arms protectively around her. Sally nestled her head appreciatively on his chest - the feeling of being wanted was something she had not experienced for a long, long time and it was so very comforting.

Chapter Thirty-One

The following day Abdullah enquired of Khalid about Sally's answer to his request for her to work at the stables and had been amused at his Secretary's struggles to assure him that it would be 'Um ... er ... soon!'

Khalid was nervous. Abdullah's instructions had come suddenly. In Khalid's carefully-ordered world, there was very little room for spontaneity – all new ideas had to deliberated, the risks carefully calculated. What His Highness was suggesting was unthinkable! A woman – working at the stables? It was unheard of! But Abdullah had not allowed time for further discussion and had refused to take further counsel on the matter. Having made his wishes known, and without further thought being given to the action he was proposing, Abdullah had proceeded to walk out onto the terrace, where he had seen Sally.

Khalid had found himself in a very unenviable position. On one hand, he could not disobey the Sheikh but, on the other, he found himself having to think on his feet! He would have much preferred to have time to at least think through the best way to approach this young woman, to consider what questions should be asked, anticipate the answers and maybe rephrase any further questions. He knew that if he did not deliver the result that Abdullah wanted, he would have failed in his duties.

However, if he succeeded, he knew he would have to face the inevitable questions from the circle of Counsellors and other elders and trusted advisors surrounding the Sheikh. As the young Sheikh's closest advisor, it was Khalid's duty to counsel caution and to curb his young master's sudden impulses.

Up until that moment, Abdullah had been compliant and level-headed, in spite of his youth. But from the moment that Sally had made him laugh over the wheelbarrows, he had felt carefree again and wanted to taste once more the freedom of youth, however briefly. He wanted to have what any other young man might have – the right to do something spontaneously. He knew that his behaviour had seriously disconcerted Khalid and he was sorry about that but, in this matter, he would have his own way.

Khalid was in a no-win situation and it was with an air of resignation that he stood before the Sheikh. He had failed to return with the answer Abdullah was expecting, but tried to console himself with the knowledge that at least there would now be time to consider how best to go about the innovative idea of a woman working at the stables.

Abdullah gazed fondly at his Secretary. Soon? Hmm ... he couldn't help thinking that he and Khalid were both learning new words in their dealings with this young woman! He chuckled to himself as he realised that Khalid, always so precise and adept in his dealings, had obviously met his match!

'Soon?' Abdullah asked, working hard to maintain a solemn and business-like tone.

'Yes. Soon.' Khalid was certain.

'When soon?'

'Er ...' Khalid was flustered – he couldn't say when. Miss Sally had refused to say 'when', so he repeated, 'Soon! She will come soon.' Khalid was sure of it.

'Very well then. We must make it ... soon!'

Abdullah felt that he had been patient long enough and could not bear the thought of Sally remaining where she was for one day longer than was necessary. Why did she not rush to take up his invitation to fulfil her heart's desire? He sensed that Sally had a natural affinity with horses and instinctively knew that she should spend her days with them, not stuck indoors, especially with the likes of Hishaam. She would be happy at his stables and he would be happy too, knowing that she was there. But like a skittish filly, she needed skilful handling, mastering even? Abdullah smiled, thinking that what Sally needed was a gentle push in the right direction.

Abdullah decided that Hishaam was to be informed that, if he wished his affairs to continue without any unnecessary interference from the authorities, he must find another secretary. Immediately!

'You will notify me, please, when this has been done!' Abdullah instructed Khalid, and dismissed him in a formal manner. Khalid bowed very low and hurriedly returned to his outer office.

For the first time since starting work in Al Khaleej, Sally felt that Monday morning really did feel like 'the morning after'. It was well past midnight by the time she had arrived back at her flat. Matthew had been sweet and she had given him her telephone number, but she had left with Caroline and Alex.

After seeing to Bouncy she had gone to bed, where she had tossed and turned as a multitude of thoughts chased each other round and round in her mind. The evening's emotional roller coaster had taken its toll and it was ages before she finally fell asleep.

First, there had been the shock of meeting Abdullah again and the realisation that he was not only a very powerful Sheikh but a member of the ruling family as well. The offer to work at his stables came as a bit of shock, too, and she couldn't work out in her mind exactly how she felt about being 'ordered' to give up her present job so that she could work for him. Automatically, she wanted to rebel at being dictated to about what to do with her life. Over the past year she had got used to being on her own and making her own decisions – but, she had to admit, it was rather thrilling to be the focus of attention of someone so powerful. And so handsome! Yes, she decided, she would love to work with his horses, but she needed time to sort a few things out first – Caroline being one of them. Inwardly she groaned, dreading a confrontation with her friend, and even more she dreaded the thought of a pompous lecture from Alex. Well, I'm not answerable to them and they can't stop me, she told herself. The thought occurred to her that it might actually be best if she could leave Hishaam's employment and start work at the stables quickly, so that by the time they found out it would be a fait accompli! In the darkness, she giggled with mischief as she imagined the look on their faces.

Although Caroline had taken the news that she had already met the Sheikh rather better than Sally had thought she would, what her friend would have to say about working at his stables, Sally knew, would be another matter!

Her thoughts moved on. Matt was nice, she decided, and sensitive – and, for the first time in a long time, she had agreed to go out on a date. When she had danced with him, it had felt wonderfully comforting and safe in his arms. She hadn't felt that when dancing with any of the other men that Caroline and Alex had set her up with.

But of all the tunes to play, the band had chosen the one that she had first danced to in Doug's arms. As she lay in her bed, she could hear the tune in her head again and she was overwhelmed with grief as she remembered Doug holding her, kissing her, making love to her – and now he was married to Moira. Only Bouncy heard the sobs, and it was Bouncy who licked away the tears from her cheeks until his mistress fell into a restless slumber. Then he gently settled down on the bed, stretching his long body out alongside hers, just as old Cloud had done on her visits to the farm.

Suddenly her alarm was going off, and she struggled to get herself up and ready for work. Ugh! Monday morning! On the way up the stairs to her office, Sally stopped off as usual to collect the telexes from Amiri and couldn't help but notice that his smile was a little wider than usual. He was positively beaming!

'Good morning, Amiri. You look very happy today.'

'Yes, Miss Sally, I am very happy today, I have the very good news. My wife is bringing a baby.' He patted his own tummy to emphasise his delight.

'Congratulations, Amiri! Which wife is this and when will she bring it?'

'My new wife!' He said proudly. 'She tells me she has baby inside and, inshallah, she will bring it after six months more.'

'What do your other wives think about this news?'

'Oh, they very, very happy now, because I am not so long with my new wife and they say when the baby is coming and crying too much I will be going to see them more.' He grinned sheepishly.

Sally congratulated him again on his good news and thanked him for sharing it with her, then climbed the stairs to her office to await Hishaam's arrival.

Having put the air conditioning on, she made herself some coffee before settling down to go through the telexes. Ahmed popped in just before ten and they shared a fresh pot of coffee while he told her more stories about his youth. Just as he was leaving, Hishaam arrived, the smell of alcohol oozing from every pore of his body. Formal greetings were exchanged and Ahmed, rolling his eyes at Sally behind Hishaam's back, wandered away down the corridor.

Hishaam stumbled heavily into his chair, squinting at Sally through hooded red eyes, the likes of which she had only seen on a bloodhound.

'Coffee, Sally! Quick! Give me coffee!' Hishaam groaned. 'My headache is really too bad. It's migraine, truly it is - only I know how much I suffer.'

Sally started off down the corridor towards the small kitchen to refill the water jug for the coffee percolator and as she did so, she could hear the telephone ringing. Fervently, she hoped it wouldn't be anything too difficult for Hishaam to cope with before he'd had his first caffeine hit of the day. When she returned to the office, she heard Hishaam slam the telephone down.

'Sally!' he squeaked, holding his head in his hands. 'I am sorry! You are fired!'

Sally paused in the act of making the coffee, not sure that she heard him correctly. Maybe, she thought, he had alcohol poisoning - however that manifested itself. He certainly drank enough to addle his brain.

'Did you say "fired"?'

'Sure, you are fired,' Hishaam repeated.

'Fired? Why? What have I done wrong?' she asked, smiling over her shoulder and humouring him as she poured water into the percolator and switched it on.

'You are fired! Why do you not listen to what I say? You are fired! Now! Today! Please leave!'

When she turned round to face him, she realised that he was deadly serious. Her eyes widened as he had raised his arms with his palms towards her in a gesture to indicate that there was nothing further to discuss. Sally still could not believe what she was hearing and, seeing the dismay on her face, Hishaam tried to ease her hurt by saying, 'My dear, you have done nothing wrong. No, no! You are, as a matter of fact, the best secretary I have ever had, but believe me when I say you are fired. You are fired. Now go! Straight away. This morning!'

Sally stared across the office at her boss, her mouth open wide in shock. 'Oh, for goodness sake,' she muttered under her breath, unable to believe what was happening. Just then, the percolator gurgled. She turned to switch it off and poured the coffee. Maybe I can persuade him to change his mind, she thought as she crossed the space between them and, standing respectfully in front of her boss with the two cups in her hands, she pleaded with him.

'Hishaam! Please ... I need this job! You can't be serious! You can't sack me! I've got rent to pay on my flat and I have to buy food for myself as well as Bouncy, and dog food isn't cheap ... and ... but ... but just a minute ...' She placed the cups on the desk. 'That doesn't make sense! If I'm the best secretary you have ever had ... why are you sacking me?'

'I am sorry, Sally. Believe me, it is totally out of my hands.' He brushed the palms of his hands together several times.

Sally had learned that hand signals were an integral part of any conversation in Al Khaleej and the brushing of the palms together in that way meant 'khalas' – finished! It meant that the topic of conversation was closed, but Sally refused to accept that this was the end of the matter. He couldn't leave it at that, he just couldn't! As she was about to remonstrate with him, the phone rang again and they both stared at it for a moment. Sally looked enquiringly at Hishaam, not sure if she should answer it, but he nodded to her, indicating that she should. As Sally picked up the receiver, Hishaam breathed a sigh of relief, blowing on his hot coffee, desperate to get the first mouthful. It was so very difficult having to deal with such unpleasant business, so early in the morning!

'Good morning, '

'Miss Sally?'

'Speaking.'

'Hold on. Please wait. I will put you through.' Sally heard crackling on the other end of the line and then a familiar voice.

'Good morning, Sally. I hope the party went well last night?'

'Good morning, Your Highness. Thank you for asking. Yes, I did enjoy the party last night.'

Hishaam had been quietly sipping and blowing at his hot coffee but, on hearing who was on the other end of the phone, he suddenly slurped an extra-large mouthful. As the searing hot liquid hit the back of his throat, he frantically leapt from his chair, spluttering and choking as he gasped in cold air to try to cool the inside of his mouth. Then, unexpectedly, he sneezed!

'Your boss is not being sentenced to death by Ahmed's flower pollen again, is he?' Abdullah inquired politely.

'Er ... no. I think it's my coffee that seems to be choking him this time. But he's no longer my boss. I've literally just been fired. No more than a few minutes ago.' Still feeling utterly bewildered by this turn in her fortunes, she suddenly remembered the conversation she'd had with the First Secretary the previous evening. No! She thought. He wouldn't dare ... or would he?

'Hey ... is this anything to do with you? Me losing my job?' Sally made no effort to hide her annoyance at the thought that this man could control her life.

Hishaam spun round. The silly girl was going to get them deported – if not worse! How dare she speak to the Sheikh in that tone of voice! He'd been hastily mopping up coffee from the front of his jacket but now he frantically leaned towards Sally, waving both of his hands inches from her face in attempt to make her stop. Sally ignored Hishaam's desperate gesticulations. On the other end of the phone she could hear Abdullah laughing.

'I can hear you are cross with me, Sally. Somehow I thought you would be pleased. Now you are free to work for me. Please be at my stables this afternoon at four. I will speak to you then and please, do not be too angry with me.'

Before Sally could reply, the line went dead and she was left holding the silent receiver in her hand. Blast the man! Clearly he was behind Hishaam's strange behaviour this morning! Slowly replacing the receiver, she realised that he had done it again. He had got the better of her – she was livid to think that he could treat her this way, but paradoxically was flattered and secretly thrilled. The upshot of it all was that now she didn't know whether to stamp her feet in anger or shout out with joy!

Hishaam watched Sally as she slowly replaced the receiver and his heart began to thud in a strange rhythm in his chest.

'What did he say? What did he want?' Quickly, Hishaam downed the remainder of his coffee, hoping it might soon wake him up to find that he was just a bystander in his own nightmare.

Standing by the side of Hishaam's desk, staring down at the phone in disbelief, Sally whispered, 'He wants me to work at his stables. I am to be there at four this afternoon.'

Hishaam wagged a finger at Sally. 'I suppose that was a stupid question. It is obvious what he wants! Did he say anything else?'

When Sally shook her head, relief flooded through Hishaam. Perhaps, after all, there were to be no recriminations laid at his door for Sally's disrespectful attitude to the Sheikh – and, indeed, why should there be? he asked himself. I have done nothing wrong.

'Take care. I warned you he was a powerful man! Now see! You have made a very big problem for yourself!'

Sally was annoyed at the abrupt way in which Abdullah had ended the phone call with the command that she should be at his stables at four. From her conversation with the First Secretary the night before, she had understood that she might at least have some time to consider the job offer. Now, it seemed, without any further reference to her or her wishes, the matter had been taken completely out of her hands!

During the past twelve months she had begun to enjoy her independence and had gradually felt as if she was taking control of her own life. When she had booked the flight and flown out to the Middle East without discussing it with anyone else, she felt that, at last, she really had come of age. The job with Hishaam was easy enough and paid enough for her to have the things that she treasured most in her life now – her own flat, her own car and her own dog. Best of all was the freedom to make her own decisions about her life. Did she really, she wondered, want to put herself into a situation where she would have to comply with the demands that this all-powerful, all-controlling man might make on her? Well, she thought, I can take care of myself! But with a smile she admitted to herself that he did have some fabulous horses, and she'd always wanted to work with horses – and he was rather handsome.

Suddenly, Hishaam's words penetrated her thoughts and she felt herself getting angry again.

'I beg your pardon. Did you say, I have made a big problem for myself? Me? I have made a big problem for myself ?' She took a step towards him and Hishaam quickly stepped back. 'I didn't make any problems for myself, Hishaam! It was you! You made the problem for me! You sent me up there, to the Palace offices, in the first place, unless of course you've completely forgotten!'

'Ah yes. The delayed horses ... that is true, Sally ... but you see, here in the Middle East, we are great believers in fate. Yes. You see, it is all the will of Allah. It is written. It is your destiny. Your destiny is already written. You cannot change it. You see, Sally, something brought you here, to the Middle East ... then that morning, well ... you could see ... I was not well ... and you went in my place ... and then your passion ... Ah yes, this great passion and love for horses. Without that, you would not have gone into his stables. It was your fate. I could wish that it were otherwise. You are a very good secretary, Sally, but now ...' he shrugged his shoulders, 'it seems you are destined to go down a very different path ...' His voice had filled with emotion in his attempt to defuse her anger by blaming local beliefs for the sequence of events. He pressed both hands to his chest while he delivered his heart-rending speech, and Sally saw his eyes fill with unshed tears. Then he bowed his head, with all the air of one resigned to fate.

Taller than Hishaam by a couple of inches, Sally stood looking down on his bowed head, knowing only too well what had brought her to the Middle East! As far as she was concerned it was all to do with the deceit of men, not bloody destiny or the will of Allah! Sally wanted to retort that it was his passion for booze, not her passion for horses, that was responsible for the change in her 'destiny', but she bit her tongue. Maybe there was something in this 'destiny' thing.

Hishaam usually spent the first few hours of the day with his hands held over his eyes to filter out the sunlight and ease the pain of his hangovers, although he still managed to bark out his orders to Sally. Today's emotional speech on her possible fate had brought him close to tears, and she had been quite touched by his poetic prophecy of what the future might hold for her. He raised his bowed head slightly, peeping up at her with sad eyes. Wanting to avoid the embarrassment of a tearful farewell, she asked, 'Before you throw me out, Hishaam, would you like me to make you one more coffee?'

Not one to waste emotion on a lost cause, Hishaam cheered up immediately. 'Good idea!' he said and promptly got on with the business of the day.

It was nearly midday when Sally left but, before she went, she found Ahmed, who was still doing his rounds in the building, and said goodbye to him. He promised that not only did he have many more tales to tell her of days gone by but that he would continue to send her flowers every week. In exchange he made her promise to come back and have coffee with him soon.

Amiri shyly said that he would keep in touch via his cousin, the dressmaker, and would let her know when the new baby arrived. Overwhelmed with their kindness and concern, she promised to keep in touch with them all, and left Hishaam's offices for the last time.

She was moving on and putting the past behind her – but she wasn't sure, as the door closed behind her, what the future might hold and whether she might be flying once again too close to the sun. Only time would tell, but she was ready for the adventure.

THE END

Seven Bands of Gold books

Seven Bands of Gold: Book Two: Sensual Love

It is 1968 and 19-year-old Sally Phillips has fled the UK for the Middle East in an attempt to heal her broken heart. Betrayal by her Scottish fiancé has made her suspicious of men and reluctant to trust them, but she remains in many ways naive.

She begins to adapt to life in the Sheikhdom of Al Khaleej, making friends and finding a job, and it is not long before she has become indispensable to her boss. So it comes as a shock one morning to find herself unceremoniously and inexplicably dismissed. Almost simultaneously, she is offered very different employment at the Royal stables. Infuriated to learn that her sacking had been masterminded by a powerful man used to getting his own way, Sally hesitates to accept, but her finances leave her no choice.

Incensed by the high-handed ways of the Sheikhdom's Heir Apparent, but secretly delighted at the thought of working with his beautiful Arabian horses, Sally resolves to keep their relationship business-like - however much her heart flutters when the handsome Sheikh is near.

Her new employer shows a keen interest in Sally. She finds his attention embarrassing but, as their friendship develops, she discovers that beneath the power and authority lurks a kindred spirit who yearns to live his life away from the spotlight. He demands that Sally treat him like any other man - and when she finds it difficult to use his first name he predicts that one day he will make love to her and that she will call it out in the throes of passion. Sally's on-going relationship with the attractive Naval Lieutenant Commander, Matthew Rawlinson, makes her sceptical of this outrageous boast. First Love saw Sally's sexuality awakened; in Sensual Love, the seductive Sheikh Abdullah takes her sex education to a new level - and the convent-educated and ill-prepared schoolgirl proves a fast learner! Torn between the comfort and security of her affair with the gentle Matt and the deep passions aroused by the experienced Sheikh, Sally imagines life could not get more complicated. But when a figure from her past casts his shadow over this curious ménage-a-trois, she realises how wrong she was.

Seven Bands of Gold: Book Three: Forbidden Love

Dashing Naval Officer Matthew, powerful and sexy Abdullah and Doug, Sally's first love, all appear in this third book. Matthew turns out to be not as reliable as Sally thought. Doug, still in love with Sally, watches unhappily from the sidelines as the love between Sally and Abdullah deepens.

Seven Bands of Gold: Book four: Enduring love.

Sally has made her decision and based on an unexpected card that fate has dealt her has decided to go it alone, but will she be allowed to make a new life for herself? Will her past loves respect her wishes? Hidden away in a Welsh valley Sally happily sets about making a new life for herself, however a past love walks straight back in to her life when she is at her most vulnerable.

About Jenny Lees

Born into an RAF family, Jenny Lees attended 12 schools in as many years. Her most vivid childhood recollections are of standing in front of classrooms of strange faces and being introduced as 'This is Jenny, who has come to join us for a while'. But the nomadic upbringing gave her the chance to live and make friends in many parts of the world.

Her lifelong passion for horses, Arabians in particular, has in recent years become her life's work. She lives in Herefordshire and owns a stud of Arabian horses where she conscientiously preserves rare and precious bloodlines of the desert. Jenny became frustrated with novels whose love scenes ended on the wrong side of the bedroom door with ' - ' - thus the story of Sally Phillips began to gestate and, before she knew it, Jenny's innate talent for storytelling had given birth to quadruplets.

You can find Jenny at
https://www.facebook.com/jennyleesauthor/

Printed in Great Britain
by Amazon